PEN American Center

congratulates

CONJUNCTIONS

on 20 years of dedication

to literature and the arts

P E N

AMERICAN CENTER

A fellowship of writers devoted to
advancing the cause of literature
and reading in the United States,
and defending free expression
around the world.

568 Broadway, Suite 401
New York, NY 10012
www.pen.org

COMING UP IN THE SPRING

Conjunctions:38
REJOICING REVOICING

Edited by Bradford Morrow

With a special portfolio guest-edited by Peter Constantine and William Weaver

It has been said that translators are the unacknowledged ambassadors of literature. With *Rejoicing Revoicing, Conjunctions* celebrates these artists for the bearers of cultural riches that they are. A special portfolio will gather works-in-progress by many of America's most renowned translators and some of the field's younger stars, inviting readers on an odyssey from Latin America to Europe, from Africa to East Asia.

Richard Howard offers poems by Maurice Maeterlinck, with a preface (each contributor provides an insightful note) about what drew him to this author. Edith Grossman, acclaimed for her translations of Márquez and Llosa, presents a chapter from her new *Don Quixote*. Kafka trans-

lator Breon Mitchell gives a first look at German novelist Uwe Timm's new book. Richard Pevear and Larissa Volokhonsky—foremost translators of Gogol, Dostoevsky, and Tolstoy—share their new version of Dostoevsky's *The Adolescent*.

Guest editors William Weaver and Peter Constantine also contribute, as do Burton Pike, Gregory Rabassa, Michael Emmerich, Keith and Rosmarie Waldrop, Peter Cole, Edmund Keeley, Forrest Gander, and others.

Rejoicing Revoicing will also present new work by Julia Alvarez, Tan Lin, Renee Gladman, Peter Gizzi, Eleni Sikelianos, and Fred D'Aguiar, among many others.

CONJUNCTIONS

Bi-Annual Volumes of New Writing

Edited by
Bradford Morrow

Contributing Editors
Walter Abish
Chinua Achebe
John Ashbery
Mei-mei Berssenbrugge
Mary Caponegro
Robert Creeley
Elizabeth Frank
William H. Gass
Jorie Graham
Robert Kelly
Ann Lauterbach
Norman Manea
Patrick McGrath
Rick Moody
Joanna Scott
Mona Simpson
Quincy Troupe
William Weaver
John Edgar Wideman

published by Bard College

EDITOR: Bradford Morrow
MANAGING EDITOR: Michael Bergstein
SENIOR EDITORS: Robert Antoni, Martine Bellen, Peter Constantine, Elaine Equi, Brian Evenson, Jonathan Safran Foer, Pat Sims
ASSOCIATE EDITORS: Jedediah Berry, Alan Tinkler
ART EDITOR: Norton Batkin
PUBLICITY: Mark R. Primoff
WEBMASTERS: Brian Evenson, Michael Neff
EDITORIAL ASSISTANTS: Micaela Morrissette, Andrus Nichols

CONJUNCTIONS is published in the Spring and Fall of each year by Bard College, Annandale-on-Hudson, NY 12504. This issue is made possible in part with the generous funding of the National Endowment for the Arts, and with public funds from the New York State Council on the Arts, a State Agency.

NATIONAL ENDOWMENT FOR THE ARTS

SUBSCRIPTIONS: Send subscription orders to CONJUNCTIONS, Bard College, Annandale-on-Hudson, NY 12504. Single year (two volumes): $18.00 for individuals; $25.00 for institutions and overseas. Two years (four volumes): $32.00 for individuals; $45.00 for institutions and overseas. Patron subscription (lifetime): $500.00. Overseas subscribers please make payment by International Money Order. For information about subscriptions, back issues, and advertising, call Michael Bergstein at (845) 758-1539 or fax (845) 758-2660.

All editorial communications should be sent to Bradford Morrow, *Conjunctions*, 21 East 10th Street, New York, NY 10003. Unsolicited manuscripts cannot be returned unless accompanied by a stamped, self-addressed envelope.

Conjunctions is listed and indexed in the American Humanities Index.

Visit the *Conjunctions* website at www.conjunctions.com.

Cover design by Jerry Kelly, New York. Previous covers designed by Leslie Miller, The Grenfell Press; Anthony McCall, Anthony McCall Associates; and Jerry Kelly. Cover photography by Robert Lorenzson.

Available through D.A.P./Distributed Art Publishers, Inc., 155 Sixth Avenue, New York, NY 10013. Telephone: (212) 627-1999. Fax: (212) 627-9484.

Printers: Edwards Brothers

Typesetter: Bill White, Typeworks

ISSN 0278-2324
ISBN 0-941964-53-1

Manufactured in the United States of America.

TABLE OF CONTENTS

CONJUNCTIONS:37
Twentieth Anniversary Issue

COVER ARTISTS: Gregory Amenoff, Donald Baechler, José Bedia, Francesco Clemente, Gregory Crewdson, Lynn Davis, Michael Eastman, Eric Fischl, Red Grooms, Komar & Melamid, Deborah Luster, Brice Marden, Elizabeth Murray, James Nares, Tim Rollins + K.O.S., Susan Rothenberg, David Salle, Richard Serra, Joel Shapiro, James Surls, and Robin Winters.

Match

Jules and Rita were rivals in the office and, therefore, hated each other. You'd often overhear, even when you didn't try, words like *sexist, racist, pig, bitch, phony, liar, chauvinist, dyke, punk* in conversations about the other each regularly engaged in with favorite colleagues. So it comes as a great surprise to learn from eyewitnesses that Rita and Jules embraced then kissed, a kiss hotter they say than the scourging fire driving them from the office to the window ledge where they joined hands and leaped, falling like birds of flame the day the 767 toppled the Twin Towers.

—John Edgar Wideman

FOREWORD

NOT FOUR, BUT A SCORE. Little magazines are not supposed to last
that long. They are the mayflies of periodicals. Nowadays, a lot of
them do last because the universities they are attached to endure—
the buildings cost too much to tear down. There, in quiet quads, they
crawl up academic walls like vines of ivy. *Conjunctions*, however,
was never little. It was born twins, one of whom was bound and
came out like a book. Littles are never clothed. Its initial issue was
a Festschrift for James Laughlin, a genre that's generally a book. Nor
was it small, running for 312 pages, longer than a Coppola film.
Nor did it shrink as time went on. Number 34's contributor page
begins on page 478. Littles usually start out well only to weaken
before they fade away entirely. *Conjunctions* is now a Samson with
hair to its knees, because it has continuously enlarged its scope—one
that was never narrow—to include important work from overseas,
and to reflect on the literature that has been made as well as to herald the literature that will be. Littles have pals and publish them, but
only too often their ambitions are only dreams. *Conjunctions* has
maintained a standard of quality that, in my opinion, is unmatched
by either Bigs or Littles, while remaining catholic in its sense of what
counts. Like the Littles, however (and the reason why the magazine
has prospered), *Conjunctions* has had one greatly gifted and ener-
getic editor throughout its lifetime. We, who contribute, are grateful
that it's Brad Morrow's magazine, and we feel honored by the others
with whom he has conjoined us.

The quality is there, spread over the pages of every issue, for anyone to read: youthful voices and hoarse ones like mine, literally conveyed from the lands of the unlikely, manuscripts rescued from some
purgatorial past, real writers recognized and fished out of the stream.
Maybe many of us feel as I do that with *Conjunctions* Brad has built
for serious writers a raft where we can thirst and cling and curse like
survivors from the shipwreck of our culture. He has enlisted the help
of good people; he has begged if not on the street in many an office
or at tavern tables; he has read his eyes out; he has kept his ear to the
alphabet, and has scrounged strange stuff from salvation's army
that's nevertheless fit to dress a prince proudly; he has taken enough

time away from his own writing to shame all of us who are less generous; he has had to suffer the slings of injured egos and the arrows of envious and carpy critics; and he has never ducked an issue or sacrificed a principle. Nothing Little in sight. I have never cottoned to close games. Personally, I like blowouts best, and Brad has run up a big score.

—William H. Gass
October 2001
St. Louis

EDITOR'S NOTE

THREE YEARS SEEMED a remote possibility, five at the outside. The idea was to map an arc of innovative literature during those first dark years of the eighties. But then, as if by benign fission, it only grew, the result of its contributors' combined energies. Now, 37 volumes later—an ugly number, not the felicitous 40 a bi-annual two decades old should wear on its sleeve, though in fact a modest reminder of those several times we nearly toppled into oblivion—*Conjunctions* celebrates its twentieth.

Manifestos, so popular among literary movements in the early decades of the last century, seem musty instruments now, salvos against philistines and aesthetic foes, decrees that for all their usefulness to lazy scholars are in fact limiting—leashes got up as whips. I have always resisted reducing my editorial aesthetics to a finite manifesto, knowing that the voices of the contributors define what *Conjunctions* intends, or *means*, at any given moment. Which is not to say the project isn't guided by a partiality in favor of writing whose language is spirited, edgy, stylistically vigorous, sometimes truly delicate, yet always out toward the brink of what is possible. In the past, I have referred to *Conjunctions* as a living notebook, and that seems still a useful image. Through over ten thousand pages of work ours has been the site of many visions—some coincident, some wildly dissimilar, but always funded by a serious devotion to idea and form in language. As the word itself suggests, *Conjunctions* is a juncture, a *tyuonyi*, a grange hall, a meeting place. A book is ever a house. And ours has been fortunate for its inspiring inhabitants.

I would like to acknowledge my debt of gratitude to the many people who have helped keep this project alive and thriving. From interns to contributing editors, designers to proofreaders, from charitable foundations to generous individuals who have donated resources, from typesetters to managing editors—to everybody who has given their support to *Conjunctions* over the years, my thanks. Ignorant in the extreme about what it takes to bring out a literary journal, I published the first few issues myself before realizing idealism and resolve weren't enough. James Laughlin introduced me to Robert M. McKinney, who underwrote the next two volumes.

A consortium of brave friends mustered enough money to get out *Conjunctions:6*, which looked to be, in the grand tradition of "little magazines," our farewell number, until the Boston publisher David R. Godine intervened. John Glusman, then an editor at Collier Books, carried *Conjunctions* forward through another crucial period.

It has been at Bard College, an institution richly deserving of its reputation as a champion of the arts, that *Conjunctions* at last found its home. Innovative itself in the best ways, Bard has, for the past dozen years, made it possible for *Conjunctions* to flourish. To Bard's president, Leon Botstein, to its executive vice-president, Dimitri Papadimitriou, and to everyone at the college involved with this project, thanks. As a poet once put it: *Onword.*

—Bradford Morrow
October 2001
New York City

Singing

Richard Powers

IN SOME EMPTY HALL, my brother is still singing. His voice can't have dampened yet. Not altogether. The rooms where he sang still hold an impression, their walls dimpled with his sound, awaiting some future phonograph capable of playing them.

My brother stands fixed, leaning against a piano. He is just twenty. It's December 1961. The country still dozes in its last days of willed innocence. No one has heard of Jonah Strom but our family, what's left of it. We've come to Durham, North Carolina, the old music building at Duke. Jonah has made it to the final round of a national vocal competition that he'll later deny ever having entered. My brother stands alone, as always, just to the right of center stage. He towers in place, an escaped tree in a massacred woods, listing a little bit toward starboard, backing up into the crook of the grand piano, his only safety. He curls forward, a lazy fiddlehead, the scroll on a reticent cello. Left hand steadies against the piano edge, while right hand cups itself in front of him as if holding some letter, now oddly lost. He seems baffled to find himself here. He should be.

One moment, the Erl King is hunched on my brother's shoulder, whispering a blessed death. In the next, some trap door opens up in the air's weave and my brother is elsewhere, teasing our Dowland of all things, a bit of ravishing sass for this stunned lieder crowd who can't grasp the web that has just slipped over them:

> *Time stands still with gazing on her face,*
> *Stand still and gaze for minutes, hours, and years to*
>   *her give place.*
> *All other things shall change, but she remains the*
>   *same,*
> *Till heavens changed have their course and time*
>   *hath lost its name.*

Two stanzas, and his tune is done. Silence hangs over the shocked hall, drifting up over seats like a balloon on the horizon. For the space of two downbeats, even breathing is a crime. But finally, there's no surviving this surprise except by killing it in applause. The noisy gratitude of hands starts time up again, sending the dart to its target and my brother to the things that will finish him.

This is how I still see him, although he'll live another third of a century, long enough to sound unrecognizable by the end. This is the moment when the world starts to find him, the night when I first hear where my brother's voice comes from. I'm up there on stage too, at the battered Steinway with its caramel-coated action. I am accompanying him, trying to keep up and not listen to that siren voice saying, *stop your fingers; throttle this piece. Crash your boat on the reef of keys and let yourself die in peace.*

That night is not my proudest as a musician, though I make no fatal fumbles. After the concert, I'll again ask my brother to let me go, beg him to find an accompanist who can do him justice. And again he'll refuse me, smiling, "But, Joey, I already have one."

I'm there, up onstage with him. But at the same time, I'm down in the hall, in the place I always sit at concerts: eight rows back, just inside the left-hand aisle. I sit where I can see my own fingers moving, where I can study my brother's face—close enough to see everything, but far enough so nothing I see can wreck me.

We ought to feel some wave of paralyzing stage fright. Backstage is a bleeding ulcer. Performers who have spent their whole youths training for this moment now prepare to spend their old age explaining why the moment didn't go as planned. The hall is full of venom and envy, families who have traveled hundreds of miles to see the pride of their lives reduced to a commonplace. My brother alone is fearless. He has already paid. This public contest is superfluous. It means nothing.

This contest is not music. Music was all those years of warm, close nights singing together in the belly of our family. This prize is no wish-granting fish, only a dried bit of taxidermy to hang on a wall. Jonah moves through the fright and nausea on a cloud, amused, as through a dress rehearsal for a performance already cancelled. Against this sea of panic, his calm electrifies. The fall of his hand on the piano's black enamel ravishes his listeners, a part of his sound.

I see him on this night from four decades on. The night of his first public triumph. He still has that quizzing look around the underside of his eyes that later life will obscure. His soft jaw quakes a little on Dowland's quarter notes. He drops his head a shade toward his right shoulder as he lifts to the high C, shrinking from the listeners he

13

holds entranced. The face ripples, a look only I can see, from my intimate perch behind the piano. The broken-ridged bridge of his nose, his brown bruised lips, the two bumps of bone riding above his eyes: almost my face, only fiercer, lighter, a year older. The public record of our family's private crime.

My brother sings to save the good and make the wicked take their own lives. At twenty, he's already intimate with both. This is the source of his power, the sound that holds his audience stunned for a few stopped seconds before they can bring themselves to clap. In the soar of that voice, the rift it floats out over.

The year is a snowy, black-and-white signal coming in on rabbit-ear antennas. The world of our childhood—the A-rationing, radio-fed world pitched in its final war against evil—falls away into a Kodak tableau. A man flies into space. Astronomers pick up pulsed signals from starlike objects. All across the globe, America draws to an inside straight. Berlin's tinderbox could flash at any moment. Southeast Asia is a smoldering brush fire. At home, a rash of babies piles up behind the viewing glass of maternity hospitals from Bar Harbor to San Diego. A hatless boy president plays touch football on the White House lawn. The continent is awash in spies, beatniks, and major appliances. Montgomery hits a five-year-old, festering impasse. And seven hundred unsuspecting people in Durham, North Carolina, disappear, lulled into the granite mountainside by a beauty their own given privilege never suspected.

No one has heard my brother sing yet but us. Now the word is out. As the applause grows, I watch his face waver with doubt. Behind the hasty barricade of a crooked smile, he gauges the size of his misstep. He looks around for a shadow to duck back into, but it's too late. He breaks into a broad, leaky grin, accepting his doom. The audience roars.

They bring us back, twice. Jonah has to drag me out the second time, to the demanding house. Then the judges call out the winners in each range—three, two, one—as if the old music building at Duke were Cape Canaveral, this music contest another Mercury launch, and America's Next Voices the likes of Shepard and Grissom. We stand in the wings with the other tenors, all fawning in a ring around Jonah, already hating him. I fight the urge to work this group, to assure them that my brother and I are not special, to lie to them that each performer has sung as well as anyone. The others sneak glances at my brother, studying his unstudied posture. They go over the strategy for next time: the panache of Schubert, to show you can do mainstream. Then the left hook of Dowland, striving for that endless, covered sustain above the high A. What they don't see—what they can never imitate—is my brother.

My brother hangs back against the fly ropes in his concert black, appraising the choicer sopranos. *Stands still and gazes.* He sings to them, encores in his mind, bending them as a psychic does spoons. Everyone knows he has won, and already Jonah struggles to make it mean nothing. The judges call his name. Invisible people cheer and whistle. Something in his victory flatters their sense of democracy. Jonah turns to me, dragging the moment out. He suppresses a grin. "Joey. Brother. There's got to be a better way to make a living." He breaks another rule by dragging me out onstage with him to collect the trophy. And instantly, his first public conquest falls into the past.

Afterward, we move through a sea of small ecstasies and epic disappointments. Improvised congratulating lines form up around the winners. In ours, a woman hunched with age actually falls on Jonah's shoulder and starts to cry. My brother amazes me, extending his performance, as if he really is the ethereal creature she has mistaken him for. "Sing forever," she keeps saying. "Sing forever," until her dark, pretty caretaker, with a knowing wink to my brother, leads the poor soul back to the plantation.

But we aren't yet through the evening's gauntlet. A few places behind the sobbing matriarch in our line of well-wishers, a ramrod retired colonel of a man twitches. A natty fellow, silvered over, in a blue seersucker suit. His face is a hostile muddle, certain that he has just been duped in a way he can't dope out. I feel the man's anger, well before he reaches us. We've lived with this every day since we left home. He waits out his moment in the line, his distress visibly mounting. Reaching the front, he charges. He offers no hand. I know what he will say before he can get it out. He studies my brother's face like a thwarted anthropologist. "What exactly *are* you boys?" His voice is the police, as if he has just come down to his wine cellar and found us breaking in.

The question we grew up on. The question no Strom ever figured out how to interpret, let alone answer. However often I've heard it, it still zeros me out. Neither my brother nor I bother to exchange looks. We're old hands at annihilation. I make some motions to placate the man, to smooth over the misunderstanding between us. But he backs me off with a look of real violation, a look that chases me for good from late adolescence's covered cove.

Jonah has his answer; I have mine. But he's the one whom the man

15

confronts. My brother inhales, as if we're still onstage, the smallest grace note of breath that would otherwise lead me in to the downbeat. For a semiquaver, he's about to launch into *Fremd bin ich eingezogen.* That would have been my dodge of choice. But Jonah pitches his sung reply, buffo style, up high in the head-toned stratosphere:

> *I am my mammy's ae bairn,*
> *Wi' unco folk I weary, Sir . . .*

His first full night of adulthood, but an adulthood of twenty, still drunk with having just been named America's Next Voice. His unaccompanied encore turns heads all around us. Jonah stares down the lot of them, an open-throated, giddy dare. It's 1961. We're in a major university town. You can't string a guy up for high spirits. They haven't strung up anyone for high spirits in these parts for, say, half a dozen years. My brother laughs his way through the Bobbie Burns couplet, thinking to win the colonel over with eight bars of good-natured cheek. The white-haired man goes livid twice over, once for being fooled in the concert hall and once again for being flipped off in the green room. He tenses and puckers, but the line of admirers moves him along, out the stage door, toward what must be a paralyzing stroke, if the look of hilarity spreading across my brother's face knows anything about the future.

At the end of the chaotic conga line, our father and sister stand waiting to rough us up. This is how I see them too, from the far side of a life. Still ours, still a family. Da grins like the infidel he is. "You pronounciate German like a Polack. Who the hell taught you your vowels? A disgrace. *Eine Schande!*"

Jonah wraps him in a half nelson. "Shh. Da. For Christ's sake. Remind me never to take you out in public. 'Polack' is an ethnic slur."

"'Polack?' Crazy, you are. That's what they're called, bub."

"Yeah, bub." Ruth, our family's perfect mimic, nails him. She has passed for the man often, over the phone. "What the hell else you call people from Polackia?"

The crowd near us turns to look again. Something about us is a flaw in their entire world view. But out here in polite, classically trained public, the anomaly eludes them. They push on to the other winners, leaving us, for another moment, a whole, safe nation. Father and eldest son reel about, drunk on the remnants of Schubert

16

still banging about the emptied hall. They lean on each other's shoulders. "Trust me," the older one tells the younger. "I've known a few Polacks in my day. I almost married one."

"I could have been a Polack?"

"A near-Polack. A counterfactual Polack."

"A Polack in one of many alternate universes?"

They babble to each other, shorthand jokes for the one whom none of us will name this night, the one for whom every note of our prize contest is offered up. Ruth stands between them, silent amid their banter, the keeper of our mother's features in this world. My mother, the woman my father almost did not marry, who came from a line longer and more American than anyone in this hall.

"You did good too, Joey," my little sister makes sure to tell me. "You know. Perfect and all."

I hug her to me for her lie, and she glows under my grasp, a time-lapse diamond. We wander over to Da and Jonah. Assembled again: the surviving four-fifths of the Strom family chorale.

But Da and Jonah don't need either of us accompanists. Da has hold of the Erl King motif, and Jonah thumps along, his uncanny three-and-a-half-octave range dropping into bass to whack at the piano's left hand. He hums the way he wanted me to play it, if I could. The way it ought to be played, in heaven's headliner concert series, following God's afternoon tea. Ruth and I draw near, despite ourselves, to add the inner lines. People smile as they pass, frightened, ashamed of us, our running violation. But Jonah is the evening's star, momentarily beyond reproach or scorn.

The audience this night will say they heard him. They'll tell their children how that chasm opened up, how the floor dropped out of the old Duke concert hall and left them hanging in the vacuum that they thought music's job was to fill. But the person they'll remember won't be my brother. They'll tell of sitting up in their seats at the first sound of that transmuting voice. But the voice they'll remember won't be his.

His growing listeners will chase Jonah's performances, hold tickets for his many cancellations, follow his career even into those last, decoupled years. Fans will search out his records, mistaking the sound on the disk for his. But my brother's sound could never be recorded. He had a thing against the permanent, a hatred of being fixed that's audible in every note he ever laid down. He lived the reverse of Orpheus's curse: Look *forward,* and you lose.

It's 1961. Jonah Strom, America's Next Voice, is twenty. This is

17

how I see him, forty years on, now eight years older than my big brother will ever be. The hall has emptied; my brother still sings. He sings through to the double bar, the tempo falling away to nothing as it passes through the fermata's blackness, a boy singing to a mother who can no longer hear him.

That voice was so pure it could make heads of state repent. But it sang knowing exactly what shape rode along behind it. And if any voice could have sent a message back to warn the past and stave off the future, it would have been my brother's.

Two Poems
Ann Lauterbach

GRID MTV

—to Stephen Westfall

Singly, out of blank, singly
as when *never* opens an eye
under the stressed
staring bud
weaves out chords
that some were insisting is music.
Not the simple reactionary sway of horizon—
freighted substitutions, Chinese shorts, panic roofs—
what were these but a pastel charity, sneaker prints
on a book jacket? Holes in
snow, what were they? Thimbles.
As if "life" could touch its metaphors, concentration
bring itself to an afterimage,
break apart, unravel,
and we still on the inside of now
where the house itself is occupying the house
with only a flickering sense
of what memory might look like from here:
"before the fact" "Berlin" "the same chalk."
Repetition is the wager of abstraction, Stephen said,
painting over and under, transgression without force.

But here is the fluid violence of wealth, white fence
lacing humped largesse, toes
bright in
snakeskin mules,
the new world's acts
coming in close, diamond and eye,

19

Ann Lauterbach

among crude
disadvantages, schematic
list, bower of chores, to dress
the imbecile in silk
the sick in the nude restlessness
of a summer night, the stars having fallen onto the meadow
in bug scraps, graves tilting, oaks opulent and straight,
the punishing vocabulary of ease pulled from the dump.
The sun might be a slingshot heaven, raking the world,
besotted with damp. *Video killed the radio star.*

Please do not hurt the ghost's sealed amphitheater, not sky, not
bright strips above the broken instance of our love,
not this unanswered provocation from afar,
formulas pulling twilight, as the girl her mother's hair.
Fractions of money launch
a pure ambition to receive, and I
am confounded in this exercise of rooms, whose brother
steps into water to skip stones. The inundated horizon,
its gift? Counting up from year to year
at the edge of the graveyard where the raccoon crossed, where the crows
speak their condition, where small wandering beasts are a currency of error.

Who lost? Under night's grin, trees
emanating faint fingers,
sun impossible, sun bewildered, sun
clasped at the root of the mountain's blue,
sun under impossible fingers, rising
to the vagrant collision of being.
Mind, you would say, wondering if the subject were that
or other impossible gifts,
their commerce wholly measured.
Ladies and gentlemen, rock and roll.

Ann Lauterbach

TO & SO

1.

Unalterable complex   unfurled shed.

Came this way   unslithered

purchase factored in as

noise (following personal

revelations of the suit)

swiftly, swiftly   "then"

glazed over visual

to

amplitude of signs

crank imperatives   tides of exact ephemera

held or foretold

to the graduated sweetness of a perfect impasse

swindle, cant, ribs cut out

to

episodes O! O! O!

Ann Lauterbach

                  The reporter lonely in Istanbul?

                      carpets, tea, blue glass, bridge

to

   perfect these

             household gods

      eyes against envy, beads against expectation

              more stones, more letters,

              and so the symmetry of good windows

   set

to remember, in distant times,

how facts

looked blank, under thrall

of a prerequisite doubt

      nothing defraged there, only terse contractions

      enjoyed up close

      riddle, whim

      apparition

clear-eyed, yes, but something

seduces even the greatest soldier to minor treason—

infatuated

tables slanted up, legs raised

a motion of tears

quotidian exhaled

       a farewell of sorts

under logic, under guess, where the bug,

without much left, the all

made small

diligent maker

shipwrecked encyclopedia

coyote racing across the graveyard toward a flock of wild turkeys

2.

OK, so

here is rain's

insistent oblique

elderly contest

she who would have seemed

before this task

what had resembled, but now

abstract, global

an abbreviated cost

there will be no generals

in our army of thieves

and the big library

will discover little poems

there is always violence

and clean elaborations of such.

What? What?

You want to ask *what?*

3.

Unjust equation   night *is* night

closes on a simple thing

recurrent in the kneeling air

collapse of particulars   say leaf say drip

what is required is attached at the outer rim

we in our love

also indicted

because the frame extends only so far

then around a corner then descent

gradual glide into viscous air

Again? Up again? Is this another never,

another cell, another impossible procedure, another

X, another unsayable,

thread lifted from a wall

steel arc leaning in the public arena

surface wax

doctrinal silence

Ann Lauterbach

huge installation of the instant

hardly any water

eyes of the fox

where there was rain.

Unmanageable   clock partition murmur

sincere, sincere

among the charmed

beyond delusion's skin or the characteristic eye

staring out again

fractured road   glossy   ravenous with suction

images among graves

so

apart from what you were saying

the tie looms

contaminated by the false

sullied by sport

slender hands of the brute

dusting his lapels

unmoved   the enchantments as dust

unpinned   fallen   as wound

sojourn of the various   ablaze as a cloister exhumed

as the cradle dumped

    darkened then darkened   entrance glued to endurance

                     so

you had to mention the will

                     so

you were led away

    doorstep forbidden

    disestablished strip of the radiant plenum

                     bare-shouldered, strapless, sky

Pictures
Robert Creeley

1.

This distance
between pane of glass,
eye's sight—
the far waving green edge

of trees, sun's
reflection, light
yellow—and sky there too
light blue.

2.

I will sit here
till breeze, ambient,
enfolds me and I
lift away. I will

sit here as sun
warms my hands, my
body eases and sounds
grow soft and intimate

in my ears. I will sit
here and the back of the house
behind me will at last
disappear. I will sit here

3.

Harry's gone out for pizza.
Mabel's home all alone.
Mother just left for Ibiza.
Give the old man a bone?

Remember when Barkis was willing?
When onions grew on the lawn?
When airplanes cost just a shilling?
Where have the good times gone?

4.

If one looks back
or thinks to look
in that uselessly opaque direction,
little enough's ever there.

What is it one stares into,
thinks still to recover
as it all fades out—
mind's vagary?

I call to you brutally.
I remember the day we met
I remember how you sat, impatient
to get out.

Back is no direction . . .
Tout passe?
Life is the river
we've carried with us.

5.

Sun's shadows aslant
across opening expansive
various green fields down

from door
here ajar on box tower's
third floor—

look out on
wonder.
This morning.

6.

I never met you afterward
nor seemingly knew you before.
Our lives were interfolded,
wrapped like a present.

The odors, the tastes, the surfaces
of our bodies were the map—
the mind a distraction,
trying to keep up.

I could not compare you to anything.
You were not like rhubarb
or clean sheets—or, dear as it might be,
sudden rain in the street.

All those years ago, on the beach in Dover,
with that time so ominous,
and the couple so human,
pledging their faith to one another,

now again such a time seems here—
not to fear
death or what's been so given—
to yield one's own despair.

7.

Like sitting in backseat,
can't see what street
we're on or what the
one driving sees

or where we're going.
Waiting for what's to happen,
can't quite hear the conversation,
the big people, sitting up front.

8.

Death, be not proud . . .
Days be not done.
Air be not gone.
Head be not cowed.

Bird be not dead.
Thoughts be not fled.
Come back instead,
Heart's hopeful wedding.

Face faint in mirror.
Why does it stay there?
What's become
Of person who was here?

9.

Wet
    water
warm
    fire.

Rough
    wood
cold
    stone.

Hot
    coals
shining
    star.

Physical hill still my will.
Mind's ambience alters all.

31

10.

As I rode out one morning
just at break of day
a pain came upon me
unexpectedly—

As I thought one day
not to think anymore,
I thought again,
caught and could not stop—

Were I the horse I rode,
were I the bridge I crossed,
were I a tree
unable to move,

the lake would have
no reflections,
the sweet, soft air
no sounds.

So I hear, I see,
tell still the echoing story
of all that lives in the forest,
all that surrounds me.

Last Resort Retreat
Mary Caponegro

AS TO THE MAJESTY OF THE animal in the road—its beauty, formidable and fragile both, its poignant vulnerability—well, all that is lost in the crudity of her scream, her bark; that's how he hears it anyway, and thinks he'd find the deer less skittish, on a daily basis, than his wife—her ever-fretful, hawking gaze and blaring trumpet vigilance. Poor, nevermore frolicsome deer, maimed-by-him-with-her-as-accessory, when what he would have wished, in all honesty—the honesty of his momentary rage—was to shut her up for once, for all the love and habituals, to have, through any means, a moment's peace. It's snowing, always snow or rain or fog on this road. To him it's no big deal, but all it takes is one flake, drop, or patch to get her started: the anxiety machine—women and weather, what *is* that about, and wouldn't you know that this would be the road to their theoretical "recovery"; is it symbolic? He suspects so, she too, and as the weekend wears on, they will come to believe, increasingly, that each activity, each event, is both symbolic and contrived.

Left, right, right to the Last Resort Retreat—that's how she memorized it, so keen as she is on infantile mnemonics: yet another item on the list of her compulsive what-we-mustn't-forget cosmologies. When they're finally done with all the winding, to the accompaniment of her whining, "Have we gone too far? We might have passed it. Are you sure we're on the right road?"; (he) "Don't *need* to ask directions, no one's here to ask"; (as she) "Don't go so fast, *please*"; (he) "*You* drive, then"; (she) "All right, fine"; (he) "No thanks, I take it back, that's all we need"; and then, of course, the deer, and finally, quite a bit the worse for wear (though obviously not to the deer's degree), they reach the elusive rural road, the final left before they are (theoretically) twice righted by the Last Resort Retreat.

Sometimes she can step outside of it, of them: their dance, their schtick, their trance, whatever New Age term their couple chemistry—lately so volatile—deserves. Look at the two of them, she thinks: They could be any couple really, any couple certain when they started up of lifelong passion, at least guaranteed compatibility;

were they not uncannily compatible? Had not everyone remarked? But lately everything seemed tentative, they felt certain only occasionally and when certain: of inevitable demise.

What really is the point, she wonders, if he has no interest, no receptivity, not a shred of generosity, about this project, this weekend, this intensive retreat that by the time it's done will feel in its duration as many years as they've been married. O poor dumb dead deer, I'll take your place, she thinks, envying the leaden flesh now nothing but a memory in the rearview mirror, wanting to have the guts, the benighted recklessness, the trusting spontaneity to leap across a road, without vacillation, into oncoming traffic, traffic likely consisting at this moment exclusively of cars whose destination is identical to theirs, a destination far too embarrassing to admit, too compromising to reveal in other than a whisper to anyone other than this poor innocent deceased creature whose last breath will be forever mingled with their memory of the Last Resort Retreat, for which she'd seen a flyer (also something on the Internet), nothing more, what were they getting into, he'd complained—no references, for heaven's sake, already its effect was exacerbation rather than amelioration.

"Come in and let's get started, sign these waivers, please."

No, it can't be that these two clowns beckoning with forms and pencils are *in charge?* And what a sorry-looking set of "peers"; from day one he'll refer to as contestants (as if they'd accidentally signed up for some game show the objective of which is consummate humiliation; tune in for the *old-ly-wed game!*—not a laugh- but a cry-track); shed their boots, get in the circle, is this kindergarten?, "take you to your cabin later, since you're late." Oh, punitive, is that it? Make them suffer publicly, what if they have to pee? (All those seventies EST anecdotes flood his brain.) She *always* has to: infernal recurring bladder infection—is particularly prone whenever any hint of conjugal connection arises. Her idea, to do this stupid thing, and she's the one who makes them late—for what? For kitty litter, or was it trash bags, not to mention the unending existential dilemma of what to wear.

"It's a retreat, for Chrissake, not a prom. What are you doing in the closet all this time," he'd yelled up to her, "masturbating?"

"Could you blame me?"

Sometimes she could be a real downer.

Pen and paper are being passed out. Like the first day of school? He begins to write atop the page: *My summer vacation,* then nudges her to display his mischief. He dares them to solicit a title for his composition: *My marriage, my time-has-not-been-flying-for-some-time-I-am-not-having-fun marriage. My whose-idea-was-this-any-way-get-me-out-of-here marriage. My hell and welcome to it, etc.,* and one presumes the rest of them to be in dire straits as well or they wouldn't be subjecting themselves to such compromising tripe? But it turns out all the form-and-pencil-waving morons want is some pedestrian, why-are-you-here-what-do-you-hope-to-gain sort of info; oh God, he hates to pay through the nose for such scams: You pay *and* you do all the work. And now the first activity.

Groups are being formed. Well, isn't that original? Placed on the left are all the couples who consider themselves to have healthy, active sex lives. On the right: those for whom sex is no longer . . . viable. Laughter at the disproportionate size of the groups.

"Do you envy them?" A few heads nodding. "Do you think there is anything in this group that the other group might envy?"

"Yeah, more time," says someone from the left.

"More sleep": another.

Under his breath, Norm volunteers, "More jerking off!"

"Let's ask them," the guy in charge continues.

"Well, yes, I have to say," says a weepy woman from the right group, "I feel even worse to go from connection on that grand a scale to missing each other in all other important aspects of our lives, you know?"

The female facilitator, earnest yet imperious, comments, "We might want to note here that the tendency seems to be so far for men to do the joking and women, the feeling."

"Yeah, and how do you think *I* feel to have my wife sob every time she has an orgasm?"—from the trembling-voiced woman's formidable-looking husband.

"Now, there'll be no defensiveness in this session. Here are the rules: We demarcate the space. No attacking, no defending except in the ways we prescribe, which we will soon provide you, and which, we promise you, will be ample. Isn't that right, Pierre?"

"Yes, that's absolutely right, Elizabeth." (It's like a game show, or a news hour with two chummy hosts.) "Aside from those constraints, there is an honor code. Sign on the dotted line, couples. These contracts bind you to your best intentions. Hug your partner, as wholeheartedly as you can. Now back to small groups."

"Do-si-do ho ho ho. Hey, when is milk and cookies? Or will it be s'mores?"

"Norm, please behave." And as if to back him up, a pitcher and plate appear, although the milk is soy and the cookies not nostalgic chocolate chip but something more resembling molten granola.

At the break, they finally get to "check in" to their cabin: rustic, but serviceable (just the sort of place, he thinks, she'd never go if *he* proposed a woodsy "getaway"—but hey, whatever).

"Look, a private bath!" Thank God, a private bath, she thinks, with him so antisocial, not to mention her cystitis. He paces, leans against the wall, surveys the place. In his peripheral vision, he sees his wife hanging up what appears to be her wedding dress, and remembers talk of some absurd "reenactment" on the final day. In the humble cabin, the garment looks like Cinderella's dowry. The tux he'd worn would never fit him now, that's for sure. He stands there, in a kind of stupor, watches her unpack her toiletries.

"Why are you brushing your teeth now?"

And he claims *she* nags. "I guess it's my business if I feel like . . ."

"Forget it, I can't hear you through the foam."

She takes the toothbrush out. "Who knows, I might just want to kiss somebody!" No sooner has she rinsed and spit than the bell rings, all the cabins start to empty out for round two. "Come on, we can't be late again."

"What'll they do, send us to the principal? Or maybe we'll get lucky and be expelled!"

"Speak for yourself. Tell me something, do you think the facilitators are married?"

"How should I know?"

"I asked you do you think, not do you know?"

"What, to each other?"

"Duhhh!"

"Well, they could be married . . . separately, outside this circus, and have a . . . professional affiliation. If you can call this bullshit professional. Besides, I think he's gay. You have the key, right?"

"Yeah, I've got it. You think every non-*he-man* man is gay."

"He's not the one you want to kiss, I hope?"

"The one I want to kiss would be my husband, *idiot!* Not that he deserves the wish."

"You know, I think I've had enough of this whole thing already, Martha."

"We just got here, Norm. Could you make just a teeny-weeny effort to cooperate?" She strides ahead. He catches up, accomplished almost instantly, his legs by far the longer.

"Yeah, what's in it for me? Just kidding." (Oh, there she goes, all sulky, he really *was* just kidding.)

When they reach the main building, there is on every chair some doughy-looking—object, like a bolster—can it be . . . a dildo?—some gigantic chunky surrogate because some secret questionnaire revealed she wasn't satisfied? Did anyone ask him if *he* was satisfied? The diameter of a small tree trunk really. So they've come all this way, laid out all this cash, for their enlightened facilitators to say, in effect, give up, you're better off with sex toys than your husband's dick? And is there any solace for said dick? It has, he supposes, to fend for itself. "This, gentlemen"—Ms. Cheekbones is making an announcement—"is your partner's throat"—there is a collective gasp from the female portion of the room and a certain new focus from the male contingent— ". . . for all intents and purposes. When you feel most frustrated in the course of these five days, you can grasp this special high-density viscoelastic foam and squeeze. The heat of your hands will make it conform."

"And what do we get?" says an indignant woman, who had held it like a trophy before its identity metamorphosed, as it were, in her hands. "To bake a cake?"

"In this case, no, you don't . . . create," the puling male facilitator says. "You, ladies . . . you get to . . ."

Cheekbones chimes in, "OK, let's not beat around the bush . . . castrate."

Once the horror, bemusement, indignation, and I-want-my-money-back protests subside, they allow themselves, one at a time, to be schooled in pseudoviolence. But their novice practice must not take place, they are told, in mixed company. Just as in bathhouses, the clientele is segregated; here, when the women take their oversized plastic bats to do the deed, the men will be sent back to their individual cabins to commence composing their legal defense for the faux murder they are about to commit (or have just committed), and when the men's hands collectively prepare to grip the vessel of breath, there will be a changing of the guard, and the women are to take up their pens and make their husbands history, by each composing, as earnestly as circumstances will allow, a eulogy. These randomly gendered writing tasks will themselves then be switched, such that by week's end, everyone will be thoroughly murdered and thoroughly mourned. All are assigned the composition of a private "missed-list," composed of all the attributes a husband or wife will miss most in a (hypothetically) permanently absent spouse.

37

"Now, sit down, each of you, sit down and hear me out. I will tell you something very sad" (something in those eyes is undeniably hypnotic). "This is what you do each day through your misunderstandings. Think of a dog that grips someone by the throat. Or the expression 'to have a man by the balls.' What do you feel when you reflect on this?"

"Do you ever get the feeling these two might not be quite—legitimate?"

"So squeeze or slice to your heart's delight, any time of day or night."

"What's this, the ax murderer's anthem?"

"Norm, hush, I can't hear. This is the most important part."

"We provide you these tools and this room to get it out of your system, but after any action with our special props, you are obliged to then sit back and observe your handiwork, and ponder the consequences of your repeated actions. The pondering, in fact, may lead you to emotional areas you have never traversed. This navigation will of course be your responsibility. Any questions?"

"May I ask why you chose these two . . . images?" someone asks.

"If you don't mind," the unctuous male facilitator says, "we'd rather let you answer that yourselves before you leave the Last Resort Retreat."

"Other questions?"

"What's the point of all this?"

"The point, participants, is this: We provide you hypothetical space to go to your emotional limit, and then we provide the means to imagine the worst-case-scenario extremes that would result. Think of it as a controlled environment in which you can be out of control. Through these means, we hope to help you achieve catharsis, healing, and ultimately, reunion."

"How many times do you think they've delivered *that* speech?"

Everyone receives another break after the segregated tutorials, to allow them to process all the information and to resume their primary pairings. (Solitary challenges lie ahead, such as a night apart in the solitary confinement cabin complete with barred windows.) On go coats and boots again and out stream couples. "I need a nap," says Norm, and when they enter the cabin he immediately flings his body like a board across the bed.

"Oh look," says Martha, "chocolates on the pillow! Just like a—"

"Let me guess"—in chorus: "bed and breakfast!" Rolls his eyes. "I'll need more than chocolate to recuperate from this day."

"The day's not over yet." She bends to scoop the foil-wrapped candy from the bed, declaring, "Well, I *never* say no to chocolate."

"You should do a commercial." Women and chocolate, what's *that* about? Like fetal alcoholism, they're born addicted. "The bed's made too. I thought you said you locked the door."

"I said I took the key, I don't remember if I locked it."

"So where do they hide the chambermaids?" Austere Elizabeth in a little black, aproned number: provocative image. Bothers him some. "I don't like the idea of people coming in when we're not here."

"I wouldn't worry about Last Resort robbers. Or privacy either." She peers down and picks one up. "You know what, they're not chocolates, honey, they're . . . they're . . . condoms."

He opens one eye, squints at the contents of her hand. "What is that—to make us feel diseased?"

"No, they're a backup, I suppose, in case we didn't bring any, knowing we'd be too busy pseudostrangling and castrating each other and so forth. I don't know, maybe they're for all the men whose tubes aren't tied."

"Once our dicks get lopped off, it's a moot point, isn't it?"

"You make it sound like the violence is for real."

"I thought that was the idea: invest fully in the illusion."

"Or maybe it's a prop to help us dump all our bad history and renew our curiosity, to pretend we just met at a bar or something."

"Yeah, or at a marriage retreat."

"You know, you're really a downer sometimes."

"Take that back." He rolls over onto his stomach.

"OK, you're right, that isn't true, you're really a downer *all* the time."

"I'm a hard-nosed realist, darling, if you haven't figured that out yet."

"Give me another sixteen years and maybe I'll catch on."

"Doesn't sound like you *want* another sixteen years." He buries his head in the pillow; she firmly pries it from its shroud, and pushes his shoulder until he's lying on his side, puts her face beside his.

"Don't do that pouting thing, OK? What I *want* is a marriage that doesn't feel like a wake."

"We'll throw a party then. A sour-sixteen party, what do you say?"

"I say that doesn't deserve a response. Maybe they're chocolate-*covered* condoms."

"Just don't swallow, ha ha; you'd choke and then I wouldn't have the satisfaction of metastrangling you anymore!"

"You know, your jokes are pretty violent on the whole. Do you think *brutal* sense of humor is an accurate description?"

"Twenty-some-odd years ago in college you called it gutsy and original."

And he was right, she had. Everyone had. Her first exposure to his scathing humor was his comedy routine at the Friday night "open mike." Everyone said he should take his act "on the road." They praised its edge, its originality. Made comparisons to Lenny Bruce, even Dick Gregory. And she, along with many of her peers, was in awe of the combination of intelligence and audacity that fueled his anti-Nixon rants as well as his critiques of conservatism, material-ism, "suburbanism, sexual uptightism, domestic nuclear monog-amism, yeasty-no-thinkism," to use his words, his sort of wordplay. An intense guy with big dark eyes, muscular build, and a black T-shirt that he sweated straight through by the time his act was done. She watched him hurl it off his body once he was off the stage, some-how entranced, in spite of herself, by the muscles of his bare back. He turned by chance and saw her, no doubt also saw her blush, and on an impulse, smiling, threw it in mock gesture like a bride does her bouquet to all the "single" girls, but threw it straight to her. She never washed it, never gave it back, not even when, ten years later, he stood beside her as she threw a real bridal bouquet, and never con-fessed, even after they'd shared countless acts of sex, how many times she had fantasized with that cloth memento between her thighs. (And that was twenty-seven years ago!) Wasn't change a sad thing sometimes? Now his trenchant humor just seemed grating, no longer seductive or unique, certainly not sexy; larger-than-life capti-vating had turned, like milk gone sour, to just plain annoying. She couldn't pinpoint when. She had no clear idea why. All she wondered then was why, of all the girls he could have taken home that night, and what's more, gone "steady" with etc., did he choose her, whole-some Martha, whose only prior boyfriend was Brian, the nerdy bio-major—oh, the privilege of having Norman Silverstein's attentions (despite the condescending surprise on the part of his admirers)— indeed it made her blush and now she cringes to think of blushing then. And then feels guilty.

"Everything changes."

"Oh, that's profound."

"Subversive at fifty just doesn't cut it, Norm, I hate to tell you, it isn't charming anymore."

"I'm forty-nine, you're forty-seven. And I don't give a shit about charm." The bell rings again in the main building, to signal the end of break and resumption of structured activity.

"Who would *ever* have guessed! Be bold and bald then!"

"What? Where did *that* come from?"

"Your head is close to hairless. Go all the way, for heaven's sake. Cut off that stupid ponytail. It's thin and gray!"

"I'll meet you over there, when you're ready to be civil."

"When *I'm* civil? That's a good one. I'll stay right here."

"I'm gonna te-ell: Martha's playing hooky."

"Hooky nothing, gotta write your eulogy."

"All right, suit yourself. I'll bring you back a veggie burger, if you're good."

What really is the point, he wonders, if she has no resilience, no willingness to roll with the punches, no stamina for the long haul? Though she would claim the greater investment in their relationship, she's the one who dwells on every minor infraction—will not let it go. She has demands, oh does she ever have demands, but he has faith. She calls him oblivious but he thinks all the molehills of their differences are made mountainous by her willful histrionics—by her hyperbolic, melodramatic preoccupation with the so-called problematic aspects of their scrutinized-to-death relationship. All she does is carry on, whereas he can overlook occasional peccadilloes on her part, he can, in the other, *positive* sense, *carry on*, from day to day: a working, functional, satisfying, healthy rather than discussion-saturated, crisis-driven relationship. But it *was* once healthy—living, breathing, satisfying—wasn't it? Their marriage? Until recently? At least initially? Before money woes, miscarriages, stagnancy, silences, intolerances, mutual disillusionments never made explicit, before their marriage landed up against a concrete wall. When their relationship was supple instead of brittle. Nubile. When she looked at him with something besides resignation; was it ever admiration? When she yearned for him. And he for her. When they considered themselves *made for* rather than *stuck with* each other. When their relationship was light instead of laden. Oh, he remembers light, one image of inexpungible light. Moth (nickname she used to love) was far too nervous on their wedding day to be considered a radiant bride, and never pregnant long enough to be radiant in that traditional maternal way, but oh was she luminous the day that declared to him their physical compatibility. It was July. First visit after the school year had ended. First opportunity to be spared negotiating dorm rooms and roommates, etc. Her parents' private cabana

41

on the shore. They had been dodging waves in the Atlantic Ocean one sultry humid day. Between the waves, he lifted her into his arms and carried her, making like King Kong and leaving footprints in the dark, wet sand, then spontaneously took her hand and ran back to the cabin, to the cramped outdoor stall where they showered off the sand and peeled off each other's clammy suits: her blue-and-green tie-dyed bikini—he still remembers how it looked, how she looked *in* it, despite her ever-self-conscious "I'm too chunky/dumpy/hippy/busty" bullshit.

"None of the above," he always said, and says, "Stand corrected, zaftig goddess; you, babe, are my brick-house." And he knows there is some feature of her physical being, some pheromonal adrenaline that made possible the spontaneous lifting of her short but buxom five-foot-three-inch body while the gulls flew above them. Can't even now remember how, on an impulse, he managed to hoist her all the way up to his shoulders. Her buttocks in his hands, her breasts falling softly over his head, as he made himself her pedestal, holding her more intimately than if she were his infant, his pooch or kitty, his doll or trophy; and if that power to be both her possessor and protector was an incredible turn-on, if so, then so what? It was to *her*, too, he was sure, even if she never said; he felt her ecstasy as he made her still more buoyant than the ocean could. When they had showered off the sand, he wouldn't let her wash what was inside: "I'll do it for you," with his tongue, and he can still taste how the ocean's salt and her juices melded into something tangy: tart and sweet together, and he never felt so capable. She said, "You'll hurt your back." "I won't," he said, "I'm Superman." But somehow he'd turned into Bozo.

And why not be true to that destiny, he thinks, fatalistically.

In an unobtrusive manner, between sessions, Monsieur Pierre and Madame Elizabeth take orders for the evening meal, gliding down the aisles where everyone is dutifully getting "in touch with" the symbolic foam shapes that lie under their hands, as if each were fashioning clay on a potter's wheel, intuitively calibrating pressure to yield form and create contour. "Vegetarian or venison, vegetarian or venison," like a stewardess making rounds up and down every aisle, he thinks, chicken or beef, coffee, tea, me. He sees her for a moment in stockings, short navy blue skirt and tucked-in shirt, maybe mock-blowing into an inflatable vest—he's never seen a stewardess that tall, though—but then she's once again in the long, flared Gypsy skirt and blouse, a flowing figure intoning veggie or venison, veggie or venison.

Martha, having kept her distance, feels suddenly famished, and makes her way over to the main building, noticing for the first time how its spacious white interior echoes the landscape. One could be peaceful here. Then she hears commotion, and peers into the auditorium to see food flying everywhere. Veggie burgers are being thrown like Frisbees and someone has organized a subversive volleyball game with the phallus necks as surrogates for a ball. Someone even got hold of a badminton raquet, it looks like: someone who couldn't resist the lure of a metaliteral shuttlecock. She has a feeling of foreboding, and as her eye moves center stage, she sees her husband, undoubtedly the instigator of all this, Norm, the court jester, with two of the dense foam cylinders affixed to his head (Lord knows how he made them stick), prancing about like a mascot at halftime, with his potbelly wobbling, mimicking a Mouseketeer, distorting the lyrics in his typical, infantile, improvisatory fashion (spelling out his own private anthem). "Forever let us hold our dick heads high!" But by the time he's gotten to the refrain: "M-I-D/ D-L-E/ MIDDLE A-G-E," she is on her way out with head down, too mortified to stick around. Unfortunately, someone recognizes her affiliation, corners her before she can escape.

"Your husband is a riot. How refreshing to find someone with a sense of humor to offset all this piety."

"If you say so." Hopes her burning cheeks are somehow not discernible.

"Tell me, though, how did he manage to make those Velcro patches stick to his head?"

"Things stick better to skin than hair!" Finally she makes her exit and races for the cabin.

Who really gives a shit, she thinks, if he's alive or dead, for all the good it's done to have a living, breathing spouse beside her day and night, the contrast of their early married years to these last few, like day to night, as gasping passion cedes, inevitably, to snoring. All those marital clichés that she, that they, resisted, felt irrelevant to *their* relationship, *their* future: Who knew or cared then whose better half was who to whom; but now, no doubt about it: Two worse halves don't make a whole. Martha and Norm, once a single entity, are a mere sum of parts that no longer cohere, or did they ever?—she can't remember now. Too remote to imagine a past existing before anger, during fervor, in the thick of incalculable ardor; yet she remembers the sensation of glorious abandon, when the certainty hormonally, emotionally, etceterally dictated *this*, good woman, is *the one*, and seize the day, this is, *at last*, the one, and who knows if there'll ever be another? And she was in her twenties then! It all comes down to this, she thinks: I'm fucking fed up with this nurtureless environment. But what sort of eulogy is that? Try it as a letter maybe. *Dear Norm, you're dead, you ain't no good to me no more.* Even she can see how sophomoric *that* sounds. (Bogus blues song, he would say.) Oh fuck it, try it later.

In the castration cubicle, she tries to put more oomph into her swing, with Pierre's coaching. His calm solicitousness is like a salve. He seems incapable of irritation as he patiently explains, then demonstrates, then asks her permission to hold her arms as she holds the bat. She senses he's athletic underneath his elegant appearance. A "batgirl" (doubling as waitress and chambermaid, no doubt) retrieves the fallen phalluses and reattaches them to the Velcro bull's-eye centered on the wall. When she's broken a sweat, she starts to get into the literal swing of it, but once Pierre moves on to coach the woman in the next cubicle, instead of being exhilarated by the exercise, it makes her feel fatigued and depressed. Maybe it's her turn for a nap. But then she has to confront Norm. She's got a better plan. She won't even let on that she saw him.

"How's the writing going?"

"Fine. I got A in argumentative/persuasive writing, remember?"

"Yeah, I helped you write those papers, if you recall."

"You couldn't have; it was sophomore year, you weren't there yet."

"No, that was expository writing."

"What, did you memorize my transcript?"

"You showed me the papers, remember? They impressed me. Except for the grammar."

"Whatever. So how'd you do on the chopping block?"

"In the end I couldn't kill you, I just ripped your dick off a bunch of times and wished you dead."

"Good job."

"I'm not even tall enough to kill you."

"That's logical."

"You know, I never liked that word."

"Tall?"

"*No.*"

"Oh, kill?"

"No, *dick.* The word dick."

"That's true, you never did. *What is the sound of one dick ripping?*"

"Is that a Zen C-o-h-e-n?"

"Pretty clever. But who can concentrate around here?—To tell you the truth, I'm a long way from done. I feel ambivalent about the whole exercise, and I would do much better after a few Z's. Do you hear them moaning next door? It's like being trapped in a bad porno flick, but on the other side of the screen! I just want a nap, this whole retreat is way too organized. Jesus, what a racket."

"Take it easy."

"If this is their idea of audiovisual aids, we could have gone to a no-tell motel instead—saved a lot of trouble and money. . . . Hey, have you got a quarter?"

"You need to make a phone call *now?*"

"No, I want to see if there's a slot somewhere on this bed to put a coin in—to make it vibrate. Good grief, why don't they cut it out?" he yells, shaking the bed violently with his arms, then attacking the wall.

"Norm, *you* cut it out, stop banging on the wall, we'll be in even more debt if we have to pay for damages. Besides, we're supposed to hear them, remember? It's supposed to . . . inspire us!"

"Oh I get it, no sex *and* no sleep—great therapy they dole out here. and what's that—stink?"

"I think it's some passion aromatherapy for . . ."

"You have to be . . . tell me you're kidding."

"You're the one in charge of kidding, darling. I'm dead serious."

"Well, seriously, then, *darling,* can you remind me why we're here?"

"Becaused we're fucking *desperate,* Norm, in case you forgot, because our marriage has cancer!"

"Desperate fucking for the fucking desperate, is that it then? Spanish fly might have been more to the point. Tomorrow, maybe they'll have us switch sheets—roll around in their come: a sort of New Age wet suit! Day 1: Rip off his dick; Day 2: Squirm in their sperm; Day 3: Dust off those vows."

"You're gross. And I have to say, even some *desperate* fucking I could go for."

"What, you didn't see the banner over the altar as you walked down the aisle arm-in-arm with your father, sixteen years ago?— *Abandon sex, all ye who enter here!*"

"I guess I was never one to see what's right in front of me."

"Hey, if you're really horny, though, I guess that deer isn't going anywhere."

"You know that's *really* gross, that . . . that's insulting on so many levels I can't even begin . . ."

"Well, look, it has its advantages . . . no HIV risk . . . only Lyme's disease."

"Try Norm's disease, or maybe *ab*norm's disease?"

"Touché."

"Touché nothing. Not only was that crude, it was cruel—don't you get it?—to me, to that . . . creature."

"Look, it wasn't directed at you personally."

"At me impersonally, I suppose."

"Look, I'll aim it at myself, my male self, will that cheer you up? I'll even sing for you. *Do a doe, a female deer*—wait a second, OK, I got it—*with a drop of golden spunk.* (See, I'm not offended, I'm amused.)"

"You're *sick* is what you are! You killed it, don't you understand? How can you?"

"*I* killed it? You're the one that screamed and made me swerve."

"You're the one that stopped relating sexually!"

"I'm the *what?* You know, if you had a church it would be named Perpetual Queen of the Non Sequitur. And could you spare me the jargon. They've brainwashed you already! What are you trying to say?"

"Don't fuck with me, *fuck* me, that's what I'm trying to say! Is that plain enough?"

"Oh that's plain all right, that's plenty plain." He shoves his feet, first left then right, into his boots and slams the cabin door. She opens it to call out after him.

"Look, Norm, Harrison Ford can do something outrageous like staple his hat to his head and be dashing as Indiana Jones, but don't you see with your cock-headed Crazy Glue antics, you're just making an ass of yourself?" (Standing in the snow, he looks, for a priceless moment, sheepish, realizing that putting himself on display meant that his wife could see him too.)

"I thought you would see me as what's-his-face, Bottom, in *Midsummer Night's Dream*."

"Don't give yourself airs. I hate to tell you, just being on stage doesn't automatically make it Shakespeare."

"Actually, now that it's all out in the open, do you have any skin cream in that cosmetics bag? Peeling that glue off really wrecked my skin."

"Find it yourself!" She flings the nylon travel case to him. "You know, Norm, it would have been a lot easier to take the thirty seconds to stick those deer warning thingies on the bumper of the car than to put those dense rubbery cones on the flesh of your fat head! But you couldn't be bothered to do the more sensible thing that might have spared a creature's life."

"Moth, I told you, those whistles don't do . . ."

"Don't call me that when I'm mad at you. And I'm not finished yelling at you, if you don't mind. You had to take on the ludicrous, I-must-be-at-all-times-the-center-of-attention challenge instead! Why'd you even bother to remove them? You should have left your donkey ears on for the trial!"

He'd forgotten the trial! The biggest event! And of course, he'll be first, right on top of Elizabeth's shit list after the food fight. He'll be grilled like venison shish kebab. And no more time to refine his defense speech.

"Sit up front to give me moral support, OK?"

"At my *own* murder trial? Are you out of your mind?"

On go boots and jacket only to remove them in the so-called courtroom. He takes with him the folded piece of paper on which he has written only this: *I don't know which is worse, the guilt or the loneliness.*

Yup, he's up first, and no surprise. He's dead meat. Somehow the gravity of even an ersatz jury is sobering, makes the thing less rinky-dink than he anticipated. Not to mention the aristocratic Elizabeth of the cheekbones, now standing over him in judgment, in judge's *robes*, no less. Hey, happy Halloween. Can you believe it? Where's the powdered wig?

"Where were you on the night of the fourteenth, right? Isn't that the script?" Ha ha.

"No, Norman, the question is not so simple or technical. The question is, why did you murder your wife?"—and something in that schoolmarmy sobriety makes him feel instantly like a criminal, persuades him he's some O. J. sans athletic prowess, and in the middle

47

of rambling that his wife was so uptight and didn't give him space and she was always in his face and didn't acknowledge his efforts or appreciate his attentiveness or attend to *his* pride (as if through mist he sees his wife's hand rise repeatedly, her mouth form syllables), or value his masculinity (such as it was), or be willing to look at *her* flaws for a change, just as diversion from her broken-record list of grievances, he starts, in spite of himself, to bawl—how mortifying—she's a witch, he thinks, her Honor, the Honorable New Age Queen of Mending Hearts is a sorceress. Eliciting emotion through coercion.

"I must tell you, Norman, you are not making the strongest case for yourself." Those big gray, rheumy eyes, loomy with pseudo-wisdom, or could it be genuine compassion? Did they drug him, for God's sake? Downers laced into the vegan *déjeuner?* Pathetic successor of the sublime hash brownies of his youth, enough of which would never fail to make for a relaxed and happy roll in the preconjugal hay, hey, wasn't that eons ago?—and for that matter, wasn't that the very eon in which, in a bliss not derived from any form of cannabis, under no influence but that of Venus, they listened to the ocean pounding in their ears and she said, "I'm so ready for you now," and he said, "No, you're coming *this* way," and his memory is a vivid wash of clitoris and tongue, wave and foam, and her irrepressible high-tide joy that seemed to him to detonate the very ocean. Could Brian, the bio-major dweeb, have provided that? Could any frat boy on campus have offered her that? Would they ever again visit that particular paradise? How long since they'd done or felt anything like that? He weeps even more now, for the beauty of the memory, for the sorrow of its status *as* memory. For the hardship he continues to inflict on his wife. He's overwhelmed, he's ashamed of his ways, of his tears.

Martha—who only now he realizes throughout his testimony was shouting "I object!"—comes to greet him open-armed, console him, so proud of his bravery in exposing a vulnerability she seems to cherish, for he suspects misguided and likely self-serving reasons. Defensive, overwhelmed, confused, he evades her embrace, goes AWOL, stalks away from the podium to clear his head, hears *her* crying. A sound he knows too well, especially lately, lately in this case constituting the last six, twelve, or twenty months—a sound you become inured to and learn, wearily, begrudgingly, guiltily, to tune out like a lawnmower, buzz saw, or trash truck, though it's probably more, in spirit, like a blaring alarm clock—attend to this, attend to this, wake up and do something or you will be too late, don't just push the snooze button—a sound, in any case, that makes you sad and angry at the same time, a sound you can't stand, a sound intrinsically incriminating, a sound you know if you let it in will overwhelm you. So what do you do? You do the obvious self-preservational thing and tune it *right* out! And here for the first time in maybe five years, *he* produces tears; nonetheless, *she* steals the show, it's got to be *her* show even though she does on autopilot what for him is cataclysmic, wrenching, devastating, never-show-his-face-again-emasculating. He'll need a retreat from his retreat, like a vacation from vacation, ha ha, ha, and no doubt there are, at this very moment, classes somewhere for healing those stressed out from healing. Overhauls for the overhealed. They put a mickey in his drink, he thinks: a New Age *sissy*-mickey, that's the ticket, some concealed cry-baby pills.

He's reeling, she who sits in judgment over him can see it, he can see her see him reeling, see right through him, through his schtick, his hype, his fright. This all-seeing queen lifts her viscoelastic gavel, which for all its foam-rubbery give would seem to make a thud of such authority it startles him . . . as she demands, "Is your grief, sir, for your murdered wife, or for your own frustration?"

Well, aren't we suddenly specific? Where's that all-embracing New Age tuna-meld now? My grief is for my wife, my life, my wrong-place-at-the-wrong-time, permanently out-of-commission deer, my dearly departed virility, my annihilated spontaneity, my definitively do-not-resuscitate marriage, how would *I* know what I'm grieving for *exactly?* How would *I* know why I feel like shit? I thought I was paying *you* for answers! For the last sixteen years, plus the decade before, I was trying my damnedest only now to find out none of it counts, I'm supposed to try harder despite the fact that it's definitively too late. But all he can manage to articulate is the much cruder, "Take that rented tux and shove it up your . . ."

"You're in contempt of court!" (Of cunt, more like it.) Oh give me a break, how far will they take this charade? He stalks out of the auditorium, finds her in the corridor, tries to reason with her, tries to embrace her, now *she's* resistant. He retreats, disconsolate, to the cabin; the only thing he has energy for is a nap. He notices a letter on the rustic desk—a Dear John note, no doubt. Yup, sure enough, "Dear Norm" it starts, but now he understands, it's what she wrote down for the eulogy:

Dear Norm,

Fuck you, you wouldn't fuck me anymore (you should appreciate the bluntness), or was it I who wouldn't you? Who knows who won't fuck whom at this point, at this juncture, is it over? At the point of dissolution who can see clearly anymore? Dear Norm, I want you back, but I'm so pissed, I want you dead (oh, right, you are dead), I wish I were dead myself: a spent, still body, me, because only over it will I admit I have a stake in this relationship, this knot we tied so tight, and now it pinches everywhere and who could care less who is pinching whom, dear Norm, I want you back, but in the old way, irretrievable. I grieve for what can't be retrieved, I grieve for my capacity to love you, Norm, I grieve for my memory of the delight of harboring you inside me, dear Norm, my stupid spouse, I'm stuck with you, I took your fucking name, I was insane in my romantic girlish glee—if only I had at least hyphenated it, but that seemed too precious, too trendy, cumbersome, awkward, too multisyllabic, your stupid name, first worse than last; the irony so fucking patent! You're the furthest thing from norm-al, Norm. You know, I never wrote a eulogy before. But should have for the deer, poor creature, my scream killed you. I'm a cartoon of that fucking Edvard Munch on every wall and even once a huge inflated doll thereof, more or less a mouth with legs, I shove our marriage in my mouth and now I spit it out. I scream and everything in earshot dies. Oh deer, your carcass is our gutted fucking. This is a eulogy for me, I think. I need to pee.

Isn't a eulogy supposed to have a certain dignity? He wants a chance, at least, to edit the thing. He wants to respond to it, but he can't quite get himself together. And he weeps again, with his head on the desk, because it also moves him. Undoes him, really. He wants someone to slap him, as someone inevitably would do the hysterical leading ladies in old movies. Maybe he can go out and find a snowbank to weep in, then freeze to death—his carcass a warning on the path like the poor, there-but-for-fortune, ex-trekkers lining Mount Everest. But if he plans to do that, he should at least be able to pass for a snowman, shouldn't he? He wouldn't want to frighten any children passing by. He rises and rummages through that cosmetics bag of Martha's and finds a cuticle scissor with which he unceremoniously shears off the offending ponytail and surrounding hair—his head, but for a thin hedge at a level with his ears, now nearly nothing but skin. Shorn is newborn in a sense, isn't it, he thinks, getting his messed-up self into fleece jacket and cap and out the door. Just what he wanted: bracing. He needs something to brace him. Almost instantly, it seems, his eyelashes are coated with tiny icicles. Fresh snow has fallen, continues to fall. If he fell asleep here in the field for years like Rip van Winkle, the whole field could be his beard and his bed; he deserves no better bed than its frozen expanse, like a while-you-were-out index of obliviousness. You need to open your eyes, Mr. Winkle. Visibility is not terribly high with the snow blowing sort of . . . sideways. There are drifts. He turns back, and sees her.

She in her wedding dress—surreal, all billowy; the expression *like a vision* never seemed so literal or less clichéd. But something's distorted, ambiguous, like she's too big or too small, displaced. He sees his wife larger-than-life, but he knows she can't be any taller than normal—walking over the snow-covered field, with her stupid down jacket all puffy on top and the giant, bustling, satin and lace, layered skirt puffy below. She looks lost, uncertain, absurd, but determined, overdressed, to be sure. As she approaches, he sees the even dumber earmuffs clamped over the wedding veil, whose train, with the dress, swish over the snow, making a broad, delicate trail that is shallower than the corrugated imprint made by the soles of her L.L. Bean boots. Every fiber of her costume and her person fascinates him but in an almost grotesque way. White deer make a ring around her, walk beside her, as if her protectors. The trail of boot prints and paw prints and veil-trail read out as if abstract musical phrases. And in his ears is "their song" from the Beatles' *White Album*, the song he would ceaselessly croon to her in their first years together. Is he dreaming, tripping? Are they white-coated creatures or are their coats coated in snow? He never believed that legend of the ostensibly albino deer from the fenced-in army depot site, some controversy about radiation vs. natural mutation, but maybe it's true after all. One who'd supposedly leapt into an acquaintance's living room. But in this crazy region with its classical place names, this ideal spot for New Age healing extravaganzas, why couldn't it be true: wild turkeys smashing like tornadoes into bathrooms and inadvertently attacking girls in the shower, white deer breaking through picture windows? Hey, why not? What is that anyway, a plea for domestication? Or a refusal to be kept in one's circumscribed "savage" place; an insistence on shattering the illusion of civilization. That might make good comic material. He'd be onstage now, on the road, if *she* hadn't preferred, years ago, to create a domestic life. Or he *thought* she preferred that. Thought she *said* she'd preferred, years ago, to create a domestic life. She lifts the front of the huge skirt as she steps, left, right, left, and apart from the clunky orange boots, all the rest of her lower half seems to merge with the snow, as if she were poured onto it. Suddenly he feels it an urgent issue, whether the deer surrounding her are snow-covered deer or intrinsically white, but in either case it seems as if they emerged from her billowing skirt, as if she'd given birth to them, one by one, and they accompany her as her attendants as well as her goslings. "I found a pen," she seems to be shouting—is it something she wants him to sign? No, silly girl, he wants to say, the vows are spoken, not written. *Martha, my dear . . . hold your hand out, you silly girl,* then I can see if there's a pen in your mittened hand *(and you will see—that you and me were meant to be—for each other).* Those lyrics make him cry anew. Or is it divorce papers she wants signed? "I found a pen; I let them out." OWWW OWWW; something hurts. The syllable expands over the ocean of snow. Or is it WOOOOWW, like the cartoon of a pothead at a party, stupid with bliss, the whole universe is singing (unless it is crying, moaning, in pain). Which is it, Norm, which? The deer too (wait, aren't deer silent creatures?) would seem to be entreating or enjoining him: Take the VOOOOWWWS, Norm. Take the VOOOWWS. You OOOWWWEE us that. All she needs is a shepherd's staff. Martha had a little fawn, and it was pure as snow, and everywhere that Martha went—*Do a doe, a female deer, with a drop of golden*—it shames him now, the *Sound of Music* gag, against this more ecstatic, authentic music of the universe. Could this be what they meant by music of the spheres? It seems to keep echoing, the sound, the syllable, mutating. They couldn't be saying Chihuahua! They do not resemble Chihuahuas at all. They are deer, and by no stretch of the imagination ordinary deer. (*Take the vows— you owe us—take the vows—you owe us.*) They are definitively deer. His cheeks and ears are red with cold. His head feels colder without his token hair, but the silver lining is that the cold anesthetizes his two head wounds. The bullet only grazed me, Officer. You see, the trouble is I ripped my dick, her neck, off my thick, yet ultimately fragile, head. My head deserves the cradle of this snowbank, wouldn't you agree? If an ostrich can put its head in the sand, Martha my dear—my deer, that's it—can't a man put his head in the snow? The damp is penetrating through his no-longer waterproof boots to his toes. Norman stands on his head and waves his legs, trying to air-dry his feet, then tumbles over. He makes snow angels all in a row. He stands up, soaked through. He is reaching his hand across the field, calling her name, hoping she will see or hear, and he feels as if he were indeed Rip van Winkle, awakening to a strange, new world.

Four Poems

Forrest Gander

GHOST SONATA

The fulcrum of the composition: a sheared-off, gnarly trunk. In apparent contradiction of death's irreversibility, it has broken into leaf. It leans slightly forward, our way, producing a visual effect similar to the entasis or swelling of a classical pillar. Its isolation magnifies a solemnity. The bark's sharp, rough texture balances the diffuse weight of the rest of the image. Beyond the trunk, a horizon lists. Foliage at the left edge is blurred as though it had been caught trying to escape the photograph even as a dark flare burns its way into the upper right corner.

The strain between active points is sustained in the *repoussoir*, the clear, centered figure of a ruptured tree. Through shifting gradients, the trunk anchors an articulated foreground to the dissolving back field. A warm black yields—immediately behind the trunk—to pale gray. From the ground itself, an ethereal, creamy light seems to rise. The photograph is mute, but implicative. A leafy explosion crowns this severed totem. At the border between a tangible and an intangible world, life climbs onto death's shoulders.

Forrest Gander

BRIDGE AND SWIMMER

Our eye goes with the swimmer who carves across the water a white wake. The track in the water parallels the span of the bridge beyond it. From there, from the railroad bridge, at the end of its tether, our gaze returns to congregate in the tree stretched over the lake. Its limbs angle like bridge girders. They reach across sullen water into the sky's reflection which spreads toward us, shimmering like a slick of olive oil. We take in the whole dreamy romance before we let our attention fall to the blemish on the face of the print. Distracting us from our nostalgia, insisting on the photograph's materiality, it sabotages all transparence. Just so, the blemish completes the photograph, conspiratorially connecting the surface, part of the viewer's realm, with the bridge and swimmer deep within. Here at the blemish, the etic perspective (we are separate from the event) and the emic (we are part of the event) collide in a dialectic whose singular resolution is the photograph itself.

BROKEN TOWER

Then this place
along Purgatory Creek, past the grist mill's
stone ruin, a road
pulled from darkness and stretched out to dry
in morning air. The image's complexity, its
shifting depths, derive
from an interplay
of directed tensions: rearing
trees and tower, prone ditch and
road. The eye stutters between axes
of symmetry unable
to pin down the beat.
Neatly into the coffin of the ditch,
the ghostly tower would fit. A tree
sashays. Are those catfish heads
scattered in the dirt? Effervescing,
the brush clamors toward
road. Ditch water dull as resin. Of
all we survey,
aren't we drawn often to
the least substantial? Weatherworn and saturated
by the density of light, the tower and
its trees blend into a compassion precisely
where our sightlines meet.

Forrest Gander

ARGOSY FOR ROCK AND GRASS

Keeled shells of snapping   turtles, their saw-
tooth tails in the river   mud. Gulping
in shallows, blowing   out water through
their nostrils so the surface   froths. Wind, that
murmur of psalmody,   runs through the distant
assembly of pin oaks.   A family graveyard, untended
in bracken fern. Five   concrete headstones
decorated with marbles: Child, Child, Child, Child, Child.
The landscape clutches   its long roots, its concealed
life animates   the loam. A drawn-out
exposure nets traces of   movement—flying birds, trembling
leaves shadow the print   like thought. A hogs-
head of tobacco lies   half-buried midstream.
Glinting in rock: mica,   feldspar, cyanide. Although
placc is depicted, no   sign in the world
corresponds to this   image. There is no source
for such radiance   outside the photograph.
The stone draws grass,   and the treeline wavers,
vague in the background,   proposed and
forgotten. It sucks us from   and returns us to
the scene, less   construal than
inquiry. Setting as   mirror, perspective
as mechanism. Not   to direct the un-
observed, to receive it. Faulting   the image for its lack
of clarity, we would   miss its fullness
coming to be. A   river named The
Holy Ghost. We   believe what we do not know.

Sleeping with Schéhérazade
Rikki Ducornet

THE NIGHT OF OUR RETURN from Fayoum, Father's and mine, I took
Theophrastus to bed with me. From my bedroom window I could see
the neighbor's roof illuminated by a full moon, and a lonely sheep
awaiting sacrifice. Pigeons were raised on that roof also, pigeons
Beybars bartered for and prepared for us so lovingly. And there was
an admirable tomato plant the size of a small tree, its fruit as sweet
as plums. For a time I sat gazing out the window holding the book
to my face, testing its fragrance. The Fayoum surged in memory:
my room and its lamp, the green lake and its birds, the still gardens
sustained by their gridworks of bright water, the gardeners and har-
vesters themselves reduced by distance to ciphers as they are painted
on the walls of tombs. I opened the book and read:

> *Moisture belongs to plants . . . this moisture is at-*
> *tended by a taste . . . all plants have most moisture*
> *at the time of making growth. Again, in some plants,*
> *the juice has a special color; in some it is white, as in*
> *those which have a milky juice; in some blood-red,*
> *as in centaury—*

These words acted upon me like a sequence of charms and as I continued to read, I felt the presence of Ramses Ragab distinctly, as I had
throughout that entire week even when he had vanished into his
laboratory to dream at his little fan-shaped table.

> *Again, in some plants, the juice is merely thick, as in*
> *those in which it is of milky character . . . the juice*
> *of the silphium is pungent like the plant itself.*

Reading Theophrastus was an operation of grace, of grace and deep
magic—as when I read my beloved *Arabian Nights* and the perceptible world dissolved:

I have known love and passion since infancy; I was nourished at my mother's breasts—

Words that spelled the night with urgency, a kind of stunning clarity:

—In all plants mentioned, the juice either forms naturally—

Something like an undiluted sublimity:

—or when the incisions are made. But it is obvious that men only make incisions in plants whose juice is sought after such as myrrh, which should be cut at the rising of the dog star and on the hottest days—

Thinking: *on the hottest days.* Thinking: *moisture is attended by a taste.* Thinking: *My longing is violent; it submerges me in heat. None like it existeth.* Reading Theophrastus: *They first pound it up in sweet wine.* Recalling these words of Schéhérazade: *and O how sweet are the nights.*

It is dark, Schéhérazade recited, *it is dark and my transport and my disease are excited, and desire provoketh my pain.*

Imagining what it would be, what it must be to be naked in the naked arms of a man; what it might be to be *incised*, penetrated by a man. *And the root is stout and sweet,* wrote Theophrastus. *The fruit is good for the eye.*

Imagining for the first time fearlessly, the reality of a girl *being sexual* (a term of my mother's) with a man. I thought of Sakkiet, wondering what it would be to be betrothed against one's will. Imagining, in a sudden fever, what it would be to be betrothed to Ramses Ragab against my will. These are the thoughts that thrust me into pleasure's heady orbit, pleasure, like an act of magic, flooding the hours of the night with fragrancy.

For Schéhérazade, love was like a game of chess played in bed upon the counterpane, its moves could not be counted. Schéhérazade enchanted the king Scháhriar not only with her stories within stories, but her moves within moves.

Rikki Ducornet

> *It is dark and desire—*

When I closed my eyes, everything vanished and all that was left was this: my resurgent secret, exotic and irresistible, that "sweet tradition of little girls," Saleh once laughingly said; all that was left was pleasure, and its attainment the only operation of sympathy that mattered. My pleasure wantoning like a wilderness in his mutable embrace, gazing into his many faces, alone in the middle of the night, having returned home from Fayoum on the hottest of days, in the season of roses, in the season of the making of attar.

> *And the beauty of delight hath appeared with perfume.*

When I awoke, the noon had abandoned my window, and both books—Theophrastus and *The Arabian Nights*—were sprawled beside me. I lay in the luxury and silence of solitude and thought about Schéhérazade, her beauty and intelligence. The first time she sleeps with Scháhriar, she offers to recite *a moral tale disguised as a licentious one*, saying that, unlike lesser mortals, he will appreciate the difference. She has just lost her virginity to Scháhriar, and in a few hours her neck will be broken. In order to survive, she needs to inebriate the king's soul. The prophet tells men to cultivate their wives as one cultivates a garden; this is just what Schéhérazade does to Scháhriar. Night after night, she cultivates him in the infinite reverie that glimmers at the heart of human sexuality. Night after night, she provokes the king's curiosity and his desire, just as she softens his lethal rage against women and reveals the feminine sympathies that animate the world: the rose, the shell, the female sex, the female face, the moon; her saliva and the nectar of flowers, the taste of grapes having ripened on the vine. She reveals the *sympathy* between sensual love and adventure; she reveals that love is both the reason for adventure and its reward. Love, Schéhérazade tells Scháhriar, is the universe's soul—indissoluble and indestructible. Without love's ardor to animate it, the universe would be as lifeless as a handful of sand. Everything is perceived through the senses, she reminds him; it is the imagining mind that makes the world intelligible and nothing animates the imagination as does love. It is love that makes us human, spontaneous, and thoughtful; it is the highest bond and the greatest good. The world and all its forms

64

belong to Eros, and when everything is ended love will persist. Ardor, Schéhérazade tells Scháhriar, is the world's cause and the world's reason. When Schéhérazade speaks, it is as if the words themselves are wantoning.

At the end of the book, the storyteller is a queen and her sister, Dinarzade, has become a woman. She, too, sleeps with Scháhriar. Dinarzade has never left her sister's side; she has listened to all her stories and witnessed their lovemaking. I imagined that Sakkiet and I were sisters, that Ramses Ragab was Scháhriar, and that we shared his embraces. Flowers were threaded in our hair, and our hands and feet were stained with henna. We smelled of *susinum*. He desired us above all others but between the two of us he could not decide. His counterpane heaved with our laughter.

In *The Arabian Nights*, the descriptions of what a desirable woman is are repeated again and again like a conjuration. Perfect beauty united:

> *The voluptuousness of the Greeks, the amorous virtues of the Egyptians, the lascivious movements of the women of Arabia, the heat of the daughters of the Ethiopians, the limitless knowledge of India's temple whores, the unbridled passions of the women of Nubia, the narrow cunts of the daughters of the Chinese, the vigor of the women of Irak, the delicacy and knowledge of perfumes of the Persians, the muscular thighs of the women of Upper Egypt . . .*

and so on. That night I wrote a letter to Ramses Ragab. And because I could not bring myself to write "Ram" or even "Ramses," and because I knew it would be ludicrous to write a love letter and use his full name, I decided simply to begin:

> It is very late and the moon which was full and bright over the neighbor's roof is gone and I am alone, no, I am not alone because my heart is full of the fragrancies of Fayoum, your mother's "Jicky" and your father's books, and always the smell of roses and the knowledge that you were near.
> I know you think I am a child but I am only one year younger than Sakkiet, who will be married soon.
> And I want
> and I wish that
>   I wish

I was unable to go further. I could not name what it was I wished for, what it was I wanted. I could not, I dared not write: *I want you to make love to me.* I could not, I dared not write: *I want you to take me.* But then, suddenly seized by my own boundless longing, I began to write quickly, as though I was about to die and needed at all costs to write everything down; as though I would die like a fish out of water if I didn't write everything down at once:

> I am dreaming of our naked bodies pressed together in a garden of roses, a garden of lilies, in a garden of henna, in the bed Schéhérazade shared with Scháhriar. You once told me that I smelled of new pencils and grapefruit and green sandalwood but I smell only of sandalwood and rose attar— the fragrance you gave me; it is a woman's fragrance. And it says in my copy of *The Arabian Nights* that dark girls have a *hidden sensibility*, and I think this is so because I always know as soon as you enter our house what fragrancies you have been making. Like the seasons of the air, your perfume changes from one day to the next; sometimes it seems from one moment to the next, as though being near you was like being in a garden where many flowers grow and their perfume is carried on the breeze; sometimes it is jasmine that scents the air; sometimes it is the flowering quinces. Or a man is passing in the street selling cinnamon and everything changes, the mood of the day changes entirely. He is selling fried dough dipped in honey; he is offering freshly roasted coffee in cups perfumed with mastic; he is roasting almonds; he is turning lamb on the spit; he is boiling the mint for tea.
>
> I cannot place or name you. You are too "volatile"—a word you taught me. I think you are mysterious.
>
> In my book (I'm still talking about *The Arabian Nights*), it says young girls smell like nard and that this has a wonderful smell. I wonder if this is true and if you were lying beside me breathing my skin would you say, "Lizzie, you smell like nard." It also says that it is best for a man to be with a girl and I think this must be so. But if you think I am still too young we could wait for a year because then I'll be fourteen, the age Sakkiet is now, and there will be no reason not to love me then if you love me now. I hope you will read my letter and tell me if you love me; sometimes I think you do. I think you love me when I look up and see you are gazing at me and your eyes warm me as though suddenly the air in the room came directly from Fayoum, Fayoum under the midday sun when everything is still—even the birds—and everyone is resting in the shade. At noon when the scent of roses is so strong everyone is dizzy.
>
> I have read that nard is found in the Himalaya Mountains

and that it grows at seventeen thousand feet! So it is very rare. And I have read that in the Tamil language "nard" is the word for everything that smells good. Once you gave me some to smell; you put a drop on my wrist. It was strange but wonderful, a little like valerian and patchouli at the same time. Green and gold, cold and hot! I wish

I want to go to you now, this instant, and ask you to put your nose to my wrist and tell me if I smell of a schoolgirl's pencils, or if I smell of *nard!*

Theophrastus says that people think that in order to harvest mandrake you have to whisper to the plant about the mysteries of love. And this is because the root of the mandrake is just like a human person: It is female or it is male. I think my letter to you is like a mandrake harvest because I am telling you my deepest mystery. Please read my letter and answer it as soon as you can because I am like a plant that needs water, I am like a mandrake that has heard all about love and wants to be pulled. I think I am dying for you. Yes. This is what is happening. I am dying for you.

Lizzie

After I wrote this letter I pressed the cipher I had tattooed to my wrist with a pin so that it pained me and bled a little, and this to ease my longing, the pain in my heart. A drop of blood pearled at the center of the cipher; it tasted sweet. I thought to needle the cipher was to *needle him,* if only a little. I took up my letter and read it.

My letter was impossible! It was ridiculous—the letter of a precocious schoolgirl. If he read it he would laugh in that quiet way he had; he would laugh indulgently; he would indulge me and be kind, nothing more. He was a man of the world—hadn't Mother once told me so? *A man of the world, even if he comes across so damned precious, you know?* I supposed it was true; clearly it was true. He was a man of the world who had dealings every day with the most beautiful, the most sophisticated women of Cairo, women whom I now imagined as versions of Mother—big-bodied, full-bosomed women with coltish legs and *wantoning* eyes who, as they received their precious purchase from his own hand—the coveted jar of cream, the unique perfume—would whisper a name and a number and an hour. They would meet, not in a field of flowers like some ridiculous Egyptian movie with someone wailing: *Habibi! Habibi!* in the background over and over again, no, but instead in a beautiful room tiled with blue stars in an impasse planted with ancient trees, a room that their husbands knew nothing about, yes: These were handsome, cynical women, divorced or married to men too busy to notice their wives vanished for hours altogether in the afternoon; foreign women, Swedish tourists, for example, unmarried and worldly, mad for Egyptian men; women unafraid to write: I want to be penetrated by you; please meet me (but no, they wouldn't plead!), *meet me*, Rue Mouizz Lidin Illah, number 5, tomorrow, the blue door behind the fountain, so that we may *pleasure one another* (a great phrase I'd also picked up from *The Arabian Nights*); women, in other words like Mother, who littered the floor with apricot underwear and fucked even when bleeding. Again, self-loathing welled up inside me: how I hated my body, just barely female, my breasts like those green plums so small one can hold half a dozen in the palm of the hand! Unlike Mother's breasts, so damned gorgeous, her long legs—*would I ever grow tall?* Mother, asleep on the other side of the river, in the arms of strangers she eyed from her balcony, in her room filled with flowers rotting in their vases. When she was awake she was the embodiment of air and this is why I felt oppressed and had to fight to breathe. Asleep she was the cipher for clay; I could imagine how heavy she would seem asleep beside her lover, all her quickness stilled, her breath smelling of the day's cigarettes, her body like a bank of sand soaking up the night, soaking up the radiant heat of another's body. I could not imagine her lying in my father's arms, only with a stranger, dark and lean, as bright as a dagger; a stranger like the one I'd seen her pressed to the afternoon Father and I returned from the Mouski and opened the door and the chess set of ivory tumbled to the floor and our lives began to fall and were still falling.

Sobbing now, I tore up my letter to Ramses Ragab, the man beyond reach, the older man, the worldly man, the gazelle man who came to our house almost every day *but not to see me*, not because he, too, longed to *pleasure me*, but because he shared—if to a lesser degree— Father's folly; the man who stretched out like an overgrown boy, having kicked off his impeccable, *man-of-the-world* shoes; having dropped his linen jacket over a chair with a nonchalance that pierced me to the quick, to stretch out with a sigh on the Shiraz saying: "*Eh, bien! Mon général! On commence?*"

Audience
Mei-mei Berssenbrugge

1.

People believe, at the theater, an audience is tricked into believing it's looking at life.

The film image is so large, it goes straight to your head.

There's no room to be aware of or interested in people around you.

Girls and cool devices draw audience, but unraveling the life of a real human brings the outsiders.

I wrote before production began, "I want to include all of myself, a broken person who hasn't worked for years, who ran away, who's simply not dead."

Many fans feel robbed and ask, "What kind of show's about one person's unresolved soul?"

2.

There's sympathy for suffering, also artificiality.

Having limbs blown off is someone's reality, but not mine.

I didn't want to use sympathy for others as a way through my problems.

There's a gap between an audience and particulars, but you can be satisfied by particulars, on several levels: social commentary, sleazy fantasy.

Where my film runs into another's real-life conditions seems problematic, but they don't link with me.

Linking, entertainment, is the flow of images, thwarting a fan's transference.

If you have empathy to place yourself in my real situation of face-to-face intensity, then there would be no mirror, not as here.

3.

My story is about the human race in conflict with itself and nature.

An empathic princess negotiates peace between nations and huge creatures in the wild.

I grappled with the theme, again and again.

Impatience and frustration built among fans.

"She achieves a personal voice almost autistic in lack of affect, making ambiguous her well-known power to communicate emotion, yet accusing a system that mistakes what she says."

"Sex, tech are portrayed with lightness, a lack of divisions that causes anxieties elsewhere."

When I find a gap, I don't fix it, don't intrude like a violent, stray dog, separating flow and context to conform what I say to what you see.

Time before the show was fabulous, blank.

When I return as to an object in space, my experience is sweeter, but not because of memory.

The screen is a mirror where a butterfly tries so hard not to lose the sequence of the last moments.

My work should reflect society, like mirrors in a café, double-space.

There's limited time, but we *feel* through film media we've more.

4.

When society deterritorialized our world with money, we
managed our depression via many deterritorializations.

Feeling became vague, with impersonal, spectacular equivalents in
film.

My animator draws beautifully, but can't read or write.

He has fears, which might become reality, but Godzilla is reality.

When I saw the real princess, I thought her face inauspicious, ill
favored, but since I'd heard she was lovely, I thought, maybe she's
ill and not photogenic today.

Compared to my boredom, I wondered if her life were not like looking into a stream at a stone, while water rushed over me.

I told her to look at me, so her looking is that around which everything rushes.

I don't care about story or look so much as, what do you think of her?
Do you like her?

She's not representative, because of gaps in the emotion, only yum-
my parts, and dialogue that repeats.

She pencils a black line down the back of her leg.

A gesture turns transparent, then proliferates into thousands of us
doing the same.

Acknowledging the potential of a fan club, she jokingly describes it
as "suspect."

She means the performance comes out through the noise.

5.

At a bar, you see a man catch hold of a girl by the hair and kick her.

You could understand both points of view, but in reality, no.

You intervene, ashamed for hoping someone else will.

It becomes an atmosphere, a situation, by which I mean groups.

In school we're taught the world is round, and with our own eyes we confirmed a small part of what we could imagine.

Because you're sitting in a dark place, and I'm illuminated, and a lot of eyes are directed at me, I can be seen more clearly than if I mingled with you, as when we were in high school.

We were young girls wanting to describe love and to look at it from outer space.

Two Poems
Brenda Hillman

STUDY FOR "THE AIR IN TRIANGLES"

Not till dawn agrees a volunteer

How downhill it was outside the world

Unicyclists with knives   Translators

When we spoke to the triangles
The letters came

First Y and N and especially A

By dusk they had settled
In the voicelet

A robin had been feeding baby isoceles heads
Beside the ski hut

Brief don't   let   me cries aflutter

Their shapes of waste she carried out
Over the chamberous meadow's yellow

Then the beaks would sink quietly down

Should the birds be subject to a geometry
Based on the mystical three points of nature

Either the middle of the figure is mind
And the points are word world and weather

Or one of the points is mind

And word is the middle
That sort of thing

A living comes in an opinion which is energy

Sufficiently touching air

Lines mostly said   The not-unsayable

DOPPLER EFFECT IN DIAGRAM THREE

Waves past the meadow viajante
Summer is almost straight
From cities from countries
They had straight-smelling shirts
Parentheses from the hawk a day sound
Only borders in the mouth
Almost no weather at all from its travels
The heat singinginging
A series of syllables not yet delivered
Families just beginning to gather
Double gather like curtains
So much not enough one said
A hope inflected from the east
Something at rest about the waves not then
Someone swell to be remembered
In the theories of the address
Blue & the palindrome of a wave
Moving against the rest

The earth's axis has been set aflame
The harlequin picks his teeth with a matchstick
It was called life those decades
Dragonflies attached one per stalk
A music staff turned sideways
Papermill Creek before the death of paper
Incandescence is its own defense one said

Periodicity of a fear moving
Off from the too bright years
A bike in a car the spokes turning
Click-click past rags and ravens
It's up to sounds to descend in sizes
To address a surprise or terror
But how does the air feel with all
Those waves inside do radio waves feel
When we're listening to them
Can any object pass through the falling
And how does the (((((((((do it

In the model an observer stands on
The platform and we grow to love him
He is wild and is thinking of nothing
Let us call all this observer A
There is a row of bending sounds
As the trouble curves rightward
Mr. Doppler is in heaven by now
A slim hush the fat springs click
The men in burgundy shorts roll
The little carts along
People think they are you but they are not
You are you and no one and everything
The oscillating quality of dusk clashes with
What is universal just as the sounds
In a person's name clash with handwriting
How lovely we seem as someone pulls away
With an identity among the abstracted
Pale diners who eat behind the cellophane

But in fact he is lost to us
As the page turner at the recital is lost
Or one who speaks of the Irish solution
Or one who names roses Peace or Sally
When it starts being unbearable
Time will not pierce the air with its death feet
In the pulling away life is continuous
The worry hyphens inside the molecule
The sentence or the train passing
As it holds out its skirts of sound

Brenda Hillman

The sentence has started its journey
But has no idea for its mystic demise
It rides in the firebox to the cave
Looking out at pines their raw huts
Bearing its constant falling
Over the laughter in the night pool of those
Who haven't stopped and may not ever

All the Lights of Midnight:

Salbatore Nufro Orejón, "The Physics of Ero^r" and Livia Bassil's *Psychology of Physics*

Mark Z. Danielewski

[As set forth by I. Maldonado in the presence of Ricardo Justiniano who translated; Abel Izquierdo who retranslated; Sergio Gutiérrez who joked about Air Force Hawker Hunters; Elena Huidobro who recalled a matter of Mapuche cosmology; Xavier Arellano who drank espresso and slept in his chair; Antonia Muños who spoke quietly of Violeta Parra's suicide; Dario Hernandez who had plenty to say about hidden variables and wave mechanics and summer swims; Serena Ortiz who arrived late but still told (again) of her stay at Villa Grimaldi; Hector Corrilla who knew nothing about pair production let alone gardening but had personally met Dyson; Gabriel de Benavides who brought with him a *charango* but spoke only of street names; Sabastian Vasquez who at one point quoted bitterly, "*Hay que guardar silencio y olividar*"; and Miguel Sepúlveda who sobbed once but still wrote it all down——all down at the Abelian Café on Spring Street on the evening of February 13, 2001, between those ever uncertain hours of dusk and dawn.]

IT REMAINS A LONG-STANDING conviction that mathematics and physics reside beyond the influences of familial and social circumstances. Purportedly both fields still maintain an autonomy undisturbed by tear or bloodstain; integers, Greek letters, even the naked back of an integral all shimmering beyond anything human. By contrast a musical composition, no matter how technical, would never be deprived of the emotional beginnings characterizing its creation, even though its language too remains so nonspecific as to verifiably sustain any relation other than to itself. Except, of course, music fulfills in its hearing, its experience. Law as well achieves preeminence in the name of ethical and social systems somehow by and for the people but still apart from the people. Though Law too necessarily fulfills in a hearing. Our citadel of equations, however, claims no need of its own experience, its own human hearing. Its view is so total, the way by which its builders come and go—their lives, their loves, their ends—is absolutely irrelevant.

In Livia Bassil's powerful and brooding *Psychology of Physics* (Lagrangian Rose Press, 2000), words such as "total" and "absolutely" are carefully scrutinized, while a word like "love" absent in the absorber theory, quantum electrodynamics, or the double-slit experiment fills her pages like some ancient ether as unsubstantiated as it is perhaps irrefutable.

By itself the prologue is a breathtaking accomplishment. More questioning than conclusive, Bassil's dexterity with syntax, the breezy compression of biography and detail can only leave one longing for the so much of the world she's contained and hence the so much more of the world she's omitted. In a mere thirty-eight pages Bassil peers into the lives of this century's greatest scientific minds, whether Meitner, Noether, Hawking, or numerous others, daring with each mention to demand what effect living has had upon the integrity of an experiment or peer-reviewed theory. Quietly she asks us to consider Schrödinger at the second battle of Isonzo in July of 1915 or imagine Tomonaga in the ruins of post–World War II Tokyo. She prods us at least to wonder whether or not the loss of Einstein's daughter, Lieserl, could have possibly "put the bend on Lorentz." And what of Feynman, who in 1945, twenty years before he won the Nobel Prize, lost his wife and childhood sweetheart, Arline Greenbaum, to tuberculosis? "Even if we concede that experience cannot alter the commutative properties of multiplication," Bassil delicately ponders, "how certain can we be that it has not already altered what figures or equations were chosen to be multiplied in the first place?"

Unafraid of all she implies and perhaps in anticipation of the accusatory declamation "what for?" surely to come her way, Bassil concludes her prologue with this brief but clear statement of purpose: "It is a political imperative for any and all free thinkers to mistrust any institution claiming to be beyond the motions of our own impulses. For without listening to what influences us, how can we ever dare to hear what is beyond what our influences continuously insist we hear?"

Of course in the chapters that follow, Bassil leaves the common greats to concentrate exclusively on that genius from Chile, Salbatore Nufro y Cuevas Ruvias Orejón Sandino, otherwise known simply as Nufro, the pale, some say misshapen, man who once stood unsteadily before an audience at M.I.T. delivering a proof with such force and vitality, one associate later declared him to be "the Byron of Field Theory." No one ever denied it—his dark eyebrows; the fantastic flutter of fingertips whenever numbers were discussed; the complicated wines he preferred; the black sweaters he always wore; the ranging trips he would take from meadow to mountain; the weeks he would lie alone in his study, suddenly infirm and deadly— all describing in near perfect opposition a man who was as defeated as he was unbeatable; rooted as he was motive; as driven by silence as he was determined by the music of his homeland. Rumors still persist that he was the only professor who had ever made a student swoon over mirror symmetry.

Nufro first became known in the United States for his early work on quantum electrodynamics, studying with the likes of Julian Schwinger, carrying on a well-documented correspondence with Freeman Dyson, and writing some highly illuminating papers on perturbation technique. Had he done nothing more, his efforts in the area of gauge theory would have assured him a place in the pantheon of quantum mechanics.

As is well known, though, it was his unpublished paper "The Physics of Ero^r," written in 1978 at the age of twenty-three, eventually resulting in the formal *Particle Alternatives* published almost ten years later, which shocked Nufro into the spotlight. In it he showed how a particle's "choice of path" actually determined "the property of the destination" despite classical expectations when taking into account decoherence and path integrals; a claim which the world at large initially viewed as incoherent but which a tiny cadre of physicists viewed as nothing short of miraculous.

For the reader unequipped for the complexities of Nufro's discovery, Bassil expertly and somewhat poetically lays out the theory in terms any high school student could understand: "With 'The Physics of Ero^r' Nufro brought to the world all its possibilities. Into every college textbook on quantum theory he introduced the concept that not only was every path between 'origination point/particle S' & 'destination point/particle M' actual and present but the observance of a path out of the so-called classical trajectory could go so far as to renegotiate the very nature of the destination point/particle 'so that M could change to F.'" As one of Nufro's colleagues explained: "Observance was once again the key. What should have been a photon, thanks to an alternative path, could suddenly end up an electron or proton. Hell, you could potentially wind up with a monkey and a cat dressed in white tails sitting around a table discussing *La Nueva Canción Chilena*, sipping tea. That caused quite a stir. The macro set gets quite ripe when the quantum crew interferes." But perhaps another chronicler of the physicist's life provided the simplest, albeit weirdest, example: "Nufro went ahead and proved mathematically that if you swim to an unknown boat out in the bay who you find owns it could be vastly different from who would have owned it had you taken a canoe there instead."

Some theorists still insist that quantum possibility dilemmas, particularly Nufro's, will eventually be resolved with advances in the area of hidden variables, much like Zeno's paradox was resolved with the mathematics of limits. In that spirited debate lie volumes. Bassil, however, has no interest in speculating on the future of quantum theory nor for that matter is she concerned with Nufro's presence in the United States, only fleetingly touching on the young South American's arrival in New York City and the paper he would soon after scribble down at the Abelian Café on Spring Street. That much of Nufro's history is already well known; as certain, perhaps, as our own knowledge of the modern world. After all, New York still stands as does the Abelian Café. Bassil's quest is rather to examine what stood before and more importantly determine those paths that ultimately led Nufro to the autonomous purity of his particle alternatives.

Born near Los Angeles, Chile, Nufro grew up wandering the banks of the Bíobío River not far from the falls of Salto del Laja. His father was a civil engineer. His mother a common gardener from Isla de Chiloé who raised her son on stories of the *Trauco* and *La Pincoya*, a blonde nymph who was said to emerge from the sea at sunrise and dance on the beach. Supposedly, if she looked inland, the ocean would seethe with fish. If, however, she looked back at the waves, all fish would vanish. Even when Nufro's family moved to Santiago, his mother continued to keep alive the rich cultural legends of the Chilean Southland.

The delicious detail Bassil musters for her project can hardly be anticipated here, be it Nufro's early determination to knit his own sweater, dying the wool in crushed cinnabar imported from the Hunan province in China, while at the same time deriving a series of odd probabilities to anticipate and then even determine stitch patterns; or his efforts to create a game combining chess and poker; or most notably his substantial musical ingenuity: "By fourteen, he was playing the guitar feverishly, regularly busking deep into the A.M. winds at the Mercado Central. It didn't matter if he was working his way down Paseo Ahumada strumming *Vals a mi padre* or singing *Ha cesado, la lucha sangrienta* near the Palacio de la Moneda, he was always learning and tinkering with new arrangements, new material, visiting *peñas* similar to Violeta Parra's famous *La Carpa de la Reina,* mingling with artists and activists, accompanying anyone who was around, often a wide array of musicians with *bombos, quenas,* and of course *zampoñas."*

Off folk and Andean baroque, Nufro earned book money. Though soon enough Bach and everything else were left behind in favor of his own improvised works, which became increasingly more difficult to hear, until rumor has it by the age of fifteen he declared to several musicians from the Technical University *peña,* some of whom would go on to join Inti-Illimani, "I have played it all," after which his fingers moved but never touched, string and fret retaining their accustomed distance, Nufro packing more and more shreds of homemade sweater into his ears so he "could hear."

Increasingly irritated by their son's behavior, his parents grew more outspoken in their condemnation of his "pranks." They were not alone. Few could understand what exactly Nufro was perceiving. Soon even his friends withdrew from his strange concerns, turning to the much more accessible musical tastes of Victor Jara or Roberto Bravo. Then at seventeen, Nufro met someone who would not go: Françisca Yepun de la Viña Escalcra. "Ycpun," as young Françisca was happy to explain, was her Mapuche name meaning *el lucero de la noche* or "evening star." (*Yeln* = to carry; *Pun* = night.) Supposedly, though likely apocryphal, one of the first things she told Nufro to do was pick her up: "Manage that Musician Boy and you'll carry all the puns of this whole wide world . . . me." Nufro easily lifted her and then went even further, walking the Alameda, all the way from the University to Cerro Santa Lucia, with the giggling girl in his arms, Nufro the whole time singing in her ear *A la mar fui por naranjas.*

As Bassil writes: "[Françisca] was bright with the sentiments of the time, surging with devotions for all an artist was supposed to mean to the poor and the silent and the weary and the forgotten and the persecuted and the ill. Upon her ankle she wore slender chains of gold. In her hair flowed silks of many colors. She beguiled him. But he beguiled her too, and whether it was his blue eyes or the stab of madness in him, Françisca found in Nufro the conscription her own future as a painter had always anticipated."

Or so she thought.

What really awaited her then awaits us all even now in Bassil's

81

book, the merest viewing of which will with awful force cast upon Nufro and his work the same shadow Heisenberg's political affiliations cast today. Somehow in the early days of Pinochet's rise to power, Nufro was seduced by a radical political organization known only as SENDA, a self-proclaimed descendant of such groups as the mythic *brujeria* from the South and the secret society *Logia Lautarina*, which back in 1818 is said to have ordered the execution of three famed Chilean revolutionaries: José Miguel and the Carrera brothers. Confirmed by the VEM™ Corporation, SENDA openly kept council with several members from the Catholic prelature Opus Dei. Most significantly, though, SENDA worked directly with DINA, *Dirección de Inteligencia Nacional*, the Chilean security force that under Pinochet's authority was responsible for the murder and disappearance of thousands, including eventually Victor Jara, who sang famously in his song *La luna siempre es muy linda: "Recuerdo el rostro de mi padre como un hueco en la muralla."*

Seeking to ensure the place of the new regime, SENDA worked constantly to insinuate itself into the world of political dissidents throughout the country. Supposedly Pinochet was referring to SENDA in 1975 when he proclaimed that not a leaf in Chile moved without him knowing it.

What attracted Nufro in the first place to such criminals remains a mystery, even to Bassil, despite page after page of tireless examination. One point, though, becomes clear: It was not long after Nufro's parents left Santiago for the North that Nufro handed his guitar over to Françisca—"Paint the strings solid to the frets," he said—and began an even closer association with SENDA, hiding it at first from Françisca and then by the spring of '74 revealing it like "a poisonous petal pushing up to kiss a new world."

On June 11th around 4 A.M. Françisca confronted Nufro on the corner of Los Pescadores and Covarrubias, not far from the Estadio Nacional, where he had arranged to meet several SENDA members. Words quickly lost their shape in the blast of shouts and screams. He struck her. She spat her blood on his cheek. And then it was over, Françisca gone, folding like an evening into a different evening of exactly the same name, edgeless and beyond illumination.

What followed Nufro himself would later describe tersely as "two and a half years of lunacy." And perhaps it could have remained just that, a silly crusade in the name of distant associations carried out with flyers, phone calls, and coffee-talk noise, were it not for the Maldonado family (no relation to Supreme Court President Luis

Maldonado); for unfortunately still interred with them lie all the horrible consequences the political exacts on unready youth; when motives derived from matters as slight as a neglected dinner invitation, loosely paraphrased public statements, unsuspected familial rudeness somehow one day become a police concern, black roots suddenly visible in a bitter winter rain, heralding low-bent rumors of headlights and pistols and knife blades and rifles and shadows lurching in wail, bewildered even, stumbling in the confusion of so sudden and unexpected an end, no matter that the crossed-stars of *melipal* still wheeled above the smoldering back of villarrica or down by the Valdivian waterfront fishermen ate *crudos* and drank glasses of *pisco* and told sour jokes, not one of them suspecting what was happening so close by, how they had fallen, the uncompromised remainder of all who would not could not hold till daybreak. And if even upon those amber-glazed tiles the murder of three generations of farmers could escape judgment, there was in addition to the old couple and their sons an infant—Izarra Maldonado—limp in a deep granite basin, nothing more than her own beautiful becoming drowning in the shadow of her own slowly unfolding rose.

Nufro had not been there. Enough evidence surfaces in Bassil's chapters to assure us of at least that. But there is also enough evidence—equal evidence—that he was the one who carried the scaled note, which, though hidden from his eyes, conveyed sentence upon a family, all of whom would perish that night with the exception of young Incendio Maldonado, who was overseas at the time.

It is thus Bassil's contention, in view of such horrendous involvements, that in spite of its integers and functions and motionless Greek letters, the pristine autonomy of "The Physics of Ero^r" was deeply influenced by Nufro's profound desire to undo the paths of his past.

Though obvious to many has been the cunning error inherent in "Ero^r" (for who could possibly ignore all the Latinate implications especially in light of the quantum subject matter?), Bassil's assessment still proves far more comprehensive. By concentrating on the story of Nufro and Françisca, Bassil reveals how Nufro's use of the letter M to indicate the point/particle of destination in his formulae suddenly takes on new meaning when M, perhaps for Maldonado, transforms to F—the first letter in Françisca's name. The point/particle of origination proves just as curious. Where A or other would have sufficed, Nufro chooses the letter S or the initial of his own first name: Salbatore.

Bassil's list of letters and symbols along with their possible historical counterparts grows from there but is still nothing compared to the most intriguing discovery of all: the results of her own inspection of the actual tea-stained page on which Nufro first scribbled out "The Physics of Ero^r." No spelling error, she finds, but a transcription error and a pen shy of ink. It seems the superscript "^{r}" was not an "r" but rather—followed by a near invisible gutter pressed into the paper, void of pigment—the beginning of an "s." In other words, not "Ero^r" but "Eros."

It appears then that Nufro's quantum miracle, autonomous before the call of all human influences, was first and foremost a love poem for Françisca, the woman he spent a lifetime regretting he'd left.

To her credit, Bassil, while delighting in the romance of this story, never goes so far as to let Nufro escape the mistakes of his past. The shadows remain. The specter of the Maldonado family possesses her book. One of course wishes it didn't. In some ways one wishes there were no "Psychology of Physics" and hence no "Physics of Ero^r" and so no brutal evening on the outskirts of Valdivia. Just a different path, a different way, where perhaps for a moment you and I might be free to imagine, if only fleetingly, scenes of alternate possibilities: quantum theory deprived of one of its most breathtaking discoveries, undone on the corner of Los Pescadores and Covarrubias, where in spite of that treacherous clan a different choice is made, her lip unbroken, his cheek unstained, the two of them fleeing for wholly other places, perhaps south to Isla de Chiloé in search of the ghost ship *Caleuche* or west to Te Pito te Henua to eat oranges and swim above the black reefs, or even east over the Andes, as far as Península Valdés, where they might linger now, forever in the shadowmatter of their dreams, Françisca with color in her hair and slender chains of gold upon her ankle, Nufro beside her, ears red from the wind, unpainted guitar on his knee, while beneath his fingertips the notes of strange coastal moans bind all the lights of midnight with the powerful prophecy of a song.

The Murder of Rabbi David Berliner Herschell

Nomi Eve

My father writes:

Our family history has not been
marked by many regular crimes. But the case
of the murder of my great-great-great-
grandfather, Rabbi David Berliner Herschell,
is a horrible exception. As Herschell was a
very prominent member of the Anglo-Jewish
Jerusalem community, his deathbed was
attended by the British Consul to Jerusalem,
James Finn. James Finn was an avid diarist—
he kept daily journals of consular affairs for
the years he spent in Jerusalem. These diaries
still exist today. They have been published
under the title *A View from Jerusalem.*
Many details about daily life in nineteenth-
century Jerusalem come from Finn's diaries.
Last fall when my daughter, Nomi, was in
Jerusalem, she went to the Central Jerusalem
Library to see Finn's original diary. The
library directors gave her permission to
reproduce the parts of the diary that are
relevant to our family history. Much of the
following information comes from the notes
James Finn took of the crime.

Nomi Eve

I write:

Rabbi Herschell was anxious about his work. This is what he wanted to know: What happens when the soul bears a bruise? He had recently come upon a definition of soul hitherto unwritten— he proposed that the soul is an Iridescent Turning Thing. "It is thick and gelatinous, and it is soft and it is constantly turning." He very much liked the sound of it—"an Iridescent Turning Thing." He would present his findings to the local council of mystics and scholars next week.

Rabbi Herschell rubbed his eyes, chewed on the end of his quill. He leaned back in his chair, and tried to make it squeak. It was a new chair, an import from Tunisia, but it had an old squeak to its legs. Herschell liked to

My father writes:

In 1848 my great-great-great-grandfather, Rabbi Herschell, a widower, emigrated from London to Jerusalem, where he came to live with his youngest daughter, Sophie, and her husband, Jacob Silverman. Silverman, an Austrian citizen, was a businessman—the part owner of a factory that produced phosphorous wicks.

Rabbi Herschell had a very impressive lineage. Not only was he the son of the chief rabbi of the British Empire but he was also a direct descendant, through the intertwining bloodlines of three daughters, of the famous spiritual teacher the Ari of Sephat. Sephat is a city in the northern mountains of Palestine. The Ari lived there in the fifteenth century. And it was in Sephat that the Ari taught the *Zohar,* or *The Book of Splendor,* which is the core text of Jewish mysticism or Kabbalah. Rabbi Herschell considered himself to be a spiritual descendant of the Ari. He devoted his later years to the study and practice of Kabbalah.

According to family tradition, during the last years of his life, Rabbi Herschell wrote a mystical treatise "in the tradition of the Ari." But no record of such a work exists today.

---

tease the squeak out of the wood. But it wouldn't always cooperate. Like now, it was silent. No squeak at all. He wondered on—he wanted to know what happens when the soul has a bruise, as it often, if not always, does. Does the bruise, in one or some of the soul's periodic and inevitable revolutions, turn into the eyes? And if it does, when it does, what does it look like? He rubbed his temples, and he bit on the end of his quill. The chair squeaked, and Rabbi Herschell smiled. When he smiled, his eyes squinted into crescent moons, tiny slits really, and laugh lines radiated out of his temples. He continued writing until the clock showed ten minutes before noon, when he put down his quill and went into the parlor for lunch.

86

> The "soul" (*nefesh*) stands in intimate relation to the body, nourishing and upholding it. Having acquired due worth, it becomes the throne for the "spirit" (*ruach*) to rest upon, as it is written, "until the spirit be poured upon us from on high" (Isa. 32:15). And when these two, soul and spirit, have duly readied themselves, they are worthy to receive the "supersoul" (*neshamah*), resting in turn upon the throne of the spirit. The supersoul stands preeminent, and not to be perceived. There is a throne upon throne, and for the highest a throne. (*Zohar* I. 83 b)

I write:

Herschell settled in before his tray of lunch. He arranged the pillows properly behind his back. He tried to make this chair squeak but it wouldn't. Taking a deep breath, he eyed the food but did not begin to eat it. Instead, he continued his ruminations. He had come to believe that the soul was made up of an infinite number of membranous layers. According to his formulations, upon birth, these layers congeal into one gelatinous mass. He would tell the council that "when a soul suffers a bruise, its layers separate. A small bruise results in the peeling apart of two or three layers. This creates a raw, rough pocket of air between the layers—a painful, dangerous condition. But also quite a common one." Herschell looked down at his platter. Chicken, some turnip soup. He wasn't very hungry. He could feel his work rumbling inside of him. This was not a bad feeling, only an itchy one. He leaned forward and began to eat so that he could quickly return to his treatise.

My father writes:

On November 10, 1851, Herschell had completed his morning studies and was in the parlor of the family house eating his lunch. After just several bites, he took seriously ill. Doctors were called immediately, as was British Consul James Finn. It was quickly ascertained that the rabbi's lunch had been poisoned.

Consul Finn writes:

<u>Nov. 10, 1851</u>: *Two Ashkenazim came to inform me of Rabbi Herschell being poisoned—I went, and in company of Dr. Macgowan, stayed till very late at night. The company was grim. Much chanting of psalms. The house is crowded with solemn words uttered by solemn souls. The sufferer lies abed. Doctor is unable to relieve his pain, which is severe.*

Nomi Eve

My father writes:

Immediately, Jacob Silverman and his son, seventeen-year-old Anshel, were suspected of the crime. This was for two reasons, both having to do with the fact that Herschell was a very wealthy man. First, there was the matter of Jacob Silverman's bad investments. Soon after Herschell arrived in Jerusalem, Silverman had wanted him to invest money in a factory for the production of phosphorous wicks. At the time, phosphorous wicks were used to kindle fire. They were considered a technological revolution. A dry wick would be laid on a flint and then struck with a stone hammer. The impact produced sparks, which set the wick on fire. Rabbi Herschell, conservative in matters of money, refused to contribute to the venture. Silverman invested in the wicks and lost a large amount of money. Not because the technology was deficient, but because his investment partners absconded to Syria with the bulk of the business's cash. But perhaps more important was the matter of Herschell's recent marriage. . . .

I write:

Chasia was standing on the right side of the bed, crying. Her sobs were so loud that the effigies lying in the catacombs of the Mary Church next door heard her sorrowing and immediately thanked their Savior that they were made of stone and would never feel such grief.

The bedroom was very crowded. Herschell lay on the bed, his limbs at odd angles. Someone was bending over him, poking his neck with a cold instrument, asking him a question. But Herschell didn't respond. He was, as usual, hard at work. He was trying to remember. Herschell and Chasia. Chasia and Herschell. He needed to introduce her to his Death with the proper degree of respect, humor, and familiarity. This was his final work.

Herschell closed his eyes. He felt her fingers on his shoulder. She leaned toward him and he could feel her breath on his neck. With tremendous effort, he called up a memory of their first month together as a married couple. He was working on his treatise. He had looked up from his books. She was sitting in the peacock chair darning a dark blue tablecloth. The long folds of the cloth draped down her lap, falling onto the floor royally, gracefully. She felt him looking. She knew what he was thinking. And she had said, as if they had been in the middle of a conversation, "After all, I could have fallen in love with Methuselah. Or Abraham Our Father. I could even have fallen in love with old Adam. Didn't he live until one hundred and sixty-four? In the grand scheme of things, my dear, you are really

88

quite a baby." He had risen up then, and walked over to her. Bending down, he kissed her lips while the fingers of his left hand reached for the nipple of her right breast in a way that told her he very much appreciated her grasp of biblical detail as well as her own private way of telling time. Stroking harder, he had brought her to pleasure right there in the parlor. Afterward, they had climbed the stairs and made love. Upstairs, in this room.

Chasia was leaning forward now, her forehead touching his shoulder, so that he couldn't see her face, but he could hear her sobs, and could feel her shaking. Herschell and Chasia. Chasia and Herschell. And now the former remembering silently and the latter crying loudly. Strange, he thought, this too, a kind of embrace.

Consul Finn writes:
At a late hour I had to draw up the will—it was done with great difficulty on account of the failing faculties of the valuable man. We had some trouble in arresting and imprisoning the son-in-law and grandson on the charge of murder. We got infunkchis from the pasha, and these led by the kawass climbed over the next house and succeeded in arresting them—also opening the strongly barred door. Shouts of the men and screams of the women were distinctly heard by us while I was leaning over the old rabbi catching his accounts in making the will. The room was filled with Ashkenazim rabbis. The cookwoman was also suffering from the poison—Dr. Macgowan as well as the wife had tasted the poisoned food and still retained a nauseous taste in the mouth. Returned very late by beautiful moonlight—Oh the difference between heaven and earth!

See how precisely balanced are the upper and the lower worlds. Israel here below is balanced by the angels on high concerning whom it stands written: "who makest thy angels into winds" (Ps. 104: 4). For when the angels descend to earth they don earthly garments, else they could neither abide in the

I write:

Toward midnight, he told himself the story of how they had met. Chasia had been calling on his daughter, Sophie. The meeting was over, and Chasia was in the hallway on her way out of the house, when she passed by Herschell's study. The study door was open. Seeing her, he called out to her. He couldn't help himself. She stopped and stared into the study. He didn't think, but he said the first thing that came to mind. He said, "Please, miss, can I share with you my new theory. I call it my Theory of Opposite Existence?"

world, nor could it bear to have them. But if this is so with the angels, then how much more so it must be with the Torah: the Torah it was that created the angels and created all the worlds and through Torah all are sustained. The world could not endure the Torah if she had not garbed herself in garments of this world. (*Zohar* III. 152a)

She didn't respond. But she also didn't move to go. It was warm. Her coat was open. Underneath her coat she was wearing a dark purple dress with a beautiful coin-hung frontpiece that hugged her bodice not tightly but tenderly. She smiled in an indulgent, absentminded way, and then she crossed her arms, and leaned back against the hallway mantel. As she did so, her big silver bracelets jangled. Now *Herschell* smiled, because the jangling seemed a close acoustic cousin to his favorite chair-squeak. But in the middle of his smile, Herschell blushed, because he was having an uncharacteristic-to-Herschell-thought: "That it would be very pleasant indeed to tease a jangle or two out of this young woman. Not at all like a chair, more like a sexy cherub." His shoes were a scuffed, dark brown, he was wearing his everyday black suit, and his beard, snowcap white, reached all the way down to his belly.

He checked this thought and continued to speak. This time *very* consciously, *not* saying the first thing that came to his mind. Instead, he said, "We know the world like fabric turned inside out. All that we think to be the right side of existence is really right side in. This hallway, that window, the dirt and sky and my own sentences. Everything we see and know. Like a pair of socks or a shirt after it has been laundered—all seams and hems and faded color and crude knots. We are deluded into thinking that this"—and now he paused dramatically while he pointed with a wide sweeping motion at the walls—"is all there is, when actually, the world's final form is much more wonderful than that."

She smiled. She smiled wider. He smiled too, so that his eyes disappeared, but still he could see. She breathed deeply, making the coins on her chest clink. She loved his deep voice and the way his beard bobbed when he spoke. She loved his theory too, though she thought it could use some work on the details. Herschell rose from his chair. He pulled on his beard and walked toward the young woman. She bit her lower lip. They stood there together for quite some time, not speaking but knowing. And that's when Herschell had a little revelation. He couldn't help but wonder, "If age isn't inside out too. All my extra seconds are like seams, and her newness like so many knots."

He felt his insides flip and flop. Looking into her gray-blue eyes, he smiled. She smiled back. Because her insides were flipping and flopping too. Together, they began their first joint investigation.

~~~~~~

Flipping and flopping. Flopping and flipping. Herschell could hear that the room was full of people praying. So many voices chanting psalms. Herschell and Chasia, Chasia and Herschell. He tried to roll over in the bed but only succeeded in rumpling up his lying still. Chasia put her hand on his shoulder, she tried to help him move, but only succeeded in rumpling up his gracious giving up. Not a defeat but a pause, a rest. A restlessness. But then he couldn't feel her fingers anymore. A Herschell here and a Herschell there. A creaking sound. "Is it the bed?" he wondered, smiling.

Consul Finn writes:
Nov. 11: Called early at the rabbi's house—found him become much worse—the doctors held serious consultation—all agreed that there is no hope.

I write:
Someone had brought the baby into the room. Herschell was glad. He loved this tiny creature, this little spot of Herschellness. He could smell the baby—a blue smell with a peachy center. Herschell breathed in deeply. Chasia, sitting by his side, had the baby on her lap. She was crying while the baby was happily gurgling and trying to stuff its whole fist in its mouth. Reb Herschell tried to sit up, to get a better view, to cheer the child on. But he could not lift himself really. He loved this baby, he thought, sinking back into his pillows. Loved his children. He was a great favorite with children in general. This was because he knew that children did not like to answer questions straight on. Instead of asking a child, "What did you do today?" he would ask, "What didn't you do today?" And the child, instantly aware of the silly illicit nature of the question, would spill out a litany of absurdities. "I didn't rebuild the Bet Hamigdash, I didn't jump on the roof while singing in French, I didn't walk around without any clothes, I didn't tell my brother that he should go and eat an onion." Herschell, with his eyes smiling in their moony way, always had the same answer, "A litany most grand, my child, you have not had quite a day, I am proud of you." The baby was now staring at his own left elbow. Herschell motioned for him to be brought closer. He kissed the baby on his little left ear, and on his little cheek.

And then the baby was gone. Herschell was tired. He could feel his soul turning more quickly than usual. And the inner iridescence was brighter too. Herschell put a hand on Chasia's wrist. She bent down and kissed his palm. As her lips fluttered and pressed on his skin, he shut his eyes and asked himself, "What didn't you do today, Herschell?" Smiling, and with closed eyes, the rabbi told himself many answers.

The psalms were growing louder. Herschell tried to distinguish voices. He heard a cousin, a student, a good friend. Chasia seemed to be the only one not reciting psalms. Herschell sighed. Long ago he had concluded that the body was a "Fleshy Concatenation of Mysteries and Membranes." The voices grew louder. Now he wondered if the mysteries and membranes were, "like the soul, iridescent." Herschell took inventory: His tongue was thick and his lips were puffy and his hands were cold and his belly was paining and there was a thick layer of nauseous tingle torturing the skin of his face. Louder. Herschell groaned and mumbled to himself, "No, not iridescent at all." He wanted the psalmists to stop. Not because he didn't appreciate their efforts, but because he knew that there was no prayer, no psalm, no special service that could blot out the cruel theology of poison unblessing his veins now. He groaned again, because he also knew that life was a prayer and that Chasia—sitting by his bed, looking at her hands, staring in a washed-out, sad, scared way—he knew that Chasia was a psalm. "My psalm," he whispered. For several seconds he lay there, eyes closed, chanting her. But then he felt bitter. Angry. And he cursed the robbers of "this, my own personal liturgy, my life." He looked to Chasia, and she looked to him, and in small voices, against the background of big voices, they prayed together, one thousand special sorrows in their eyes.

Consul Finn writes:
Nov. 11: The doctor left. Shortly afterward the chanting of Shma Yisrael rose up with the screams of the women announcing that the sufferer was no more! Murdered by his own family! The rabbi's wife was inconsolable. There was the corpse surrounded by portraits of his illustrious father, chief rabbi of London, grandfathers, all rabbis of important congregations. I remained till the executor removed the valuables into one room and sealed it with wax. The funeral will be tomorrow. Upon leaving, I found Jews pouring through the streets. The event is one of great horror in the Jewish quarter. Who has before heard of one Jew killing another!

Or of killing his father or grandfather? When I formerly saw old Rabbi Herschell in silk and gold presiding in the great synagogue of Dukis Place, who could have foretold I should have this melancholy task to perform for his family?

Consul Finn writes:

Nov. 12: The unfortunate Rabbi Herschell was buried today on the Mount of Olives. The funeral was attended by several hundred of the rabbi's co-religionists. In all aspects a most venerable ceremony. I was impressed and moved. But as I walked away, I couldn't help but think of our Savior who cried for the fate of Jerusalem here on this same mountain. Woe that such sacred ground should now endure the morbid effects of poison, of murder. This is certainly a horrible day. I attended the ceremony with Dr. Macgowan. Later, I and my wife paid a visit to the house of the new widow. There was much sorrow and weeping.

I write:

From here he could see many things, but from a different vantage. Before, he had felt himself far away. "As if," he had once mused, he was "born to traverse the inner layers of soul, the ones far back." Consequently, it always seemed as if a million dark and invisible leagues separated him from the outer world. But now everything had changed. The far had turned to near. He was skimming the surface—floating on the silky upper layers. Herschell touched his face. This was indeed a revelation. Close up. Thrust forward. He patted his nose, pinched his cheeks, tugged on his beard, feeling the skin pull up and down, prickly and good, thinking, "Yes, the distance is gone, and when my soul turns into my eyes I will see and will be close up. Finally." He laughed, feeling a happy weird intimacy with the way his face cleaved to his soul "nicely, snug but not uncomfortable, a perfect fit. The Blessed Creator is a Master Tailor indeed." Herschell touched his face again. Soon, his soul commenced its Iridescent Turning. And when it spun into his eyes, the color astounded him. A million rainbows had replaced the million leagues of dark. And though he was alone now, he gave thanks for this.

Consul Finn writes:

Nov. 14: The Silvermans were arrested. It is believed that the father planned the crime and goaded the boy on in order to prevent

the rabbi from making a new will. The tainted meal was determined to have been liberally laced with a noxious powder.
Investigation points to Anshel Silverman. On the morning of the
crime, the boy had been to visit his grandfather. Before the visit,
Anshel stopped into the kitchen and conversed with the cookwoman's daughter. I suspect that Anshel Silverman diverted the
girl and poisoned the food.

My father writes:

After a lengthy trial, the defendants were acquitted for lack of "irrefutable
evidence." However, they were always popularly considered guilty. So much
so that even today, over one hundred and forty years after the crime was
committed, at large family gatherings if any descendants of the Silvermans
are present, someone from our branch of the family will inevitably point to
them and whisper, "Murderers!"

Chasia Herschell inherited her husband's fortune. The only part of the
inheritance that remained in our family was a pair of silver candlesticks
willed by Herschell directly to his eldest daughter, Esther, my great-great-
grandmother. Today, the candlesticks are in possession of my distant cousins
who live in Jerusalem. I have seen this treasure only once.

Not long after her husband's death, Chasia left Jerusalem with her young
son. They moved to Sephat, where she remarried. There is a legend in
our family that in addition to the inheritance, Chasia also made off with
Herschell's "mystical treatise." And since her destination was the city of the
Ari, Sephat, the seat of Kabbalah, it would seem most fitting if she had in fact
brought the rabbi's work to the source of his inspiration. But of this there
is no proof.

I write:

Rabbi Herschell was anxious about his work. "Bruises?" He was
almost finished with bruises, having formulated that "Yes, the
bruise does spin into the eyes. And when seen there, just above pupil,
but below iris, it is not iridescent but is dark, dark maroon, the color
of dried blood." The council of mystics and scholars would surely be
interested. He would present his findings soon. Next week. Or the
week after. Herschell shifted in his chair, and once again, he smiled
because it was very, very squeaky. And then he smiled again, this
time wider, his eyes disappearing into tiny slits, smiling because he
knew that his sense of humor was predictable, and this, he thought,
quite a silly and endearing quality of "me, Herschell, one particular
little man." Herschell leaned his elbows on his writing table, and he

thought of Chasia. Herschell and Chasia, Chasia and Herschell. He began to work on another theory. A follow-up, a logical extension. Something to do with the notion of a "family soul." Something to do with the shared layers. The ones that sift into each other, "like vascular sand." He worked deep into the night. And deep into the night's night.

―――――――――

Acknowledgments:
Quotations from the *Zohar* are taken from *The Wisdom of the Zohar*, arranged by Fischel Lachower and Isaiah Tishby. Translated from the Hebrew by David Goldstein. The Littman Library of Jewish Civilization. London, 1994.

Quotations from Consul Finn's diary are taken from the original pages of the *Consular Diary of James and Elizabeth Finn, 1849–1858*. Some quotations are fictional, some are actual.

Foam
(Essay with Rhapsody)
On the Sublime in Longinus and Antonioni

Anne Carson

SPILL

The Sublime is a documentary technique. "Documentary: of, related to, or relying on documentation; objective, factual." Take for example Longinus' famous treatise *On the Sublime*. This work is an aggregation of quotes. It has no argument, no organization, no paraphrasable conclusion. Its attempts at definition are incoherent or tautological. Its key topic (passion) is deferred to another treatise (which does not exist). You will come away from reading its forty chapters with no clear idea what the Sublime actually is. But you will have been thrilled by its documentation. Longinus skates from Homer to Demosthenes to Moses to Sappho on blades of electricity—who cares what his theory is, the skating is a joy! Sublime quotes are their own reason for being.

What you enjoy in a documentary technique is the feeling that you are crossing back and forth on the frame of facts, skating from document to document, while retaining your own point of view—which is called "objective" because you make facts into objects by viewing them this way. You are not so swept along by the facts as to forget your own viewing, as you would be in the midst of a story or poem or dramatic film. Instead you insist on seeing the edge of the frame wherever you look. In a good documentary the facts spill over the frame, then spill again.

Consider Chapter 20 of *On the Sublime,* where Longinus congratulates the Greek orator Demosthenes because he knows how to make his nouns rain like blows when recounting a violent scene:

> By attitude! by look! by voice! the man who hits can do things to the other which the other can't even describe.
> (Demosthenes, *Against Meidias* 72; Longinus, *On the Sublime* 20.2)

96

"With words like these," Longinus smiles, "the orator produces the same effect as the man who hits—striking the judges' minds with blow after blow"—and he quotes again:

> By attitude! look! voice! when he with insolence, when he like an enemy, when he with bare fists, when he with a slap on the side of your head—

Longinus' point is that, by brutal juxtaposition of coordinate nouns or noun clauses, Demosthenes transposes violence of fists into violence of syntax. His facts spill over the frame of their courtroom context and pummel the judges' minds. Watch this spillage, which moves from the man who hits, to the words of Demosthenes describing him, to the judges hearing these words, to Longinus analyzing the whole process, to me recalling Longinus' discussion of it and finally to you reading my account. The passionate moment echoes from quotation to quotation. Quote by quote, your soul enjoys it.

Why does your soul enjoy it? Longinus answers this question by addressing the psychology of watching, listening, reading, being an audience. This psychology involves a shift and opening out of power:

> Touched by the true sublime your soul is naturally lifted up, she rises to a proud height, is filled with joy and vaunting, as if she had herself created this thing that she has heard.
> (Longinus, *On the Sublime* 7.2)

To feel the joy of the Sublime is to be inside creative power for a moment, to share a bit of electric extra life with the artist's invention, to spill with him. Consider another example. When Michelangelo Antonioni was filming *Story of a Love Affair* with actress Lucia Bosé in 1950, he found he had to step out from behind the camera, cross the set, and adjust her psychology himself:

> How many blows Lucia took for the final scene! The film ended with her beaten and sobbing, in a doorway. But she was always happy and it was hard for her to pretend to be desperate. She was not an actress. To obtain the results I wanted I had to use insults, abuse, hard slaps. In the end she broke down and wept like a child. She played her part wonderfully.
> (Michelangelo Antonioni, *The Architecture of Vision* 186)

97

In between Antonioni and Lucia in the doorway is an area of small, hard, restless excitement. It is a documentary excitement. I mean this in two ways. "Documentary" refers generally to a dependence on documents, as I believe I mentioned earlier. "Documentary" also implies, cinematically, a preference for factual over fictional subject-matter in the preparation of a film. When he steps from behind the camera and crosses down into *Story* to improve Lucia Bosé with his wonderful slaps, Antonioni breaches a boundary between fact and fiction. But we would never know this had he not documented the moment himself—Antonioni recounted this anecdote to a reporter from *Corriere della Sera* in 1978 and later reprinted it in his book *The Architecture of Vision* (New York, 1996)—acting as his own Demosthenes and then as his own Longinus. So too we might never have known of Demosthenes' effect on a courtroom of judges had Longinus not praised it in *On the Sublime*. We might never have known of the violence of "the man who hits" had Demosthenes not denounced it in his speech *Against Meidias*. In each case a passionate moment is created, quoted, spilled. You may feel your own hands tingle, your soul lift.

The original expert in this kind of spilling of power, Longinus tells us, was Homer. Here is Longinus describing how Homer crosses down into his own poem to become as sublime as his subject-matter:

> Look this is the real Homer who storms like a wind alongside the fighting men, none other than Homer who "rages as when spearshaking Ares or ruinous fire in the mountains rages, in folds of deep forest, and foam is around his mouth."
> (Longinus, *On the Sublime* 9.11; Homer, *Iliad* 15. 605-7)

Foam is the sign of an artist who has sunk his hands into his own story, and also of a critic storming and raging in folds of his own deep theory. It is apparent to most of his readers that Longinus moves through the chapters of *On the Sublime* covered with foam himself. "Longinus *is* the great Sublime he draws," says Boileau. "What is most Sublime, Homer's battle of the gods or Longinus' apostrophe upon it?" asks Gibbon. "Sublime natures are seldom clean!" is Longinus' way of putting it (*On the Sublime* Chapter 33). Slap.

STOP

The Sublime is big. "Bigness" or "magnitude" is one of Longinus' synonyms for it throughout his treatise. Its bigness is always threatening to go out of control, to submerge and vanquish the soul that seeks to enjoy it. Threat provides the Sublime with its essential structure, an alternation of risk and salvation, which other aesthetic experiences (e.g., beauty) do not seem to share. Threat also furnishes the Sublime with its necessary content—dire things (volcanoes, oceans, ecstasies) and dire reactions (death, dread, transport) within which the sublime soul is *all but lost.*

Foam is a sign of how close the threat came. In fact a sublime soul is threatened not only from without but from within, for this soul's own nature is too big for itself. The sublime orator, the sublime poet, the sublime critic is a man wildly lost in his own art, hurried out of himself, heedless, rash, wrong—"they burn all before them as they are carried along!" (33.2). Longinus insists on ecstasy, on genius spinning out of control, like the Rhine or the Danube or even Mt. Aetna, "whose uprushings send rocks and whole riverbanks from down below and pour out rivers of that weird, spontaneous, earthborn fire" (35.4). But notice how, on the brink of Aetna, documentation intervenes. Longinus has been quoting Pindar's famous description of Mt. Aetna (*Pythian* 1.21ff), now he shifts his frame into view:

> Could we not say of all such examples that . . . the monstrous always excites wonder! (35.5)

Suddenly you are not lost in the Sublime—you are standing at a safe distance, regarding it as it spills, enjoying its relative desperation, apostrophizing its monstrous, unclean fire. "So now it is on film, the rest is up to you," as Antonioni says (C. T. Samuels, *Encountering Directors* [New York 1972] 20).

Antonioni's films involve different kinds of playing with the passionate moment, different ways of spilling its contents. He enjoys, for example, drawing attention to offscreen space by placing a mirror in the middle of the scene so that you glimpse a stray piece of world there. Or he likes to give you two successive shots of the same portion of reality, first from close up, then a little further away, scarcely different yet noticeably not the same. He also uses a procedure, called *temps mort* by French critics, whereby the camera is left

Anne Carson

running on a scene after the actors think they have finished acting it:

> When everything has been said, when the scene appears to be
> finished, there is what comes afterward . . . the actors con-
> tinue out of inertia into moments that seem "dead." The
> actor commits "errors." . . .
> (S. Chatwin, *Antonioni or the Surface of the World* [Berkeley 1985]
> 126 and n. 24)

Antonioni likes to document these moments of error, when the
actors do unscheduled things, act "back to front," as he says. Possibility of foam. He began opening out the frame in this way while
working on *Story of a Love Affair.* Later he took to letting the shot
run even after the actors had made their exit. As if for a while something might be still whispering around there amid the chairs or
cobblestones.

You may not think Antonioni's films are sublime, nor do I, but I
think Antonioni's use of Antonioni is sublime. As is Longinus' use
of Longinus. "Sublimity is the echo of a great mind—as I believe I
have written somewhere else," (9.2) says Longinus, echoing gently.
You get an echo effect from Antonioni too, especially when he tells
the story about the day he went to the asylum, which is repeated in
every interview, conversation, or study of his work. He says (originally in "Fare un film é per me vivere" in *Cinema nuovo* 138 [1959])
that the first time he put his eye to the camera was in a lunatic
asylum. He had determined to make a film on the insane. The director of the asylum looked insane too, or so Antonioni noted when he
met him on the day of the shoot. But the inmates themselves were
efficient and helpful in setting up props and equipment and getting
the room ready. "I must say I was surprised by their good cheer," he
says. And then he turned on his big lights.

The room "became hell." Inmates were screaming. They crumpled,
twisted, and rolled themselves over the floor, trying to get away.
Antonioni stood numb, his cameraman too. At last the director
of the asylum yelled, "Off with the lights!" The room grew silent
with a slow and feeble movement of bodies leaving agony behind.
Antonioni says he never forgot this scene. Had he shot film that day,
it would have been a documentary of foam. But the mad people, who
knew a lot about spillage, laid themselves low. You have to admire

100

the mad. They understand how to focus a passionate moment. So does Longinus. His treatise ends like this:

> Best to leave these matters and to proceed to what comes next—the passions, concerning which I undertook to write in another . . .

—here the manuscript of *On the Sublime* breaks off. The next page is too damaged to read and after that you cannot say how much is missing. Longinus skates away.

THE DAY ANTONIONI CAME TO THE ASYLUM
(Rhapsody)

> *It was a restless moment. He came closer.*
> —Lucia Bosé

It was the sound of her writing that woke me. Since you ask, this is what I remember. Her desk is just outside my room. Some days I hear sounds too loud. Some days I hear a crowd and there is no crowd.

At her desk she keeps notes. She lists our medications. She does the crossword puzzle or puts checkmarks in the margins of *Classified*. A grinding glasshard sound. Others are unaware. These differences are hard to bear.

Then there it was, mutiny. They told us we had to come downstairs to the salon early and "participate" so we all took our clothes off. Eighteen naked people in the hall. She said not a word. That's what scared us. We got dressed again. Overalls, no more women and men.

What the eye saw was a pile of documents on her desk with tiny paragraphs and signatures and staples. These documents were not seen again in the salon or elsewhere. I keep my eye on documents.

101

Documents are how most of us ended up here. *That's him,* said someone as we descended the stairs. Antonioni wore a small brown sweater and looked like a cat. I wanted to give him a lick or a pat.

Swoony was the mood I would say in the room. A suddenly arriving beautiful man will not so much fool people as keep them awake—drunk with our own awakeness we rushed around doing his bidding. To be awake was a thing many had dreamed of, while continuing to sleep for years, like the famous princess in 'her coffin of glass. Once I opened a Chinese fortune cookie that said, *Some will attain their heart's desire, alas.*

He got behind his 16mm Bell & Howell. Two of his men gave instructions. Patty and Bates and I were dragging chairs out of the way. The big black cords had to be run out to plugs. We were making no mistakes. We were being extremely careful. No jokes. No sleep. No staring. And she in her place by the wall, refolding her crossword and trying to look calm. Because it contains the word "hyssop" the 51st is my favourite Psalm.

Hyssop is (as you may know) a purificatory herb that smells like mint from outer space. *Create in me a clean heart O God.* I got a whiff of hyssop just when those big black cords lit (light starts to smell when there's too much of it) and some sudden radiance aligned me with the rugs on the floor. So there we all were on the floor and Patty yelled *Keep turning* so we did (to ward off death) and every time Bates turned past me we kissed which is one of our interior arrangements in group activities (of which there are a lot here), life being short and burning yearning being burning yearning.

Patty's view is that if I weren't in this place I wouldn't have time for someone like Bates. I told

her I'm a practical fellow and Bates is my practice
right now. "Have time for" is exactly the point—
days here are two hundred years long. Outsiders
(Antonioni) come in at the wrong velocity. I bet he
knew that. His face had the look of someone who
enters a room and there's no floor. Meanwhile we
rolled all the way to the wall and at a signal from
Patty reversed and rolled back—beautifully, I
thought, it was somehow like bowling. He seemed
pained by everyone yowling.

To yell is the rule here—rule of the mad—it dis-
guises the kissing and makes us less sad.

Antonioni opened his eyes. She left her place by
the wall and came over to him. *The patients are
afraid of the light,* she explained, *they think it is
a monster.* This kind of spontaneous misinforma-
tion is typical of the medical profession. Well I
suppose she could hardly say, *The patients wor-
ship life-giving Aphrodite every chance they
get, thank you for furnishing this opportunity.*
Anyway I'm not sure how smart she is. One day I
told her about evolution—how in the beginning
people didn't have selves as we have selves, there
were arms heads torsos what have you roaming
about by the breakers of the shore of life, ankles
unattached, eyes needing brows, until at last what
made the parts come together as whole creatures
was Love—and she said, *Do you know a 6-letter
word for loose or wanton woman derived from
the sound of a horse's hooves going down the
road at night?* To which I replied, *Yes I do and I
can shower with Bates tonight, right?*

Always planning ahead, that's me, practical as
purgatory my mom used to say. *That the bones
which thou hast broken may rejoice.* But now
there we were eighteen terrible people in a room
trying not to look at one another as we got up off
the floor. Antonioni gave himself a tidy cat shake

and returned to form. The director of the asylum was beside him murmuring low in a Let's See What We've Learned Today tone. Sober nods all round. I would have liked to hear from Antonioni. Cats don't spend themselves but they notice everything. I saw he noticed Bates. How close for an instant we grazed our fates.

New white snow had fallen over dark slush outside. Patty expressed disappointment in the morning's pitch and tenor overall. *Fuckin sketchy gig, man*—was I believe her phrasing. Still we take our blessings where they fall. Nothing improves community life like an hour of aerobics first thing. *Purge me and I shall be clean, wash me and I shall be whiter than snow.* The yelling is mild all the rest of the day. And it was Friday, angel cake for supper, hot showers later and who knows what interior arrangements there. Since the day I gave her "tittup" she treats me with extra care. *Don't be a mourner,* she says and juts way back on two legs of her chair.

Good Old Neon
David Foster Wallace

> *Hay un concepto que es el corruptor y el desati-*
> *nador de los otros.*
>
> —Borges, *Discusión*, 1932

MY WHOLE LIFE I'VE BEEN a fraud. I'm not exaggerating. Pretty much all I've ever done all the time is try to create a certain impression of me in other people. Mostly to be liked or admired. It's a little more complicated than that, maybe. But when you come right down to it it's to be liked, loved. Admired, approved of, applauded, whatever. You get the idea. I did well in school, but deep down the whole thing's motive wasn't to learn or improve myself but just to do well, to get good grades and make sports teams and perform well. To have a good transcript or varsity letters to show people. I didn't enjoy it much because I was always scared I wouldn't do well enough. The fear made me work really hard, so I'd always do well and end up getting what I wanted. But then, once I got the best grade or made All City or got Angela Mead to let me put my hand on her breast, I wouldn't feel much of anything except fear that I wouldn't be able to get it again. The next time or next thing I wanted. I remember being down in the rec room in Angela Mead's basement on the couch and having her let me get my hand up under her blouse and not even really feeling the soft aliveness or whatever of her breast because all I was doing was thinking, 'Now I'm the guy that Mead let get to second with her.' Later that seemed so sad. This was in middle school. She was a very large-hearted, quiet, self-contained, thoughtful girl—she's a veterinarian now, with her own practice—and I never even really saw her, I couldn't see anything except who I might be in her eyes, this cheerleader and probably number two or three among the most desirable girls in middle school that year. She was much more than that, she was beyond all that adolescent ranking and popularity crap, but I never really let her be or saw her as more, although I put up a very good front as somebody who could have deep conversations and really wanted to know and understand who she was inside.

David Foster Wallace

Later I was in analysis, I tried analysis like almost everybody else then in their late twenties who'd made some money or had a family or whatever they thought they wanted and still didn't feel that they were happy. A lot of people I knew tried it. It didn't really work, although it did make everyone sound more aware of their own problems and added some useful vocabulary and concepts to the way we all had to talk to each other to fit in and sound a certain way. You know what I mean. I was in regional advertising at the time in Chicago, having made the jump from media buyer for a large consulting firm, and at only twenty-nine I'd made creative associate, and verily as they say I was a fair-haired boy and on the fast track but wasn't happy at all, whatever *happy* means, but of course I didn't say this to anybody because it was such a cliché—'Tears of a Clown,' 'Richard Cory,' etc.—and the circle of people who seemed important to me seemed much more dry, oblique and contemptuous of clichés than that, and so of course I spent all my time trying to get them to think I was dry and jaded as well, doing things like yawning and looking at my nails and saying things like, '*Am I happy?* is one of those questions that, if it has got to be asked, more or less dictates its own answer,' etc. Putting in all this time and energy to create a certain impression and get approval or acceptance that then I felt nothing about because it didn't have anything to do with who I really was inside, and I was disgusted with myself for always being such a fraud, but I couldn't seem to help it. Here are some of the various things I tried: EST, riding a ten-speed to Nova Scotia and back, hypnosis, cocaine, sacro-cervical chiropractic, joining a charismatic church, jogging, pro bono work for the Ad Council, meditation classes, the Masons, analysis, the Landmark Forum, the Course in Miracles, a right-brain drawing workshop, celibacy, collecting and restoring vintage Corvettes, and trying to sleep with a different girl every night for two straight months (I racked up a total of thirty-six for sixty-one and also got chlamydia, which I told friends about, acting like I was embarrassed but secretly expecting most of them to be impressed—which, under the cover of making a lot of jokes at my expense, I think they were—but for the most part the two months just made me feel shallow and predatory, plus I missed a great deal of sleep and was a wreck at work—that was also the period I tried cocaine). I know this part is boring and probably boring you, by the way, but it gets a lot more interesting when I get to the part where I kill myself and discover what happens immediately after a person dies. In terms of the list, analysis was pretty much the last thing I tried.

The analyst I saw was OK, a big soft older guy with a big ginger mustache and a pleasant, sort of informal manner. I'm not sure I remember him alive too well. He was a fairly good listener, and seemed interested and sympathetic in a somewhat distant way. At first I suspected he didn't like me or was uneasy around me. I don't think he was used to patients who were already aware of what their real problem was. He was also a bit of a pill-pusher. I balked at trying antidepressants, I just couldn't see myself taking pills to try to be less of a fraud. I said that even if they worked, how would I know if it was me or just the pills? By that time I already knew I was a fraud. I knew what my problem was. I just couldn't seem to stop. I remember I spent maybe the first twenty times or so in analysis acting all open and candid but was in reality sort of fencing with him or leading him around by the nose, basically showing him that I wasn't just another one of those patients who stumbled in with no clue what their real problem was or were totally out of touch with the truth about themselves. When you come right down to it, I was trying to show him that I was at least as smart as he was and that there wasn't much of anything he was going to see about me that I hadn't already seen and figured out. And yet I wanted help and really was there to try to get help. I didn't even tell him how unhappy I was until five or six months into the analysis, mostly because I didn't want to seem like just another whining, self-absorbed yuppie, even though I think even then I was on some level conscious that that's all I really was, deep down.

Right from the start, what I liked best about the analyst was that his office was a mess. There were books and papers everyplace, and usually he had to clear things off the chair so I could sit down. There was no couch, I sat in an easy chair and he sat facing me in his beat-up old desk chair whose back part had one of those big rectangles or capes of back-massage beads attached to it the same way cabbies often have them on their seat in the cab. This was another thing I liked, the desk chair and the fact that it was a little too small for him (he was a large guy) so that he had to sit sort of almost hunched with his feet flat on the floor, or else sometimes put his hands behind his head and lean way back in the chair in a way that made the back portion squeak terribly when it leaned back. There always seems to be something patronizing or a little condescending about somebody crossing their legs when they talk to you, and the desk chair didn't allow him to do this, if he ever crossed his legs his knee would have been up around his chin. And yet he had apparently never gone out and gotten himself a bigger or nicer desk chair, or even bothered to oil the medial joint's springs to keep the back from squeaking, a noise that I know would have driven me up the wall if it had been my chair and I had to spend all day in it. I noticed all this almost right away. The little office also reeked of pipe tobacco, which is a pleasant smell, plus Dr. Gustafson never took notes or answered everything with a question or any of the cliché analyst things that would have made the whole thing too horrible to keep going back whether it even helped or not. The whole effect was of a sort of likable, disorganized, laid back guy, and things in there actually did get better after I realized that he probably wasn't going to do anything to make me quit fencing with him and trying to anticipate all his questions and show that I already knew the answer—he was going to get his $65 either way—and finally came out and told him about being a fraud and feeling alienated (I had to use the uptown word, of course, but it was still the truth) and starting to see myself ending up living this way my whole life and being totally unhappy. I told him I wasn't blaming anybody for my being a fraud. I had been adopted, but it was as a baby, and the stepparents who adopted me were better and nicer than most of the biological parents I knew anything about, and I was never yelled at or abused or pressured to hit .400 in Legion ball or anything, and they took out a second mortgage to send me to an elite college when I could have gone scholarship to U.W.–Eau Claire, etc. Nobody'd ever done anything bad to me, every problem I ever had I'd been the cause of. I was a fraud, and the fact that I was lonely was my own fault (of course his ears pricked up at *fault*, which is a loaded term) because I seemed to be so totally self-centered and fraudulent that I experienced everything in terms of how it affected people's view of me and what I needed to do to create the impression of me I wanted them to have. I said I knew what my problem was, what I couldn't do was stop it. I also admitted to Dr. Gustafson some of the ways I'd been jerking him around early on and trying to make sure he saw me as smart and self-aware, and said I'd known early on that playing around and showing off in analysis were a waste of time and money but that I couldn't seem to help myself, it just happened automatically. He smiled at all this, which was the first time I remember seeing him smile. I don't mean he was sour or humorless, he had a big red friendly face and a pleasant expression, but this was the first time he'd smiled like a human being having an actual conversation. And yet at the same time I already saw what I'd left myself open for—and sure enough he says it. 'If I understand you right,' he says, 'you're saying that you're basically a calculating, manipulative person who always says what you think will get somebody to approve of you or form some impression of you you think you want.' I told him that was maybe a little simplistic but basically accurate, and he said further that as he understood it I was saying that I felt as if I was trapped in this false way of being and unable ever to be totally open and tell the truth irregardless of whether it'd make me look good in others' eyes or not. And I somewhat resignedly said yes, and that I seemed always to have had this fraudulent, calculating part of my brain firing away all the time, as if I were constantly playing chess with everybody and figuring out that if I wanted them to move a certain way I had to move in such a way as to induce them to move that way. He asked if I ever played chess, and I told him I used to in middle school but quit because I couldn't be as good as I eventually wanted to be, how frustrating it was to get just good enough to know what getting really good at chess would be like but not being able to get that good, etc. I was laying it on sort of thick in hopes of distracting him from the big insight and question I realized I'd set myself up for. But it didn't work. He leaned back in his loud chair and paused as if he were thinking hard, for effect—he was thinking that he was going to get to feel like he'd really earned his $65 today. Part of the pause always involved stroking his mustache in an unconscious way. I was reasonably sure that he was going to say something like, 'So then how were you able to do what you just did a moment ago?,' in other words meaning how was I able to be honest about the fraudulence if I was really a fraud, meaning he thought he'd caught me in a logical contradiction or paradox. And I went ahead and played a little dumb, probably, to get him to go ahead and say it, partly because I still held out some hope that what he'd say might be more discerning or incisive than I had predicted. But it was also partly because I liked him, and liked the way he seemed genuinely pleased and excited at the idea of being helpful but was trying to exercise professional control over his facial expression in order to make the excitement look more like simple pleasantness and clinical interest in my case or whatever. He was hard not to like, he had what is known as an engaging manner. By way of decor, the office wall behind his chair had two framed prints, one being that Wyeth one of the little girl in the wheat field crawling uphill toward the farmhouse, the other a still life of two apples in a bowl on a table by Cézanne. (To be honest, I only knew it was Cézanne because it was an Art Institute poster and had a banner with info on a Cézanne

109

show underneath the painting, which was a still life, and which was weirdly discomfiting because there was something slightly off about the perspective or style that made the table look crooked and the apples almost square.) The prints were obviously there to give the analyst's patients something to look at, since many people like to look around or look at things on the wall while they talk. I didn't have any trouble looking right at him most of the time I was in there, though. He did have a talent for putting you at ease, there was no question about it. But I had no illusions that this was the same as having enough insight or firepower to find some way to really help me, though.

There was a basic logical paradox that I called the 'fraudulence paradox' that I had discovered more or less on my own while taking a mathematical logic course in school. I remember this as being a huge undergrad lecture course that met twice a week in an auditorium with the professor up on stage and on Fridays in smaller discussion sections led by a graduate assistant whose whole life seemed to be mathematical logic. (Plus all you had to do to ace the class was sit down with the textbook that the prof had edited and memorize the different modes of argument and normal forms and axioms of first-order quantification, meaning the course was as clean and mechanical as logic itself in that if you put in the time and effort, out popped the good grade at the other end. We only got to paradoxes like the Berry and Russell paradoxes and the incompleteness theorem at the very end of the term, they weren't on the final.) The fraudulence paradox was that the more time and effort you put into trying to appear impressive or attractive to other people, the less impressive or attractive you felt inside—you were a fraud. And the more of a fraud you felt like, the harder you tried to convey an impressive or likable image of yourself so that other people wouldn't find out what a hollow, fraudulent person you really were. Logically, you would think that the moment a supposedly intelligent nineteen-year-old became aware of this paradox, he'd stop being a fraud and just settle for being himself (whatever that was) because he'd figured out that being a fraud was a vicious infinite regress that ultimately resulted in being frightened, lonely, alienated, etc. But here was the other, higher-order paradox, which didn't even have a form or name—I didn't, I couldn't. Discovering the first paradox at age nineteen just brought home to me in spades what an empty, fraudulent person I'd basically been ever since I was four and lied to my stepdad because I'd realized somehow right in the middle of his asking me if I'd broken the bowl that if I said I did it but 'confessed' it in a sort of clumsy, implausible way, then he wouldn't believe me and would instead believe that my sister Fern, who's my stepparents' biological daughter, was the one who'd actually broken the antique Moser glass bowl that my step-mom had inherited from her biological grandmother and loved, plus it would lead or induce him to see me as a kind, good stepbrother who was so anxious to keep Fern (whom I really did like) from get-ting in trouble that I'd be willing to lie and take the punishment for it for her. I'm not explaining this very well. I was only four, for one thing, and the realization didn't hit me in words the way I just now put it, but rather more in terms of feelings and associations and cer-tain mental flashes of my stepparents' faces with various expressions on them. But it happened that fast, at only four, that I figured out how to create a certain impression by knowing what effect I'd pro-duce in my stepdad by implausibly 'confessing' that I'd punched Fern in the arm and stolen her Hula Hoop and had run all the way down-stairs with it and started Hula Hooping in the dining room right by the sideboard with all my stepmom's antique glassware and figurines on it, while Fern, forgetting all about her arm and hoop because of her concern over the bowl and other glassware, came running down-stairs shouting after me, reminding me about how important the rule was that we weren't supposed to play in the dining room. . . . Meaning that by lying in such a deliberately unconvincing way I could actually get everything that a direct lie would supposedly get me, plus look noble and self-sacrificing, plus also make my steppar-ents feel good because they always tended to feel good when one of their kids did something that showed character, because it's the sort of thing they couldn't really help but see as reflecting favorably on them as shapers of their kids' character. I'm putting all this in such a long, rushing, clumsy way to try to convey the way I remember it suddenly hit me, looking up at my stepfather's big kindly face as he held two of the larger pieces of the Moser bowl and tried to look angrier than he really felt. (He had always thought the more expen-sive pieces ought to be kept secure in storage somewhere, whereas my stepmom's view was more like what was the point of having nice things if you didn't have them out where people could enjoy them.) How to appear a certain way and get him to think a certain thing hit me just that fast. Keep in mind I was only around four. And I can't pretend it felt bad, realizing it—the truth is it felt great. I felt power-ful, smart. It felt a little like looking at part of a puzzle you're doing and you've got a piece in your hand and you can't see where in the larger puzzle it's supposed to go or how to make it fit, looking at all the holes, and then all of a sudden in a flash you see, for no reason right then you could point to or explain to anyone, that if you turn the piece this one certain way it will fit, and it does, and maybe the best way to put it is that in that one tiny instant you feel suddenly connected to something larger and much more of the complete picture the same way the piece is. The only element I'd forgotten to anticipate was Fern's reaction to getting blamed for the bowl, and punished, and then punished even worse when she continued to deny that she'd been the one playing around in the dining room, and my stepparents' position was that they were even more upset and disappointed about her lying than they were about the bowl, which they said was just a material object and not ultimately important in the larger scheme of things. (My stepparents spoke this way, they were people of high ideals and values, humanists. Their big ideal was total honesty in all the family's relationships, and lying was the worst, most disappointing infraction you could commit, in their view as parents. They tended to discipline Fern a little more firmly than they did me, by the way, but this too was an extension of their values. They were concerned about being fair and having me be able to feel that I was just as much their real child as Fern was, so that I'd feel maximally secure and loved, and sometimes this concern with fairness caused them to bend a little too far over backwards when it came to discipline.) So that Fern, then, got regarded as being a liar when she was not, and that must have hurt her way more than the actual punishment did. She was only five at the time. It's horrible to be regarded as a fraud or to believe that people think you're a fraud or liar. It's one of the worst feelings in the world. And even though I have had no real direct experience of it, I'm sure it must be doubly horrible when you were actually telling the truth and they didn't believe you. I don't think Fern ever quite got over that episode, although the two of us never talked about it afterward except for one sort of cryptic remark she made over her shoulder once when we were both in high school and having an argument about something and Fern was storming out of the house. She was sort of a classically troubled adolescent—smoking, makeup, mediocre grades, dating older guys, etc.—whereas I was the family's fair-haired boy and had a killer G.P.A. and played varsity ball, etc. One way to put it is that I looked and acted much better on the surface then than Fern did, although she eventually settled down and ended up going on to college and is now doing OK. She's also one of the funniest people on earth, with a very dry, subtle sense of humor—I like her a lot. The point being that that was the start of my being a fraud, although it's not as if the broken-bowl episode was somehow the origin or matrix of my fraudulence or some kind of childhood trauma that I'd never gotten over and had to go into analysis to work out. The fraud part of me was always there, just as the puzzle piece, objectively speaking, is a piece of the puzzle even before you see how it fits. For a while I thought that possibly one or the other of my biological parents had been frauds or had carried some type of fraud gene or something and that I had inherited it, but that was a dead end, there was no way to know. And even if I did, what difference would it make? I was still a fraud, it was still my own unhappiness that I had to deal with.

Once again, I'm aware that it's clumsy to put it all this way, but the point is that all of this and more was flashing through my head just in the time of the small, dramatic pause Dr. Gustafson allowed himself before delivering his big reductio ad absurdum argument that I couldn't be a total fraud if I had just come out and admitted my fraudulence to him just now. I know that you know just as well as I do how fast thoughts and associations can fly through your head. You can be in the middle of a creative meeting at your job or something, and enough material can rush through your head just in the little silences when people are looking over their notes and waiting for the next presentation that it would take exponentially longer than the whole meeting just to try to put a few seconds' silence's thoughts into words. This is another paradox, that many of the most important impressions and thoughts in a person's life are ones that flash through your head so fast that *fast* isn't even the right word, they seem totally different from or outside of the regular sequential clock time we all live by, and they have so little relation to the sort of linear, one-word-after-another-word English we communicate with each other with that it could easily take a whole lifetime just to spell out the contents of one split-second's flash of thoughts and connections, etc.—and yet we all seem to go around trying to use English (or whatever language our native country happens to use, it goes without saying) to try to convey to other people what we're thinking and to find out what they're thinking, when in fact deep down everybody knows it's a charade and they're just going through the motions. What goes on inside is just too fast and huge and all interconnected for words to do more than barely sketch the outlines of at most one tiny little part of it at any given instant. The internal head-speed of these ideas, memories, realizations, emotions, and so on is even faster, by the way—exponentially faster, unimaginably faster—when you're dying, meaning during that vanishingly tiny nanosecond between when you technically die and when the next thing happens, so that in reality the cliché about people's whole life flashing before their eyes as they're dying isn't all that far off— although the *whole life* here isn't really a sequential thing where first you're born and then you're in the crib and then you're up at the plate in Legion ball, etc., which it turns out that that's what people usually mean when they say 'my whole life,' meaning a discrete, chronological series of moments that they add up and call their life-time. It's not really like that. The best way I can think of to try to say it is that it all happens at once, but that *at once* doesn't really mean a finite moment of sequential time the way we think of time while we're alive, plus that what turns out to be the meaning of the term *my life* isn't even close to what we think we're talking about when we say 'my life.' Words and chronological time create all these total misunderstandings of what's really going on at the most basic level. And yet at the same time English is all we have to try to understand it and try to form anything larger or more meaningful and true with anybody else, which is yet another paradox. Dr. Gustafson—whom I would meet again later and find out that he had almost nothing to do with the big doughy repressed guy sitting back against his chair's beads in his River Forest office with colon cancer in him already at that time and him knowing nothing yet except that he didn't feel quite right down there in the bathroom lately and if it kept on he'd make an appointment to go in and ask his internist about it—Dr. G. would later say that the whole *my whole life flashed* phenomenon at the end is more like being a whitecap on the surface of the ocean, meaning that it's only at the moment you subside and start sliding back in that you're really even aware there's an ocean at all. When you're up and out there as a whitecap you might talk and act as if you know you're just a whitecap on the ocean, but deep down you don't think there's really an ocean at all. It's almost impossible to. Or like a leaf that doesn't believe in the tree it's part of, etc. There are all sorts of ways to try to express it.

And of course all this time you've probably been noticing what seems like the really central, overarching paradox, which is that this whole thing where I'm saying words can't really do it and time doesn't really go in a straight line is something that you're hearing as words that you have to start listening to the first word and then each successive word after that in chronological time to understand, so if

114

I'm saying that words and sequential time have nothing to do with it you're wondering why we're sitting here in this car using words and taking up your increasingly precious time, meaning aren't I sort of logically contradicting myself right at the start. Not to mention am I maybe full of B.S. about knowing what happens—if I really did kill myself, how can you even be hearing this? Meaning am I a fraud. That's OK, it doesn't really matter what you think. I mean it probably matters to you, or you think it does—that isn't what I meant by *doesn't matter*. What I mean is that it doesn't really matter what you think about me, because despite appearances this isn't even really about me. All I'm trying to do is sketch out one little part of what it was like before I died and why I at least thought I did it, so that you'll have at least some idea of why what happened afterward happened and why it had the impact it did on who this is really about. Meaning it's like an abstract or sort of intro, meant to be very brief and sketchy . . . and yet of course look how much time and English it's seeming to take even to say it. It's interesting if you really think about it, how clumsy and laborious it seems to be to convey the smallest thing. How much time would you even say has passed, so far?

One reason why Dr. Gustafson would have made a terrible poker player or fraud is that whenever he thought it was a big moment in the analysis he would always make a production of leaning back in his desk chair, which made that loud sound as the back tilted back and his feet went back on their heels so the soles showed, although he was good at making the position look comfortable and very familiar to his body, like it felt good doing that when he had to think. The whole thing was both slightly over-dramatic and yet still likable for some reason. Fern, by the way, has reddish hair and slightly asymmetrical green eyes—the kind of green people buy tinted contact lenses to get—and is attractive in a sort of witchy way. I think she's attractive, anyway. She's grown up to be a very poised, witty, self-sufficient person, with maybe just the slightest whiff of the perfume of loneliness that hangs around unmarried women at thirty. The fact is that we're all lonely, of course. Everyone knows this, it's almost a cliché. So another layer of my essential fraudulence is that I pretended to myself that my loneliness was special, that it was uniquely my fault because I was somehow especially fraudulent and hollow. It's not special at all, we've all got it. In spades. Dead or not, Dr. Gustafson knew more about all this than I, so that he spoke with what came off as genuine authority and pleasure when he said (maybe a little superciliously, given how obvious it was), 'But if you're constitutionally false and manipulative and unable to be honest about who you really are, Neal' (Neal being my given name, it was on my birth certificate when I got adopted), 'how is it that you were able to drop the sparring and manipulation and be honest with me a moment ago' (for that's all it had been, in spite of all the English that's been expended on just my head's partial contents in the tiny interval between then and now) 'about who you really are?' So it turned out I'd been right in predicting what his big logical insight was going to be. And although I played along with him for a while so as not to prick his bubble, inside I felt pretty bleak indeed, because now I knew that he was going to be just as pliable and credulous as everyone else, he didn't appear to have anything close to the fire-power I'd need to give me any hope of getting helped out of the trap of fraudulence and unhappiness I'd constructed for myself. Because the real truth was that my 'confession' of being a fraud and of having wasted time sparring with him over the previous weeks in order to manipulate him into seeing me as exceptional and insightful had itself been kind of manipulative. It was pretty clear that Dr. Gustafson, in order to survive in private practice, could not be totally stupid or obtuse about people, so it seemed reasonable to assume that he'd noticed the massive amount of fencing and general showing off I'd been doing during the first weeks of the analysis, and thus had come to some conclusions about my apparently desperate need to make a certain kind of impression on him, and though it wasn't totally certain it was thus at least a decent possibility that he'd sized me up as a basically empty, insecure person whose whole life involved trying to impress people and manipulate their view of me in order to compensate for the inner emptiness. It's not as if this is an incredibly rare or obscure type of personality, after all. So the fact that I had chosen to be supposedly 'honest' and to diagnose myself aloud was in fact just one more move in my campaign to make sure Dr. Gustafson understood that as a patient I was uniquely acute and self-aware, and that there was very little chance that he was going to see or diagnose anything about me that I wasn't already aware of and able to turn to my own tactical advantage in terms of creating whatever image or impression of myself I wanted him to see at that moment. His big supposed insight, then—which had as its ostensible, first-order point that my fraudulence could not possibly be as thoroughgoing and hopeless as I claimed it was, since my ability to be honest with him about it logically contradicted my claim of being

116

incapable of honesty—actually had as its larger, unspoken point the claim that he could discern things about my basic character that I myself could not see or interpret accurately, and thus that he could help me out of the trap by pointing out inconsistencies in my view of myself as totally fraudulent. The fact that this insight that he appeared so coyly pleased and excited about was not only obvious and superficial but also wrong—this was depressing, much the way discovering that somebody is easy to manipulate is always a little depressing. A sort of corollary to the fraudulence paradox is that you simultaneously want to fool everyone you meet and yet also somehow always hope that you'll come across someone who is your match or equal and can't be fooled. But this was sort of the last straw, I mentioned I'd tried a whole number of different things that hadn't helped already. So *depressing* is a gross understatement, actually. Plus of course the obvious fact that I was paying this guy for help in getting out of the trap and he'd now showed that he didn't have the mental firepower to do it. So I was now thinking about the prospect of spending time and money driving in to River Forest twice a week just to yank the analyst around in ways he couldn't see so that he'd think that I was actually less fraudulent than I thought I was and that analysis was gradually helping me see this. Meaning that he'd probably be getting more out of it than I would, for me it would just be fraudulence as usual.

However tedious and sketchy all this is, you're at least getting an idea, I think, of what it was like inside my head. If nothing else, you're seeing how exhausting and solipsistic it is to be like this. And I had been this way my whole life, at least from age four onward, as far as I could recall. Of course, it's also a really stupid and egotistical way to be, of course you can see that. This is why the ultimate and most deeply unspoken point of the analyst's insight—namely, that who and what I believed I was was not what I really was at all—which I thought was false, was in fact true, although not for the reasons Dr. Gustafson, who was leaning back in his chair and smoothing his big mustache with his thumb and forefinger while I played dumb and let him feel like he was explaining to me a contradiction I couldn't understand without his help, believed.

One of my other ways of playing dumb for the next several sessions after that was to protest his upbeat diagnosis (irrelevantly, since by this time I'd pretty much given up on Dr. Gustafson and was starting to think of various ways to kill myself without causing pain or making a mess that would disgust whoever found me) by means of listing the various ways I'd been fraudulent even in my pursuit of ways to achieve genuine and uncalculating integrity. I'll spare you giving you the whole list again. I basically went all the way back to childhood (which analysts always like you to do) and laid it on. Partly I was curious to see how much he'd put up with. For example, I told him about going from genuinely loving ball, loving the smell of the grass and distant sprinklers, or the feel of pounding my fist into the glove over and over and yelling, 'Hey batterbatter,' and the big low red tumid sun at the game's start versus the arc lights coming on with a clank in the glowing twilight of the late innings, and of the steam and clean burned smell of ironing my Legion uniform, or the feel of sliding and watching all the dust it raised settle around me, or all the parents in shorts and rubber flip-flops setting up lawn chairs with styrofoam coolers, little kids hooking their fingers around the backstop fence or running off after fouls. The smell of the ump's aftershave and sweat, the little whisk broom he'd bend down and tidy the plate with. Mostly the feel of stepping up to the plate knowing anything was possible, a feeling like a sun flaring somewhere high up in my chest. And how by only maybe fourteen all that had disappeared and turned into worrying about averages and if I could make All City again or being so worried I'd screw up that I didn't even like ironing the uniform anymore before games because it gave me too much time to think, standing there so nerved up about doing well that night that I couldn't even notice the little chuckling sighs the iron made anymore or the singular smell of the steam when I hit the little button for steam. How I'd basically ruined all the best parts of everything like that. How sometimes it felt like I was actually asleep and none of it was even real and someday out of nowhere I was maybe going to suddenly wake up in mid-stride. That was part of the idea behind things like joining the charismatic church up in Naperville, to try to wake up spiritually instead of living in this fog of fraudulence. 'The truth shall set you free'—the Bible. This was what Beverly-Elizabeth Slane liked to call my holy roller phase. And the charismatic church really did seem to help a lot of the parishioners and congregants I met. They were humble and devoted and charitable, and gave tirelessly without thought of personal reward in active service to the church and in donating resources and time to the church's campaign to build a new altar with an enormous cross of thick glass whose crossbeam was lit up and filled with aerated water and was to have various kinds of beautiful fish swimming in it. (Fish being a prominent Christ symbol for charismatics. In fact, most of us who were the most devoted and active in the church had bumper stickers on our cars with no words or anything except a plain line drawing of the outline of a fish—this lack of ostentation impressed me as classy and genuine.) But with the real truth here being how quickly I went from being someone who was there because he wanted to wake up and stop being a fraud to being somebody who was so anxious to impress the congregation with how devoted and active I was that I volunteered to help take the collection, and never missed one study group the whole time, and was on two different committees for coordinating fundraising for the new aquarial altar and deciding exactly what kind of equipment and fish would be used for the crossbeam. Plus often being the one in the front row whose voice in the responses was loudest and who waved both hands in the air the most enthusiastically to show that the Spirit had entered me, and speaking in tongues—mostly consisting of *d*'s and *g*'s—except not really, of course, because in fact I was really just pretending to speak in tongues because all the parishioners around me were speaking in tongues and had the Spirit, and so in a kind of fever of excitement I was able to hoodwink even myself into thinking that I really had the Spirit moving through me and was speaking in tongues when in reality I was just shouting, 'Dugga muggle ergle dergle' over and over. (In other words, so anxious to see myself as truly born-again that I actually convinced myself that the tongues' babble was real language and somehow less false or inadequate than plain English at expressing the feeling of the Holy Spirit rolling like a juggernaut right through me.) This went on for about four months. Not to mention falling over backward whenever Pastor Steve came down the row and popped me in the forehead with the heel of his hand, but falling over backward on purpose, not genuinely being struck down by the Spirit like the other people on either side of me (one of whom actually fainted and had to be brought around with salts). It was only when I was walking out to the parking lot one night after Wednesday Night Praise that I suddenly experienced a flash of self-awareness or clarity in which I suddenly stopped conning myself and realized that I'd been a fraud all these months in the church, too, and was really only saying and doing these things because all the real parishioners were doing them and I wanted everyone to think I was sincere. It just about knocked me over, that was how vividly I saw how I'd deceived myself. The revealed truth was that I was an even bigger fraud in church about being a newly reborn authentic person than I'd been before Deacon and Mrs. Halberstadt first rang my doorbell out of nowhere as part of their missionary service and talked me into giving it a shot. Because at least before the church thing I wasn't conning myself—I'd known that I was a fraud since at least age nineteen, but at least I'd been able to admit and face the fraudulence directly instead of B.S.ing myself that I was something I wasn't.

All this was presented in the context of a very long pseudo-argument about fraudulence with Dr. Gustafson that would take way too much English to relate to you in any detail, so I'm just telling you about some of the more garish examples. With Dr. G. it was more in the form of a prolonged, multi-session back-and-forth on whether or not I was a total fraud, during which I got more and more disgusted with myself for even playing along. By this point in the analysis I'd pretty much decided he was an idiot, or at least very limited in his insights into what was really going on with people. (There was also the blatant issue of the mustache and of him always playing with it.) Essentially, he saw what he wanted to see, which was just the sort of person I could practically eat for lunch in terms of creating whatever ideas or impressions of me I wanted. For instance, I told him about the period of trying jogging, during which I seemed never to fail to have to increase my pace and pump my arms more vigorously whenever someone drove by or looked up from his yard, so that I ended up with bone spurs and eventually had to quit altogether. Or spending at least two or three sessions recounting the example of the introductory meditation class at the Downers Grove Community Center that Melissa Betts of Settleman, Shannon got me to take, at which through sheer force of will I'd always force myself to remain totally still with my legs crossed and back perfectly straight long after the other students had given up and fallen back on their mats shuddering and holding their heads. Right from the first class meeting, even though the small brown instructor had told us to shoot for only ten minutes of stillness at the outset because most Westerners' minds could not maintain more than a few minutes of stillness and mindful concentration without feeling so restless and ill at ease that they couldn't stand it, I always remained absolutely still and focused on breathing my prana with the lower diaphragm longer than any of them, sometimes for up to thirty minutes, even though my knees and lower back were on fire and I had what felt like swarms of insects crawling over my arms and shooting out the top of my head—and Master Gurpreet, although he kept his facial expression inscrutable, gave me a deep and seemingly respectful bow and said that I sat almost like a living statue of mindful repose, and that he was impressed. The problem was that we were all also supposed to continue practicing our meditation on our own at home between classes, and when I tried to do it alone I couldn't seem to sit still and follow my breath for more than even a few minutes before I felt like crawling out of my skin and had to stop. I could only sit and appear quiet and mindful and withstand the unbelievably restless and horrible feelings when all of us were doing it together in the class— meaning only when there were other people to make an impression on. And even in class, the truth was that I was often concentrating not so much on following my prana as on keeping totally still and in the correct posture and having a deeply peaceful and meditative expression on my face in case anyone was cheating and had their eyes open and was looking around, plus also to ensure that Master Gurpreet would continue to see me as exceptional and keep addressing me by what became sort of his class nickname for me, which was 'the statue.'

In the final few class meetings, when Master Gurpreet told us to sit still and focused for only as long as we comfortably could and then waited almost an hour before finally hitting his small bell with the little silver thing to signal the period of meditation's end, only I and an extremely thin, pale girl who had her own meditation bench that she brought to class with her were able to sit still and focused for the whole hour, although at several different points I'd get so cramped and restless, with what felt like bright blue fire going up my spine and shooting invisibly out of the top of my head as blobs of color exploded over and over behind my eyelids, that I thought I was going to jump up screaming and take a header right out the window. And at the end of the course, when there was also an opportunity to sign up for the next session, which was called 'Deepening the Practice,' Master Gurpreet presented several of us with different honorary certificates, and mine had my name and the date and was inscribed in black calligraphy *Champion Meditator, Most Impressive Western Student, the Statue.* It was only after I fell asleep that night (I'd finally sort of compromised and told myself I was practicing the meditative discipline at home at night by lying down and focusing on following my breathing very closely as I fell asleep, and it did turn out to be a potent sleep aid) that while I was asleep I had the dream about the statue in the commons and realized that Master Gurpreet had actually in all likelihood seen right through me the whole time, and that the certificate was in reality a subtle rebuke or joke at my expense. Meaning he was letting me know that he knew I was a fraud and not even coming close to actually quieting my mind's ceaseless conniving about how to impress people in order to achieve mindfulness and honor my true inner self. (Of course, what he seemed not to have divined was that in reality I had no true inner self, and that the more I tried to be genuine the more empty and fraudulent I ended feeling inside, which I told nobody about until my stab at analysis with Dr. Gustafson.) In the dream, I was in the town commons in Aurora, over near the Pershing tank memorial by the clock tower, and what I'm doing in the dream is sculpting an enormous marble or granite statue of myself, using a huge iron chisel and a hammer the size of those ones they give you to try to hit the bell at the top of the big thermometer thing at carnivals, and when the statue's finally done I put it up on a big bandstand or platform and spend all my time polishing it and keeping birds from sitting on it or doing their business on it, and cleaning up litter and keeping the grass neat all around the bandstand. And in the dream my whole life flashes by like that, the sun and moon go back and forth across the sky like windshield wipers over and over, and I never seem to sleep or eat or take a shower (the dream takes place in dream time as opposed to waking, chronological time), meaning I'm condemned to a whole life of being basically nothing but a custodian to this statue. I'm not saying it was subtle or hard to figure out. Everybody from Fern, Master Gurpreet, the anorexic girl with her own bench, and Ginger Manley, to people from the firm and some of the media reps we bought time from (I was still a media buyer at this time) all walk by, some several times—at one point Melissa Betts and her new fiancé even spread out a blanket and have a sort of little picnic in the shade of the statue—but none of them ever look over or say anything. It's obviously another dream about fraudulence, like the dream where I'm supposedly the big pop star on stage but really all I do is lip synch to one of my stepparents' old Mamas and Papas records that's on a record player just offstage, and somebody whose face I can't ever look over long enough to make out keeps putting his hand in the area of the record as if he's going to make it skip or scratch, and the whole dream makes my skin crawl. These dreams were obvious, they were warnings from my subconscious that I was hollow and a fraud and it was only a matter of time before the whole charade fell apart. Another of my stepmother's treasured antiques was a silver pocket watch of her maternal grandfather's with the Latin RESPICE FINEM inscribed on the inside of the case. It wasn't until after she passed away and my stepfather said she'd wanted me to have it that I bothered to look up the term, after which I'd gotten the same sort of crawly feeling as with Master Gurpreet's certificate. Much of the nightmarish quality of the dream about the statue was due to the way the sun raced back and forth across the sky and the speed with which my whole life blew rapidly by like that in the commons. It was obviously also my subconscious enlightening me as to the meditation instructor's having seen through me the whole time, after which I was too embarrassed even to go try to get a refund for 'Deepening the Practice,' which there was now no way I felt like I could show up for, even though I also still had fantasies about Master Gurpreet becoming my mentor or guru and using all kinds of inscrutable Eastern techniques to show me the way to meditate myself into having a true self . . .

. . . Etc., etc. I'll spare you any more examples, for instance I'll spare you the literally countless examples of my fraudulence with girls—with the ladies, as they say—in just about every dating relationship I had, or the almost unbelievable amount of fraudulence and calculation involved in my career, not just in terms of manipulating the consumer and manipulating the client into trusting that your agency's ideas are the best way to manipulate the consumer, but in the inter-office politics of the agency itself, like for example in sizing up what sorts of things your superiors want to believe (including the belief that they're smarter than you and that that's why they're your superior) and then in giving them what they want but doing it just subtly enough that they never get a chance to view you as a sycophant or yes man—which they want to believe they do not want—but instead see you as a tough-minded independent thinker who from time to time bows to the weight of their superior intelligence and creative firepower, etc., etc. The whole agency was one big ballet of fraudulence and manipulating people's images of your ability to manipulate images, a virtual hall of mirrors. And I was good at it, I thrived there, remember.

It was the sheer amount of time Dr. Gustafson spent touching and smoothing his mustache that indicated that he wasn't aware of doing it and in fact was subsconsciously reassuring himself that it was still there. Which is not an especially subtle habit, in terms of insecurity, since after all facial hair is known as a secondary sex characteristic, meaning what he was really doing was subconsciously reassuring himself that something *else* was still there, if you know what I mean. This was some of why it was no real surprise when it turned out that the overall direction he wanted the analysis to proceed in involved issues of masculinity and how I understood my masculinity (my 'manhood' in other words). This also helped explain everything from the lost-female-crawling and two-testicle-shaped-objects-that-looked-deformed prints on the wall, plus the little African or Indian drums and little figurines with (sometimes) exaggerated sex characteristics on the shelf over his desk, plus the pipe, the unnecessary size of his wedding band, even the somewhat overdone little-boy clutter of the office itself. It was pretty clear that there were some major sexual insecurities and maybe even homosexual-type ambiguities that Dr. Gustafson was subconsciously trying to hide from himself and reassure himself about, and one obvious way he did this was to sort of project his insecurities onto his patients and get them to believe that America's culture had a uniquely brutal and alienating way of brainwashing its males from an early age into all kinds of beliefs and superstitions about what being a 'real man' was, such as competitiveness instead of concert, winning at all costs, dominating others through intelligence or will, being strong, not showing your true emotions, depending on others seeing you as a real man in order to reassure yourself of your manhood, seeing your own value solely in terms of accomplishments, being obsessed with your career or income, feeling as if you were constantly being judged and on display, etc. This was later in the analysis, after the endless period where after every example of fraudulence I gave him he'd make a show of congratulating me on being able to reveal what I felt were shameful fraudulent examples, and said that this was proof that I had much more of an ability to be genuine than I (apparently because of my insecurities or male fears) seemed able to give myself credit for. Plus it didn't exactly seem like a coincidence that the cancer he was even then harboring was in his colon—that shameful, dirty, secret place right near the rectum—with the idea being that using your rectum or colon to secretly *harbor an alien growth* was a blatant symbol both of homosexuality and of the repressive belief that its open acknowledgment would equal disease and lethality. Dr. Gustafson and I both had a good laugh over this one after we'd both died and were outside linear time and in the process of dramatic change, you can bet on that. (*Outside time* is not just an expression or manner of speaking, by the way.) By this time in the analysis I was playing with him the way a cat does with a hurt bird. If I'd had an ounce of real self-respect I would have stopped and gone back to the Downers Grove Community Center and thrown myself on Master Gurpreet's mercy, since except for maybe one or two girls I'd dated he was the only one who'd appeared to see all the way through to the core of my fraudulence, plus his oblique, very dry way of indicating this to me betrayed a sort of serene indifference to whether I even understood that he saw right through me that I found incredibly impressive and genuine—here in Master Gurpreet was a man with, as they say, nothing to prove. But I didn't, instead I more or less conned myself into sticking with going in to see Dr. G. twice a week for almost nine months (toward the end it was only once a week because by then the cancer had been diagnosed and he was getting radiation treatments every Tuesday and Thursday), telling myself that at least I was trying to find some venue in which I could get help finding a way to be genuine and stop manipulating everybody around me to see 'the statue' as erect and impressive, etc.

Nor however is it strictly true that the analyst had nothing interesting to say or didn't sometimes provide helpful models or angles of looking at the basic problem. For instance, it turned out that one of his basic operating premises was the claim that there were really only two basic, fundamental orientations a person could have toward the world, (1) love and (2) fear, and that they couldn't coexist (or, in logical terms, that their domains were exhaustive and mutually exclusive, or that their two sets had no intersection but their union comprised all possible elements, or that

$$'(\forall x)\ ((Fx \rightarrow\ \sim(Lx))\ \&\ (Lx \rightarrow\ \sim(Fx))),'\ \text{or}\ '\sim((\exists x)\ (Fx\ \&\ Lx))'\ ),$$

meaning in other words that each day of your life was spent in service to one of these masters or the other, and 'One cannot serve two masters'—the Bible again—and that one of the worst things about the conception of competitive, achievement-oriented masculinity that America supposedly hard-wired into its males was that it caused a more or less constant state of fear that made genuine love next to impossible. That is, that what passed for love in American men was usually just the need to be regarded in a certain way, meaning that today's males were so constantly afraid of 'not measuring up' (Dr. G.'s phrase, with evidently no pun intended) that they had to spend all their time convincing others of their masculine 'validity' (which happens to also be a term from formal logic) in order to ease their own insecurity, making genuine love next to impossible. Although

125

it seemed a bit simplistic to see this fear as just a male problem (try watching a girl stand on a scale sometime), it turns out that Dr. Gustafson was very nearly right in this concept of the two masters—though not in the way that he, when alive and confused about his own real identity, thought—and even while I played along by pretending to argue or not understand quite what he was driving at, the idea struck me that maybe the real root of my problem was not fraudulence but a basic inability to really love, even to genuinely love my stepparents, or Fern, or Melissa Betts, or Ginger Manley of Aurora West High in 1979, whom I'd often thought of as the only girl I'd ever truly loved, though Dr. G.'s bromide about men being brainwashed to equate love with accomplishment or conquest also applied here. The plain truth was that Ginger Manley was just the first girl I ever went all the way with, and most of my tender feelings about her were really just nostalgia for the feeling of immense cosmic validation I'd felt when she finally let me take her jeans all the way off and put my 'manhood' inside her, etc. There's really no bigger cliché than losing your virginity and later having all kinds of retrospective tenderness for the girl involved. Or what Beverly-Elizabeth Slane, a research technician I used to see outside of work when I was a media buyer, and had a lot of conflict with toward the end, said, which I don't think I ever told Dr. G. about, fraudulence-wise, probably because it hit too close to the bone. Toward the end she compared me to some piece of ultra-expensive new medical or diagnostic equipment that can discern more about you in one quick scan than you could ever know about yourself—but the equipment doesn't care about you, you're just a sequence of processes and codes. What the machine understands about you doesn't actually *mean* anything to it. Even though it's really good at what it does. Beverly had a bad temper combined with some serious firepower, she was not someone you wanted to have pissed off at you. She said she'd never felt the gaze of someone so penetrating, discerning, and yet empty of care, like she was a puzzle or problem I was figuring out. She said that it was thanks to me that she'd discovered the difference between being penetrated and really known versus penetrated and just violated—needless to say, these thanks were sarcastic. Some of this was just her emotional makeup. She found it impossible to really end a relationship unless all bridges were burned and things got said that were so devastating that there could be no possibility of a rapprochement to haunt her or prevent her moving on. Nevertheless it penetrated, I never did forget what she said in that letter.

Even if being fraudulent and being unable to love were in fact ultimately the same thing (a possibility that Dr. Gustafson never seemed to consider no matter how many times I tried to set him up to see it), being unable to really love was at least a different model or lens through which to see the problem, plus initially it seemed like a promising way of attacking the fraudulence paradox in terms of reducing the self-hatred part that reinforced the fear and the consequent drive to try to manipulate people into providing the approval I'd denied myself. This period was pretty much the zenith of my career in analysis, and for a few weeks (during a couple of which I actually didn't see Dr. Gustafson at all, because some sort of complication in his illness required him to go into the hospital, and when he came back he appeared to have lost not only weight but some kind of essential part of his total mass, and no longer seemed way too large for his old desk chair, which still squeaked but now not as loudly; plus a lot of the clutter and papers had been straightened up and put in several brown cardboard banker's boxes against the wall under the two sad prints, and when I came back in to see him the absence of mess was especially disturbing and sad, for some reason) it was true that I felt some of the first genuine hope I'd had since the early, self-deluded part of the experiment with Naperville's Church of the Flaming Sword of the Redeemer. And yet at the same time these weeks also led more or less directly to my decision to kill myself, although I'm going to have to simplify and linearize a great deal of interior stuff in order to convey to you what actually happened. Otherwise it would take an almost literal eternity to recount it, we already agreed about that. It's not that words or human language stop having any meaning or relevance after you die, by the way. It's more the specific, one-after-the-other temporal ordering of them that does. Or doesn't. It's hard to explain. In logical terms, something expressed in words will still have the same *cardinality* but no longer the same *ordinality*. All the different words are still there, in other words, but it's no longer a question of which one comes first. Or you could say it's no longer the series of words but now more like some limit toward which the series converges. It's hard not to want to put it in logical terms, since they're the most abstract and universal. Meaning they have no connotation, you don't feel anything about them. Or maybe imagine everything anybody on earth ever said or even thought to themselves all getting collapsed and exploding into one large, combined, instantaneous sound—although *instantaneous* is a little misleading, since it implies other

127

instants before and after, and it isn't really like that. It's more like the sudden internal flash when you see or realize something—a sudden flash or whatever of epiphany or insight. It's not just that it happens way faster than you could break the process down and arrange it into English, but that it happens on a scale in which there isn't even time to be aware of any sort of time at all in which it's happening, the flash—all you know is that there's a before and an after, and afterward you're different. I don't know if that makes sense. I'm just trying to give it to you from several different angles, it's all the same thing. Or you could think of it as being more a certain configuration of light than a word-sum or series of sounds, too, afterward. Which is in fact true. Or as a theorem's proof—because if a proof is true it's true everywhere and all the time, not just when you happen to say it. The thing is that it turns out that logical symbolism really would be the best way to express it, because logic is totally abstract and universal and outside what we think of as time. It's the closest thing to what it's really like. That's why it's the logical paradoxes that really drive people nuts. A lot of history's great logicians have ended up killing themselves, this is a fact.

And keep in mind this flash can happen anywhere, at any time.

Here's the basic Berry paradox, by the way, if you might want an example of why logicians with incredible firepower can devote their whole lives to solving these things and still end up beating their heads against the wall. This one has to do with really big numbers—meaning really big, past a trillion, past ten to the trillion to the trillion, way up there. When you get way up there, it takes a while even to describe numbers this big in words. 'The quantity one trillion, four hundred and three billion to the trillionth power' takes twenty syllables to describe, for example. You get the idea. Now, even higher up there in these huge, cosmic-scale numbers, imagine the very smallest number that can't be described in under twenty-two syllables. The paradox is that *the very smallest number that can't be described in under twenty-two syllables,* which of course is itself a description of this number, only has twenty-one syllables in it. So now what are you supposed to do?

What actually led to it in causal terms, though, occurred during maybe the third or fourth week that Dr. G. was back seeing patients after his hospitalization, although I'm not going to pretend that the specific incident wouldn't strike most people as absurd or even sort of insipid, as causes go. The truth is just that late at night one night in August after Dr. G.'s return, when I couldn't sleep (which happened a lot ever since the cocaine period) and was sitting up drinking a glass of milk and watching television, flipping the remote almost at random between different cable stations the way you do when it's late, I happened on part of an old *Cheers* episode from late in the series' run where the analyst character, Frasier (who went on to have his own show), and Lilith, his fiancée and also an analyst, are just entering the stage set of the underground tavern, and Frasier is asking her how her workday at her office went, and Lilith says, 'If I have one more yuppie come in and start whining to me about how he can't love, I'm going to throw up.' This line got a huge laugh from the show's studio audience, which indicated that they—and so by demographic extension the whole national audience at home, as well—recognized what a cliché and melodramatic type of complaint the inability-to-love concept really was. And, sitting there, when I realized that once again I'd managed to con myself, this time into thinking that this was a truer or more promising way to conceive of the problem of fraudulence—and, by extension, that I'd also somehow deluded myself into almost believing that poor old Dr. Gustafson had anything in his mental arsenal that could actually help me, and that the real truth was more that I was continuing to see him partly out of pity and partly so that I could pretend to myself that I was taking steps to becoming more authentic when in fact all I was doing was jerking a gravely ill shell of a man around and feeling superior to him because I was able to analyze his own psychological makeup so much more accurately than he could analyze mine—the flash of realizing all this at the very same time that the huge audience laugh showed that nearly everyone in the United States had probably already seen through the complaint's inauthenticity as long ago as whenever the episode had originally run—all this flashed through my head in the tiny interval it took to realize what I was watching and to remember who the characters of Frasier and Lilith even were, maybe half a second at most, and it more or less destroyed me, that's the only way I can describe it, as if whatever hope of any way out of the trap I'd made for myself had been blasted out of mid-air or laughed off the stage, as if I were one of those stock comic characters who is always both the butt of the joke and the only person not to get the joke—and in sum I went to bed feeling as fraudulent, befogged, hopeless and full of self-contempt as I'd ever felt, and it was the next morning after that that I woke up having decided that I was going to kill myself and end the whole farce. (As you probably recall, *Cheers* was an enormously popular series, and even in syndication its metro numbers were so high that if a local advertiser wanted to buy time on it the slots cost so much that you pretty much had to build his whole local strategy around those slots.) I'm compressing a huge amount of what took place in my psyche that next to last night, all the different realizations and conclusions I reached as I lay there in bed unable to sleep or even move (no single series' line or audience laugh is in and of itself going to constitute a reason for suicide, of course)—although to you I imagine it probably doesn't seem all that compressed at all, you're thinking here's this guy going on and on and why doesn't he get to the part where he kills himself and explain or account for the fact that he's sitting here next to me in a piece of high-powered machinery telling me all this if he died in 1991. Which in fact I knew I would from the moment I woke up. It was over, I'd decided to end the charade. After breakfast, I called in sick to work and stayed home the whole day alone. I knew that if I was around anyone I'd automatically lapse into fraudulence. I had decided to take a whole lot of Benadryl and then just as I got really sleepy and relaxed I'd get the car up to top speed on a rural road way out in the extreme west suburbs and drive it head-on into a concrete bridge abutment. Benadryl makes me extremely foggy and sleepy, it always has. I spent most of the morning on letters to my lawyer and CPA, and brief notes to the creative head and managing partner who had originally brought me aboard at Samieti and Cheyne. Our creative group was in the middle of some very ticklish campaign preparations, and I wanted to apologize for leaving them in the lurch. Of course I didn't really feel all that sorry—Samieti and Cheyne was a ballet of fraudulence, and I was well out of it. The note was probably ultimately just so that the people who really mattered at S. & C. would be more apt to remember me as a decent, conscientious guy who it turned out was maybe just a little too sensitive and tormented by his personal demons—'Almost too good for this world' is what I seemed to be unable to keep from fantasizing a lot of them saying after news of it came through. I did not write Dr. Gustafson a note. He had his own share of problems, and I knew that in the note I'd spend a lot of time trying to seem as if I was being honest but really just dancing around the truth, which was that he was a deeply repressed homosexual or androgyne and had no real business charging patients to let him project his own masculinity conflicts onto them, and that the truth was that he'd be doing himself and everybody else a favor if he'd just go over to Garfield Park and fellate somebody in the bushes and try honestly to decide if he liked it or not, and that I was a total fraud for continuing to drive all the way in to River Forest to see him and bat him around like a catnip toy while telling myself there was some possible nonfraudulent point to it. (All of which, of course, even if they weren't dying of colon cancer right in front of you you still could never actually come out and say to somebody, since certain truths might well destroy them—and who has that right?)

I did spend almost two hours before taking the first of the Benadryl composing a handwritten note to my sister Fern. In the note I apologized for whatever pain my suicide and the fraudulence and/or inability to love that had precipitated it might cause her and my stepdad (who was still alive and well and now lived in Marin County, California, where he taught part-time, and did community outreach with Marin County's homeless). I also used the occasion of the letter and all the sort of last-testament urgency associated with it to license apologizing to Fern about manipulating my stepparents into believing that she'd lied about the antique glass bowl in 1967, as well as for half a dozen other incidents and spiteful or fraudulent actions that I knew had caused her pain and that I had felt bad about ever since, but had never really seen any way to broach with her or express my honest regret for. (It turns out there are things that you can discuss in a suicide note that would appear almost bizarre if expressed in any other kind of venue.) Just one example of such an incident was during a period in the mid '70s, when Fern, as part of puberty, underwent some physical changes that made her look chunky for a year or two—not fat, but wide-hipped and bosomy and much more broad than she'd been as a pre-teen—and of course she was very, very sensitive about it (puberty also being a time of terrible self-consciousness and sensitivity about one's body image, obviously), so much so that my stepparents took great pains not to say anything about Fern's new breadth or even ever to bring up any topics related to eating habits, diet and exercise, etc. And I for my own part never said anything about it either, not directly, but I had worked out all kinds of very subtle and indirect ways to torment Fern about her size in such a way that my stepparents never saw anything and I could never really be accused of anything that I couldn't look all around myself with a shocked, incredulous facial expression as if I had no idea what she was talking about, such as just a quick raise of my eyebrow when her eyes met mine as she was having a second helping at dinner, or a quick, quiet, 'Are you sure you can fit into that?' when she came home from the store with a new skirt.

The one I still remembered the most vividly involved the second-floor hall of our house, which was in Aurora and was a three-story home (including the basement) but not all that spacious or large, a skinny three-decker such as many you always see all crammed together in Naperville and Aurora. The second-floor hallway, which ran between Fern's room and the top of the stairway on one end and my room and the second-floor bathroom on the other, was cramped and somewhat narrow, but not nearly as narrow as I would go out of my way to pretend that it was whenever Fern and I passed each other in it, with me squashing my back against the hallway wall and splaying my arms out and wincing as if there would barely be enough room for someone of her enormous breadth to squeeze past me, and she would never say anything or even look at me when I did it but would just go past me into the bathroom and close the door. But I knew it must have hurt her. A little while later, she entered an adolescent period where she hardly ate anything at all, and smoked cigarettes and chewed several packs of gum a day, and used a lot of makeup, and for a while she got so thin that she looked angular and a bit like an insect (although of course I never said that), and I once, through their bedroom's keyhole, overheard a brief conversation in which my stepmother said she was worried because she didn't think Fern was having her normal time of the month anymore because she had become so underweight, and she and my stepfather discussed the possibility of taking her to see some kind of specialist. That period passed on its own, but in the letter I told Fern that I'd always remembered this and other periods when I'd been cruel or tried to make her feel bad, and that I regretted them very much, although I said I wouldn't want to seem so egotistical as to think that a simple apology could erase any of the hurt I'd caused her when we were growing up. On the other hand, I also assured her that it wasn't as if I had gone around for years carrying excessive guilt or blowing these various incidents out of proportion. They were not life-altering traumas or anything like that, and in many ways they were probably all too typical of the sorts of cruelties that kids tend to inflict on one another growing up. I also assured Fern that neither these incidents nor my remorse about them had anything to do with my killing myself. I simply said, without going into anything like the level of detail I've given you (because my purpose in the letter was of course very different), that I was killing myself because I was an essentially fraudulent person who seemed to lack either the character or the firepower to find a way to stop even after I'd realized my fraudulence and the terrible toll it exacted (I told her nothing about the different realizations or paradoxes, what would be the point?). I also inserted that there was also a good possibility that, when all was said and done, I was nothing but just another yuppie who couldn't love, and that I found the banality of this unendurable, largely because I was evidently so hollow and insecure that I had a pathological need to see myself as somehow special or exceptional at all times. Without going into much explanation or argument, I also told Fern that if her initial reaction to these reasons for my killing myself was to think that I was being much, much too hard on myself, then she should know that I was already aware that that was the most likely reaction my note would produce in her, and had probably deliberately constructed the note to at least in part prompt just that reaction, just the way my whole life I'd often said and done things designed to prompt certain people to believe that I was a genuinely outstanding person whose personal standards were so high that he was far too hard on himself, which in turn made me appear attractively modest and unsmug, and was a big reason for my popularity with so many people in all different avenues of my life—what Beverly-Elizabeth Slane had termed my 'talent for ingratiation'—but was essentially calculated and fraudulent. I also told Fern that I loved her very much, and asked her to relay these same sentiments to Marin County for me.

Now we're getting to the part where I actually kill myself. This occurred at 9:17 P.M. on August 19, 1991, if you want the time fixed precisely. Plus I'll spare you most of the last couple hours' preparations and back-and-forth conflict and dithering, which there was a lot of. Suicide runs so counter to so many hard-wired instincts and drives that nobody in his right mind goes through with it without going through a great deal of internal back-and-forth, intervals of almost changing your mind, etc. The German logician Kant was right in this respect, human beings are all pretty much identical in terms of our hard-wiring. Although we are seldom conscious of it, we are all basically just instruments or expressions of our evolutionary drives, which are themselves the expressions of forces that are way larger and more important than we are. (Although actually being conscious of this is a whole different matter.) So I won't really even try to describe the several different times that day when I sat in my living room and had a furious mental back-and-forth about whether to actually go through with it. For one thing, it was intensely mental and would take an enormous amount of time to put into words, plus it would come off as somewhat cliché or banal in the sense that many of the thoughts and associations are basically the same sorts of generic things that anyone who's confronting imminent death will end up thinking. As in, 'This is the last time I will ever tie my shoes,' 'This is the last time I will look at this rubber tree on top of the stereo cabinet,' 'How delicious this lungful of air right here tastes,' 'This is the last glass of milk I'll ever drink,' 'What a totally priceless gift this totally ordinary sight of the wind picking trees' branches up and moving them around and laying them back down is.' Or, 'I will never again hear the plaintive sound of the fridge going on in the kitchen' (the kitchen and breakfast nook are right off my living room), etc. Or, 'I won't see the sun come up tomorrow or watch the bedroom gradually undim and resolve' and at the same time trying to summon the memory of the exact way the sun comes up over the fog of the humid fields and the wet-looking I-55 ramp that lay due east of my bedroom's sliding glass door in the morning. It had been a hot, wet August, and if I went through with killing myself I wouldn't ever get to feel the incremental cooling and drying that starts here around mid-September, or see the leaves turn or hear them rustle along the edge of the courtyard outside S. & C.'s floor of the building on S. Dearborn, or see snow or put a shovel and bag of sand in the trunk, or bite into a perfectly ripe, ungrainy pear, or put a piece of toilet paper on a shaving cut. If I went in and went to the bathroom and brushed my teeth it would be the last time I did those things. I sat there and thought about that, looking at the rubber tree. Everything seemed to tremble a little, the way something reflected in water will tremble. I watched the sun begin to drop down over the townhouse developments going up south of Darien's corporation limit on Lily Cache Rd. and realized that I would never see the newest homes' construction and landscaping completed, or that the homes' white insulation wrap with the trade name TYVEK all over it flapping in the wind would one day have vinyl siding or plate brick and color-coordinated shutters over it and I wouldn't see this happen or be able to drive by and know what was actually written there under all the exteriors. Or the breakfast nook window's view of the big farm's fields next to my development, with the plowed furrows all parallel so that if I lean and line their lines up just right they seem to be rushing together toward the horizon as if shot out of something huge. You get the idea. Basically, I was in that state in which a man realizes that everything he sees will outlast him. As a verbal construction I know that's a cliché. As a state in which to actually be, though, it's something else, believe me. Where now every movement takes on a kind of ceremonial aspect. The very sacredness of the world as seen (the same kind of state Dr. G. will try to describe with analogies to oceans and whitecaps and trees, you might recall I mentioned this already). This is literally about one one-trillionth of the various thoughts and internal experiences I underwent in those last few hours, and I'll spare both of us recounting any more, since I'm aware it ends up seeming somewhat lame. Which in fact it wasn't, but I won't pretend it was fully authentic or genuine, either. A part of me was still calculating, performing—and this was part of the ceremonial quality of that last afternoon. Even as I wrote my note to Fern, for instance, expressing sentiments and regrets that were real, a part of me was noticing what a fine and sincere note it was, and anticipating the effect on Fern of this or that heartfelt phrase, while yet another part was observing the whole scene of a man in a dress shirt and no tie sitting at his breakfast nook writing a heartfelt note on his last afternoon alive, the blonde wood table's surface trembling with sunlight and the man's hand steady and face both haunted by regret and ennobled by resolve, this part of me sort of hovering above and just to the left of myself, evaluating the scene, and thinking what a fine and genuine-seeming performance in a drama it would make if only we all had not already been subject to countless scenes just like it in dramas ever since we first saw a movie or read a book, which somehow entailed that real scenes like the one of my suicide note were now compelling and genuine only to their participants and to anyone else would come off as banal and even somewhat cheesy or maudlin, which is somewhat paradoxical when you consider—as I did, sitting there at the breakfast nook—that the reason scenes like this will seem stale or manipulative to an audience is that we've already seen so many of them in dramas, and yet the reason we've seen so many of them in dramas is that the scenes really are dramatic and compelling and let us communicate very deep, complicated emotional realities that are almost impossible to articulate in any other way, and at the same time still another facet or part of me realizing that from this perspective my own basic problem was that at an early age I'd somehow chosen to cast my lot with my life's drama's supposed audience instead of with the drama itself, and that I even now was watching and gauging my supposed performance's quality and probable effects, and was in the final analysis the very same manipulative fraud writing the note to Fern that I had been throughout the life that had brought me to this climactic scene of writing and signing it and addressing the envelope

135

and affixing postage and putting the envelope in my shirt pocket (totally conscious of the resonance of its resting there, next to my heart, in the scene), planning to drop it in a mailbox on the way out to Lily Cache Rd. and the bridge abutment into which I planned to drive my car at speeds sufficient to displace the whole front end and impale me on the steering wheel and kill me instantly. Self-loathing is not the same thing as being into pain or a lingering death. If I was going to do it, I wanted it instant.

On Lily Cache, the bridge abutments and sides' steep banks support State Route 4 (also known as the Braidwood Highway) as it crosses overhead on a cement overpass so covered with graffiti that most of it you can't even read. (This sort of defeats the purpose of graffiti, in my opinion.) The abutments themselves are just off the road and as wide as this car. Plus the intersection is isolated way out in the countryside around Romeoville, ten or so miles south of the southwest suburbs' limits. It is the true boonies. The only homes are farms set way back from the road and embellished with silos and barns, etc. At night in the summer the dew point is high and there's always fog. It's farm country. I've never once passed under 4 here without seeming to be the only thing on either road. The corn high and the fields like a green ocean all around, insects the only real noise. Driving alone under creamy stars and the little cocked scythe of moon, etc. The idea was to have the accident and whatever explosion and fire was involved occur someplace isolated enough that no one else would see it, so that there would be as little an aspect of performance to the thing as I could manage and no temptation to spend my last few seconds trying to imagine what impression the sight and sound of the impact might make on someone watching. I was partly concerned that it might be spectacular and dramatic and might look as if the driver was trying to go out in as dramatic a way as possible. This is the sort of shit we waste our lives thinking about.

The ground fog tends to get more intense by the second until it seems that the whole world is just what's in your headlights' reach. High beams don't work in fog, they only make things worse. You can go ahead and try them but you'll see what happens, all they do is light up the fog so that it seems even denser. That's kind of a minor paradox, that sometimes you can see farther with low beams than high. All right—and there's the construction and all the flapping Tyvek wrap on houses that if you really do do it you'll never see anyone live in. Although it won't hurt, it really will be instant, I can tell you that much. The fields' insects are almost deafening.

136

If the corn's high like this and you watch as the sun sets, you can practically watch them rise up out of the fields like some great figure's shadow rising. Mostly mosquitoes, I don't know what all they are. It's a whole insect universe in there that none of us will ever see or know anything about. You'll notice the Benadryl doesn't help all that much once you're under way. That whole idea was probably ill-conceived.

All right, now we're coming to what I promised and led you through the whole dull synopsis of what led up to this in hopes of. Meaning what it's like to die, what happens. Right? This is what everyone wants to know. And you do, trust me. Whether you decide to go through with it or not, whether I somehow talk you out of it the way you think I'm going to try to do or not. It's not what anyone thinks, for one thing. The truth is you already know what it's like. You already know the difference between the size and speed of everything that flashes through you and the tiny inadequate bit of it all you can ever let anyone know. As though inside you is this enormous room full of what seems like everything in the whole universe at one time or another and yet the only parts that get out have to somehow squeeze out through one of those tiny keyholes you see under the knob in older doors. As if we are all trying to see each other through these tiny keyholes.

But it does have a knob, the door can open. But not in the way you think. But what if you could? Think for a second: What if all the infinitely dense and shifting worlds of stuff inside you every moment of your life turned out now to be somehow fully open and expressible afterward, after what you think of as *you* has died, because what if afterward now each moment itself is an infinite sea or span or passage of time in which to express it or convey it, and you don't even need any organized English, you can as they say open the door and be in anyone else's room in all your own multi-form forms and ideas and facets? Because listen—we don't have much time, here's where Lily Cache slopes slightly down and the banks start getting steep, and you can just make out the outlines of the unlit sign for the farm-stand that's never open anymore, the last sign before the bridge—so listen: What exactly do you think you are? The millions and trillions of thoughts, memories, juxtapositions—even crazy ones like this, you're thinking—that flash through your head and disappear? Some sum or remainder of these? Your *history*? Do you know how long it's been since I told you I was a fraud? Do you remember you were looking at the RESPICEM watch hanging from the rearview and seeing the time, 9:17? What are you looking at right now? Coincidence? What if no time has passed at all?* The truth is you've already heard this. That this is what it's like. That it's what makes room for the universes inside you, all the endless inbent fractals of connection and symphonies of different voices, the infinities you can never show another soul. And you think it makes you a fraud, the tiny fraction anyone else ever sees? Of course you're a fraud, of course what people see is never you. And of course you know this, and of course you try to manage what part they see if you know it's only a part. Who wouldn't? It's called free will, Sherlock. But at the same time it's why it feels so good to break down and cry in front of others, or to laugh, or speak in tongues, or chant in Bengali—it's not English anymore, it's not getting squeezed through any hole.

So cry all you want, I won't tell anybody.

But it wouldn't have made you a fraud to change your mind. It would be sad to do it because you think you somehow have to.

It won't hurt, though. It will be loud, and you'll feel things, but they'll go through you so fast that you won't even realize you're feeling them (which is sort of like the paradox I used to bounce off Gustafson—is it possible to be a fraud if you aren't aware you're a

---

*One clue that there's something not quite real about sequential time the way you experience it is the various paradoxes of time supposedly passing and of a so-called present that's always unrolling into the future and creating more and more past behind it. As if the present were this car—nice car by the way—and the past is the road we've just gone over, and the future is the headlit road up ahead we haven't yet gotten to, and time is the car's forward movement, and the precise present is the car's front bumper cutting through the fog of the future, so that it's *now* and then a tiny bit later a whole different *now*, etc. Except if time is really passing, how fast does it go? At what rate does the present change? See? Meaning if we use time to measure motion or rate—which we do, it's the only way you can—95 miles per hour, 70 heartbeats a minute, etc.—how are you supposed to measure the rate at which time moves? One second per second? It makes no sense. You can't even talk about time flowing or moving without hitting up against paradox right away. So think for a second: What if there's really no movement at all? What if this is all unfolding in the one flash you call the present, this first, infinitely tiny split-second of impact when the speeding car's front bumper's just starting to touch the abutment, just before the bumper crumples and displaces the front end and you go violently forward and the steering column comes back at your chest as if shot out of something enormous? Meaning that what if in fact this *now* is infinite and never really passes in the way your mind is supposedly wired to understand *pass*, so that not only your whole life but every single humanly conceivable way to describe and account for that life has time to flash like neon shaped into those connected cursive letters that businesses' signs and windows like so much to use through your mind all at once in the literally immeasurable instant between impact and death, just as you start forward to meet the wheel at a rate no belt ever made could restrain—THE END.

fraud?]. And the very brief moment of fire you'll feel will be almost good, like when your hands are cold and there's a fire and you hold your hands out toward it.

The reality is that dying isn't bad, but it takes forever. And that forever is no time at all. I know that sounds like a contradiction, or wordplay. What it really is, it turns out, is a matter of perspective. The big picture, as they say, in which the fact is that this whole seemingly endless back-and-forth between us has come and gone and come again in the same instant that Fern stirs a boiling pot for dinner, and your stepfather packs some pipe tobacco down with his thumb, and Angela Mead uses an ingenious little catalogue tool to roll cat hair off her blouse, and Melissa Betts inhales to respond to something she thinks her husband just said, and David Wallace blinks in the midst of idly scanning class photos from his 1980 Aurora West H.S. yearbook and seeing my photo and trying, through the tiny keyhole of himself, to imagine what all must have happened to lead up to my death in the fiery single-car accident he'd read about in 1991, like what sorts of pain or problems might have driven the guy to get in his electric-blue Corvette and try to drive with all that OTC medication in his bloodstream—David Wallace happening to have a huge and totally unorganizable set of thoughts, feelings, memories and impressions of this little photo's guy a year ahead of him in school with the seemingly almost neon aura around him all the time of scholastic and athletic excellence and popularity and success with the ladies, as well as of every last cutting remark or even tiny disgusted gesture or expression on this guy's part whenever David Wallace struck out looking in Legion ball or said something dumb at a party, and of how impressive and authentically at ease in the world the guy always seemed, like an actual living person instead of the dithering, pathetically self-conscious outline or ghost of a person David Wallace knew himself back then to be. Verily a fair-haired, fast-track guy, whom in the very best human tradition David Wallace had back then imagined as happy and unreflective and wholly unhaunted by voices telling him that there was something deeply wrong with him that wasn't wrong with anybody else and that he had to spend all of his time and energy trying to figure out what to do and say in order to impersonate an even marginally normal or acceptable U.S. male, all this stuff clanging around in David Wallace '81's head every second and moving so fast that he never got a chance to catch hold and try to fight or argue against it or even really even feel it except as a knot in his stomach as he stood in his

139

real parents' kitchen ironing his uniform and thinking of all the ways he could screw up and strike out looking or drop balls in right and reveal his true pathetic essence in front of this .418 hitter and his witchily pretty sister and everyone else in the audience in lawn chairs in the grass along the sides of the Legion field (all of whom already probably saw through the sham from the outset anyway, he was pretty sure)—in other words David Wallace trying, if only in the second his lids are down, to somehow reconcile what this luminous guy had seemed like from the outside with whatever on the interior must have driven him to kill himself in such a dramatic and doubtlessly painful way—with David Wallace also fully aware that the cliché that you can't ever know what's going on inside somebody else is hoary and insipid and yet at the same time trying very consciously to prohibit that awareness from mocking the attempt or sending the whole line of thought into the sort of inbent spiral that keeps you from ever getting anywhere (considerable time having passed since 1980, of course, and David Wallace having emerged from years of literally indescribable war against himself with quite a bit more firepower than he'd had at Aurora West), the realer, more enduring and sentimental part of him commanding that other part to be silent, as if looking it coldly in the eye and saying, almost aloud, 'Not another word.'

[for N.M.N.80.418]

Seven Minds
Martine Bellen

*"The only wisdom we can hope to acquire
Is the wisdom of humility: endless humility."*
—T. S. Eliot

1. ASYLUM

Fissured plates,

Self-condensing music moves to evaporate

When growing in an open field

The girl's ears sealed with only tones of her own

Subtle senses carry her world (one not finished

More invisible and bliss

Full of menacing might,

Lampblack

A birdlike fear sleeps on deciduous cones,

———————

Bedouins and begonias, belladonna and two lions

Creep into arroyo for courage

In less than a minute a sparrow appears

141

          To be them

Flutters, chips, nervous

Sandy uplands spatially level with god

———————

    Found object or iris / lotus

         Living in a pool of living

         Quantity transparency

Narrow wings / octave alight air, retrenching

———————

Abundant tree

Guests run through its blood

Fall and spring

    Into a fish, now a bunting

The girl escapes through a new skin on the pond

Turns (as eyes, thoughts

    Sees

    Distance between awe & asyle de nuit

2. MOCKER

Relative mystery

        Leafless in late spring

To glimpse the way

               Worship balances

               When crushed

Practice turns to fragrance

—————

Fog lifts from her pool

          How thoughts melt

          Moments house intercourse

          Pond affairs

          Develop oblong through reflection

—————

Inundated

        Undulating river bottoms

Ungraspable

Unable to remember the was

So when

Reminded her mistake is another's memory

———————

Sassafras   tulip tree   pubescent petiole

Twigs   tomentose   aments red anthers

Sweet seed

Still point or suchness in which the object presents no-self

3. INSTRUCTIONS

Her voice still in her ears

(Dear old hole on the pond)

Rings dangle off lobes, fishes clap the surface

Mind atmosphere wind

Impossibly remote

4 sutures prominently winged

Inside an important personage though rarely visible

Around the edge of the mirror grow vigorous shoots:

pipewort, timothy, goatsbeard, enchanter's nightshade

Chitter chatter bottomlands or actional love

———————

Deep north

Essential principles of the mind

Bud a bright yellow

Vanished cravings

An incurable magnet

She a fountain of fleeting weather

Like a vanquished star's beacon

Like aurora subtle body

Like whispers form faraway prayer

Martine Bellen

4. SUBSTANCE

Take special care

The chipmunk doesn't fall in and hurt

Hostile   frightened   separate dwellings

Dehiscent or gaping fruit

Part of an error present in each

Clean sand from seaweed, seaweed from sand

Genius

Preconceptions transmute into conceptualizations

Soul-consoling semidark

Easy victim to poisonous emanations

Enough to stop a breath

Red and orange pearlescent tints doubled around the pond's skirts

Fruit poisons those who feel

A rarely forgotten beauty

Phantom existence surrounds

Low miry banks

Maims or spreads name

Over the abodeless present

Balancing on long loose panicles of a branch

& a tiger's wing

The pageant of her pond, a full mind looking-glass

Below the hard edge

Deeply rugose and very bitter

5. EXPERIENCE

One can swallow an ocean, its fish, mariners, coral reefs,

Hardened lava that coats its floor

Hide-and-seek

& handsome:

Describe in inches, tensile

Martine Bellen

A suture and Buddha injection

What melts besides

        forms

               of water?   loss of color / nature

      Pyramidal deeds that intend him   Who encounters providence

As the counter-image of freedom

––––––––––

        Branchlet

          Where they embrace, inform

          Meaning,   infer grace

          Staminate yellow light

Solitary spirits with radial symmetry who move the swamp

                            fill enthusiasms

                            limitations

Proceed toward destiny without knowing

It's here

Madness)

The current oracle

    & smooth-sculled winter

Obstacles

Or harms disappeared

How would you describe the wind?

6. WILL

Weapons such as the tongue

Illuminating multiplicities

A gate through which non-one proceeds to the residence proper

Martine Bellen

(Delusion and intriguing)

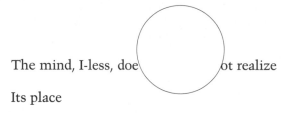

The mind, I-less, doe   ot realize

Its place

When the marksman's is lost

Tongue-lashing

———————

Her pursuit of being too concrete

True spirit, the third self

Her wood is light

When clouds are part of the sky

When they part the sky, part from the sky,

When the still sky is cloudless,

Empty, when clouds fall in the pond,

When sky adjusts before your eyes

Sky

Blue describes ocean

In minds that reflect & are often stormy

(Black clouds   Black willow)

Detached catkins of empty capsules

Weeping at their roots

———————

What's at work behind the field?

No one / one is you

The moon in the white bucket washed away by wave ripples

Or vanish behind the eye's wink

So large a space lost in the dynamic instant

Obeys the dictates of an absentee monster

60 or 70 feet give or take

Her appressed scales and ability

To deadlock dreams

7. INHUMAN

Not from the stuff of cloud

Horizon latitude

Sings at night as the girl flies, her music swallowed by hungry air

Ear ulterior

A glass sinks through the pond,

The agency of clouds

Impenetrable, its avowal transmitted

Through dense muslin maps of weather

(Not in sound

Observing rooks & the underside of an invisible leaf

Beautiful form mounting in the open field

Slender drooping joints

Ought never be expressed other than by ideogram

Tree full of birds

They leave winds of birds

The leaves—wings of birds

The birds leave their wings & spirits

Rise sunward, ramify, curve outward

Columnar, indomitable

Resting in the wind their mountain the composure of mind

Three Poems
Elaine Equi

A SENTIMENTAL SONG

We feel more than see
the stars white as radishes
and as sharp.

To we who always look down,
it's right that they be *in* the ground.
We love winter because it makes inner

seem even more inner
                            and crackling.

*

Cold is a fragrance
that clings to the skin
and smells cold.

Imagine a perfume called "Snow"
and another called "Drizzle"
and another called "January"

and all of them—free.

*

Just for today, I'd like to
step into someone else's list.
Run their errands. Wish their wish.

Today is St. Ita's day (the most famous
woman saint in Ireland after Brigid).
She is said to have reattached

the head to the body
of a man who'd been beheaded
and to live only on food from heaven.

Meanwhile the weather here is gray
but optimistic, aspiring to (I'm not sure what).
The slant of something moving up and away.

CAN'T COMPLAIN

We were just a sea of talking heads
getting carried away on a moving sidewalk
with space around the names
we kept dropping and picking up.

And though we thought it normal to think
one day the whole shebang would collapse,
our stories kept telling us elsewhere.
It was the antiapocalypse and it wasn't

going to go away because we were bored.
Try thinking less of progress and more of others
is what it said. What's wrong with everyone
being rich? Oh nothing, nothing at all, we chimed

as we slipped past the scarlet beast at the door
with the sign that read: too much allegory
may be hazardous to your health. You see,
we were trying to return to an earlier motif

when "outside" was an aspiration in and of itself
and one could eat natural phenomena for breakfast
and live like a king cockroach on a cloud-stained
couch. All our rainy days saved up for this.

Elaine Equi

FOR AUGUST IN APRIL

Now that we are back
to the beginning
of the alphabet—

its green apron
          and aquarium days,

its archers who aim
          at nothing at all,

who prefer to let
the targets come to them.

Suddenly, we are ashamed
of trying to connect things
with artifice and would prefer
the actor speak his part
in a series of asides.

We aspire to an assortment.

The asylum shines
          with symptoms

that are, at first, at attention
then later, at ease

as if consciousness
were nothing but an auction house.

The radio is not on, yet
much is still audible—

          auguries, aubades.

View of Kala Murie Stepping Out of Her Black Dress

Howard Norman

I HAD ARRIVED AT CHURCHILL, Manitoba, on September 11, 1926. I would soon discover that it was Kala Murie's wedding night.

About this new life I had no expectations. That kept manageable my fear of disappointment. It sufficed that I was no longer in Halifax. For the time being that was enough. What happened was, I'd simply answered an advertisement in the Halifax newspaper, the *Herald:*

> GENERAL ASSISTANT. Knowledge of the art
> of photography. Darkroom experience required.
> Contact: Vienna Linn, Churchill, Manitoba.

I qualified, especially the "darkroom experience," since by that time I'd worked in the *Herald*'s darkroom for nearly five years. I immediately posted a letter. Just short of five weeks later came the reply:

> *Dear Peter Duvett,*
> *You have the position secured, if you still*
> *want it. Write travel plans—to same address.*
> *Vienna Linn*

No "Sincerely yours" or "Best wishes." A man of some directness, I thought. Keep your expectations reasonable.

Wanting to put things in motion right away, I then wired Vienna Linn. His return message was prompt and encouraging. Its only note of concern was put as a question: *Have you located Churchill on the map? It's no walk in the park up here. Your services, however, will be most welcome.* I happily gave notice at the *Herald*, put what few pieces of furniture I owned in the basement of my apartment house on Water Street, paid my last month's rent as was owed, purchased a train ticket to Winnipeg. I was on my way.

I sat up in coach and hardly slept the entire journey, scrimped on meals, navigated the swaying aisle of the train, keeping to myself. Mostly I read my book, *The Strange Life of Mrs. J. Doyle.* It was about a real-life woman, Mrs. John Doyle, who'd lived her entire life in Dublin. One day, at age eighty-five, she fell down a flight of stairs in a neighbor's house. When she woke in the hospital, she had what the doctors called "selective amnesia." She could now only remember things from the year 1895. All other years had been erased from her memory. The Dublin paper ran the headline: KNOCK ON HEAD SENDS MRS. DOYLE BACK TO 1895. Somehow, tumbling down the stairs had given Mrs. Doyle a "photographic memory," but only for 1895. A kind of fame then pursued Mrs. Doyle. Historians, journalists, scholars of every sort—plus the occasional psychic—appeared at her door, wanting Mrs. Doyle to verify certain rumors, help decipher unsolved mysteries, look at photographs and talk about what was in them, "as if," the author, Walter Manning, wrote, "it was a chance for humanity to fully recapture Time itself." There Mrs. Doyle sat, day after day in her shabby room in Dublin, as visitors came and went and Mrs. Doyle told what she remembered. And in fact no one disputed a single detail she offered. At the same time, Mrs. Doyle couldn't for the life of her remember any number of her family—certain nieces, nephews, grandchildren, that is—because they hadn't been alive in 1895.

I read the book pretty much straight through. Every page, I wanted to know what happened next. To feel some nervousness, excitement, agitation, even fear about *what happened next* was how I judged a book as good or not. In terms of *The Strange Life of Mrs. J. Doyle,* I thought the author had a lot of skill to keep a reader paying close attention for 409 pages chronicling poor Mrs. Doyle's fate—it was quite an accomplishment. The author was sympathetic to Mrs. Doyle. I could tell that from page one. I myself would've liked to have spoken with her. With a day's travel to Winnipeg yet to go, my nerves a bit frayed from lack of sleep, I set down the book for awhile and thought, *Too bad you don't get a choice in the matter—which years to forget. I'd throw myself down the stairs, if I could pick and choose.* I laughed quietly to myself in the darkened train car. Passengers all around were snoring, mumbling in their sleep, staring out windows, curled up in as many shapes as an alphabet. I couldn't sleep. I thought up about thirty captions, describing my fellow passengers. I might've slept a little.

*

By arrangement, the pilot Driscoll Petchey met me at the train. He accompanied me by taxi to the small airport—a landing strip and one building. We boarded his single-prop plane. On its side, more or less scrawled in big black cursive writing, it read: D. PETCHEY KNOWETH CLOUDS, which struck me as comical and religious. Around 11 A.M., we set out north. Petchey was about fifty, give or take, with a weather-beaten, handsome face, thin lips that disappeared into deep clefts on either side of his mouth, a protruding Adam's apple, uncomfortable to look at, because it was like watching a gear fitting inside a human body. The entire journey, Petchey talked a blue streak. Actually, we both had to shout over the sound of the wind and engine. "My life" and "the godforsaken beauty of the north," Petchey went on about this, that, or the other subject. It was distracting entertainment. I was grateful, since I was such a jittery passenger. Did not like flying at all. He said he lived in Churchill but also rented a room in Winnipeg. I asked why he chose to live in Churchill. He thought for a moment. "The real truth is," he said, "all tourist bureau summer bird-watching nonsense aside—hey, reach in that metal box at your feet, get out the government brochure, will you?"

I unfolded the brochure. "Read the first part," Petchey said.

"Okay, sure," I said, glancing at a photograph of a bunch of children, Eskimo and otherwise, standing in front of the Hudson Bay Company store. I read: "The town of Churchill is located on the western shore of Hudson Bay at the mouth of the Churchill River. In summer, white beluga whales abound. Churchill's residents maintain a frontier spirit, in a town where Eskimos and Cree Indians thrive at the outskirts, and best understand the beautiful starkness of the surrounding tundra and sea. The occasional polar bear saunters past the post office, surely a sight to behold! Yet each spring the twentieth century arrives in full regalia, when European ships arrive to load grain sent up from Canada's western provinces."

"Enough—goddamn it!" Petchey spoke and laughed at the same time. "As I was saying, rarely do people travel up to Churchill, look around, and say, 'Home sweet home.' People live there because there's more *oxygen*. Or to flee some demon or other. Of course, there's families, a church, I don't contest that."

"Well, I just answered an advertisement in the newspaper," I said. "I wanted a new job. No more, no less."

"There's always more or less—but no matter, you've got yourself a new job, eh? And you're now employed by Mr. Vienna Linn. You're employed by quite an unusual man."

"Is he civil? That's what I care most about. Is he a civil man, because my last employer—"

"He's always been civil to me. But my opinion? He's on the lam from something. Some *deed*. I don't know this as a fact, mind you. But I've seen fugitives from justice—I'm not saying he's that. I've seen escapees from their own past lives—I'm not saying Vienna Linn's that, either. It's just that I've got a nose for such individuals, eh? Yet in diction and how he carries himself, he's somewhat the opposite of a lowlife. And here's something else. See, I was the one who flew Vienna Linn and his fiancée into Churchill. From that day on, it's struck me he's a type of genius, or expert at affecting as much successfully. Fiancée in tow, he settled right down in Churchill and stayed the godforsaken winter, which is the real test. Staying the winter, that does speak for the man. For her, too—Kala Murie is the fiancée's name. I don't know what nationality's that. Vienna right away set up shop. His camera work is topflight—at least to my eyes, his tripod camera work is. And here's something. Thomas Swain, who owns and runs the Churchill Hotel, your new home—Swain told me Vienna paid for his and, separately, his fiancée's room a year—that's twelve full months—in *advance*. Now, mind you, that phenomenon, Peter Duvett, made a prominent item in the *Hudson Bay News*."

"Seems like nobody's business," I said. "It was in the newspaper?"

"Funny thing, isn't it? Small towns. You'd think, if the smallest, most insignificant item of someone's life was written up for all to see, it'd eliminate rumor. But rumors fly around Churchill, too, just like any other northern town, I suppose."

"I'll remember that."

Vienna Linn did not meet my plane. I was surprised by that. The rutted landing strip was two hundred or so meters from the hotel. From the air, as we circled on approach, the configuration of Churchill was such that it made me wonder where the center of the town was. As Petchey calibrated the wind for landing, he pointed out the post office, the school, the Hudson Bay Company store, and I also noticed a road of sorts lined with small houses, a group of squalid shacks along the river. I saw no people out and about.

I stood next to my suitcase as the propeller ratcheted down. I thought, *Man standing next to leather rectangle*, a caption no doubt borne of the fact that I sensed my life had been reduced to its most basic properties and proportions. Without fully realizing it, I lifted the suitcase and clutched it to my chest.

"That's how a little boy holds his suitcase, waiting for Mum and Dad," Petchey said. I set the suitcase down. He walked past, lugging a sack of letters and packages. Then he stopped, turned toward me. "I recognize the look," he said. His face exaggerated a wild-eyed disbelief, which made me laugh a little. "City boy wonders, 'Will there be slippers by the bed?'"

"That's not how I lived in Halifax," I said. "Not even close to that."

"My point is, Churchill's a place where you've got to get truly acquainted with yourself. Be your own best friend. See how deep your well runs. Are you resourceful, I'm talking about."

"I think I'm resourceful."

"Time will tell, eh?"

"Thanks for the advice."

"It's free advice. And you're welcome."

He walked on ahead to the Hudson Bay Company store and I went to the hotel. I noticed it was three stories high. I stepped inside; nobody was behind the check-in counter. I set down my suitcase for the second time. The staircase had scrolled banisters. There was a fire blazing, the fireplace looked like a small cave. The lobby had two sofas opposite each other, both facing a low wooden table. There was a rocking chair in each corner. The table had a few newspapers and magazines on it. And an oil lamp. Standing ashtrays next to each sofa. Along the wall, to the right if you faced the fireplace, was a writing desk and chair. There were two electric floor lamps, but also a candle on each surface, two iron candelabras on the mantel. I studied the fireplace again. It didn't strike me as being intelligently built. I thought most of the heat would get swallowed up. The draw was good, though. I went over and stood by it. It threw off heat, but didn't heat the entire lobby. A coal stove stood in a corner nearest the entranceway. It wasn't burning a fire. The lobby seemed cozy enough, but there was nobody in it. I walked back to the counter and tapped the bellhop's bell—nobody. So I wrote my name in the leather-bound registry, crossing each *t* in Duvett individually, the way my first form teacher, Mrs. Bromie, had bent over me and insisted.

I looked across and read a placard set on a tripod at the doorway to the dining room:

161

KALA MURIE

will lecture on

"THE UNCLAD SPIRIT"

The life and philosophy of Georgiana Houghton

—learn the truth about spirit-photographs—

I had never heard of a spirit-photograph. I walked past the placard and into the dining room. The half dozen or so tables had been placed at the back of the room. Chairs were set in neat rows in front of a lectern.

For some reason—I can't account for it—I only took small notice of Kala Murie at the lectern, and instead studied the audience. That was easy, because it consisted of only four people. One elderly Eskimo man and two elderly Eskimo women sat side by side in the front row, directly opposite the lectern. In the back row was a man who, at first glimpse, seemed about Driscoll Petchey's age. He was leaning forward in rapt attentiveness, the lecture already being in progress. I sat in a chair at the far left end of the last row. He hadn't noticed me yet. He was wearing a herringbone jacket, white shirt buttoned at the collar, black shoes. His short beard was neatly trimmed, his black hair combed back tightly to his head in what appeared to be slick black triangles on either side of a part down the middle. I thought right away that it was Vienna Linn. I attempted a caption, but the words *drawn forward* were all that came to mind. Listening to Kala Murie, his expression was somewhat childlike in its excitement. *Go on, what happened next?* Yes, of course, that's what you most want to know in any good story. He shifted in his chair, leaned forward again, nodded slowly, every nod an encouragement. He in turn looked somber, amazed, distraught, drinking in every word spoken by his fiancée.

The Eskimo men and women handed something along their row. Each took a bite; whatever it was, it stretched like taffy.

This tableau (I took two years of French in school)—the near-empty room, the woman speaking passionately—struck me as both pitiable and strange; you can't help how feelings suddenly combine, and, besides, this was my new employer and his fiancée, I had best pay attention. Though I didn't know, of course, exactly what I'd just walked in on. I moved to the center of the row. Kala noticed, narrowed her eyes, scowled as if reprimanding me for being late and drawing attention to it, all the while never breaking stride in her lecture.

Then I truly looked at her. And could not look away. Simply put, she was the most exquisite woman I'd ever seen. *Exquisite* was not a word I had ever needed before, a word in waiting. It was as if seeing Kala had suddenly given me the ability to describe her, if only to myself. She wore a formal black dress—it could have served as a mourning dress, I thought. It had a high collar held by a cameo pin. As she spoke, she absentmindedly fidgeted with this cameo, touched it lightly like a talisman. She had dark red hair that fell shoulder length, but also, on either side of her head, swirled up in waves held by embroidered combs. I had seen women's hair done up like this in magazines. Kala had a slightly upward tilt to her chin as she spoke and a strong, alert face, though even from my first station at the back of the room and then in the last row, I noticed deep circles under her eyes. "World-weary," my mother might well have said. As I later discovered, my private estimation that Kala was thirty-two or thirty-three years of age fell short. She was thirty-eight.

Kala leaned slightly forward, resting her elbows on the lectern. Her voice seemed now to push past a natural shyness—this might've been a theatrical trick, I didn't know. The placard had said "lecture," but what I saw and heard seemed both lecture and performance. As I listened, I thought that there was a restrained tone to her voice, even a flatness, which allowed any rise in pitch to seem a small excitement. It was a voice not without fervor, yet not preacherly—it was striving. I had attended two stage dramas in my life. Kala Murie, I thought, could hold her own with both featured actresses. Now and then she glanced down at a notebook or loose pages, it was difficult to see which, but it appeared that for the most part she'd memorized her lecture.

Kala now stopped talking. She composed herself, rubbed the sides of her head as if trying to erase a headache, closed her eyes, opened them again. Taking a deep breath, she said, "As if speaking in the voice of Georgiana Houghton, I shall now relate a letter from Mr. Anthony Slater of London, England, sent to the *Spiritualist*—it is dated May 8, 1872."

I have the book in front of me now. Let me turn to the passage she read. Here it is, on page 114:

> "I visited Mr. Hudson, told him my object in calling, and after a few preliminary remarks on both sides, he proceeded to take a negative of me. It turned out to be a very good, clear, sharp negative—nothing more. I requested he try another, which he did, selecting indiscriminately from some *previously* used and dirty glasses for this occasion, and after going through the usual routine of cleaning, done in my presence, he poured on the collodion, and placed it in the bath. I remained in the darkroom all the time the plate was in the bath. I saw it put into the camera frame and then into the camera, which had been previously focused to me, and all that Mr. Hudson had to do was uncover the lens. I saw the slide drawn up, and when sitting saw the cap or cover of the camera removed, and, after the usual exposure, replaced on the lens. I then accompanied him into the darkroom and saw the developing solution poured on the plate, but not the vestige of anything appeared, neither myself nor background, but a semiopaque film all over the plate, as if it had been somewhat overexposed. I then asked for another attempt, which was carried out under precisely the same circumstances, namely that I witnessed the whole proceedings from beginning to end. I must now, in justice to the 'psychic force,' gentlemen, tell them what I asked mentally, and *felt what I asked*—that if it were possible for the spirit of my mother to come and stand by my side, and with me to portray her presence, to please do so. The result, you may or may not have seen, is a fine female figure draped in white, standing before me with her hand resting on my head. I need not say I was as pleased as I was astonished, and felt determined to further investigate the matter, as I believed Mr. Hudson played no trick on this occasion. Having read in the *British Journal of Photography* that the editor thought it very unlikely that he would get any spirit-pictures if he took his own instrument and plates, I took the hint, and did as he suggested, not that I doubted the artist or the spirits in the least. I accordingly made a new combination of lenses, and took also a new camera and several glass plates, obtaining, in the same manner as before, a fine spirit-picture.
>
> "It was again repeated with another sitter, and with like success; *collusion or trickery was altogether out of the question.*"

Having completed her reading of this letter, Kala lapsed into silence a moment, near to the edge of a swoon, but seemed to recover quickly, and caught her balance by clutching the lectern. Now she looked directly at the three Eskimo people and said, "Mostly—*mostly*, it should be said, Georgiana Houghton wrote about the 'uninvited guest,' which I've defined for you"—she cast me a glance of disappointment—"at the beginning of my lecture. But Miss Houghton was also aware of a blessed and astonishing phenomenon, spirit-pictures as a kind of séance, evidenced by the letter I have just read to you, the testimony of Mr. Slater, *documented* testimony."

The Eskimo people, it seemed to me, appreciated Kala's excitement, but looked puzzled and spoke in low tones amongst themselves a moment. Kala took a drink of water, set down the glass, and said, "I know. I know. It's remarkable, isn't it? But it all happened. It's all the truth."

"Yes, Mr. Slater felt sad about his mother being dead, eh?" one of the Eskimo women said.

"Yes," Kala said, "and, emboldened by grief, he physically and mentally"—Kala pointed to the side of her head—"he *willed* a 'return crossing,' over the bridge from one station in the afterlife to another. That is, from heaven to a spirit-photograph. And a journey to permanent residence in the photograph. She now lived in the photograph—the photograph was now her home, you see. She survived all difficult tests put forth by natural human skepticism. Therefore, ladies and gentlemen, let me say again *clearly* that Mr. Slater's letter proves an example of spirit-photography as successful séance. Mr. Slater's mother was called back."

"When I was a little girl," the same woman said, "I saw a group of ghosts out in a kayak."

Kala held a direct gaze at the Eskimo people for a moment, which made them look, to my mind, uncomfortable. "Thank you for your kind attentions," she said, bowed slightly, and waited for applause.

Wild applause from Vienna Linn, and when she heard only his clapping, she gestured for him to stop. He immediately stopped clapping. "Perhaps there are questions?" she said. "Are there any questions at all?" Kala said.

Vienna stood up. "It was splendid, dear," he said. "Endlessly fascinating. Bravo! Shall we have tea?"

The Eskimo people had gathered at the end of their row, waiting to see what happened next.

Kala stepped from behind the lectern, walked directly up to Vienna. He kissed both of her hands, she said, "Thank you, Vienna dear," so then I knew for certain that he was my new employer. It seemed to me that Vienna's affections buoyed up Kala with happiness. Her face was flushed and beaming. They held hands. It didn't appear to be for show. I now noticed another man standing at the back of the room. He did not seem interested in the proceedings really; he was glaring at me.

Vienna caught my attention. "Ah," he said, "you must be Peter Duvett. I know most everyone else in Churchill—you must be Peter."

We met halfway down an aisle and shook hands. Viewing him close up, I saw that he had a rather long face, sardonic smile, and that his sideburns were flecked with gray. He was about six feet tall, with the narrow shoulders of a child really never quite grown out of gawkiness. Yet what was unusually striking was his eyeglasses. His eyes seemed to waver like stones beneath the surface of two tiny ponds. The lenses were so thick, I imagined Vienna Linn could merely see into the glass, not through it.

"Taken aback, no doubt," he said. "It's the eyeglasses, isn't it?"

"My apologies. I didn't mean to—"

"I'm quite used to the reaction, Mr. Duvett."

"Peter."

"Peter—quite used to it. I've had poor eyesight since I was a boy, which might be why I stubbornly chose photography. I've had good lenses all along. But these latest ones are a miracle. Utterly changed my life. Obtained them in Budapest. Ten years ago, was it? I had three pairs made. They fairly work magic with glass in Budapest. These lenses afforded me a new life. Feeble eyesight, as you can well imagine, would've been quite a cross for a photographer to bear. My new spectacles are quite a spectacle, I like to say. One has to have some humor about one's natural flaws, don't you think?"

"Well, I'm glad they came up with such good lenses."

"Not inexpensive, mind you. When I wear them, I see almost perfectly. But when I don't wear them, my fiancée, Kala Murie, well—she has to lead me around breakfast to bed to bath, in whatever order the day may bring. But otherwise—for instance, looking out the window just now, I see the snow's picked up."

"Summer's just ended down in Halifax."

"Think of that! Our Reverend Painter—H. Dawson Painter. You'll meet. He said, 'Weather goes from angelic to annoying to deadly on any given day up here.' Painter's sickeningly quaint, but his weather report is accurate."

"I think I saw his church from the air."

"It so happens—did Petchey tell you? It's a mere few hours away

166

from my and Kala's wedding. I'd bet Petchey told you."

"He mentioned your fiancée but not a wedding."

"Well, the wedding's tonight and that's why I'm nervous as a schoolboy, and there's still, what? Two hours, almost three, before church bells. Except the wedding's here, in the hotel. No bells, in fact. Painter will officiate because someone legally has to."

I glanced over at Kala.

"Oh, of course Kala will change into her wedding dress," Vienna said. "And I'll get dressed to the nines. She always wears that black dress for her lectures."

"This is an important night then."

"*Important* hardly suffices, young man."

"Of course not. I said it awkwardly—just to say something."

"No offense meant, none taken."

"Sorry—thanks. Thank you."

"We'll have a small amount of get-acquainted time before I take my leave of you, Peter. Join Kala and me for tea in the lobby, why don't you?"

"Maybe for a few minutes. I'm a bit worn-out from my flight up here."

"The weather coming in?"

"Rough, I'd say."

"Nothing new in that."

"I hadn't flown before."

"Good to be on solid ground then."

"Yes."

"Good."

"What are those shacks along the river?"

Over Vienna's shoulder I saw Kala greet the Eskimo men and women, each with a kind of smiling forbearance.

"Basically," Vienna said, "it's the Eskimo part of town. There's Cree Indians, too. They've lived here forever, of course. From before any wooden structure. You might say it's their abode—not Churchill per se, but the surroundings. Even somebody as unenlightened as me knows that much. Europeans are just interlopers, though might be interlopers for ten centuries to come, the way history works, you see."

"Nobody was around the shacks. I didn't see a single person from the air."

"Well, most Eskimo families are downriver just now, hunting, fishing, to return shortly, I'm told. Reverend Painter keeps track of such comings and goings. The freeze-up isn't that long off—two months, give or take. After December 15, Driscoll Petchey doesn't fly out until around May, with certain exceptions. Emergencies. So get your letters to loved ones written and sent out by December 15, Mr. Duvett."

"I won't be sending any letters."

"I see," Vienna said. He studied my face a moment. "Well then. The hotel's got a room waiting. Two nights paid in advance, as my return letter to you promised."

"That helps, thanks."

"Allow me to ask, while Kala Murie's occupied there with admirers. Considering the remoteness of the place, why would a handsome young man like yourself, Peter, come to Churchill?"

"Plain and simple, I was sick to death of my job. At the newspaper. As I wrote you, Mr. Linn."

"Vienna, please."

"Vienna."

"And rest assured, I read your letter carefully, and I'm pleased that you've traveled all this way. Rest assured."

"I'm relieved to know that."

"However, you might find one similarity between your old job and your new one not to your liking."

"What's that?"

"The hours. In one of your communications to me, you mentioned upward of ten hours a day in the newspaper darkroom, didn't you?"

"Yes, I did."

"Some days—not all, but some—and possibly on into the night, ten hours in a row might be required. But with no café to unwind in afterward, no beautiful young ladies promenading by and such. I've lived in cities, Peter. London. Paris. Budapest. Amsterdam. Copenhagen, for a short while. In fact, we came here, Kala and I—living in sin—directly from Montreal, about a year ago."

"Mr. Petchey said you'd been here through the winter."

"Ah, Mr. Petchey. He once told me that he knew—by intuition—just *knew* that my face was on a WANTED poster somewhere in Canada."

"And wanted for what?"

"Mr. Petchey did not divulge."

"He talked a lot in the plane."

"He talks a lot; what he divulges is quite another matter."

"Anyway, Mr. Linn—Vienna. It wasn't the hours. At the newspaper, I mean. It was the sameness. Of subject. Local dignitaries.

Weddings. Tourists walking down the gangplanks of steamers in from Europe, all of that. Besides which, Halifax doesn't have cafés like in Paris."

"Again, my concern is you'll mainly be developing portraits. In the main, nothing but."

"That's fine. I feel different about things already. Thanks for hiring me."

"See if you thank me in a few months."

"Half of being somewhere new is that I'm not in Halifax is how I see it. The rest I'll take day by day."

"The only choice in life, eh?"

"I guess so."

"Sameness—but wasn't there the occasional murder, for instance? There, in your city, a murder photograph to develop, some incident that spiced things up a little?"

"Well, of course I didn't hope for that."

"Of course not. What sort of person would?"

"I did develop a photograph of a drowned person once. They even used my caption: *People watching a resuscitation.*"

At the bottom of the front page of the *Halifax Herald* had been a photograph of people standing in a circle, observing a doctor trying to resuscitate a woman. But she had already died by the time the doctor arrived.

"Could you say that again?" Vienna said.

"*People watching a resuscitation.* But my first suggestion was *People, aghast, watching a resuscitation,* but the editor took out 'aghast.'"

"Unfortunate," Vienna said.

"I offered up captions most every day, but that was the only one they ever used. Maybe because the regular caption writer was out sick that day."

Driscoll Petchey came into the dining room, walked up to us, and said, "Vienna, when're you going to take my picture, eh? I could secure your future with one of those rich gentleman patrons of yours over in England you're always hinting at. My mug in their drawing room would put the fear of God into those lords 'n' ladies, eh? Look at me, I'm an authentic type. Roustabout grizzled pilot daring bad weather, dive-bombing the occasional white bear, catapulting high amongst the Christian and pagan gods fighting it out over the god-forsaken Arctic wastes. . . ."

"I'd have to make up lies about you, just in order to counteract all the lies you tell about yourself, Mr. Petchey," Vienna said. To me it was friendly banter. "However, yes, you would seem to be photogenic. I work by commission only, as you know."

"How about I'll trade you a free escape in my plane to anywhere you choose, in exchange for the chance to photograph me? Plus you keep fifty percent of whatever you're paid from London—for my portrait."

"I'll think it over."

Driscoll Petchey then started toward the lobby, turned, and said, "Don't let Vienna Linn there tire himself out telling lies about me, Peter. It's his wedding night. A man needs his strength." Then Petchey walked out into the lobby.

Now each member of the audience came up to have a look at me. "Peter Duvett," Vienna said, "meet Mr. Moses Nuqac." I shook hands with the elderly Eskimo man. "On his right is Mrs. Nuqac—Mary. And on his left here, Mrs. Naniaqueeit—also Mary." I shook hands with the two women.

"I'm baptized," Mr. Nuqac said. His roundish face, red-brown, was friendly in a solemn way, and when he grinned, I saw that many of his front teeth were missing. Intelligent hard-set eyes. His face struck me as somewhat Oriental in structure. His wife's and friend's faces struck me similarly. They were stout in their tattered dresses, leggings, sweaters, patched woolen coats. "My wife, Mary, here is also baptized. Mary Naniaqueeit is not."

"I'm pleased to meet you," I said. The three laughed and shook my hand again, and Mr. Nuqac, in thick-tongued yet more than competent English, said, "Vienna—I know that in Kala Murie's talking I missed a lot, eh? But tell me: Why's she so surprised by what happens in them photographs, because down at our house, there's spirits coming by for visits all the time, eh? One way or another they visit. They're gone a while, then they come back." He then spoke his language to the women, obviously translating what he'd just asked Vienna. The women each gave him a quizzical look: *Yes, what is so surprising?*

Vienna did not know how to answer.

Now another man entered the room. He was about five feet eight, stocky, with thinning pale blonde hair and an unkempt thick beard.

"And here we have Martin Swain," Vienna said. "Martin—Peter Duvett, recently of Halifax."

Swain offered me a smile that was actually a downturned mouth, accompanied by a sharply exhaled "Yes, yes, hello" and a stiff hand-shake, not at all unfriendly. "You're in Room 22," Swain said. "Up the stairs to your left. Just reach around behind the counter, get your key."

"All right."

"You have two nights already paid for."

"That helps."

"My hotel's not serving dinner tonight," Swain said. "I'm sure Vienna Linn mentioned that he and Kala are getting married. On these very premises. But otherwise, dinner is served from 5 P.M. to 8 P.M. After cleaning up the kitchen, our chef, Mr. Berthot, sets out for his house promptly at 8:55. You can set your watch by it."

"What should I do for dinner tonight then?"

"Mr. Berthot's no doubt finishing up the wedding cake just about now," Swain said. "But he'll prepare your dinner ahead of time. I'll bring it up personally at 7:30, if that suits you. That'll give me half an hour to spruce up for the festivities."

"I appreciate it."

"This one time only," Swain said.

Swain walked into the lobby. Vienna Linn then noticed that Kala had slipped out, no chance to introduce us. He appeared to be genuinely baffled. "I don't know why Kala disappeared like that," he said. "Perhaps—well, often she avoids a group of men talking. Yet she said she'd looked forward to meeting you, Peter."

"No harm done," I said. "She must have a lot on her mind. That lecture and getting married on the same day."

"Yes, it's probably that it's so close to the wedding. Emotional enough on its own. Then there's her bath to take, wedding dress to get just right, some privacy before the event. By the way, Peter, please don't consider it ill-mannered, our not inviting you. Kala wishes to keep it—"

"It never crossed my mind."

"Let's sit in the lobby then."

In the lobby, we sat on opposite sofas. Then Vienna Linn said, "What was I thinking—forgot the tea!" He went into the kitchen, returning with a tray on which was a teapot, two cups and saucers, a bowl of sugar cubes. He poured each of us a serving and we sipped our tea.

"I apologize for not meeting your plane," he said.

"No bother at all."

"Quite a small turnout at the lecture."

"It was interesting. I might've caught more—spirit-photographs and such. But I came in late."

"New subject to you, I imagine."

"That's right."

"You'll be spending time with us, Peter. You'll hear all about Kala's work."

"Anyway, she looked pleased. Everyone in the audience—"

"Every one, plus one, plus one—"

"—a small turnout, but they all seemed to say nice things to her afterward."

"So few people. You might imagine Kala—truly—to be humiliated."

"But the Eskimo woman—Mrs. Nuqac, she had a response."

"One thing to know straightaway, Peter. What you heard was *not* Kala rehearsing for the larger world. She brings to each and every lecture the utmost preparation. The utmost dedication. Even if, finally, she manages to preach to the converted. Or further convince only herself of Miss Houghton's—worth."

"I envy your dedication to Kala Murie," I said.

"Diplomatic fellow, aren't you?"

"Sounds like damning with faint praise."

Vienna laughed and said, "Well, she only searches for the one face in the audience, really. The possible like-minded person. Or perhaps she can more or less pick out the person who *desires* to be like-minded and just needs a little encouragement."

After more tea, I said, "Can you tell me a little more of what work I'll be doing for you? You said portraits."

"What I do here in Churchill?" Vienna set down his cup, leaned back on the sofa. "My present employment is quite sedentary, truth be told. I'm hired by the local church, Jesuits of course, Reverend Painter's flock. He has a group of missionaries all over the territory, you see. They call him 'Father.' Jesuits do that. I call him 'Reverend.' Each time he corrects me. Missionaries, of course, have been up around here for a long time. Painter for about three or four years. A very busy man, Painter. His immediate predecessor had some luck in converting Eskimo people to the faith. Not a lot of luck, however. So I was told. Painter's first year here was spent more or less settling in. Going through church records, meetings with townsfolk every week, that sort of thing. He let people get acquainted with him. Then he cranked up his efforts considerably. Now he brings in people from Padlei, Eskimo Point, other villages north along the bay and so forth.

I'm—myself—not God-fearing. In fact, I'm a wretched unbeliever, so therefore consider myself in one sense a mere hireling of the Jesuits. I'm building up a collection of portraits of Eskimos Painter baptizes, you see. Should I have told you precisely this in my letter?"

"I wanted to get out of Halifax."

"Painter's *lackeys,* who come and go, while by no means stupid people, strike me as quite desperate."

"How so?"

"Well, to *convert* the primitive savage—that's the basic idea, isn't it? Painter reports to his superiors, I suppose you'd call them. The important thing for him is his annual report. So, by *desperate,* I mean, he gets a five-year-old to memorize the Lord's Prayer—whatever prayer—some such thing. And that apparently qualifies them for membership. Plus, the numbers, if you will. My portraits provide the evidence of his good works here in the hinterlands. Mostly—to my mind—it's employment. Don't judge me too harshly there, please. Otherwise, I do enjoy my conversations with the native people, when they choose to converse. Keep it close to the vest, most of them. Not all have been or ever will be baptized, by the way. You met Mrs. Naniaqueeit—she doesn't submit to Painter's charms. She'll go down fighting. No matter to her that Painter offers a sum of money. She won't submit, even as a kind of social etiquette, just to get along."

"I read somewhere that Eskimos shun getting their photographs taken. The camera steals their souls."

"Historical rumor, call that. Camera stealing the soul. I'd heard that, too. But after a month or so here in Churchill, it struck me as the worst sort of condescension. Because look: Whatever can be called the Eskimo idea of the *soul*—and they'd no doubt have some private word for it, if they bother with such a notion in the first place—couldn't be so easily captured as by a camera. A camera couldn't reach that deeply. You know what might capture a soul? Some sort of spirit-folk—they've got hundreds. You hear a lot about spirits up here. So, yes, revengeful spirit-folk might nab a soul, but not a goddamn camera, Duvett. Never a camera. Never a European contraption.

"Cameras stealing souls. That's a good example of how stupid you can feel after learning certain things firsthand, things that utterly contradict everything you'd thought was true."

"What's Painter think about all this?"

"Oh, Painter and I haven't actually had any long discussions. But my feeling in general about him is, if he believed a camera could actually capture an Eskimo soul, he'd pay me or someone else a fortune to burst in at night on Eskimo families sleeping and get some photographs. He'd go to any length."

"And would *you* do that for money?"

"Ah, an ethical inquiry. Are you a philosophical man, Duvett?"

"I had a little university. I read a lot of my mother's library. She had a big library. But when it comes to philosophizing, I'd most likely disappoint you."

I don't know why I lied about having some university.

"But do you have a life of the mind? Do you still read books, for instance?"

"In fact, I read one on the train, Halifax to Winnipeg."

"I ask, because if books are of interest, my wife-to-be has a number of them. In the hotel she's a veritable lending library, one might say. I think, in fact, she's left a book in your room. Her favorite book. A kind of welcoming gesture. And I've placed an album of portraits in there, too. Hope you don't mind."

"Not at all."

"I'll finish my tea, then it's upstairs."

"Same for me."

"I enjoyed our conversation, Peter. It bodes well. Not too many things bode well, do they?"

"I haven't thought about it."

"Funny thing, I don't consider myself a talkative man, despite all my chatter just now. Kala says I'm half mute all the time. Or is it mute half the time? I suppose she's right. In the darkroom, I might not say all of ten words. Don't be offended."

"Now that I know what to expect—"

"You'll likely not see Kala and me at breakfast," he said. "You and I can start in the darkroom, let's say 3 P.M. tomorrow. Between about midnight and 3 P.M. will have to suffice as our honeymoon."

"Three P.M. is fine with me."

"The darkroom's really a large storage room, third floor, turn right and go to the end of the hallway. You'll see a door marked STORAGE. It works well enough. Swain lets me use it gratis. He's a churchgoer, it turns out. He likes that I work for Painter."

We both stood and shook hands.

"All great good fortunes to you and your bride," I said.

I picked up my key from the wooden mail-and-key hive behind the counter. As I reached the second-floor landing, weariness set in hard.

I stopped and looked across the lobby to the opposite side of the second floor. There was a small, high-ceilinged room, a kind of sitting room or library, with a wall of bookshelves, holding only a scattering of books. The books leaned at odd angles. Some were stacked up. There was a table, three chairs, a reading lamp, candles in candleholders. Just to further acquaint myself with the hotel, I started down the hallway to the right of the landing, toward the sitting room. It was completely dark outside now. As I turned the corner, I glanced to my left. The room at the end of a separate brief hallway had its door wide open. Without thinking, I stepped closer and saw that the room led to a bedroom; the rooms were roughly the size of my apartment in Halifax.

Kala Murie stood in front of the three-sided bedroom mirror. I viewed her in profile. She lowered the black dress to her waist. Now, her breasts fully exposed, she held up her hair with both hands. I hadn't noticed that she wore earrings at the lecture. And when she turned to set an embroidered comb in a small wooden box on the left side of her bureau, she saw me. Her face was all candor, the fullness of her composure was, I felt, well met with the fullness of her body; looking at her, I had to consider the wholeness, because to consider any part, the curve of her breasts or hips—she simply now let the dress fall to the floor and stepped out of it—would have got me halfway to madness. The loftiest or most exaggerated caption of shocking romance and possibility would merely have been a crude understatement. I was smitten by my employer's wife-to-be, with whom I had not exchanged a word. Mere hours after arriving in Churchill. Smitten by what the moment contained. The drift of her dress to the floor was of such heart-stopping clarity that not only was I bereft of all familiar balance and emotion, but she was so singular a presence, I was blind even to Kala's reflection in the mirror. It had to be there but I didn't notice. She slowly walked from her bedroom to the main doorway. She grasped the doorknob.

"There's no way to be properly introduced now, is there?" she said.

"I'm Peter Duvett," I said, but by then she'd closed the door.

Four Poems
Jorie Graham

THE COMPLEX MECHANISM OF THE BREAK

From here, ten to fourteen rows of folding and branching.
Up close, the laving in overlappings that pool sideways as well as suck back.
Filamentary green-trims where the temporary furthest
                    coming-forward is lost.
Suctions in three or four different directions back from pinnacle-point.
Encounter of back-suck by the foremost,
                    low-breaking, upstitching really,
arrivals,
          where it seems pebblings of sandbits ruffle-up and are ruffled
                    back into the foam of
                    the breakwater browning it.
Glassy meanwhile the frontmost arrivals, their sheets filling momentarily
                                        with sky, with
clouds fully formed (in which gulls [of sand] glide) even as they all
                              are drawn back
into the ruffling front-thunder
into which direct backmotion
feeds—is fed—(over which real rows of low-flying pelicans)—
(backmotion into which retreat itself feeds, slides, you'd have to say dissolves)—
(though strangely nothing of the sea dissolves).
Behind: the crystalline green risings of just-before furling,
then the furling. Between: the wild-carrot lacings and
                              spume of
breakages the eye hardly caught. Lifting the eyes away one sees
in the near/far distance large upwallings
in which sometimes fish calmly ride sideways
                         above one,
high above, while close-up, the sky unfolds, deep, here, at our
                                        feet—
(the eyes look down to see up)—(then, squinting, out, to see
          the see-through slow uprising

holding its school). The mind doesn't
want it to break—unease where the heart pushes out—the mind
wants only to keep it coming, yes, sun making the not-yet-breaking crest
                                        so gold where the
pelicans turn as they glide—flapping then gliding—
as long as possible without too much dropping—
here and there trying to stay with the just-breaking ridge,
turning towards or away from the
                        watching-eye
to origami trick, artichoke wing—sheen—crank—beaks dragging the
gold-fringed, gathered garment-furl through which
                the fish themselves drive (thread)
the only momentarily unbreaking line. And how there is always something
else. Up close four different brown retreating furls just now [being forced
                                        to forward-break] re-
entering themselves. Each tripping over each as they are also forced
                                        into retreat.
What is force? My love is forced from me as in retreat
from love. My gaze is forced back into me as it retreats
from thought. Sometimes the whole unraveling activity
                        for just an instant
pools, all its opposing motions suddenly just pattern on these briefly
lakelike flats—the shore's upslant unspooling then in only two
                dimensions—(close your eyes)—
(although it's only when you open them you hear the seven
                                kinds of
sound: hiss-flattenings and poolings-out [sand-suctions in the
                                flat],
the pebbled wordlike pulling down and rolling up, the small
hush of the small first-line of white, it lowering its
                        voice as it proceeds
to crash, the crash where the larger one behind is hit and hits
                        the one of yet more force
behind it now, the singleness—(the one loud
thunder-break)—the backmost individual wave,
the lowering and sudden softening of all betweens [of which
every few minutes one] out of which the first crash
yet again can rise. Also the momentary lull: which now lets in
the sound of distance in itself: where your eye might
look up, further out: to where, it seems,

177

nothing but steady forward progress in its perfect
time occurs: onward, onward: tiny patterns which
seen from above, must: it is imagined: perfectly: shine).

KYOTO

Commentary continues, slanting downward.
Ah what am I carrying, what's this load, who's that
                                out there,
why all this dust? I remember "the oldest of trees."
We drove through it. I "looked." I remember
"all manner of being may swim in my sea."
Slanting upward, tiny bits of rain murmur in my gaze.
Slanting upward, the gaze senses, right *in* the looking—[so
                                fresh][after
rain, early spring]—the gaze cannot but sense [since
                        it's not in the
visual field] [not at all]—cannot but: the slantline down towards
                                                dis-
appearance. Remember:
                        the statues you were looking at [in the
old world] row after row in the beautiful garden,
veined-marble after spring rain (so-called), weight placed on the one
leg or the other, as if in gravity, although also actually
                                in gravity,
arm on a hip, arm holding a
book, a sword, a severed head—a bow, stone quills—some grapes
proffered, long gazing out, long avenues of principles, adorned, with self,
                                                with
representation, naked for the most part, trees just-in-leaf all down
                                        the lanes,
and everywhere *principle,* hidden but manifest, what we have made
                                link up in the
spine of time [the body of human making]—right there along with the
million grasses waving [in the new world] right there—aspen visible
at medium height on the near slope, just budding out—
ah what am I carrying, what is this on the ground—
or the ocean lying on its side

whispering—or the silkworm-mulberry, the damasks and brocades covering the
globe,
the hush of sateen-foldings over stone, the hiss in the human walk,
in palaces, in dancehalls—or vineyards sloping away near hilltop—
or look down on sea-top, you'll see wind-design—yes—from
here—
[where are we][who's that in the dust?][is there sleeping
anymore]
["whispering": will it always exist]["mirroring": will it always
exist]
[breath on the mirror if you should get so close]
priorities, humilities, imitation, dew-drenching, intellectuality,
[meet near the resting-place][the white-rose wall][equal to][un
equal
to]—so that if [uneasiness in the face of sunset][uneasiness in the face
of sunrise] I ask you now [with unexpected ease]
[with rapid extension of mind, leaping] to come back from
here
to the statues lining the avenue [mind/gaze now darting down it with
a strange foraging hope][as if feeding very quickly and furiously],
ask you to see them blow up: to dust: all "at once": or "one at a time":
down the wide avenue: lining both sides: dawn slowly creeping toward
the rim of
visibility: something maybe observing this: from somewhere: the air
soft, warm, known to the bluebird and swallow: then ask you to
rewind [for just][two seconds]
and see [even eyes closed] see this: wings touching then overlapping
each other slowly as the landed bird re-
settles. This
I was thinking today: all you can know: then plants and
animals: names of: movements of: your love: your hands: of
when I was ten in Kyoto mother insisting I take
flower-arranging classes: every morning in a city building:
white stone! with many steps up: then a vast room:
acidy smell of fresh-cuttings, thousands: oozing stem-ends:
eyes: hundreds of greens: and
perfumes: and shinings of movement where two hands lift
stem-ends:
and color-flash through air to angled-anchorings: said to reveal the
truth of *us*: the
four elements: "represented": the harmonies: to give a state of

mind [not pleasure][what is pleasure] what is she
carrying the young woman still bringing the still-wet branches of blossom in
through the small door to the left under her arms: almond and
cherry: changes: not dream not at all that
would be disappearance: who rules this:
more brought in every day: the birds of the finished
arrangement (flight your eye's flight around it). See,
you have picked many flowers. You will pick many more.
As for instance in this "thinking" "today" [two blossomheads
there]. There will be flowers forever. This is: Spring, today, April, 2001.
This I am carrying. These branchings, these cuttings. With a whole heart.

The questions:
What is longest? oldest? truest? plenty?
Wisdom? Peace? Wavering? Misfortune?

The rules:
One must be blameless.
One must come to loneliness and be lonely.
One must know half from whole.
One must hear the "broken carriage springs" and know them for
the cowbird's unoiled-gate-hinge
song. Nothing is partial. One must know partiality.
She picks it up and puts it down again.
One must see the cowbird spread its tail—just so—and
shut it again, clean, just
after landing. One must know. The rut is the carriage-trail.
Which carriage. The passage through trees—which bird. When.
Feeble sounds. Harsh. Missed perchings. Repetition: its
insistent coolness: me me me me says one bird, nameless,
who has heard what is dead. It's invisible. It must be heard
of.

Invisible bouquet:
[a generation ago][the forests
were][I assemble my books][we plan to]
[formerly][assume the posture][of]
[rushing]   [just a moment ago]
[suddenly]
[breathless with excitement she]
[best not to]

[is different now]
[crown the color of]
[hearing the wild birds in their]
[although it's early morning, I]
[dark forelock combed back, damp]
[days]

EBBTIDE

I am a frequency, current flies through. One has
                              to ride
                              the spine.
No peace [of mind] [of heart], among the other
frequencies. How often and how hard are answerings.
The surf, receding, leaves successive
hem-line trims of barely raised institching sand—
bridal-wreath puckerings—
glassy (this side), packed smooth (that).
Making one's way one sees the changes.
What took place before one
              looked.
Snakeskin of darker sands in with the light.
Slightly more raised and wider alligator-skins.
Crabtracks' wild unfocusings around firm holes.
The single tubefish, dead, long as a snake, half-snout,
rolled over and over as the waves pick up, return, return
less often, go away. For a while he is incandescent
white, then blue, deep green, then white again, until he's
                              left, half-turned,
eyes sandy till one wave, come back
this far as if in error, cleans him off.
Greenish with rising/falling weed-debris, shoremist
fingering long streaks of sun.
Graphed beachlength on the scallop-edged lapping retreat:
                    christmas-ornament red shrimp
punctually all long the highs of each
        upskirting arc—prongs upright,
stiff. Swift ticks of sunlight count them
                              out.

Jorie Graham

Who has enough? A little distance
                    back
two vultures feeding on a pelican. Later, claws and beak
float in the brack. Foam-bits lace-up the edge
of the retreat. Something feels like it's not
coming back. In the tidepool
sand-grains advance along a long
walled avenue, in ranks—at the conjunction of
                    two rocks, algae
signaling the entry point—(swarming but
                    swaying in
unison, without advancing) (waiting for
                    some arrival)
(the channel of them quickening)(the large espousal)(light
beginning now to *touch* what had been only
                    underwater story)—
until the gleaming flow of particles is finally
                    set down, is
                    stilled: the grains
drop down and mat, silt in, begin to dry: the wandering tribe is
                    gone, the
city's gone, the waiting gone. The individual grains
are not discernible. I'm squatting so I hear
sand sucking water in. Gravity. Glistening.
I take a stick and run it through
the corridor of wilderness.
It fills a bit with water the first time. Is self-erased.
The second time it does not fill. It leaves a
                    mark where
my stick ran. I make
another (cursive) mark. How easily it bends to cursive, snakes towards
                    thought.
                    Looking back

I see the birds eating the bird. The other way my
gaze can barely reach shore-break.
The (little) weight of the stick in my hand. The meditation
place demands. My frequency. This hand, this
sugar-stalk. The cane-fields in the back of us,
the length of tubefish back there too. And
if I write my name. And how mist rounds the headland
                    till the sea

182

is gone. One feels word should be sent us
from some source. It is all
roar and cry and suck and snap. The pebbles on the
pebbles roll. One feels one has in custody
what one cannot care for for long. Too much is
asked. Nothing is coming back the way it was.
But one can wait for the next hem, next bride,
next oscillation, comedy. Done, the birds fly
off. I can see through the trees,
through the cane grove, palm grove, out far enough into
the clearing where
the spine of the picked-clean story shines.

THE TIME BEING

I.
(Todos Santos)

Cluster of bird-chatter a knot at the center of a supreme
unfolding. Large river-pebbles almost filling a jar.
Turn it over: where they collide and recollect: that grainy quick
clatterfall: cluster: [of birdsound]: knot.

Near it a browner sound, closer-up, a
single note of it a very thick rope, stiff with age, knotted
to a rusted hinge: in it a higher and lower pitch (intermingling)
(rope squeak and hinge). But that only if the one note (repeated
more or less rapidly) (in clusters of up to five) is singled
out.

Nothing can be singled out.

*

We wait for the dog-bark, hearing sun (utterly without
glow in it) (a thing that blanks out into what we call
blindness each thing it washes) in the highest background
lymph-system screeches. Clap of banana leaves, long as a
tall child or marlin. Then the dog-bark to the
far left—for a moment just *itself,*

183

then the dog-bark drawn in, percussive, in
relation. Then we wait for the first car.

*

Engine rising [we know there's a hill] then evening-out to a
smooth hum, then into the story with fictive
presence, even as it crosses through the length of town then out.
When the woman calls out, it's not as if the netting
caught her. She knots up the far left of
the listening. A small boy suddenly very near to the
right taps a glass jar with a metal
implement, then he taps a different openness.

*

The listening: one is the first of
the fishermen. The net builds. It casts
still further. The trucks on the highway passing town. The
goatbells and cowbells intermingling at the edge of the
canefields. One is first first. Then there is a
portal, saints pass through, light
over all of it without nearing, but shadows
striating our shadows' passing-in, adding-through.
One is first then one is suddenly unable to be
first, it is a strange quick grace. The net
shifts hands, is held at the other side, at the
far side (churchbell for 17 repeats like lower
goatbell) (all sounds always reproducible
[if one rejects name] as something damaged or
frayed or about to break
from wear). One feels sound deepest in the apparently
most worn. In this sunlight, for
instance. Here. Just as I say this and the
chatter rises in a clump I know not in
response to what. Just here where the
sunlight crosses my sill and the
window-sashes lay firm gray-black marks
aslant the terracotta tiles of floor. Here
where the whiteness of the "vacancy" the palmfronds (full of
transparency and motion) carry back and forth over floortiles' grout-lines—here
where that whitening (wind really) juts wild through
all strands of

the netting (sash, grout, palmfrond) and is, of a sudden, made to let up, slow
                                                        down, as the
caught fish must.

II.
(Palm Beach, Todos Santos)

The whole of the unfolding like a skin
coming-off. Sand striated everywhere by tide-action
packing hard onto it in tiny color variations and
speckling and runs of diamond-pattern where tide
has receded. Monkfish with their porcupine-quilled
tapering backs, all head and side-eyes and quickly
left by the tides. At tide-line, with each
lapping, shrimp left at the greenish fanning wave
                                                        edge.
Retreat and more retreat. Tiretracks
recriss-crossing the marbled sandskin. Footprints,
birdprints, feathers, broken glass. The fishermen
in the distance on the rocks casting out.
Wallbreaks, the filament where the backwash
breaks and retreats leaving a pooling, white and green,
and also brownish marbled slicknesses [a tiny
stilling, really, in the regrouping of powers] and on
that slickness: filmy slownesses like lung
tissue, or the white netting from
stomach-lining they wrap lamb-kidneys in in the window
display—slightly fatty and good in baking where it
holds the parts together then melts off—
Here melting off: the skin of the
momentary lull where forward and backward
motion are ever so briefly equal—and feathery too [so soft] but
mostly marbled [so hard]
yet sloughing snakeskin off with the very next
wave and laying that skin onto shore, at
our feet. In sand: on sand:
palmfronds, feather-layerings: accumulations of differently-gapped nets at
angles not exactly overlapping: drifts of
miniscule dune-structures building like sound-waves
then lowering in sun in fast-moving clouds: making

for the time being, the time being: tide coming back
in and the fishermen now walking this way carrying off
an unusually large catch. The
story that got me here. The breaking waves tossing
spume the whole length of the beach. The glassy
tidal-retreat zone where the reduced
incline allows for a full measure of sky
every eight seconds or so to be strewn over the
otherwise dark-wet sand—a sun, a blueness,
clouds clearly moving, the skin of water
[giving] us "where-the-earth-opens" [it must open],
sun in there one cannot look at any
more than one can look at the one above—then the retreat—
sun, clouds, blue, all being taken back
into the shorebreak, tossed-up, in-ruffled
airily into huge plumes and upcast mists, the looking-down
leaving tiny holes where clam and crab and tubeworm
suck back under and the water goes *down* as well as *out*
and the earth is filling and the earth is
shut. The time presses.
The sense of one's *person*
numbs as in having been too long in too
strong a wind. The idea won't
hold as I push it out. Then it will. Then it
is held [not by me]. Then it is all gone.
The fishermen seen from the back as they
disappear through the palms.

Cloud Chamber
Reginald Shepherd

1.

He dreamt he was a renaissance,
relief from the other's body.
Event without the person was place

and time and what became of words
he couldn't read. A French troubadour
is singing German, boot prints

and tank treads march across
the music. Then I remember he is me,
and all song ends.

2.

Someone stepped on my shadow (the white
underbearing it, snowed-under
old wounds): a god again, no telling which

("with whatever name it pleases you
to be called"). He equals
or doesn't equal x, a series of events

occurring near the body, proximities
and failed connections
domesticating myth.

3.

There will always be a *he*, undoer, dew
clinging to damp skin. How
sweet a ghost, smokebitter,

fog-homed, mist and found again
amid the midst of tinder, kindling
drowned in green rain, remnant

burned fields, blind gas.
The bruised river is in flames
again, it's him I haunt.

4.

Called him *tropical storm
stalled just offshore,* or
danger falling rocks, but those

aren't boys' names either. Desire
is so self-figured, and constantly
changes his mind.

5.

My life in hiding wintered
in him, even lacking language
his skin burns. I fiction out my pride

and fade farther into him,
where what to get is only get to see.
Even the snow knows wait.

6.

Six things no longer in mind,
the bitter box of him. Lord
Not For You, Prince Nothing

Left, Sir No Still Not Enough:
called him all kinds of things,
insulting by surmise.

7.

I steer toward the jutting rocks
(blind man's stutter of stone),
create him from my wreckage:

leave the boat to burn
and watch the pain away.
Less light, the more I see.

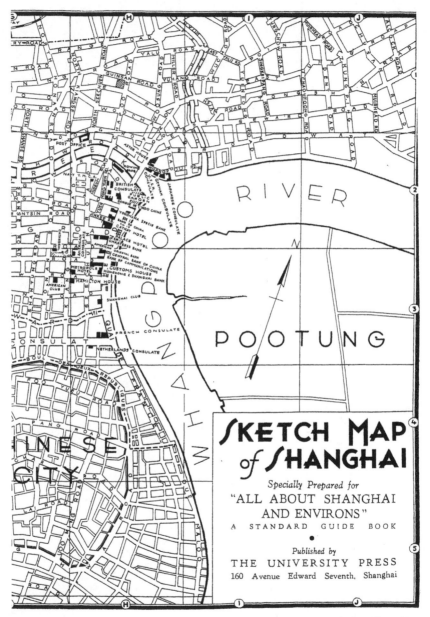

Central Shanghai, 1935

Shanghai

Walter Abish

COMPARED TO THE round-the-clock carpet bombing of Germany or of the Japanese mainland, bombarding Shanghai late in the war must have been small potatoes, a mere sideshow for the allies. We were a secondary target. Never more than a dozen bombers overhead. All along I'd been convinced that we were bombed by B-17s until, recently, checking a copy of *The Army Air Force in World War 2* (June 1944 to August 1945) in the library, I established that the planes bombing the Shanghai docks and warehouses, the shipping and airfields, the railroad marshaling yards in the Hangchow area, as well as mining the confluence of the Hwangpoo and the Yangtze, were predominantly super fortress B-29s. Much as I disliked the bombing, it was the discordant chatter of the antiaircraft batteries located on the roof of the massive Ward Road prison nearby—sometimes firing, it seemed, without pause whether or not planes were overhead—that I found most unnerving. The sound of their combined fire was deafening—it paralyzed one. Ironically, the huge prison compound which housed an air-raid shelter the public was encouraged to use might soon have become a legitimate target due to the vast quantity of ammunition we later discovered to have been stored there, not to mention its manufacturing enterprises employing cheap prison labor—another tempting target. The most severe bombing occurred on July 17, 1945, an overcast day, when this time twin-engine A-26 bombers missed their target, the Chiangwan Airdrome—an earlier claim that the Japanese radio station was the target is now disputed—striking instead a market in Hongkew. Of the more than two hundred and fifty fatalities, over thirty were Jewish refugees. At least five hundred people at the market or living nearby were wounded and hundreds made homeless.

By now, at the first sound of the alarm, we'd grab a few belongings and, hearts pounding, madly race down the stairs to the dubious sanctuary—deemed the safest place in the building—of Dr. Zimmer's ground-floor office. He'd greet us pleasantly enough, though there was never an attempt at conversation. It was clear what we were there for. As a rule, the air raids from start to finish lasted under an hour. Though my parents never revealed anything the least bit unfavorable about Dr. Zimmer in my presence, I could discern if not outright disapproval, a lack of that unqualified esteem they were wont to show Dr. Kaufmann, our family doctor, no doubt on account of Dr. Zimmer's patients: those tantalizing ladies who came and went at all times of the day, many of whom I found, arrayed in their heavy makeup, expensive furs, and high heels, exceptionally captivating.

On July 17 there was no early warning: By the time the sirens began to wail, the antiaircraft batteries were already in action. I was drawn to our window by the sound of singing, not the muted everyday sound of prayer or even the exultant chanting that greeted the high holidays. Looking across the courtyard, I could make out the members of this tightly knit orthodox community, dressed in black, thronging the lower floors of the Ward Road synagogue, swaying in prayer, their voices pitched high, filling the air with such acute urgency, such passion, that for once I, by heart a skeptic, a doubter, felt all my resistance fade. Their sustained singing, marked by passion and intensity, was unlike anything I'd previously heard—it seemed to shape an impenetrable field, albeit one of sound, to fend off destruction. At that unforgettable moment, before tearing myself away from the window to follow my parents to ground-floor safety, it wouldn't have surprised me to see the four-story structure housing this community that had stuck together, through all kinds of vicissitudes, soar skyward in response to their thunderous rhythmic appeals to the almighty.

It was the heaviest raid to date. In Dr. Zimmer's consultation room my parents were seated on the couch, clasping hands and, as far as I could ascertain, so self-absorbed that not once did they glance in my direction. The other couple from the second floor were sitting further to the rear while I occupied the chair at Dr. Zimmer's desk, with the chipped and somewhat stained-looking white enamel medicine cupboard containing rows of ominously gleaming surgical instruments to my left and the old-fashioned examination couch with its shiny metal leg supports where the, to me, ever-mysterious female ailments, maladies that were never discussed in public, could be diagnosed and presumably treated, to my right. If anything, the couch with its silver stirrups only heightened the distinction of male

192

and female. Though the sound and vibrations of detonating bombs soon intensified to a crescendo, Dr. Zimmer—who, I later determined, bore a close resemblance to Trevor Howard, who was to become one of my movie heroes—remained immobile in his chair, pensively staring into thin air, in marked contrast to my parents and the other couple, who by then were huddled on the floor, with my father protectively covering my mother with his body. At first, despite the explosions ominously rocking the building, seeing how indecorous my parents looked on the floor, I was determined to follow Dr. Zimmer's example. Nervously clutching the arms of the chair, I kept glancing at Dr. Zimmer—was it to gauge his expression, which appeared as fixed as if set in stone? After another nearby eruption, this time fully expecting the ceiling to cave in, unable to contain my terror, I threw myself headlong, a bundle of fear, to the floor, inhaling the carpet's dusty odor as my nose squashed against the finely worn Turkish fabric that had once graced the doctor's Berlin living-room floor, while my hands pressed down as if to infiltrate myself into the solid trembling floor. I prayed as I had never prayed before for the detonations to stop. With each successive thud the house shook and the floor, after a microsecond delay, shuddered in response. In the occasional lull between detonations, for what seemed an eternity, I studied Dr. Zimmer's trouscred legs and his shoes beneath the dcsk. When the bombing finally subsided, though the antiaircraft continued their maniacal chatter, I glanced up to confirm that he hadn't budged. I tried to make the transition from my ignominious cowering position on the floor back to the chair as inconspicuous as possible, though from Dr. Zimmer's frozen expression, he remained oblivious of my movements. We returned to our apartment, too stupefied by the intensity of the bombardment to exchange a single word. The religious community, when I checked, was quiet, and intact.

The following day, a friend and I, as if drawn by a powerful magnet to the area that had sustained the worst damage, managed to slip through the barbed-wire barricades erected to keep out looters. The guards and police paid no attention to our presence. Scattered here and there were still-smoldering blackened pieces of wood. The acrid smell of burnt wood and charred flesh became more penetrating the further we went. I recognized nothing. On a deserted square which must have been the site of the market, the many dead and dismembered bodies were still piled high in three or four almost fastidiously neat heaps. Without a word my friend turned to retrace his steps, while I, handkerchief pressed to my nose, grimly forged ahead, crossing the desolate square—having to pass between the heaps of bodies in order to do so. The only exit was a narrow lane that was swept clean except that here and there, randomly scattered, lay a hand, a leg, body parts that the otherwise thorough cleaners appeared to have overlooked. Back home, claiming to have come down with a cold, I went straight to bed, ineffectually trying to blot out the experience.

The war's ending was anticlimactic. It took everyone by surprise. Evidently Shanghai rated so low that when the war ended we still found ourselves under Japanese control until, what seemed an eternity, actually two weeks later, the tardy American navy finally materialized. The first inkling I had of Japan's defeat was one afternoon when, on leaving our house, I saw a man jubilantly waving his hands, almost skipping, announce to one and all that the war had ended. Yet there was something about his appearance—his decidedly goofy face—that made him a less than reliable messenger. He was just conveying news someone had heard on a shortwave set. But in no time he, this unlikely emissary, was followed by a more credible individual, bearing the identical message: "The war's over!" Forever skeptical, I headed for the Japanese gendarmerie on nearby Ward Road— disappointed to see, as always, an armed Japanese guard at the gate facing the deserted square. I tried to decipher the expression on his face with little success. If Japan had been defeated, why was the Rising Sun still fluttering from the police station's flagpole?

That night, the square was teeming with hundreds of Chinese of all ages hurling invective and, from appearances, clamoring for the death of the lone Japanese sentry—was it the same soldier who had been on duty that afternoon? Though the crowd could easily have overwhelmed him, they kept a safe distance. Now and then, a more venturesome Chinese youth darted forward, doing a little Oriental dance to taunt the soldier, only to retreat the moment the soldier lifted his unwieldy-looking rifle to which an immense bayonet was attached. Sometimes, as many as three and four young men, exhorted by a ringleader, advanced to act out in pantomime their loathing, their detestation of the Japanese—leaping in the air, wildly gesticulating, their hands cutting the air to convey a humiliation upon the recipient—the short peasant soldier—who seemed unresponsive to what was a performance more suited to the stage, until they came a little too close. The instant he raised his rifle, they retreated. It was a letdown. The war was over, but not quite yet. As I watched from the safety of the outer rim I saw no one at the gendarmerie windows. The lights were out. After fruitlessly waiting for something to happen, I left.

A protracted void followed. To me it appeared endless. Time seemed to stand still. Just as before there had always been rumors about the war, now there were rumors of riots and vandalism. The victors failed to materialize. The despised but still intimidating Japanese army remained in control, albeit less visible than before. Still, no one was prepared to challenge them—that is, until the Americans arrived. For the time being, the vast city of Shanghai lay there, submissive, patiently waiting to be occupied, waiting to place its bottomless resources, its treasures, its harbor, its hotels, its bars and whorehouses at the feet of the victors. Shanghai waited the way a courtesan, having just rid herself of a former lover, might timorously await the arrival of the next, still uncertain as to his taste, his experience, his desire for love, determined, however, at all costs, to overcome any doubts she might have had about her fading beauty. All she needed was to be desired and she'd blossom once again. But until the victor's arrival there was a lassitude, a sense of fatigue. Everything was suspended and motionless. However, along certain streets there was a sudden inexplicable burst of activity, as Chinese workers were constructing bars while the stores and warehouses along Broadway were feverishly restocking the lacquered junk, the carved figurines, the crafted teak coffee tables, the lacquer trays, the screens, everything the jubilant Americans, Australians, and Brits would want to take home as mementos of the Orient. And the women? Those incredibly eroticized wide-cheeked Chinese, Eurasian, and White Russian women. Were those small-breasted, slim, quick-moving women rehearsing their acts? Perfecting their stories of past tribulations and survival? Readying themselves for the day the allies finally made their appearance?

Then, one day, without any warning, without any fanfare, they arrived. No celebratory fireworks, no twenty-one–gun salute—not even a tugboat to hoot a welcome. At first, on seeing the white-helmeted MPs and shore patrol at the harbor facilities on Broadway looking so unruffled as they cursorily checked IDs and waved cars through, I felt let down by the absence of hoopla—by the everyday appearance of it all. What had I expected? Surely, the end of the Second World War deserved something more ebullient. Something more jubilant. In a sense, the ensuing four years of America's presence were already concentrated into those first days of their arrival. Everything there was to know about the Americans was to be absorbed in those first twenty-four hours. Everything!

The Seventh Fleet might have been tardy, but once having arrived and promptly occupied every possible space on the docks along the length of Yangtzepoo Road, the fleet more than made up for the delay with an avalanche of commodities. One had the impression that the sailors, whooping it up on the streets, were packing the newly opened bars before the ships had adequately docked. Not to be outdone, the Chinese merchants responded in kind with a lavish display of their wares—those familiar lustrous Oriental icons: Chinese dragons engraved on silver cigarette cases, Chinese dragons on the backs of garish silk shirts, teak Oriental furniture and ornamental screens with dragons and glazed pottery, and Oriental jewelry emblazoned with little dragons, while on Nanking Road one could see marvelous Chinese women in their tantalizing *qui pao* or *cheongsam,* the tight-fitting dresses slit to reveal the upper leg, their impassive faces—really masklike—conveying a purposeful sexual attitude as they strode rapidly on some assignation as deliriously scripted as Robbe-Grillet's *La Maison de Rendezvous.* The gleaming destroyers and cruisers remained at anchor in mid-river amidst the chaotic traffic of sampans and junks, in full view of the Bund, while the drab workhorses of the navy—the LSTs, LCDs, the cargo vessels, ships lacking glamour—tied up at the Hwangpoo docks next to PT boats and an occasional submarine. Officers in starched whites, with a virginal look of satisfaction, as if they had just received priestly absolution for all past shortcomings, were striding along Nanking Road. The Seventh Fleet was a veritable food emporium, much of it destined for the sidewalks of Broadway, where the stacked American supplies, the cumulative packaging feat of the mid-century, everything advertised in those glossy magazines *Time* and *Life,* went on display in its original wrappers and boxes on the sidewalks only days after the fleet had docked. It's the name of the game. Shanghai was a city without shame or self-restraint. A constant traffic of trucks shifted American merchandise from one warehouse to another. Was there anyone who had not yet tasted Hershey bars and Rocky Road? How could Germany or Japan have ever contemplated defeating the

U.S.? One need only buy a pack of Wrigley's or Camels or the *Saturday Evening Post* to acquire one of the icons of this powerful nation. Unlike Europe, America's history was far more agreeable—for it accommodated Walt Disney and Donald Duck . . . even the LSTs and Liberty ships presented an enticing invitation. . . .

Overnight, the Japanese seemed to have vanished. Though the moment the vast armada, the conquering fleet, some of it already rusting and ready for the scrap heap, made its presence felt, a number of the more brawny Germans and Austrians in our community, seeking redress, somehow ferreted out several of our former Japanese captors, including Ghoya, whose unpredictable conduct as the official in charge of issuing passes out of the ghetto made him by far the most feared and detested official. Anything—it might be the most innocuous response to one of Ghoya's unexpected queries, or the composed bearing and dignified appearance of an applicant—could trigger Ghoya's rage. There were no end of stories circulating of Ghoya's oddities. An amateur violinist, he was known to visit refugee musicans and play chamber music with them. A short, stocky man, Ghoya displayed a particular animus to tall men—on occasions, working himself into a lather, he'd step on his chair in order to more easily reach the applicant's face, which he slapped rcpeatedly.

There exists a photo of Ghoya just after he had been roughed up by an avenging group of young Jews. As if to gainsay the black and blue marks on his face, evidence of the pummeling he has received, Ghoya tries to smile, as he stands stiffly at attention, holding his hand in a pathetic salute. There's something utterly incongruous about the photo. Divested of power, the erratic former "ruler," who had referred to himself as "king of the Jews," seemed to have shrunk, much to the disappointment of his pursuers, into the insignificant, petty bureaucrat he'd once been. One of the participants in the beating, an amateur boxer, later disclosed to me almost sadly: "He didn't try to flee or put up any resistance. . . . He just stood while we bashed him about."

In those first exuberant days, it was not unusual to see several American sailors goading each other—how to explain this first startling impression—as each one, gripping the rickshaw handlebars, blithely raced down Broadway with a flustered-looking rickshaw coolie uneasily occupying the passenger seat. Could these nineteen-year-olds be the victors? It seemed so improbable. They lacked, was it dignity? Those first few days were memorable as the city, after taking its measure of the "invading" Americans with the ease of an accomplished courtesan, took note of their wants and their so-called menu: Coke, hamburgers, ketchup, and beer. We can handle this, Shanghai seemed to say. After the lengthy Japanese occupation, this was a breeze. Indeed, it was the beginning of a mutually profitable relationship—wasn't that also the purpose of the victory?

The Chinese laughter conjoined discomfiture and mockery as they observed these overly large yet childlike creatures who seemed to lack an essential Oriental ingredient of manhood—namely dignity, sense of self. The word shame simply did not appear to exist in the American lexicon. In turn, the city wasn't at all coy, it did not pretend to be a former crown colony. There were few guides to monuments, estates, or museums. Shanghai didn't even have any museums worth mentioning. The guides, having quickly mastered the essential lexicon—"young girls" and "fucky, fucky"—promptly steered the new arrivals to a myriad whorehouses and bars. Entire lanes were now devoted to these decrepit makeshift establishments. No one alluded to China's former greatness. What greatness? No mention of the Tang or Sung dynasties. After all, Shanghai must have been a swamp at the time. One need only dig a few feet into the ground to arrive at the rich watery mud of that period. Isn't Shanghai's mercantile history, above all, the history of foreign domination? The history of England's opium trade, of inordinate European greed and opportunism?

I concocted elaborate stories of how I spent my afternoons and evenings—to my surprise, my mother, who had become surprisingly indulgent, didn't question me closely. She accepted the fact that I and a number of my friends—there's always safety in numbers— seemed to be spending our free time onboard American warships.

By now the Japanese had faded from memory. How quickly they had become yesterday's news. Overnight, the American presence expunged everything I had experienced. With one magic stroke our "European" past had been erased. No loss to me! For the time being, my brain accommodated only American products. What now mattered was the new convertible Buicks, the latest songs on the hit parade, and a series of intoxicating movies, *The Purple Heart, The Ox-Bow Incident, The Shanghai Gesture.* Everything America produced was irresistible—down to the mini-packs of four Chester-field cigarettes in the Four-in-One, or the canned rice pudding with small chunks of pineapple. Yet America itself remained elusive, too vague for me to grasp. I began to devour the best-sellers with a passion. Friends would come over to listen to the songs of the hit parade and programs such as *Duffy's Tavern* on XMHA. Now that all—or at any rate, most—restrictions had been lifted, I acquired a lethal knife my mother made me return, a silver cigarette case with an engraved dragon, and a massive silver ring. In my loafers, colorful Hawaiian shirt, aviator sunglasses, smoking Camels, I was indistinguishable from the multitude of young men who hung out at the race course. . . .

Late one night, on the deck of a PT boat gently swaying on the odorous Hwangpoo River, I watched *The Big Sleep*. It was the first time I'd seen Humphrey Bogart, the private eye who doesn't tolerate shit from anyone. That much I could readily understand. In China, however, there was an excess of excrement. The city wallowed in it metaphorically and otherwise. At times ankle-deep shit was unavoidable. Each morning, on my way to school, I'd pass a small group of faceless men pushing inadequately covered wooden carts to collect from households less fortunate than ours the still-steaming "night soil" that would fertilize the fields outside the city with every disease known to mankind. As for Bogart's much vaunted self-restraint? Bogart, who duly confronted his share of inscrutable Hollywood "Orientals," had no compunction in showing them who was boss.

I expended a great amount of energy sneaking past MPs and SPs at the harbor facilities but then, having achieved my goal of boarding a ship, be it the hospital ship, *USS Repose*, or an LST or even a lowly PT boat, I was at a loss as to what to do next. To me the sailors, mostly good-natured if somewhat bored, still possessed the attractive shine of all things American. What I do recall is their total lack of curiosity. They had no idea of who I and my friends might be and what in the world we might be doing in Shanghai of all places. We were there and so were they—and wonders of all wonders, we spoke the same language.

In what was to be a final glimpse of the Japanese in 1945: I saw about a dozen of the previously feared soldiers in loincloths only, crouching in that inimitable Asian fashion, waiting to board a nearby anchored converted LST that was to transport them back to Japan. They looked and acted so inoffensively, it was hard to imagine they had ever been a component of a powerful army.

I wonder if the two Chinese policemen I passed on my way to school laughingly kicking a bulky package, actually a dead infant neatly wrapped in newspaper and tied with cord, back and forth across the street, were by imitating the behavior of their European superiors simply passing the time, or was this mindless cruelty a grotesque antidote for their sense of powerlessness? No. Of course not. They were simply kicking the package—the content was insignificant—as they might a ball, for recreation, unthinkingly. I still recall the whoosh the package made as it slid over the hot pavement. The package lent itself to kicking and they needed a pastime. Nothing more, nothing less. I tend to theorize, to speculate too much about motives. Sometimes, motives are simply an afterthought.

A group of us, all a little tipsy, went in search of Mom's Place near the race course. Having finally located the small building, we boisterously pounded on the front door, calling for "Mom," our voices revealing both our age and inexperience. Finally, in response to our commotion, a young woman opened an upper window and, looking down on us, in a throaty, inviting voice, said: "Sorry, boys, there are just the two of us." I was thrilled by her voice and by her acceptance of us as adults. After some long-distance negotiation, a servant let us in. To my distress, Mom, a plump maternal-looking lady of advanced age, materialized to take charge—"Come," she said, protectively putting an arm around me, singling me out as the youngest, "you chat with me," while the others scurried out of sight. She talked nonstop until I was completely befuddled. I don't rememer how much time passed. Somehow, I doubt that for the others much of anything transpired. For a long time, I kept thinking of the woman in the window saying: "Sorry, boys"—words that sent an electric charge through me.

It was around that time that I happened by chance upon a maze-like building in which Chinese jugglers, puppeteers, actors, magicians, singsong girls, and storytellers in long gowns carrying folding fans entertained the audience, which sauntered from one chamber to the next. Losing all sense of direction, I walked down long corridors, circling one courtyard then another, now stopping to buy something to eat, now watching a puppet performance, then a man on stilts, then a peacock chained to a table . . . all the while aware that I was the only non-Chinese in the crowd. When I described my experience, my friends showed a complete lack of curiosity. In retrospect this doesn't come as a surprise, for China and all things Chinese were not only excluded from our textbooks at school, but also from our minds. We behaved as if what was Chinese could not possibly carry much significance. I vividly recall drawing the maps of Africa and Australia in class but not once the map of China. I can recall being made to memorize a long list of Israelite kings following the split under King Rehoboam into the Northern Kingdom of Israel and the Southern Kingdom of Judah, but not once did I hear mention of a Chinese emperor. After all, why study China? The thinking went that one could look out of the window and pretty much absorb all there was to see of China. It seemed as if everyone was quite prepared to over-look China's vast history, its astounding culture, accepting the Spenglerian premise that a society unable to repel invaders was somehow lacking a crucial will and purpose—an inner strength—as a result of which it deserved its fate.

With two friends I found myself in the Little Club across from the race course, swilling Tom Collinses with three bar girls. I was all of fifteen. I disliked the alcoholic drinks almost as much as the ciga-rette burning my throat, but it felt decidedly cool. The other tables were occupied by carousing American sailors only a few years older than we. No one paid any attention to us. In the bathroom American sailors were throwing up with a gusto that seemed rehearsed. What on earth prompted me to invite the bar girl at my side to go to the movies if she could get off the following afternoon? To my dismay, she accepted.

When a friend and I stopped in the entrance to stare into the large gaudy-looking Chinese dance hall, two men at a table beckoned us to join them. As a lark, I waved back. When they kept on beckoning, we joined them at their table. Speaking a broken English, both pre-tended to know us. At first I thought it fun to go along with the cha-rade, but the effort at small talk that the Chinese men seemed to enjoy soon became more and more taxing. When the band struck up, my friend and I, along with dozens of young Chinese men, headed for the long line of dancing girls in slit dresses daintily perched on tiny three-legged bamboo stools. The young woman I approached didn't have a single word of English. It was a relief not to talk. Dancing on the crowded floor with the doll-like Chinese woman became an ordeal as well once it dawned on me that payment was required, since I had no idea of how or where to obtain the necessary tickets. After thanking the dancer I made my way back to the table to continue the torturous exchange. The initial pretense was wearing thin. I couldn't tell which was the more arduous, dancing or the contrived conversation. At the deafening sound of the orchestra we, once again, dutifully set off for one of the two gigantic dance floors. When I chose the same expressionless dancer with too much rouge on her cheeks, she looked resigned. She didn't ask for a ticket if only because she didn't know how to in English. My poor dancing must have been an additional discomfort to her—though, at least outwardly, on the crowded floor, I was able to disguise my ineptitude. Back at the table I said that we had to be leaving. Our quasi host promptly said that they would be leaving as well. The evening was not over since we all took the same tram, which entailed added strained attempts at conversation. More and more, our polite exchange sounded like an English lesson for beginners: "How old are you? Do your parents live in Shanghai? Do you speak French?"

Somewhere, within, still restless, still uneasy, sixteen lies quiescent. Sixteen going on seventeen, an age that doesn't wear well. *Tell me something about yourself.* Go on! Instantly the pimples threaten to erupt. Sixteen, an unread text? Go on! *Treat us to sixteen.* Wasn't the sporadic unsightly rash, the field of pustules on my chin, a dead giveaway? Let's face it, I didn't even shave yet. The inflamed skin housed my discomfort. The voice cracking the sound barrier as I struggled to implant a minimal authority into a mild statement. And what about the tortured expressions, the excessive burst of laughter that verged on lunacy, the strenuous attempt to compose myself—to *appear* adult? Acknowledging, *It's me!* as I gravely studied myself in a mirror, smoking a filter cigarette, only to conclude: *I'm an impostor!* Somehow pleased by the acumen it took to arrive at this insight. At sixteen the face was able to entertain a disproportionate capacity for doubt, bellicosity, derision, irritability. Let's not omit an alertness, a wariness, even a storehouse for shame? And a vagrant intelligence? In addition to bursts of an all-too-ready enthusiasm and expectation, an indiscriminate craving for books and movies to blot out the commonplace, to blot out the ungratifying present. Was I still recalcitrant? Always.

There were no less than three movie theaters, the Broadway Cinema on Wayside, the Wayside on Broadway, along with a third just off Ward Road, a few blocks from our house, the name of which I don't recall. Remnants of another age, they were rundown, and except for Sundays, poorly attended. I'd select an empty row light-years from the proximity of others to watch righteous American and English soldiers being tested as they stoically battled the Germans and the Japanese. Sitting through a double feature of *The Purple Heart* and *Blood on the Sun*, I wondered if, under similar circumstances, I'd measure up. In the gilded theater lobby on display neatly arranged under glass were the Hershey bars, Oh Henry! bars, and Rocky Road. In addition to the local fizzy orangeade there was Coke and 7UP. And always, filling in the background, neutral, noncommittal, nonthreatening faces as inscrutable as wallpaper. As the houselights dimmed, we stood up for the Chinese national anthem, which I can hum to this day. I'd enter the movie emporiums in the full glare of a Chinese afternoon to emerge after dark—always mildly unsettled by the transition. Walking home, still dazed by the daring exploits I'd seen on the screen, I felt like a space traveler returning from another dimension, not completely reabsorbed into the drab world surrounding me. Oddly enough, it didn't occur to me to question my surroundings as I braced myself for the reality awaiting me at home. With no past to speak of, I preferred not to contemplate the future beyond the next day.

In all my reading at sixteen I had not yet come across the line *Je suis un autre*, "I am another," a line by Rimbaud that was to strike me with the force of a sledgehammer. At sixteen, I was nonplussed when a kid I hardly knew revealed his hatred, angrily accosting Betty, the only girl I knew with a *sexual* history, in my presence no less: "I don't care who you go to bed with, as long as you don't sleep with *him*. If you do, I'll break every bone in your body." What was he to her? She to him? If I avoided her henceforth, it was not so much out of fear but embarrassment. I couldn't begin to understand why he threatened her and not me! For sixteen an unforgettable vituperative display. *I hardly know him but he hates my guts.* Sixteen, an ungraceful loser. At sixteen I reserved my fondness for Mushy, our cat.

My farewell to Shanghai ... timorously ringing the doorbell of an imposing townhouse on the Soochow Creek diagonally across from the post office. A former merchant's residence. Who had given me the address? I persuaded a friend to accompany me. At sixteen it was not the kind of journey one undertakes by oneself. To my relief, having passed scrutiny, in itself a kind of test, we were admitted into the large drawing room, which was cluttered with bric-a-brac, underscoring not only refinement and wealth but a decorum. Weren't the tapestries, paintings, tall statuettes all of dubious origin, like so many cherished icons there to reassure the visitor: a home away from home? Or was it an attempt to exemplify Shanghai's lustrous history? The severe-faced White Russian lady who came to greet us eyed us critically. To her right the curved white marble staircase with its gleaming banisters. Our exchange was limited to a few words. Mercifully they sufficed. A sixteen-year-old was not yet polished in these matters. What time was it? Afternoon, of course. Movie rather than brothel time. The time at which sixteen flourishes. The Chinese servant led us into a bright red wallpapered long narrow room to the left of the stairs. Four docile, doll-like young women in sleeveless Chinese costumes entered and stood in a line, not moving a muscle, while the madame remained a censorious presence in the doorway. To my left, reaching to the ceiling, were glass vitrines filled with tiny objets d'art—gifts from appreciative clients? Not wishing to dawdle, I chose blindly. I followed my selection upstairs. At the far end of the corridor, a Chinese servant, squatting on his heels next to a portable vacuum cleaner, didn't look up. The bedroom was antiseptically clean. It resembled a lab rather than a bedroom. Nothing in it encouraged lewdness. By comparison with the parlor below it was almost chilling. I took note of the electric shaver, to me another potent American emblem, next to a hairbrush on a pristine glass shelf in the immaculate bathroom, to which the door was wide open. I was reflected in a number of large mirrors. The woman, not wasting time, lay down, taking extreme care not to muss her elaborate hairdo. She pulled up her beautiful robe, exposing her slim legs and waist. She wore nothing underneath. With a petulant expression she listened to me nervously ramble on about myself—the way one does in a dentist's chair in order to postpone the treatment. The elongated tilted mirror facing the bed depicted a partially undressed slim Chinese woman. I glanced at the mirror, at her slender, smooth ivory body, overwhelmed by a feeling of unreality and, worse yet, a sudden decided lack of desire. . . . The only sound the woman made was a cricketlike *tsk, tsk* of impatience. Afterward, I comforted myself with the thought that it was the visit, itself an accomplishment, to this luxurious bordello that mattered. Not that I had gone there for the interior, for the museum effect, for the history. When I finally walked down the carpeted steps, the madame stared pointedly at her watch, to indicate disapproval, while my friend, with a puzzled smile, misconstruing my lateness, asked: "Whatever took you so long?"

Everyone was leaving—everyone anticipated the stormy conclusion. Soon, any day, Mao's army would materialize. This time, however, the Chinese forces wouldn't resemble the long, ragged undisciplined army columns I'd observed shuffling into the city in 1945.

A week or two prior to our departure a friend and I stopped at a sidewalk shooting booth on Wayside Road. It was noon, the sun was out. People, mostly Chinese, unhurriedly walked past as I took aim with a pellet gun at one of the colorful targets in the ramshackle booth. I had no reason to fear an attack from anyone. When I was grabbed by the throat from behind, I let out a yell and furiously jabbed the person behind me, convinced that my assailant was someone I knew—finding it inconceivable that a group of young Chinese would, without provocation, attack me so close to the heart of the European quarter. All my prior clashes with Chinese boys had been peculiarly stylized. On the one or two occasions I had been attacked on my way to school, the Chinese boys would invariably advance, screaming, "*Tang, tang,*" one open hand rigidly extended, challenging us to respond in kind, while we, my school friends and I, after gaping uncomprehendingly at what, to us, might as well have been a ritualized dance, ignorant of the appropriate response, settled the matter energetically with a few effective punches. . . . Now, while being assaulted in a decidedly untraditional Chinese manner, I saw my friend glancing over his shoulder as he scooted away for dear life. Presumably, with the imminent arrival of Mao's army, my attackers considered my aiming a rifle an act of sheer provocation. After trading punches, I managed to extricate myself only to be pursued up Wayside Road, all the while conscious of the incongruity of being chased like a thief caught picking someone's pocket. Near Chusan Road I made a dash for a middle-aged European couple standing in the entrance to their house. Letting myself into their small front garden I approached them with my not unreasonable request. Didn't they resemble my family? Out of breath, I explained my predicament, while my pursuers, their hatred polished to a fine gleam on their

205

faces, stood expectantly at the garden gate, awaiting the outcome. I was not yet accustomed to such a reversal of roles. To the rear of the couple, in their hallway, I could see stacked wooden crates with their names and destination stenciled on them—indication of their impending departure. In the genteel, cultivated voice of a lady from Berlin or Vienna, a voice that still resonates in my ears to this day, she not only asked me to leave: *"Sie können nicht hier bleiben!"* but, at the same time, seemed to reproach me for placing her in such an awkward predicament. "Five minutes is all I need," I pleaded. "They'll soon be gone." Emphatically she shook her head—*"Sie müssen weggehen!"*—a statement her husband meekly echoed as he retreated into the house. This isn't possible, I thought. "These men wish to beat me up." Stepping back, following her husband into the house, she shut the door in my face. All the while people were passing by, a few casting curious glances in my direction. But no one lingered, no one offered to intervene.

Having withdrawn with the dexterity of conjurers, the European couple left me no option but to exit as well. As soon as I swung open the low metal garden gate I was, once again, enveloped in the warmth of the three men's angry embrace—I could taste their rage on my lips. After another exchange of blows—in that close proximity, each of my frantic punches landed on target—I broke free, bolting down the road, barely conscious of the retaliating hits, racing toward Chusan Road, the center of our shrinking enclave, where my pursuers finally gave up their pursuit. I was so cowed by the incident that I didn't leave the proximity of our house for days. I couldn't even bring myself to mention the assault to anyone—suddenly, to discover myself to be the enemy!

A friend showed me a photo of his cousin lounging on the beach in Tel Aviv, a Sten gun in his hand. It was the weapon that held my attention, not the houses in the background, or the scruffy-looking beach. At sixteen I was inordinately captivated by weapons. I may not have had an idea of what Israel looked like, but to me the photo of the young man casually holding a Sten provided an essential and promising piece of information. It seemed as if we were traveling to a country where it was essential to carry a weapon. . . .

I was a few days short of seventeen when we left Shanghai. The Chinese on the street were already wearing their padded winter garments. I was going to miss the arrival of the Red Army. Would it be all that different from the entry of Chiang's troops in 1945? Then most of the transportation was on the shoulders of young barefoot carriers balancing supplies from the ends of a long flexible bamboo pole. The city we were leaving still retained a foreign presence. However, the number of large ships in the harbor had dwindled. There were still the few naval rejects, LSTs and Liberty ships, along with a number of rusty merchant ships at anchor in the vast harbor. By then the Japanese POW had been repatriated, and the gleaming white hospital ship, the *USS Repose,* was long gone on some distant goodwill mission. Despite all propaganda to the contrary, the Chinese Red Army was inexorably drawing closer. By then there was markedly less activity on the Bund—fewer lines of chanting coolies loading and unloading the barges. Still, the city presented an appearance of normality. Everything still seemed to function—businesses were open, and so were the banks and government offices. Foreigners were still to be seen—but looking more somber, introspective, as if on some demanding personal errand. The ending—an outcome one could only dread—was drawing near. For a city that had experienced countless transitions, one could hardly speculate what form the arrival of the Red Army would take. It was plain to see the city was resigned to what was about to develop. Resigned? It was the end of a hectic postwar party. Defeat was in the air—it coexisted with a denial that anything had changed. Even as everyone awaited the Red Army, one could always reason: But there are still the movies, the trams are running, there's food, there's electric power. . . . Even the Kuomintang officers were still to be seen, though in their tailored uniforms with the exaggerated wide shoulder boards out of a Viennese operetta, they didn't inspire confidence. It was common knowledge that the Kuomintang, perennially short of cash, was selling its U.S.-made weapons to Mao. As for the wealthy and the Chinese ruling class—they did what the affluent and powerful do so well in an emergency, namely flee pell-mell for Formosa—soon to be renamed Taiwan. We'd still stand when the Kuomintang national anthem was played in the movie houses, but no one was deceived. Think of it, a peasant army under Mao that had never been to a city this size would soon arrive—to gawk at the colorful displays in the windows of WingOn and Sincere, the two largest department stores. No longer could WingOn or Sincere depend on my father's seemingly endless supply of Molinard's intoxicating perfumes and colognes to counter Shanghai's fetid odors. This time there was no attempt, as there was prior to the arrival of the Americans, to spruce up the bars, the dance halls, the brothels. It was only a matter of time. In our immediate area the money changers, more brazen than ever, were openly trading on Chusan Road. The price of the U.S. dollar kept rising by the hour. Trying to beat inflation, I invested all of my capital and acquired $3.35.

At the time we left China, Cartier-Bresson was framing the retreat of the undisciplined Kuomintang forces in his Rollei's viewfinder. Photographing Chinese officials, coolly, imperturbably practicing tai chi on the grounds of the Imperial Palace days only before Nanking, then still the capital, fell to Mao's advancing and now unstoppable army. Only a year before, impelled by a deep dissatisfaction with my life, I sought out the *Life* magazine photographer, hoping to persuade him to take me as his assistant along on his trip to the interior. What would I have done if he had agreed? Along Nanking Road one could still see the occasional tall, blonde, leggy wives and companions of American officers entering and leaving the Palace Hotel. By then the Little Club was closed. It wasn't just the winter of inflation, of successive defeats of Chiang's army, it was the rout of the Americans, who, despite their overwhelming power, could not sustain Chiang in power—could not sustain the level of corruption.

In another telling photo by Cartier-Bresson that's fixed in my mind, a long line of retreating Nationalist soldiers on a narrow village dirt road were passing a joyous wedding procession proceeding in the opposite direction. The ornately dressed members of the wedding party, carrying banners and musical instruments, and the demoralized soldiers, fleeing Mao's advancing army, appear oblivious to each other's presence. It's as if to the villagers, the defeated and dejected soldiers are from another world, one that has no significance to their lives.

Late in December 1948, my parents and my grandmother and I boarded a converted Liberty ship with an Italian crew, bound for Israel. To avoid passing through the Suez Canal we circumnavigated Africa. On the final stretch, from Italy to Haifa, we transferred to two smallish freighters. For several days we endured a rough crossing, made worse by the lack of food. The young kibbutznik in charge of the passengers tried to describe Israel to me. I recall whenever I passed his cabin door hearing from within his tiny cabin snatches of

208

Hebrew folk music being played over again and again on a portable record player—if nothing else, the music filled me with a longing for a similar dedication, a similar purpose, a similar unshakable sense of identity.

Three Poems
Ange Mlinko

RUSTICITY

Smiling boughs most certainly mocked us:
Where are you? they asked like hypnotists
& we ventured, "In your green brain,
with your thoughts singing, & each note
is a small inflation, squaring the shoulders
& jarring the wings. Here are other thoughts,
giving off wild strawberry & mock orange
to which we add the smell of our fresh scratches."
The attars & moulderings were so nonhuman
as to render feeling into continual summonses.
Felicity crinkled, we backed into tick season,
shrouded in tenses which we liked to apply
liberally to our surroundings, as when
asserting these mountains were not built
they were cut over time by waterfalls
whose crazy & spontaneous writing created
its own context, & if it scored a new form
it avoided feeling pious about it. The casual intelligence
we are the sensorium of breeds a disparity
so georgic are the bells that fill the skies
burned clear like stubble fields with fireworks.
& if all it takes is for words to turn to perfume,
butter-, fire-, and damsel-flies to move
their hemistichs in tandem round
the cognates whirling in our fiery lobes,
one of these mornings, rising up singing, etc.
it is to be sovereign without imprint
of a particular day, just rest
& mirrored pathways one never disappeared from,
or got lost on, in the framework
of a conventional stroll, clichés.

Ange Mlinko

ANGEL ENGLISH

What a punk tree surgeon of the anti-Versailles
would do to these right angles and rastered rosebushes!
while silk trees drop duds all over the august lines
of straight staircases, cursive as they fall
in whatever language the dividuous waves
use against the ramparts. Within the *castelo*,
goldfish write in strange sigils; words continue
their siege til three birds map a plane with song.
The song makes of space an integument
across which leaps the language of business.
The king worriedly writes something on black paper;
a tourist does the crossword, unconcerned.
The riddles he must answer at the northwest gate
resemble those clues, but in coin form.

———————

My graffiti flunks me from Shakespeare's party.

Last call a hose blast on a trash can.

As the U.S. charts bomb the waitress is our witness,
the placemat's puzzles devolve into contests
of who can see the words for the forest.

A painting or a stenciling of a scene on the window
of men on horses coursing through some desolate meadow:

bare staves of trees, snow, bundled figures looking fearful
—consulting—as they land, aslant, bending their hard hats
to earth; and easily chipped as a rim, a hoof.

Through the stencil, A) the real December, 1) chimney smoke,
2) an evergreen around which a town grew to schedule,

B) a cathedral.
Pillars, figures, columns; total row at the bottom; etc.

211

Ange Mlinko

THE DOCENT OF EVENING

The museum of the sun is closed.
He wanted to read again for the first time.
Copies of copies, the serifs of buildings, evenings
before the museums close. Some places don't have museums,
they are still at their beginning. The evening
has a beginning, we have a whole museum to it
hidden in the park. It is always open, even free
to the always-student.

The rebarbative steeples over the trees
whence a peacock, the picture of a picture
which the sometime-tourists mix up with the phoenix
exist as a receding mirage where
leaves mill shade, doubling dark.
The evening had a beginning as
the vein in your arm runs down to a book.
A beginning reaches one from far away.

The Shunra and the Schmetterling
Yoel Hoffmann

—Translated from Hebrew by Peter Cole

1. a.

FROM OBLIVION THERE ascends, like that
legendary bird rising from its ashes, the veranda on
which my father's father, Isaac Emerich, sat, along
with my grandmother Emma. The veranda of the
world itself, whose heart is an electric lightbulb.
Beside it, on the wall (like Eve, naked within
that X ray we call the Garden of Eden), sits a
transparent lizard. This is the veranda on which
my grandfather sat and sent out his hand like
Napoleon, looking across the battlefield toward
the villages of Hayriyya and Saqiyya, when he
said to me in his voice which exists on the right
side of creation entirely—I was a child at the
time—"*Dort ist Arbein.*" (There is the land of the
Arabs.)

It is extremely hard to see him stand and go. He is
located now in another time, and the air is filled
with cordless voices. "Have a Good Week"* no
longer gets played on the radio.

  He sits, dead, within a time that isn't his,
and points at a place that no longer exists.
Something like the big blocks of ice we would
wrap up in a white cloth and put in the bottom
drawer of the icebox—or the ball that fell from
the school playground onto the back porch—
brings that time around like a cosmic loop.

  If my grandmother Emma now recited the
song of the egg (*kod kod kod kod kod kodaa-sh
minden napra et toyaa-sh*), time would split open
and reveal the time hidden within it, where—

*a song sung at
the end of the
Sabbath

213

preserved in a baking mold—was the scent of
French potatoes.

b.

I give my father's father the cat. My father's father
releases white butterflies into the space of the
house, and the old cat chases them as though in a
slow-motion movie. But when a butterfly rises in
the air, my grandfather performs an act like that of
the one who was crucified, and in his hand he lifts
the cat toward the skies of the room, which are
fashioned in the form of a ceiling.

   On the top floor (the sky's sky), the
Heymans are calling in Jewish between the tubs
set out for the laundry. If there is a mouse in the
worlds-on-high, they say *meiss*,* and I—a child—
hear Johann Sebastian Bach on Arlosoroff Street,
by the Monkey Park, while the *shunra*** *shunra*
shunra and the *schmetterling**** . . .

c.

How does one draw a veranda after two thousand
years of exile? A broken railing. Grillwork like
Auschwitz. A floor with tiles of pogroms and the
Nuremberg laws in the wall's plaster. . . .

   I know. The earth turns like a carousel, and
in this revolving everything's rinsed in the air.
Autumn yields rain and spring the fragrance of
grass, a banal song, and—spreading out on the
table, day after day, like a patient's sheets, my
math notebook and in my place writing the
correct digits beside the equals sign—my
grandfather diverted the evil winds that blew from
school (numbers and the lines of geometry).
Someone shattered the great union, and my
father's father, who loved me, concealed from me
the sight of fractions.

d.

Mr. Tsehayek, who had a grocery store, wandered like the cranes from Baghdad to the Land of Israel.

His golden monocle and gabardine pants, which hindered the movement of the wings, and also the need to look respectable among the cans of peas . . . all these composed the pure logic of Ramat Gan. What-was-created wore an exterior such as this, and was rounded at the ends, as in the form of Mrs. Zoller, whose name was associated with the health clinic, but whom I saw feeling a peach.

And within all these—the large closet with a mirror inside it, and in that mirror were always reflected, as seas are reflected in the skies above, two bronze beds. On the right side of the mirror was the bed of Isaac Emerich, and on the left side, the bed that belonged to Emma, and the measure of the depth in the picture reflected was the measure of the depth of outer space.

2. a.

If I want to remember, I remember only in tinted shades, and something like a gull, or gulls.

Childhood, as it recedes, becomes . . .er. My mother in her various outlines and my father in his single outline are, believe me, enough.

At the cemetery, two marble columns rise up toward the clouds. *There* I grow cannabis plants. Plant after plant, among the remains of flesh and bone.

I remember steps in the sun. A flight of stairs, as they say.

My wife, whose name is Nicola, polishes the mirrors at home. I know, I tell her, where every pot is. Try me.

She does, but I forget one—in which she

once made orange marmalade, though the pot is
clearly in view.

b.

The sun comes and the sun goes, like a noise on
the top floor of the building, where it is not
possible to tap on the ceiling with an iron-tipped
umbrella or a parasol.

My raison d'être you'll have to seek in
biology books. *There* the learned explain, like a
roofer placing roof tile next to roof tile, how I
take a silver watch out of my waistcoat pocket.

I remember autumn. My right hand was in the
Atlantic. Five fingers on the ocean floor.

Ancient fish surrounded it, like extremely
religious Jews. The trunk of the arm rising from
the depths must have seemed, in their eyes—
which bulged from their sockets—like the divine
revelation.

c.

In that meeting of clear and obscure I grew
up.

My grandfather sailed on that Arlosoroff
Street veranda, looking across toward Hayriyya
and Saqiyya, to the place where the ball of earth
sailed along, carrying with it the thin layer of air
that encircled it, as all of us breathed.

Trees, in a way, were much like lungs. And the
upper boughs—where the birds stood still—gave
forth the sound of the water they held.

Each tree was an *individuum*. There was
the one that "would come home late at night
bent over." And the one that "laughed last," and
so on.

Butterflies stood at the edge of the eye.

The warning sirens (there were wars then) completed themselves like circles one draws with a compass.

Sometimes stars were doubled by the lesser lights.
There was an upper light and there were lights below, and jackals howled in the great space between the two worlds.

In your mind's eye you could see a man, on his way from Ramat Gan to Petah Tikvah, being torn to pieces.

d.
My grandfather bent his head because the burden of the memory of women drew him, with the gravity of the pelvis, toward the floor. Like Solomon the king, he ate apple cakes at Café Kapulsky next to the Ordea Cinema.

The biblical air surrounded him in his bed with bronze bars as the angel closed the shutters of my eyes. I dreamed of coins, and he already knew a thing or two, and wouldn't even think of suggesting to the pair of mothers that they divide the only infant. He'd have revived the dead baby with the power of thought's indolence.
His death (he missed two breaths) was so peaceful because he knew he was destined to return, dead, to the streets.
Whoever sees him sees and enters a restaurant, or the cosmetics store, and doesn't bother to say, "I just saw a dead man on the street" —since his life walks alongside him.

3. a.
My uncle Ladislaus, who was a doctor, received a donkey from the Health Fund.
At night, the donkey stood on Bialik Street

217

between the stars in the sky and the stars in the sand and brayed like Arkady Dukhin.*

*a popular singer

All sorts of women whose names were Hilda tossed in their sleep. A kind of line, like the pale lightning they call a *decree*—descended on Moshe Shertok's** house and it was possible to see the purple flowers of the bougainvillea, though no one looked at them.

**Israel's first foreign minister

The donkey's heart most likely went out toward another donkey, one larger and stripped of all corporeality. At night this divine donkey filled the space, and by day—a man from Vienna whose right hand held a parasol.

b.
The word *fertig* rolled like thunder between the middle of the night and the hours of the dawn. You know how the sun comes up. A ball made of molten gold, because someone's bare feet have touched the floor.

Imagine a primordial jar of kefir. Before there was "chaos and void." And not a table in the world. Not a single bed. The jar contains no memories, nor does the kefir it holds.

c.
Uncle Ladislaus hung an imaginary violin where one normally hangs up jackets and coats, and took hold of a razor.
    The face he saw in the mirror he silently called the face of morning, but in fact he did not understand the reflection.
    Outside, the donkey, too, gazed at the inner reflection, and each of them saw behind his world. It is extremely hard to rescue time from

these sights, which freeze like the subtle vapors given off by ice a moment before the movement begins.

You can see the Argaman* factory just like in love poems by Ibn Gabirol. How that colorful fabric emerges from the machines. Or those long cords that are stretched and woven at the Yerushalmi plant beside the Yarkon.**

*here the name of the factory, but also a "sensuous purple"

**a river in Tel Aviv

d.

Mr. Katchko is already standing by the flower pots on the porch, waiting for my uncle Ladislaus to come out and go to the donkey.

The white parasol Uncle Ladislaus is holding in his right hand teaches Mr. Katchko that even the Trade Union of Hebrew Workers flies in the air. Uncle Ladislaus's stethoscope amplifies the sound of the Messiah's footsteps.

And I haven't yet spoken of the beads of dew in the low-level world. Of Mr. Katchko's daughter who has angina. But Uncle Ladislaus lets nature run its course and simply wiggles the muscles of his ears until she laughs though her throat is full of phlegm.

When it comes to the wild doves that came to me (the great miracle of my childhood), a healing power moves through all ten of my fingers and the sun rises toward the zenith (or, as they say, toward the nadir).

4. a.

If I could sing to my mother like Allen Ginsberg sang to his, I would. *Yisgadal veyisqadash*, like that, which is one of the too-late additions to that great book, the beginning of which is In the beginning.

Her name. The dead babies she gave birth

to like a blind typesetter who prints combinations of letters according to the smell of the lead.

Her moving toward death like a carpenter into an old piece of furniture he'd carved and planed without looking back even once.

b.

At the oil press of dreams, she removes her white apron and I can see she's a very thin woman. A blind cat is chasing me, and I have a hard time telling her: Was the birth difficult? And what time is it *now?*

Take the Maccabees, and the elephant in the history book, and rise, rise, rise, dead woman—if you've left at least a neck.

Explain the air. The rain. The movement of my mouth when I speak and the peculiar appearance of other people amassed as though at a Quaker meeting the length and breadth of this flattened plain mouthing complex words such as "if" or "or," though there's nothing to say before these sights: skies, and other skies that are wrapped within them, as the stars are all gathered toward the interior.

c.

I give your dresses names:
Dress one, or the dress of distant goats.
A dress made of plaids that are white and red. One could call it the café table dress.
A transparent dress whose number is seven, or eight.
A dress whose name is "the last one," and in which one could still discern the many bodies of yours that it held.

Or I could list the parts of the body: Leg. Leg. A foot. The place beneath the arms we call *pits.*

The walls of the heart. Pores or maybe not. Hair. Or maybe also not. Ten toes of the foot until the soul gives out and all the rest as in Pompeii, where only the paintings on the wall remained: a woman bathing, with a kingfisher over her head.

5. a.

I can tell you of the many windows I saw after you died. Six, six, and in every window—the child Avremaleh and his mother feeding him from a large spoon that she brought from Theresienstadt. And a mulberry tree in the yard, and under the tree there were kittens, and even Mr. Reimalt (the General Zionists' honorable delegate) had a walk-on part upon this stage, which grew distant from you, like the celestial bodies.

I also saw Mrs. Yoel, who hid a bottle of raspberry concentrate at the back of the pantry. Up and down the length of Rav Kook Street, she alone said, "Hambursh" (when she spoke of Hamburg). There was something, my mother, reminiscent of an umbrella about her pelvis, and because the Germans tracked down attorneys' wives, who widened from the waist on down, she did well to sail with the winds of time.

b.

I also saw the tailor who had sewn, from his foot on up, eternal trousers.

A large transparency came through the Singer sewing machine, which stood in the middle of the store like an ancient altar for human sacrifice: On the wall hung pieces of unfinished suits, and people went behind the curtain and took off their clothes. What was the tailor's name? Everyone I could ask is dead.

*come out,
Yiddish, as in a
children's song

("Schneider, Schneider, *kim arvis*,"* we can call to him, as one calls out to a snail in its shell, and he'll emerge from his store waving a ruler.)

c.

In those days there were seven days to the week.

The first day was the day of the wild pigeon. From the child Hanan's house, countless wild pigeons emerged whose color was the color of wine. These ancient sons of men the size of turtle doves wandered from tree to tree, an upper sea of wild pigeons, as though the soul of the earth were floating on air.

The second day was the day of the crow. This is the crow created from within the days of my childhood and into the history books overhead, and it called out—for me alone—the unutterable name of God. The third day was the day of ebb and flow. I could see the heart of the cloud in the upper waters coming and going. The fourth day was the day of tremendous sleep. The two sides of time were gathered to the middle until they were cancelled. Its other name was the day of the great equilibrium.

The fifth day was the day that the sun grew clear, and it wore the face of the moon until the end of the sixth day, which was the final day of the counting of the fowl and the celestial bodies—the day that came before.

The Sabbath was the day of my life, because on that day, masculine and feminine, I was spun by two guinea pigs whose eyes were like black buttons and whose wisdom was deeper than the infinite number of days.

d.

I know that you lived on like a shadow within my living father, in the full length of his figure, and when he spread his arms wide, one was whiter

222

than the other, as on the telephone, when he said the name "Andreas" and the end of the word disappeared.

All sorts of signs, like sirens, taught me that your death evolved into my life, through an act of kindness and grace, because it was not possible to absorb these three letters* without mediation.

*I-m-a, mother, Hebrew

6. a.

My father wore the crow suit of Mondays, despite the hot winds from the East.

From within his walking to the insurance company at the corner of Allenby, I recall gray legends: princes who were partially paralyzed placed an LP on the gramophone. The outer side of the world (neckties and BBC broadcasts) was set free.

A man came from out of the blue and suddenly said, "My name is Rivkin." Stories were concocted as one installs a window frame and places the glass pane within it, then opens it, and shuts it, even though it was all transparent from the start.

In the book *Between the Grass and the Stars*,** a young man named Heaven loves a young woman whose name is Forfend, in the grove next to Sheikh Munis, where the chain of my Raleigh bicycle slipped out of the gears, and I saw, through the thin metal rods called spokes, Rachel Sirotta among the myrtles.

**Hebrew children's stories

b.

If I could take off like a light plane, I would. It was already evening, and the moon was in the Ayalon Valley, and the sun was over Gibeon; these were all ordinary phenomena in those days, like the new Hebrew, which gave rise to the word for "tulips."

What could I have done, when my singularity is so very clear, as clear as it was at the instant of creation.

It's extremely hard to remember how the chain got back into the teeth of the gears, because there are wonders greater still. I saw my face in the water and how that face had come to appear, and also the motion of the arm, which I had to watch out for—because who knows what might be hanging from it.
We didn't then realize that within us there lay another man dying to get out, though someone had already seen to it that we knew the formula for salicylic acid and the caloric value of an egg. But Rachel Sirotta, what does all that really matter—Galileo's climbing to the top of a tower to throw objects off of it?

c.

On the way from Sheikh Munis, we saw a praying mantis. The mantis was standing on a clump of weeds, alone, like a muezzin who had forgotten his lines. We were four or five, and Ehud Kaplan, who two years later wrapped himself up in cotton and burned, raised the mantis and placed the creature on the front light of his bike, and when we got to Ramat Gan, the praying mantis was standing on the light, magnified and sanctified be his great name—*Yisgadal veyisqadash shemei rabbah.*

Solstice

Carole Maso

HE COMES IN HIS solstice suit at last—so dapper. On his lapel, a winter rose. *Father, sit down, how have you been?* He opens his hand. Ash in the palm. In the other, sand. Rose of evening in his palm. All is calm. Bright star shape—last hope. Cattle are lowing. So they say—so they say. A few more tests, days, until the blood exchange. Mother to donate her cup of blood—marrow now—and if this. And if this is why she survived—to save her daughter, Ava Klein, she thinks to herself—would it not have been worth it—the war—the toll, the terrible toll on everyone's lives—and if this is why.

Ava sings a little song from childhood. *Bluebird, bluebird, fly through my window....* She must have needed to sing to her a little. *Mother—*

In the fluorescence the mother rose to greet the night. Visitations of the doctors making their last rounds.

I dreamt my mother smiled and smiling said, live with me next to the falling feeling—the world gives way—stay with me and we'll build a little place of shadows falling, little bird. A certain sadness marking each day, intensified the joy, when it came.

She opens like music, softly swerving now, the nurses skid against icy floors—branches falling across the path—all roads closed—past midnight—how are you feeling, Ava Klein? Rather well. And here, my parents. My mother, the heroine of this particular episode—her blood the star of this show. Icy cracks in the perfection of the fever dream—snow on snow—bellwether, she looks up, tracing her name at the child's grave, once more in her mind. Snow falls, an incredible music, the hospital doors. I feel a bit as if I am stuck inside a snow globe, all this glass—here at this very same hospital once—another floor—another circumstance—maternity wing—the opening of mouths—so long ago—I cherish that memory despite everything— even now. Long ago—or so it seems—perhaps not so long. O I feel so sleepy all of a sudden so—with a suddenness like—it's hard to say. Mother pats my head. Recalled now: a border of roses and inside that border a circle of women hand in hand.

There will be time of course for counting and uncounting. 3:33 by the digital. Something in me grows light: silvery, pliable. The wet nurse gesturing. The opening of mouths—on another floor once. Dark thorn and berry where you perch, once perched.

These internal wings beating ceaselessly against my rib cage. From the white blaze of nurses and hospital directives. As we near the darkest, longest evening of the year. Last bones cast a luminous light. The cadence of these days.

Father with his web of cello. Thank you for bringing it here to this room tonight. It might be a celebration of sorts. Last chances. On the day the earth tilts furthest away. I have not fogotten: how the music saved you once. The war in blackest bloom. Perhaps a little Fourth Symphony, Father, right now, without orchestra.

Past midnight never known such silence. . . .

Father in his overcoat. He helps Mother bend a white wing into the hollow of the sleeve—*there you go.* . . .

They wave in the dark brightness of the corridor. *Good night.*

He's left behind the blueprint of the house we summered in. As requested. Lozenges. Honey. As requested. Are you—even you, Father—just an apparition then? Having been checked into this hospital room again tonight. Having believed I had made what they had once assessed as a "full recovery."

I allow myself on rare occasions to wander in my mind from one room to another of that house. The way the porcelain tub—light streaming, the whiteness and the shape of the soap in its brass cradle. *She will die holding in one hand that dissolving oval,* Father says.

She is sure he's brought her bergamot tea, lip balm, soap, but now, looking for them . . . Are you an apparition then?

The world a muffled remote star—distant—with or without snow. Draped in darkness. *Mother.* Asked to save once more. Or am I only dreaming? Salvation. A star rising. A star rising in her nighttime eye.

I might roam every room of that childhood house tonight—allow myself to linger once more in every corner, go up the back stairs to the attic, dream under the eaves. *That beach.* . . . Back down again, through the summer kitchen and—

Behind the cellar door Swan is weeping, on this hospital corridor. Like then she believes I do not hear her. How past, future seem to collide. The dream more often than not Mother: to walk, both of us, into any room, unafraid. She laughs—a little demented laugh.

Swan, he called her. Luminous one. It was as if she carried the light of all the exterminated life in her. It was more of a burden than anything else. Why hadn't they taken her? But if this is why . . .

Left unfinished for reasons unknown.

I stare at *cygnet* merged with *enigma*.

One talks ceaselessly to her in these days before the blood exchange—most intimate of all procedures—shall I become her in part?—of course I shall. For as long as you shall live—your blood shall be her blood.

Yes, one could talk ceaselessly to her, though much of the time she did not respond, certainly not to the questions you asked—but it was enough to know that she was there.

The sadness of survival.

I watch *speechlessness* fall into *abyss*. I watch *silence* rise from *sand*. What is another word for *periphery?*

An incision in the hip. A packet of glycerin. A bag of bone fragments. The blood of the saved in this pouch—and in this one, the corrupted blood. Traversing an open field, traversing doomed and saved, sick and well, the revelers, as the century moves toward its melancholy close. They lift a glass to the year's longest night. Falling into the past and the future at the same time: We call it the present. The distant past is inchoate, is terror—solstice: the vegetation all but disappeared, the birds have fled, these darkening days—the animals are sleeping and they do not wake.

The near past is Father lifting the hollow of the coat to her.

The future, time hurtling, is a random handful of alphabet. EG, SD. 3 across: *a covering for the human foot.* 10 down: *a word for the peripheral blood.* Left behind on the hospital night table: my father's crossword puzzle.

Evening and the prayers. Morning and the prayers. *Help us to find the value in suffering.* Each night the world tipped a little bit farther away. Indifference of the day. Indifference of the night. It's OK. And there in the distance, the supreme indifference of the story. It did not care what we wanted for it. It was not concerned with us.

"Beneath a sky without memory of morning or hope of night," as Father always liked to quote. Oddly, it was a consolation to him. Like so much sand passing through us. The body transparent. The body an hourglass.

He unrolls his bundle of treasures, brought to cheer up his ailing (once more) daughter.

Laid out on the bed:
honey
lip balm

lozenges
the winter rose

Blueprint:

I'm told there was pure pandemonium on the beach. A large trench dug in the sand had collapsed. After the collapse the sand was utterly serene. No one had any idea where the child was. She was submerged suddenly, and utterly, leaving no trace. The sand simply closed up over her.

Laid out on the bed now:
sundial.
hourglass.

The moon's slow sweep past the window.

From Mrs. Trollope's
Life of Frances Wright

Edmund White

NOTE: Mrs. Trollope, the mother of the famous novelist, was born in 1779, the daughter of a Bristol clergyman. She married a barrister, Thomas Anthony Trollope, and had several children by him. For a few years their marriage was happy, but soon Mr. Trollope began to administer larger and larger doses of calomel to himself for his headaches and came to suffer from mercury poisoning. He was no longer able to work and their finances collapsed. In order to save the family fortune, Mrs. Trollope traveled to America with the Scottish reformer Frances Wright and planned to settle at Wright's utopian colony in Tennessee. The experience, a complete disaster, provided Mrs. Trollope with the material for her scathing first book, *Domestic Manners of the Americans*, the satire that infuriated Americans but launched Mrs. Trollope's long and prolific career as a writer. What follows are the opening pages of a historical novel in progress in which the author purports that this manuscript was found among Mrs. Trollope's papers at the time of her death. The brackets are Mrs. Trollope's notes to herself for later revisions.

NOW THAT HER LIFE is over I have been asked to write it. To be sure I knew her only for a few intense years, but our friendship was spent on the high seas and in the United States (which she admired and I despised). We seldom agreed on anything, and her followers, if there be any left, will doubtlessly question my right to be her biographer.

But her numerous enemies, not her few friends, are the readers I address in the hope of vindicating her honor. Nor will I pretend that this is the definitive biography she merits; I'm far too burdened with other literary products to be able to track down the minutiae or verify even the main dates of Frances Wright's painful and all too controversial passage on earth. And I'm writing here in the French countryside, far from a library or the confirming or abetting reminiscences of other civilized, educated English men and women. In fact, the road outside this cottage is dusty, the peasant farmer shouts all day in an incomprehensible *patois*, there's a particularly boisterous rooster.... Fortunately, in a few days I'll be on my way to Florence and my beloved Villino Trollope.

Fanny Wright had undeniable virtues [develop this thought by the bye].

But she had, just as undeniably, many grave faults which I, as her friend and confidante, was particularly privileged to observe. Above all, she was arrogant: overweening in her pride, haranguing in her discourse (which never descended to the mere mutuality of conversation). Despite her wealth, beauty, intelligence, and cultivation, she was singularly naive, if that conveys my conviction that she knew nothing of the world, which always demands the courtesy of compromise. Picture a blazing, ten-log fire *sans* fire screen and you'll have a notion of Fanny Wright's heat and intensity (some would say her *glare*).

She had red hair, she was tall and slender, her complexion was as pale and lucent as opals—but she was the good kind of redhead, without freckles, though she did have that distinctive scent of the true redhead when she was overexerting herself, or, as the French would say, *tout en nage.* [Delete remark on her bodily scent? In dubious taste? Though she had, in truth, the smell of a wet collie when she was sweating.]

She proposed the most ungodly ideas on concubinage and equality that pen ever traced on paper. Indeed, she preached these ideas just as freely—I'll never forget our seven-week passage together to the New World aboard the *Edward* in 1827, a voyage during which Fanny Wright spent the entire time engaged in reading *Hume's Dialogues Concerning Natural Religion* to a lowly sailor. For days she was crouched on a coil of greasy rope as he was patching his trousers. I suspect he could tolerate her atheistical importuning only because he was deaf as an earthworm. Of course, Fanny Wright never drew a breath so he had no opportunity to speak. I'd imagined we— she and I and my two daughters, Cecilia and Emily; and sixteen-year-old son, Henry, my pride and beacon, my little husband and son; as well as the great French painter Auguste Hervieu—that we might more profitably have passed long hours preparing for our new lives by discussing the geography, economics, Indian habits and customs, methods of agriculture, and all else pertaining to an existence on Fanny's Tennessee plantation of Nashoba.

But Fanny seldom climbed down to the level of the actual and when she did had the most eccentric opinions; she believed, simply because her darling Thomas Jefferson had told her so, that America's two million black slaves were insufficiently prepared for freedom, as could be seen from the sorry lot of its hundred thousand freedmen, though in fact Fanny, I now realize, had never met a freedman at that time and how did she know when they'd be ready for liberty? Given their degraded status as slaves, what would ever get them ready? In any event, my children and I later met numerous respectable and enterprising freedmen, including a most attractive Mr. Jupiter Higgins, a blacksmith in Mount Auburn on the outskirts of Cincinnati, who obtained some practical, even pretty, secondhand shoes for my Cecilia when we were truly destitute and to whom I showed my gratitude as best I could. Had it not been for Mr. Higgins and the great Auguste Hervieu, who did portraits of all the local notables in order to support us, we would have starved in the land of plenty.

But I anticipate. I am sitting here in *déshabille* on a broken straw-bottomed chair in a room so noisy with clucking and the farmer's screeching to his fowl and the ripe smell of wet straw (this house is covered with thatch) that I might as well lay an egg myself, except I'm not up to it and am waiting here until my fever subsides and one of my children sends additional funds to complete my overland trip to Tuscany.

Frances Wright . . .

Well, I should begin at the beginning. Her problems began with her parents and then their early exit from her life. She was born on September 6, 1795 [verify? I'm certain this is correct], in Dundee, a city almost as crowded and filthy as Edinburgh before the New City was constructed. I can't remember who it was who told me that in Edinburgh, in the Old City, though the streets were only five feet wide and the buildings ten stories tall, the "gentle folk" waited until ten of the evening and then, when the last watch was called, all had permission to throw their slops out the window onto the street below. To be sure, whoever was passing would be foully bespattered and the rising stench was so great one could sleep only with rose petals pressed to the nostrils. Mind you, Dundee was as dark and densely settled but the Wrights lived on a floor of an ancient house, since torn down, by the Nethergate, I believe, whence the fields and gardens were visible and where the citizens would descend and bathe directly in the cold salt waters of the Tay [or are they sweet?].

Fanny was preceded by an older brother and followed by her beloved little sister, Camilla, but when Fanny was only three her mother died, and her father passed away three short months later. Despite this early disappearance, her father, James Wright, a prosperous Dundee merchant, left his mark on the child, for James was the worst sort of free thinker. He'd paid to have Thomas Paine's *The Rights of Man* reprinted in a ha'penny edition available to the poor, and this infamous egalitarian tract, full of mischievous sophistry, could have condemned the rash man to Botany Bay had he not been so well connected. He belonged to several numismatics clubs and possessed very valuable coins; typical of his Jacobin views, he wondered why government mints employed "the silly morsels of heraldry" in designing coins rather than "emblems of industry and commerce." Doubtlessly he wanted our shillings not to present the royal profiles but to show milkmaids plying swollen teats, and our crowns to enshrine dustmen wading through ordure.

He would have been arrested for belonging to the infamous Friends of the People, a communistical phalanstery in Edinburgh, had he not ridden all alone, one misty night, out into the murky Tay, where he drowned his devilish papers. . . . Years later, Fanny Wright read through the few notes her father had jotted down that had not been destroyed that night—and naturally found surprising similarities in their turns of mind. He'd written, "The spirit of law and the tenor of the conduct of governments in order to be well adapted to the mutable and ever-varying state of human affairs ought continually to change according to existing circumstances and the temper of the age." Notice his emphasis on mutable Circumstance rather than eternal Nature and its Laws. She marveled at the "coincidence in views between father and daughter, separated by death when the first had not reached the age of twenty-nine, and when the latter was in infancy." I, too, alas, find a terrifying symmetry there, a family habit of reckless disregard for tradition and a total capitulation to Wanton *Flux!*

Fanny's older brother was engaged in the navy and died in a sea battle with the French off Madeira when he was not yet seventeen. Fanny and her sister, Camilla (Fan and Cam, as they were called), were parceled out to various relatives. They lived for a while in London with their maternal grandfather, Major General Duncan Campbell of the Royal Marines, an indolent and convivial man who expressed intense satisfaction that he never dined alone and that he knew nobody but lords and generals and when he dined with them, it was always with ten or twelve wines and a gaggle of tired, opinionated women in brocaded gowns and lopsided coiffures, for they kept very late hours indeed.

Miss Wright was repelled by these bibulous Tory relatives of hers in London, for even if her father had died when she was still only a toddler, nonetheless she clung to her *Idea* of him, and an Idea is always more tenacious than a Reality. I myself have always rejected long evenings at table with the great and good of this world in favor of gay family gatherings, amateur theatricals, meals on the wing, and ardent conviviality. I far prefer a simple farmhouse, a mulled cider, the cries of happy children, and the drolleries of artistic friends to the dull paneled majesty of the Mayfair dining room with its twelve wines. Of course, I did become an intimate of Prince Metternich in Vienna long after I went to America with Fanny Wright, but the prince was so temperate he ate nothing but brown bread and butter while his guests feasted. Apparently even Napoleon III hates lingering at table and gets everyone up after an hour in order to play charades and dance Scottish jigs.

We have the record (from her own hand, *d'ailleurs*) of but one conversation between Fanny, still a child, and her florid-faced bold beau of a kinsman, General Campbell. One day when a starving beggar woman and her dirty child were turned away from her grandfather's door, Fanny asked him, "Why are those people so poor?"

"Because they are too lazy to work," the good general replied.

"But you don't work, Grandfather."

"Certainly not," said the indignant old man. "I could not associate with the rich if I worked. It is a shame for a rich man to work."

What a pity she did not grow up, as I did, the child of a sensible if impecunious clergyman. My dear mother died when I was only five, but Nature saw fit to spare my father, who instructed me in the beauty and moral superiority of Dante and Petrarch and introduced us, his children, to a wide circle of Bristol merchants and his fellow alumni of Winchester and New College. I spent my whole girlhood dancing, and I would have gladly made dancing more general and of more frequent occurrence than it already is.

Frances Wright's sufferings as a girl were indisputable, since she was deprived of the comfort and love of her own hearth. I myself knew the sorrow of growing up without a mother to help me dress, to advise me on my corsage, to set the bon ton, to warn me against the advances of one rash youth or other.

But perhaps because all those clergymen surrounding my father as well as all those scientists (for he was also an inventor, Papa, and invented plates lined with silver to soften the scraping sound of cutlery on porcelain, a noise he could not tolerate)—because all these men had wives and I a sister, I was never deprived of female counsel and company.

Frances Wright was not a comfortable woman, the sort of wifely woman whose hand unreflectingly tucks in a shirtwaist or adjusts a collar, a woman who kisses a scraped knee or remembers the man of the house likes his postprandial brandy by the fire, the sort of huswife always in motion, stirring a soup, preparing a poultice, inviting a confidence from an unhappy bride who's still a maiden a month after her nuptials. No, she wasn't one of those women who coo with others, who coolly and wordlessly survey the damage the children have made at the nursery table and calculate the time needed to repair it, who flatter men, sustain one another, and comfort the old, whose fingers are always busy with some useful needlework and who seldom censor a thought rising to their lips.

No wonder Fanny, who had no gift for feminine companionship, irritated her young aunt, her mother's only sister, who took her and Cam in charge and moved them to the Devonshire village of Dawlish along the coast of Lyme Bay, there where the English Channel debouches into the Atlantic. This young aunt, Miss Frances Campbell, lived there in some state in a twenty-room house called "the Cottage," for she was an heiress, especially after the sudden, some say apoplectic, death of her father, General Campbell. Miss Campbell's brother, Major William Campbell, also died soon before or shortly after, I forget which. He was killed in action somewhere in India, and left vast estates in Bengal, Bihar, and Benares [I remember these three B's] to his sister and his two nieces. Ironic that Fanny Wright's future and eventual power and freedom to hand down lessons to her inferiors was based on a colonial fortune founded in the Orient. She never let herself admit that irony or brood about it.

Miss Campbell hoped to raise Fan and Cam in the strict eighteenth-century manner to which she herself had been submitted, but Fanny bitterly resented it. She said, speaking of herself in the priggish third person, that "experience taught her, in early childhood, how little was to be learned in drawing rooms, and inspired her with a disgust for frivolous reading, conversation, and occupation." Oh la! The truth of it is that this tall, red-haired girl with the low voice and solid, confronting gaze, the thin body and overly frank manner, devoid of all winning coquetries—that this paragon had no sense of humor. She knew no rhymes, played no games, sang no songs, never ogled at a man or giggled at an absurdity; she alternated between noble complacency and nobler rage; if she were to have found a young man to her liking she would have matter-of-factly taken his hand and led him off to a corner, though in saying that I do not mean to impugn her modesty. Quite the contrary. She was lamentably without any manner at all and as innocent as the wheat standing in the field.

Her young aunt in her stately Cottage deeply offended Fanny in attempting to make her conventional. She was a lady who knew how to choose a taffeta, tie a shawl, say three words in approximate French, and rattle off a rondo on the spinet, but she took no interest in the American or French Revolutions, Fanny's new hobbyhorses. She dared to instruct our Green-Eyed Athena, and Fanny never forgave her for that! Fanny, after all, was Brilliant, though she knew no Latin and less Greek, but Brilliant in the way of her great-great aunt, Lady Mary Wortley Montagu, the blue-stocking muse of Dr. Johnson and Richard Savage, the very woman who'd defended Shakespeare when his extravagances had come under attack from the overly nice Mr. Voltaire. Lucky Shakespeare to have a Montagu; fortunate America to have a Fanny!

Fanny bitterly resented her young aunt and not because she'd been flogged or starved or neglected but merely because her aunt, Miss Campbell, had dared to introduce her into ordinary, brainless, respectable, provincial society and had seen fit to instruct Fanny in the ordinary occupations of a rich young woman—pouring out tea, dancing a quadrille, paying and receiving calls, and poking needles into fabric in a frame.

Nor was Fanny's anger a girlish moment of petulance but rather a form of savage indignation, nursed over five years in silence, delivered with frigid deliberation long after the fact, and never regretted or even doubted in the aftermath. This sort of unfeeling dismissal of her closest living relative makes the blood run cold:

"I now sit down, Madame, to address to you a letter which it was as little my desire as my intention to have written, had you not yourself called me to do so.

"First let me say that I write as leisurely and coolly . . ."

Imagine the impertinence! As if Miss Campbell had been the ward and not the legal guardian, the kind, administering angel.

"I spare you, Madame, a review of the days of my childhood, days that wrung such a drop from my heart—and have left me in the sad experience of life and of the nature of my fellow creatures, which, under your tuition, I, at an early age, acquired, tokens of bitterness that I shall carry with me to the grave."

Imagine invoking the grave at age eighteen! The grim extravagance of it all, when Miss Campbell's only vice was that she backed the Tories. Already we are in the deadening presence of Fanny's leaden, opaque style, which always sounds as if translated from the

Romanian when it doesn't break down into complete incoherence.

The rest of the letter darkly hints that when Fan and Cam left the Cottage, Miss Campbell explained the departure by maligning the girls' character in letters to friends and relatives—perhaps Miss Campbell feared that she'd be held accountable for Fanny's relentless campaign against her and hoped to fend off all blame.

Obviously, Fanny was already her own creature. For if I've invoked Athena, the Warrior Goddess, I could just as readily have referred to Minerva, the deity who stepped fully formed out of her father's brow—with this difference: that Minerva embodied Wisdom, not untutored Will.

I forget the details, but Fanny had staged her first *coup* by extricating her sister and herself (and their considerable fortune) out from under her aunt's control in 1813, before they were of legal age. They went back to Scotland, this time to Glasgow, to their great-uncle, James Mylne, and his wife, Agnes. There they lived in the good doctor's crowded but lively establishment. Dr. Mylne, as don of moral philosophy, taught at Glasgow (in English, of all things, but the Scots always considered themselves frightfully progressive). Everything in this cramped, contentious household was to Fanny's taste. They dined richly, the women drank brandy along with the men after supper, and everyone discussed ideas, the women all the more volubly the less they were instructed. It was about this time that Fanny announced that she preferred to God "His Majesty with the tail and the cloven hoofs." She added, with serene impiety, "I think I have done with churches. When I can hear of one that does honor to God and good to man it shall have my presence and love." To atheism she joined treason; the Glaswegians were Whigs, hated poor George III, and wanted Parliament to rule in his stead. In her great-uncle's house everyone talked Adam Smith, Thomas Paine, Mary Wollstonecraft— ah, it makes me weary, contemplating *The Rights of Man* and even *The Rights of Woman!*

Fanny, to be sure, thought she was in sole possession of the truth. She decided she was an Epicurean. I'm not too clear what that means but I gather what she had in mind was an imperviousness to Opinion and an indifference to Reputation. She published a little book several years later in London (in 1822, I believe) at her own expense. She wanted to call it *Epicurus* but was obliged to rename it (for fear of scandal and censorship) *A Few Days in Athens; Being the Translation of a Greek Manuscript Discovered in Herculaneum.* Miss Wright resorted to this innocent little fiction in order to put forth her own epicureanism, which was not the doctrine of licentiousness one might imagine at first blush from reading the title but instead a rather insipid brand of tranquillity; as she put it, "Happy life is like neither to a roaring torrent nor a stagnant pond, but to a placid and crystal stream, that flows gently and silently along."

Poor Fanny, whose life pressed forward like a broad, cold lake that inches soundlessly toward a suspiciously close horizon and then, without warning, plunges in a great foaming cascade hundreds of feet down onto punishing rocks.

I suppose few people alive today can think their way back into that distant period when Utopian schemes flourished, naive principles were fervently proposed, and everything seemed possible and perfectible. The American Revolution—or the Tax Dodgers' Rebellion, as I prefer to call it—was still recent, and the French Revolution all the closer in time, and Jacobins of Fanny Wright's ilk ignored the bloody excesses and wanted nothing save the gains in rhetoric, for that was the time of talk and more talk. Fanny was only a child, she hated her Tory aunt and worshipped the Glasgow Whigs she was living amongst. She'd begun to dress in simple muslin that she draped around her slender, statuesque body as if she were an Athenian—or Athena. And most becoming it was, to be sure. Her hair, which she cut short, gleamed in red curls she pressed forward onto her snowy brow and along her pure nape, which since the Terror inevitably appears to be the tenderest part of any noble body.

Consecrated monarchs had been rudely shaken after centuries of dozing on their thrones, and philosophical youngsters—privileged, for the most part, and angry at their parents—were strolling about in togas preaching reform and radicalism. To be sure, in England and its former colonies no great harm had yet come of these experiments, mostly verbal; only later would we all discover the bloody consequences of so much rash optimism. I myself was radical enough back then before I had made my great Voyage. Like so many others I departed for America a Progressive and came back a Conservative.

Dirt Roads
Robert Kelly

Who's heart?
We have to know
the littlest things.

1.

every rock
is where once was

some pain
that once said me

2.

stall for time's
vocabulary

make a video
of common light

play it in the hollow

scooped out of night
with your wanting

the plunge of one into

3.

Aporias.

Somebody's word

come to the end
again and again

no end to the end
no before to before

every footstep
the final
every breath the last

every road a wall

4.

or reaching out in the dark
find the hollow
place below your throat

a jewel might rest there
amber amethyst
a god

5.

sparrows soar
out from underneath her skirts
rebel watchfires
flicker prairie

inside the fusebox serpent coiled

sometimes nostalgia
for an old country
never seen
a home you never had

travel the way a steeple stands

6.

geologist of the merest argument
you can't win with me
I stand under your last word
staring straight up at the moon it means

Robert Kelly

7.

Someone spoke
of the flight of cranes

we live of course
by other people

their deaths their agonies

8.

who gives a breath
gives a sign

we are all too drunk
to fail to understand

9.

give waiting to music
the way you'd give
water to horses

10.

Going to sleep
is like reading a Chinese dictionary

everything is new in your hands

we sleep at night
because the birds stop talking then

our teachers
and all the rest of life
must answer them

and waking up
the book falls out of your hands

everything has meaning
and nothing makes sense.

11.

who is this light on the carpet
who wrote this silence

12.

In our century the destiny of the individual
presents itself under the symbolism of the window
peered into at night from outside, the garish spectacle
of our private lives thrown on the walls of the mind

or gazed out of in silent mornings
a householder from the dubious security of her house
stares blankly at the enterprise of otherness
we vaguely call The World.

The night vision and the day version
are psychoanalysis and politics,
the Voyeur and the Commissar.
In both cases the window signifies

Other people are strange and probably don't love me,
are dangerous, have things I don't have, and are far.
So when we say A Person
we mean A window of one's own.

13.

Dear window
who knows
where I stand

who knows
where the light comes from
that makes me see

that makes me me?

14.

Dear Color
everything lives in you.

Kandinsky and Albers
do business here with us,
as us, the rest
is just the checks we write
drawing on the everlasting Red.

Dear Color
let me sleep and wake with you,
and dine in your arms,

Color does all our thinking for us,
Color answers all questions
With its single own,
Color asks us in all its voices
                    Are you me yet?

How can there be a book
colored like a bruise
like the silk she wore
in a dream only I had I thought

but you had too
whose hands stained this paper
long before the words got here
to stain the stains.

How can there be a color
nearer to me than my skin

or her skin even,
that never-ceasing violin?

15.

Unclothe the other
from the veils of time
the sleazy double-knits of history

I am the elder
nuder than Susannah
no matter all my tallises

you see my naked time

16.

Belshazzar's feast in every glass
interpret the scary words
as kanji of light
caught in our eyelashes
we stare at the sun and read

The words the light tells me
I have told

17.

the mind fumbles with their names
like a drunk with his girlfriend's bra
trying to get each memory open
to feel the actual flesh of who they are

18.

I'm an air sign,
air signs don't prepare.
Instead they despair.
Generally things work out
a little better than they feared.

This modus operandi
comes in handy
when you wait for transportation
in some calamity,

or walking to the podium
with not an idea in my head—
that's the best way, see what comes up
when my back is to the wall

that's the part of life that interests me:
to see what I'll say in such extremity.

19.

it helps me not to take too seriously
what is so mysteriously
obvious in daily use,
a fuck-up with sixty volumes of excuse.

20.

ragamuffin clouds
begging some
baksheesh from the sun

21.

five swans flying
south in a line
low over river

past steel oil tanks
on the Kingston shore
ice floes, a sheet

of ice midstream
moving with the birds
I am rigid with cold

and something more
the warm thing too
that sends the swans

22.

and who told you
to be me

who let the pronouns
breed in their blessed cages of our flesh

and spawn such monstrosities of love

23.

bundle of strings
we hold together
and hold one another
to this strange
dream we call a fact

24.

the similitudes of Lord Jesus
may be likened to Dew
deposited on a desert rose.
Or a cluster of blue grapes
proffered to a dusty traveler.
A chest full of old books.

We have marched into the sky
to find our roof, tectum,
the head of our house

to weave from light
our text. All we are
is answers to a lost question.

25.

for language cannot swim
language is the ocean

waves move only up and down
the movement we call meaning
stirs along the swell

never gets there never gets lost

26.

The parachute.
Ménage à un,
this love affair
falls down the air.

Everyone
is going to die
except I.
I was never born

is nowhere
to be found
just hangs around.
Were you ever

a brick wall
mermaid library
postcard of the full moon
sent home

as if you'd been there
and there is some here
to which the mail
can come,

this is winter
that Irish music

and ice is a diamond
of impediment

a Roman word that means valises
the airline loses
full of underwear and socks and manuscripts
purporting to be by me.

27.

makes no sense to keep a diary
since all I am is telling

and no seabird does
mournful creature Whitman celebrates
some lonesome gannet falling through a porphyry
cloud like a fleshy smile, a lonely bird
whose mate made not this rendezvous alas
o God the solemn absences of space
with winter crashing on the empty shore

28.

and churches think they need an organ—
just open the fucking window and the wind will
weep all the Jesuses you'll need
truth upon truth till the year is green again

never, and Armand doesn't die, and Mary didn't,
or Paul, Charles, Robert, Marcia, April,
Joel, Louis, Jack, Steve, Amy, Allen, Ruth,
or my root Lama or my father or my mother

or anybody's anybody, and in one
of Fomenko's columns of brainless statistics
thank God Adam too is still alive, all the numbers
happen all at once, the organ plays,

nobody dies, "nothing happens," we call it music,
it is time rushing past the shabby porches of our ears

and I am just a terrible mistake.

29.

You never have a clue to who you are
until you feel your back against the wall
and there is nowhere to go but who you are.

30.

the dome and its minarets float above the sea

everything is a reflection of their desires
who persuaded it to be

only the skin knows everything.

Our Delius
Paul West

I.

WATCH HOW THE PHOTONS BLUR the two of them, almost as if he was blind already and, out of the body, saw them standing reluctantly on view, he in drainpipe pants and partly buttoned frockcoat, letting his cigarette droop right there in the doorway to the paradise garden, eyes aimed downward, big brow over (depending on that shattered light) an almost simian face. Nattily dainty, he looks lost among those motes, in very much the arranged posture of one who cannot see: a painter's model, perhaps. One step behind he stands, as if Stroheim had positioned him thus. Our Delius.

Did he compose enough? Just about. Did he write enough letters, to Bartók and Kodály, say? Almost. Did he write enough to Elgar? Nowhere near; they ran into each other too late, although having admired each other from a distance for a long time. I am overcome, in these early days of my enterprise, by the usual trite regrets. He did not have the right life, as a colleague of his used to say; yet it would be hard to devise for him, granted his genes and fads and his bluff, almost decadent temper, a life different from the one I am about to gather my lamenting wits to tell. Were I better prepared, I would not begin, but I do so only because, in this elegiac fidget, I need something relevant to do, with me merely incidental. I am his echo.

Better that I say it first before some assiduous reader tax me with self-importance, I, Campion Apsley, the companion who grew into an accompanist over the lifetime of the composer herein limned. I say accompanist only in jest, not being of course any such thing or person, not his accompanist on a musical instrument (that chore left for others), but the person who increasingly sat by him as his condition evolved, soaking up his table talk and sometimes writing it down. Often enough I was in the position of someone, a house owner say, confronted by one of those springtime irruptions of moth-flies: tiny black bumbling creatures that pour from beneath, behind, a baseboard and swarm across a bathroom floor. Day after day. You mop them up and wait for more. Just so: I mopped up what he offered and awaited his pleasure, growing, if I may say so myself, all the way from overseer and overhearer into amanuensis, guide, philosopher, and friend to him who, having soared so high, found himself cast down among the infidels; I scurrying about to gather the least crumb, morsel, with which to amplify my account of a life not so much wasted, oh no, as overspent, raising a cautionary finger against anyone who suspected me of providing only what the French call an *amuse-bouche*, that tickles the mouth and distracts it while it is waiting for something solid to bite on. No, even my interstices have significance of some kind because *he* furnished the wherewithal, and whatever he did, granted my brief, could never be trivial, not if you assumed from the first, as I did, his true eventual majesty.

Better to get it off my chest now that I sometimes was too humorous for him, who was of a more somber disposition, especially with illness. If anyone, in the modest crescendo of increasing friendship, or intensifying acquaintance, waxed the more facetious, it was always I, younger than he and proportionately sillier, my excuse being that I had vowed to pledge my life to his, asking little beyond a pittance and a chance to bask in his shadow or his radiance. It was mostly radiance until, well, let that keep. Let it be said that I tried to cheer him up a little, extending that principle so far as to imagine I was at his side even when I was not—a kind of imaginary apprentice, forever piecing together into a life the little he told me afterward about, say, letting oranges rot or ending all compositions with a quietus appropriate to nature declining, sinking into ooze or magma, slime and slop, yet always with a cheerful benison incorporated into the cadences so you knew he was happily surrendering. You will see that I, Campion, grew up while tending (attending) him, not with any hope of being like him, but merely in hopes of being a better listener, a more acute sympathizer, which is perhaps what in our more benign moments we would all like to be. He usually heard me out and nodded while I put pen to paper, sometimes changing a word even as I wrote. He spoke as smoothly as he composed, never tense or strict.

Already I discern two "betters" dogging me at the beginning of the previous two paragraphs. It would be only too easy to begin paragraphs thus, ignoring all he told me about self-consciousness and letting things flow. I was never the composer, never nature's archangel as I once called him. It was only yesterday that we disinterred his body from its French grave and reburied it in Limpsfield churchyard to the tunes of "On Hearing the First Cuckoo in Spring" and "Summer Night on the River": beneath a tree, the grave illumined by hurricane lamps and lined with laurel. What a day on which to begin recall, a year after he died with the taste of triumph poignant on his lips. 1935, when I told myself I was wrong to think I remembered him so well because I had not recovered from his death; it was wiser to think I remembered his life so well because his death had little to do with it. I mean, in no other case had a man's music flowed out into nature and become *more of it*, so much so that it sometimes did not seem even to leave him behind—he went with it out into the mellow plenitude and his body, carcass, whatever, stayed deployed like a cloud rack neither here nor there but diffused, an account given back, a form of imitation without a name, the thing rendered so much as itself that it merely drifted back into what it had come from, ravishingly akin. You will see now why I devoted so large a part of my life to his gift. His work was never *about* something, it *was* it.

The bizarre thing is that, if I were to attempt one of those lightning bolts of portraiture (what sort of man was he?), I would disregard, for the moment, his massive creative energy and his lyrical, ecstatic output, as well as his passion for high altitudes and orange groves, steamy rivers and negro spirituals (his distaste for Beethoven quartets too!), and say outright he was a man of the world, as I once saw during the night at Grez, when, with Jelka bleeding all over their primitive bathroom (taken short in the female way), he fumbled in, scooped up all that miscellaneous mess of towels, kerchiefs, pads, and rags and shoved them into a paper bag he then disposed of at speed, the while reassuring her in the depths of slumber that all was well and natural and that, above her inaudibly, there were nightingales and canaries saluting while envying her for, what did he call it that night, such an estimable bouquet of involuntary nature! He was like that, in tune with some mighty being we could all sense, but in the most intimate, calibrating way. How many times he reassured her in this way I do not recall, but he would often accomplish his feat while murmuring "*sanies, sanies,*" which word he associated with tipped-out blood, to him a condign part of the music he worked in. It was all music to him, even when gross and maybe even foul to others. No shirker he, not squeamish at all.

So he was a man, as we say, of the world, paddling his hands in it, extending to nature the same kind of obvious indulgence a mother extends to her baby. I think *sanies* meant to him more than it did to

251

anyone else; it must have been a kind of code, an electron brew all his own, so that, you might say, he saw no barrier between what he called *sanies* and the meconium of a newborn child. He was into all that, oh yes, but in the tenderest way, except that he found it hard to keep his hands to himself with women around, on ocean liner or at village dance. He got around, at some expense to his marriage, and later, to his well-being. He claimed to be of Dutch lineage, but some said he was German, although his manners and speech were those of a Yorkshireman "born and bred," as it's said. Myself, after admitting that, I would say he was a Parisian Floridian or a Floridian Frenchman: something similar, what you might call a permanent misfit, as far from someone such as the incessantly obliging Spohr, say, as could be. When he was much younger, they called him Fritz, I know not why, but this could have been an allusion to his mythical German blood. It was not American, of course, no reference to anyone's or anything's being on the fritz. Life in his zone was international, but not that colloquial, though had he lived longer, being interviewed to death, he might have succumbed to slangy usages.

II.

The boy came from prosperous wool merchants and, destined for business, was not expected to make music, as he did repeatedly, both piano and violin, without the faintest hint of instruction. His father deserves some credit, I suppose, for persisting with commercial impetus for so long in the face of his son's musical inclinations. Thus the son did not escape a severe business training, actually being sent to Germany to make a firsthand study of the wool business. Alas for his commercial career, while there he witnessed a performance of Wagner's *Die Meistersinger,* an instructive epiphany that took him beyond bales and bulk into a sublime never-never land. This performance haunted him ever after, even when he entered upon his father's business, confined to a desk while golden loops of something deliciously impossible formed in his mind. He soon formed the habit of dreaming up exotic places, not Germany, of course, or even England, but the Caribbean and Florida, where it was warm, and primitive peoples took life easy in a climate of languor and sultry peace. Begging his father to let him go see, even if only to sample the forbidden fruits of that exotic peninsula, he at last prevailed, though not without having to make all kinds of false promises. At this point, his father went from one extreme to the other, purchasing an orange plantation in Solano, Florida, so as to provide both some kind of commercial training and enable the precocious lad to fulfill his yearning for things subtropical. It is amusing to watch the father, far from yielding without a fight, observing the gradations that presumably lead from the wool trade to fruit in crates rather than wool in bales, and thence through subtle shifts to the lotus-eating life of an aspirant musician, conducted amid a community of primitive, unschooled singers, every bit as unlettered as himself. All the son had to do was look after the plantation, with the aid of account books, work schedules, and some kind of inspired pragmatism.

At home in the plantation on the Saint Johns River, to him as virgin and unexplored as Siberia or Alaska, the composer gave way to his unruly self, perhaps even so early freeing the epicurean side that led him ever after into the finest registers of swooning and languishing, a mode he found as natural as breath. Truth told, he went on a binge beginning in 1884, of reading and pondering, canoeing with his newfound and intensely relished black friends so different from the sallow, uncouth Bradfordians and the sullen, gruff Germans among whom his father had planked him, either to do harder and harder sums or to learn new ways of trading. Dances and choruses occupied his time. His oranges rotted in or out of sight, and he developed the epic image of himself as the sole white on an alligator hunt, an outsider with deep pockets, sentenced to a lustrous jail.

For the first time in his life he was happy, trapped in that timeless continuum of heat and repose, doing what he wanted only when he wanted to, which of course included work on the violin he had brought with him from Bradford. Yet, enveloped in his wild and remote world, he felt other cravings and was soon commuting to Jacksonville (a three-day trek) in search of a piano, there running into Thomas F. Ward, an organist from Brooklyn. There were few pianos to be had, even for a landed immigrant of a plutocrat, but there was musical talk aplenty. There he was, dabbling on the keys with his accustomed sweet fervor and there was Ward offering to guide him in this and that, off the cuff, as if it were perfectly normal for a Brooklyn organist to find a teachable booby in a Jacksonville music shop. Captivated by the youth's bizarre and sensuous chords, Ward interrupted the spell and, waving in half-dismissory fashion at the several pianos grouped in the shiny salon of the store, rattled off a list of his cherished composers, hard to ignore if you had been waiting all your life for just such a recital. They were friends before they met, of course; the composer had met his first antifather, with whom to take allusive dinner and thenceforth elaborate, compelling lessons. Seeming to have no urgent business to attend to, Ward went off to Solano, just a little prevailed upon, and stayed there six months.

III.

Have I said enough in this fairly straitlaced manner, benignly suppressing (as I should) the entire terminal moraine of hindsight, in which the man's genius turns like Dick Whittington to haunt the youth's onset? Safer, I surmise, to delineate the nascent gift rather than insist on its futurity; what he was going to be is what he is going to be, so it is important to show him dabbling, pounding, fiddling about, jockeying for position in the musical world of bass-baritone indigenes. Here was a man inspired by his presence among those wholly unlike him, except for their bond in music; hardly surprising, then, if all his motions in life—chewing a slice of cake, laying his head on its pillow at night, rinsing his face with water in which tadpoles swam—became rhythmic. He knew what was coming, and translated all of life into almost sickly strident phrases on the piano, at once delighting Ward and making him shiver. Thank Bach I am not writing these pages for posterity, for publication. They will remain with me forever, a talisman, I suppose, so I will not be hounding or aligning them. They will fall from the tree only to delight me in an old age, *d.v.*, in which I can no longer recall everything that went on in his life, which I heard about, had him recall, or joined with him in extracting from a dream. Such my one and only literary foray, about the one and only giant I ever met. *But what giants?* it says somewhere in *Don Quixote*, as if there were no giants anywhere: "What giants?" I know of one, though hardly doing him justice, not even the justice bestowed by Thomas Ward as our prodigy pounded the keys or caressed them with a creeping lilt. "What are you doing?" asked Henry Cowell when he caught Carl Ruggles elbowing the keys, only to be told, "Giving them the test of time." The fragments of a musical education botched will get in the way sometimes, as you see, if you exist. It is really myself reminding myself to salute the analogy before it falls by the wayside, as so many hitherto apposite analogies do, and you recognize that you are only a semiliterary man doing his best not to squander his memory with some such flummery as "last look at a too brave man" or "fades, alas, like our youth too soon." After all, I am only a narrator; indeed, I am hardly that, but only the interceptor of some golden code vouchsafed me by a passing starling. What I am being so bold to say is not polemical but chemical. There. That's the kind of thing I should be coming up with all the time, just like Delius; in the piano stores of Jacksonville, impressing the hades out of his tutor-to-be, rapture's catalyst on leave from Brooklyn. Only the dead know Brooklyn, it is said, and only the rotten at heart know the music of true decadence. If only I can keep from overloading things, I may yet get it out of my own system into, well, wherever.

Quite without malice, but stirred into some recoup of European idiom, he called me Caca, thus doubling my initials, intending no harm by it, and no vile innuendo either, but determined to have me thus: CA-CA. How would you like *that,* like dumping porridge into your pants each time he addressed you. However, I never called *him* giant, of course, though tempted; I was often inclined to sir him or to address him by surname, but never a Caca or a Pipi either. You have to swallow a peck of muck sooner or later once you recognize your exact station in life, and how much you will endure from whom. I did attempt some shy "Fredericks" from time to time, but only noticed him ducking away from them, as if an antelope had shied away from being called a zebra, or a monarch butterfly had dived away from being called a slug. That was not the way to do it. Who was it, addressing T. E. Lawrence, whose number was 231556, asked, "May I call you 231?" It must have been Noël Coward, but I may have got the number wrong. The more famous our composer became, the less of a name he had, until only his surname remained: the very thing required, as if he were now Sibelius, say, or Bartók. When that transition happens and a man becomes a commodity, his personality somewhat congeals and he has to be dealt with at a distance. That was how Bartók, Kodály, and Elgar addressed him, like bales of wool at last come to rest.

IV.

Almost my only way of doing this is not to try to write it at all, but to wait and see it come unbidden, some kind of overflow, his extraordinary talent overpowering me and making me tell the truth. In that way, I need never try to be engaging; the charm, his or mine, will come across and win you over. I see everything afloat. There is the year, 1935, he died in. There is this year, 1936. There are the next few years, in which Europe seems likely to erupt in war. There are, surely, the ongoing further years of this portraiture, '37, '38, and so on, in which all the unknowns in the world will float in parallel with other unknowns. The adventures of this manuscript will bounce off the adventures of the man himself as he advances from his time in Solano. And then there are the later years, *d.v.*, in which I might not even then have finished my chore, the forties and fifties, through which my ambition may tour like a troop of butterflies, fitful and spasmodic, indicating my subject while depicting it scattered. In a sense, I dread what is to come, to tell, knowing all that I know, and knowing more as time fans out going by. It is not a story I desire to tell in full, but it is a story that will tell itself, once dragged out of the closet, unsnippable as a cobweb. Was anyone closer to him than I? He has yet to be heard from if so, no doubt inditing in worthy copperplate in some creaky, academic library his portion of the truth he oversaw or overheard. Such is not my affair, but an attempt to delineate us in our interplay, not him wholly, nor myself, but the pair of us meshing. I sometimes think of my chore as an ancient folkway, with me chained to it as to a tome in some ancient college, unable to get away yet far enough from the cadaver of my friend to achieve distance upon him.

He might have stayed forever in Florida, taking infinite lessons from Ward, whose instruction he said was by far the best, perhaps hoping at seventy to create a masterpiece, or rather the masterpiece of a lifetime, an Orange Symphony, say, or *The Messiah of Jacksonville*, a work utterly purged of rigmarole and forged with discreet aplomb: too perfect to be praised, as he would sometimes say after a particularly splendid sunrise when the supposedly traditional hues had failed to show and, instead, a pewtery salmon had taken over, ramming into the sky opposite a pother of ocher cloud that seemed not to be cloud at all, but a divine steam.

Schooled by him in identifying such shifts, I remain his colorist, wishing him weather in the grave, for he was nothing if not atmospheric. I am not claiming that his music came to him dictated by some force, though it would not be too difficult to do, but that he always lolled in the same brew of elements, not so much designing works and sections and parts as permitting certain movements of his flux to greet the outside world, in this perhaps owing more to Scriabin and Suk than to others. Had he become familiar with American composers, he might have become more of an Apollo, but he was more like his friend Bartók, gathering up folk song, taking a lead from his black friends and their spirituals, so that much of his work seemed, to this auditor anyway, a kind of celestial humming, what is sometimes termed melismatic as being in no language, but a sort of glottal pantomime. He might have claimed to have invented such stuff, but he was too modest for that, and he believed, anyway, that all creativity began with nature, created by that forceful entity and chopped up by men. He reveled in free form, joining fantasias to the natural topography that sponsored them. An earth-ecstatic? I have heard that phrase somewhere, but think it doesn't quite fit him as much as another: élan vital, intellectual detritus of Monsieur Bergson, once fashionable to read and succumb to. No, there is no simple, smartypants phrase for what simultaneously ailed and advantaged him; it remains one of the mysteries of our being here at all; but to have set apart, from all the other noise in the universe, his own sweet, poignant microcosm, that was as a lovely a feat as I have ever known. He remains to be explored and intuited as best I can, maybe for my own sake; perhaps I need to have my memories fed back to me, jammed as I might be in the old contraption called the Iron Maiden, a mannequin with internal spikes to keep you wincing.

V.

In such an enterprise as this, one might be trapped and convicted for almost anything, not merely errors of fact, common to all humankind, but errors of imagination too. Times were when I thought his image preceded him, moving forward with silky rapidity, almost like the blindness-to-be afflicting Saul on the road to Tarsus, so that he saw the ailment as a shimmering lattice on the very point of terrible descent. This composer preceded himself, much as, I always surmised, he knew beforehand, before actually putting it down, the phrase to come in a moment's time. He leaned forward and I leaned after him, sometimes anyway, and I agree that does not make a very firm basis for matter-of-fact report—just to say you *thought* he did such and such. And the more you know someone, the better you can sense these slopings-forward into the realm of destined finitude.

I write to him.

I arrive.

I introduce myself, someone between leper and acolyte, eager to be sucked in, but, in being made over in his image, also being elevated into a higher, nobler version of myself.

"Oh," he murmured, ever prescient, "in being made over you are to be reborn. I think we can arrange something like that. Proteus meets Procrustes. Now, which is which?"

It was clear that I was never to forget the instruction he had received from Thomas Ward, who had shaped him forever without, I thought, changing his basic impulses. I would never forget my opening image of him as the Yorkshire *ingénu* rippling his fingers across the keys of pianos in far-off Florida, elegant orphan of inspiration who, in the August of 1885, took a riverboat up the Saint Johns River to Jacksonville and opened his career by singing in the choir of a synagogue. With cordial letters of admiration, he next found his way to Danville, Virginia, almost like some young prince reclaiming his inheritance, and became music teacher at the Old Roanoke Female School, a captivating but somewhat stern dandy, impressing old Mrs. Belle McGhee Phifer as a charmer: "He charmed all of us," she gushed, "this modest young Englishman with such nice manners. My husband was quickly convinced of his virtuosity at the piano, especially the chromatic quality of his extemporizations which seemed to violate the known rules of harmony. I remember my husband used to sit entranced as the young man played and often remarked *That man has music in his mind, but when he sets it down it is almost impossible to play it.*" Thus Mrs. McGhee Phifer in 1942, shortly before her death, the young man in question having beaten her to it by a dozen years, all his music said, all his theories spelled out.

His playing of the Mendelssohn Concerto was what seduced them most. He became a local notable, an alien graft, receiving the aspirant daughters of local well-to-do planters for instruction, though not in his own style ever. After a year of this, he had saved enough to take leave of them, dropping behind him shreds of minor praise to keep the daughters socially viable, and head for Leipzig, much commended to him by Thomas Ward, where the Conservatory beckoned. Thus extolled by a rabbi and a Brooklyn organist, who seemed to have lost all touch with his native heath, he offered himself for grooming in the summer of 1886, studying with Jadassohn, Reinicke, and Sitt, haunting the Conservatory concerts and trekking off to Norway during vacations, as if dogging the footsteps of Edvard Grieg, who spent the winter of 1887 in Leipzig, forming a good impression of the young composer-pianist, who by now had amassed some sketches into a suite he named *Florida,* huge on atmosphere in a Norwegian way.

"Something reclaimed," he said, "and made visionary."

To which Grieg is supposed to have answered, "Something visionary reclaimed. The vision goes with you, wherever, as it should, and you tag it to this and that. Blood-idyll, I call it." Some of us, denied the opportunity to hear *Solano* until much later, and so not as fortunate as Grieg, or as influential, have envied the man his abandoned, sumptuous quality, his being able to ferret out from people in all sorts of conditions, not all lounging in riverboats crooning spirituals, the ancient pastoral yearning that makes just about any human crave a window, a view of grassland or lawn, a waterfall pounding or a rainbow self-flung through the upper ice. He had that. He divined that in people, later on in places, and imposed it on his work. Had some of us not occupied ourselves with his every whim, we might have achieved something similar, spurning music of a dustier, more diagrammatic kind, but we never got around to it, and never would, becoming more and more immersed in his imperious gorgeousness. You could see, even in such early work as that *Florida* suite, an inclination to desert the world and soldier on in visionary privacy, even after having eyed the world and treasured it. He was going to go inward, even after what some would think the worldly overtures of rabbis, Mrs. McGhee Phifer, and the daughters of the well-to-do, not to mention the lordly, sagacious Thomas Ward and the great Grieg. Going so far inward might well cripple or mute him, but go there he would as other creative people have, inwardly fabricating what they hoped was a microcosm of the real, to which I would say something almost cantankerous: Since the macrocosm includes all microcosms or it is not complete, the macrocosm is never enough, and therefore the desire to minify it will always fail. What will emerge will be a pseudomicrocosm only because, even as you minify, or seek to, other micros are being made of just as incomplete macros. It is the sort of hectic rambling I get into when trying to make sense of a genius's plunges, knowing the thing is wrong from the start and therefore predicated on something quite different—say a lyrical surge of the imagination, based no doubt on what has been observed (since nothing is underived; try it). I mean the active provocation may have long ago been forgotten, freeing the imagination to deploy itself, but not really: Music derives from music, does it not, although I am at something of a loss to figure out from what came the first thumping of a tom-tom in a jungle somewhere. That, I confess, makes me pause because it looks as if, from the very first, it might have been underived, a mere freak of fidgety hands and the coincidental presence of a hollow tree.

You see the bind I am sometimes in, especially when brooding on such matters in the presence of his memory and the constant imprint of his music (in concerts only in those days). Surely, truly, there had been nothing like him, not even in the way that in Vaughan or Herbert there had been a pre-Wordsworth.

VI.

It is often said you can get the boy out of Westphalia, but not Westphalia out of the boy. One wonders what Westphalians were doing in Bradford, Yorkshire, to begin with. It could hardly have been for the cricket, a game that would have drawn in thousands if only they had been able to stomach working in wool. He himself clung to the old idea that they were Dutch, but the fourth of twelve children is apt to become blurred from the sheer noise of breeding. What he is likely to have remembered without pause is that his father was a typical Prussian domestic tyrant, with, hidden away in or on his being, like a tick on a cuckoo, a certain liking for music. Which could have been worse for him? The father's ironclad pragmatism or the only slightly less severe policy of the mother, a woman so uninterested even in music that lifelong she never heard a note of her son's. The astounding thing is that, from time to time, amid that harvest of children, genuine artists came to visit the home and play there: Joachim and Piatti, distilling beauty among the crags and of course infecting the boy, already bemused by traveling circuses, bareback riders, and trapeze artists in particular, not to mention more obvious addictions such as walking and riding, to which, in green on white like a fretwork pattern in slow motion, he added the grim, intense local sport of cricket, played up there with a curmudgeonly relentlessness deriving from the Wars of the Roses centuries ago, commemorated in the so-called Roses game played annually between Yorkshire and Lancashire. Bat on ball appealed more to the young composer than carryover from ancient days of feuding, and he rejoiced in the comparative silence amid which the game at whatever level was played.

Bradford Grammar School brought him out and the International College at Isleworth near London indoctrinated him with the rudiments of business life over three years of unnecessary tedium, after which, as he recalled with tender affection, he was sent to Chemnitz in Saxony, not that far from Leipzig and Dresden. He had gone through the motions of going home, at least if he thought of home as Germany rather than Holland. I had always thought of him as well prepared for life as a cosmopolitan, forever sprinkling his table talk with vignettes not only of Florida, New Zealand (these culled from his elder brother, sent there to investigate sheep farming), but also, naturally, of Chemnitz and Norway, but also of Sweden, Saint-Étienne (a wool town), and Monte Carlo, where he gambled his all on the roulette tables and won, thus managing to finance a few weeks on the Riviera: an orgy of recitals and concerts and violin lessons. Having been to Norway, he developed an interest in Ibsen's plays, actually following them in the original language. His memories, I noticed, had this scenic, commercial flavor, as of places where to send the functioning dead except (in his case) the dead were refusing to cooperate, but mingled with more chromatic recollections of oatmeal and thick molasses, huge enveloping fogs made of vapor from the Pennines, rough-spoken provincials to whom London was the devil's playground, weird smoky brands of toffee, especially the kind cooked in a shallow pan and smashed with a small hammer, housewives whitening their front doorsteps with what they called a donkey-stone, rumbling big-bellied men stinking of beer amid that other stink of hops brewed in the neighborhood. Cold wind, thick rain, Yorkshire lasses with wind-stung pink cheeks, all fair-haired with a Scandinavian look, half-inviting him with what he came to think a nurse's demeanor. More than anything there was the sound of his own speech, far from the mincing elocution of the top public (i.e., private) schools and the famous universities. He spoke broad Yorkshire and kept to the idiom of that huge, bluff land, faintly aware that half the words he uttered came from the Norsemen. So, although he may well have been chatting about the way disdain was based on refined taste, he spoke of it in the idiom of the Yorkshire farmer, patronized and ridiculed in the South, where the regional speech was just as coarse. Larded in among his gab, his French and Norwegian allusions made for an odd mix, revealing him as a man of half the world, but an industrial peasant as well.

A certain fondness for the sounds of local speech, akin perhaps to the comfort squirrels and birds felt on hearing it although without understanding, enabled him to murmur to himself in his cups a few treasured local expressions whose uncouth abruptness made him smile and brought to mind the prows of Viking ships, the flaxen beards of the invaders, the uncraven voices of their beckonings and exclamations. *Eigh-up* was a call to attention, bringing the whole of Yorkshire up short. *Don't thee thou me, thou tharrer* was an instruction not to use intimate forms of speech, or else. And *redlar*, mispronouncing regular, had to do with normality and being all right. These rank phonemes tied him to the soil up there, never mind how far off he was in France or Florida, sounds incomprehensible to others, but just as good as any other noises and almost the glottal equivalent of a piece of his he called *The Procession of Protracted Death*. Getting used to his ramblings and his introverted barks, you ended up endorsing Sir Thomas Beecham's pithy cameo of his speech as "a polyglot mish-mash." His speech through music, however, was a totally different matter, ethereally languageless, culled from nowhere and nobody unless the Farn Islands and the Hebrides (and, if so, how and when?). He could never abide the sounds of day and therefore worked at night, smoking and drinking, founding melody on an iceberg of approximate silence marred by the occasional barking of a dog. Had he worn earplugs, his music might have been quite different. It is interesting to notice how full his music is of sounds overheard, the faint crepitations of eager nature coming to the boil, stuff caught on the wing, the scuffle among dead leaves, the bawling of crows. No, I go beyond my brief, I am no doubt thinking of a much later composer. I mean he arrives at strictly musical replicas of such overhearings, but musical they are and not equivalent.

I wonder, was Scandinavian culture, to which he always turned, the true ghost of his music? It is often suggested that no composer is more English, but I can think of half a dozen much more obvious choices—Bridge, Howells, Butterworth, Gurney, Stanford, Perry, et cetera (I counting Welshmen as well)—whereas this fellow was as much Greek as French, as much Norwegian as German. In one sense he is more international than any of them, which was why I came to call him Pan, though not to his face until quite late on. Or was he the true hymnodist of Brooklyn, New York? Had Thomas F. Ward schooled him in an alien idiom that reciprocated the tunes of Florida plantation workers? It is worth noting his ability to merge into the background, like ink into blotting paper. When his tyrannical father decided to hale him out of Florida, he had to track him through a private inquiry agent.

VII.

On Ilkley Moor without a hat, irrelevantly runs an old Yorkshire song, all kinds of terrible things can happen to you. You become embroiled in the digestive processes of nature until, in the end, worms take you. This happens to be the Yorkshire version of Shakespeare's demonstration in *Hamlet* of how a king may go a-progress through the guts of a beggar. In his early days, Fritz, as he liked to be known then (sending off small songs to little magazines such as the *Dome*), knew something of this morbid, sordid side of the Yorkshire character, then let it slide away from him, only to find it returning in later years under the impulsion of disease. It may be said that he never lost it, but merely attuned to its occasional transit underground. It was the other side of Yorkshire hardheadedness: an assent to fertility, a submission to overpowering rot. I think such an assent appears often in his music; he recognizes the malady in human beings, their susceptibility to decay and the putrid, not that this happens to be morbid through and through, but more a Bachian acceptance that life is not here entirely for our gratification. It is the grown-up version, I think, of greenhorn disgust, in which the bleakness of biological process on the Yorkshire moors meets the magma of the Florida swamps.

Hence, perhaps, what he allowed to happen to his oranges, rather enjoying their decay because it demonstrated something cardinal. A grove full of rotting oranges became for him a mass of nature, festering into muck and therefore a memento of what happened to all humans. This flow into decay brought him an inkling of a universal principle that few other composers reckoned with, or even knew how to portray in music. There are the bright golden ecstasies, frequently evoked, and there are the gruesome disintegrations in which, eventually, all things come together and make—as the Ilkley Moor song reveals—a kind of compost without which there would be no continuance in nature, human or otherwise.

This was the man whom Thomas Beecham, his steadfast devotee, described, at least on first impression, as "a cardinal or at least a bishop in mufti, I kept on saying to myself, for his features had that noble cast of asceticism and shrewdness one mentally associates with high-ranking ecclesiastics." An astute romantic? A generous-looking accountant or solicitor? An introverted philatelist? He had many more faces than the one he presented to Thomas Beecham, one of them being a sobersides look, a commonsensical scrutineer, far from the swooning romantic many have thought him. If I am wrong in thinking his a Yorkshire face, I must concede that I also found it the hesitant face of a man ever on the brink of a wave, and his gaze penetrating.

Was the gaunt, withered face of his last years implicit in this judiciously well-tempered multiple mask? I think not, I regarding his emaciation as an external extra, something brought about by circumstance and perhaps the torments of an exile's career. Bony head of standard *senex* is what I discern in his last face, one that has listened too hard to everything, including the feral whisper of the slow spirochete. Of course, one does not see the face, one hears the music, in which the face somehow subsumed itself, so that listening to it one somehow became acquainted with his brain flowing by behind the death mask of the living man. Having been invited to compose incidental music for the Norwegian political comedy *Folkeraadet* (Parliament), he was conducting in Oslo when some university student fired a blank at him, upon which Delius fled the pit and the theater for the Grand Hotel, where Ibsen, conveniently on the spot, consoled him. When he returned to the podium, the play succeeded and sold out for the next three weeks. Such alarms became predictable, in both Norway and Germany; he was trying to do something different, even if he himself was unsure what it was. Those who heard his music, however, were less unsure and subjected him to hostile displays, perhaps educating him in his favorite finale, the dying fall. He was undertaking something he perhaps wished he had not trained himself to do.

VIII.

His face, when I first saw it, lacked any hint of the playboy he might have been, not so much of the Western world as of the fjords and the Hebrides. Indeed, something Nordic and unfulfilled kept on coming through, as it does in Bax, say; I might even say faery or elfin, but another side of him kept that under control, more inclined to subdue such fantasy to a warm night on the river or a sunrise scalding his retinas. It is not easy to formulate it, but I think he had a tropical side he underrated, and a Scandinavian side he treasured a little too much. He was several men, of course, and he knew many more composers and musicians than he has received credit for, among the ones I have already mentioned Christian Sinding and Florent Schmitt. He also knew Ravel, who made a piano score from his third opera, as well as Gauguin and Strindberg. From Gauguin, we must note, for about twenty pounds he bought the painting *Nevermore*. I babble. It is my way, which I sometimes apologetically call associative meander. Perhaps he drove or urged me into it as I struggled to keep pace with his sweeping mind, his tumbling thoughts. Florent Schmitt, in fact, did the piano scores of the first two operas. That is how my mind works, not organizing but assembling, and out of such assembly creating patterns I never observed in him during his lifetime. This, I suppose, means I am getting into his act, now and then anyway, but I justify the tic by telling myself that, when someone you revere is dominant, your little wanderings and your impetuous deviancies are as much his as your own. It is a matter of osmosis, I suppose, with (as I sometimes used to say) the great god Pan calling the tune, not only giving you back the great hymn of nature you thought lost but also inspiring you to novel gestures you would never have dreamed up in earlier, less influenced years. Short of doting or fawning, I took him more seriously than the English did, for much of his life anyway, and that must count for something.

"Campion," he would say in that Yorkshire-voweled Florida drawl of his, "don't you wish *you* could compose?"

He certainly did not mean compose myself. "Not with you around me," I told him. "One's enough. Without you, I perhaps would, but why would I do that without you? With you, there is no need, seeing as how there is so much of you to assimilate anyway."

"Campion Apsley," he would muse, "isn't that a Catholic name? I mean the Campion. I must be thinking of some old Catholic brought up in a Yorkshire school, Stonyhurst, say."

It was my turn to go blank; as far as I know I was named for a flower and remained quite content with that allusion. But he would go on, dreaming and gesturing, at some point shifting from language to music and quite losing me in the melodic transfers.

My head clears immediately when I think of him in Paris (the city in which I first joined up with him), as it never did or does when I link him with Norway and Germany. Something in the French air, I mean the atmosphere of Paris, sobers me up, gets me out of *finesse* into *géométrie*. In Paris he can hardly be said to have been sociable, apart from his few—Schmitt, Ravel, Gauguin—but he did in the January of 1896 encounter Jelka Rosen, from an old Schleswig-Holstein family, studying painting in Paris. They fast became attached and he took to visiting her home in Grez, as if he needed a retreat from a retreat. They kept to themseles although frequenting the cafés and boîtes, which makes it all the stranger that he allowed me any contact with him, perhaps just because, to begin with, I was studying music in Paris, though with less than titanic avidity. He doted on her and, having her to sustain him, permitted my attentions, which initially amounted to no more than a glass of wine (his treat) and an occasional line of Mallarmé. If I courted him at all, it must have been the mystic in me responding to the romantic in him (and her). She, I guessed, had decided from the first that he was the man for her— languorous, cordial precision—whereas he took pleasure in other women, whether she understood this or not, and potential discord always seemed to flutter behind their more conventional niceties, even when in Grez for a while he took lodgings to be near her (they timed their excursions there well, like two coordinated metronomes). She had one big idea and that was him, whereas he, almost always on the erotic qui vive, took an interest as many men will in what is politely called the field, which he played and did not relinquish even after he and Jelka became engaged. Over Christmas, he declared he needed to go back to Solano Grove for several months, and this shocked her, to find him going his own way. She might have been even more shocked had she known that one of his Parisian amours was booked to sail on the same ship to New York, disguised as a young man, and go off with him to Florida. This knack he had for what I came to call simultaneous intensity caused him no upset at all, almost as if he were conducting the orchestra of his personality. He returned in June, resumed his lodgings and his affair in Grez, and got on with the third act of *Koanga* and his tone poem *Over the Hills and Far Away*, which is indeed where he had been. And now he was only ten miles from Paris, disguised as nothing at all except a thoroughly fulfilled swain, all thought of inconsistency boiled away like the froth off milk. He married Jelka in the summer of 1903, having presumably confronted his demons and settled them. Or not.

Speaking of his women friends, he invariably referred to their voices, their timbre and tempo, as a musician might, though he got from their speech (those whom he liked) an infallible grandeur, citing one's Dutch composure, which led her to a quiet, unemphatic enunciation. She did not disturb or provoke him, he said, but spoke each word with equivalent reverence, matter-of-factly, so the net effect was one of chiseled calm. I was amazed at how much he got from this aspect of his philandering, almost expecting from him a setting to music or even the orchestration of the voice. He preferred the ebullience of another speaker, however, delighting in her deep earthy delivery, more Italian than German, and the hearty laugh she mingled it with. There balanced, he thought, on her vocal cords metallic globes of resounding metal, even after her voice had been resting unused, and this he inexplicably related to the quiescence of her gonads; the quieter she was hormonally, the deeper and more commanding she sounded. I then realized that what he was always after, in this cult of the dark brown voice, *was* something German or perhaps Italian: a voice thickened and corrupted by liquor and smoke, a threnody of the nightclubs, a lazy, sated, page of estrus, a bedroom contralto he might fit into whatever was taking shape in his head.

With this in mind, indeed safely so, I advanced to another thought in my unending quest to fathom him. He may have womanized, but he did so not in a spirit of "so many realities" that freed him to treat each woman as a discrete entity, but as if all women were one, and jointly available. To possess one was to possess all, even if his passion extended only so far as dark-haired women with deep voices. Maternal perhaps. I never dismissed the notion that he remembered being in his mother's womb and hearing from above the distorted mellow melody that was his shawl, his sounding board. He always needed that above him, soothing and getting ready for him, a platform of staves, say, never to be found among the brittle sopranos tweeting and squeaking and warbling, the tunes of the empyrean, say. What he yearned for was of the earth earthy, as they say, because it nearly exempted him from music altogether. This was just another, I told myself, of his Pan thoughts, as I named them, akin to thoughts of God in a thunderstorm tupping the soil, as some author of this period had already insisted in a book. I forget who. If this was pantheism or panentheism, I have no idea (the -isms leave me cold), but he was certainly attuned to the vision of the gods as magic agricultural trolls.

"Hear that voice, that epiglottis?" He often said this, while lounging in a café and absently eyeing the physique that went with it. "Now *there's* a bedside manner."

So where, you may well ask, did the rather dumpy Jelka fit into this program of physical need? Well, she had a satisfactorily low, pagan voice, enough for him certainly, but by no means entitling her to a monopoly. What would you make of her face? That of a proud possessor, one of the overdevoted faces above a brawny

German body often enough encased entirely in velvet. Seen, at least by me, looking down at him as he sat in wheelchair or lay on bed, twice his size, and no doubt a woman confounded by his saintly, ecclesiastical mien. She remained bonny while he became quite beaky, especially in his last years. No man, though, is privy to the squirmings of another's penis, and still less to the proddings of the libido. No doubt a good deal of his erotic yearning stayed private, unacted upon; he thought his lascivious thoughts and turned them into rhapsodies and airs, dances and (after his famous cuckoo piece) what I fondly referred to as "On"s. This habit of transformation made him a wizard; I presumed that, had he wanted to, he could have turned all natural phenomena to sex. He was a shape-changer, a man who, unlike many, lived his youth in old age and vice versa, remaining an ageless paragon, the Dorian Gray of dreamland.

Perhaps his illicit desires only made his Cowper's glands flow, and that was the end of it, and the liquidity became his music. I could never be sure, but I knew that his eternal *leman* (to use an old Anglo-Saxon word for lover; he rather fancied it) was the *foison*, or plenty, of the planet. In some ways he was an atmospheric astronomer, captivated by evolution. I have heard astronomers saying how glad they were to have made a living out of what delighted them, and I never heard him say anything so obvious; but it was clear that he felt always something magical going on around him, generating in him an ecstasy, a joy in suppuration and flow. In a sense, this made him less a person than anyone else, for he floated away into the mighty never, leaving only his music behind him, findable on the distant shore only as a hulk or husk saying thank you. Such a man is delighted to have been born, I suppose, and to have happen to him whatever bodily shifts came his way, and even to lapse back into the cosmic slop as at least having been chosen to do so, submitting to yet another chemical experience.

I go back to what he once told Eric Fenby, stressing the need for soul to speak to soul. "You can't teach a young musician," he said, "to compose any more than you can teach a delicate plant how to grow, but you can guide him a little by putting a stick in here and a stick in there. Composition as taught in our academies is a farce. Where are the composers they produce? Those who do manage to survive this systematic and idiotic teaching either write all alike, so that you can say that this lot belongs to this institution, this lot to that, or they give us the flat beer of their teachers, but watered down."

I am still unsure if I understand this, but I do get the drift of his animus. He abominated and despised counterpoint. The tone poem or rhapsody was what he loved most, and what he was most envied for, having dumped all that cerebral baggage behind him under the influence of Thomas Ward. In a sense he gains and never loses the barbaric yawp of his beloved Whitman, whose words he set to music in the *Sea Drift* of 1903. It was enough for him to have written about being alive, not as heedless of circumstances as some have thought (walks, sails, drifts, hearings, climbs, sits all figure in the iconography of his titles). I think the subtlest giveaway to his process appears in the instructions to *Song of the High Hills*, a sublime work for orchestra and chorus; he writes that the choir must sing on the open vowel best suited to the character of the music—the vocal parts are wordless all through, which means the chorus is an instrument. He does not need them to be articulate, but, in hymning, say, the section headed "The wide, far distance—the great solitude," to be awestruck. As he himself said, "The human voices represent Man in Nature—an episode that becomes fainter and then disappears altogether."

IX.

It is easier to recall him at Grez, standing with hands clasped behind him, one step behind tubby Jelka, whose paintings of their tiny French hamlet graced the walls alongside work by Gauguin and Munch. The garden outside was her true masterpiece, though, and perhaps the ramshackle, uncoordinated house was his with its windows flung wide open, espaliers growing up to the roof, the front courtyard's garden crammed with vegetation, so much so that both merely edged their way into it to be photographed. The house stood, an L-plan, on the village street between the old church and a ruined keep, its lofty stone walls slanting down past the orchard to the river Loing. At home he kept a handful of scores, half of which were music by Richard Strauss, from whose example he was learning counterpoint, by this time (1900) no longer Delius the man-about-town (Paris), the importuner and voyeur, the expatriate picaro, but Delius the introvert and recluse, harvesting not so much isolation or rootlessness, as the vision of consummate Pan. It is as if the composer, brought here from abroad, lifted from Florida to Norway and Paris, then disappears into himself and comes out again pastoralized, laid

269

to rest in the bower of his own fecundity, a scene not far from that of October 1929, when, blind and paralyzed, he attended the week-long festival organized in London by Sir Thomas Beecham: six concerts, to which Delius, no longer the impassioned composer wriggling about in an armchair and bathed in sweat, was carried in his invalid chair, propped up on cushions, down the ship's gangway to a waiting ambulance. Silver hair, gray felt hat, heavy overcoat, tortoiseshell glasses, pale, wrinkled, ascetic face, as his sister noted at the time.

He next lay on a litter, swathed in flowers, perched on a balcony, managing to rid himself of a few syllables: "This festival has been the time of my life." After that, like one of his own human voices among the high hills, he dwindles and soars into a delirium of pain and morphine, spasms and violent twists as Fenby reads to him from a favorite novel. First buried, as he wished, near a church "where the winds are warm and the sun friendly," in June of 1934, he resurrects himself from the South of France to Limpsfield churchyard, where the winds are keener, the sun sterner, to the tunes of his cuckoo and, on a summer night on the river, his punt.

Those who judged him a creator of formless rhapsodies had got him back. Those who believe all tone poems end in mystery reclaim him from the ether, perhaps committing themselves to words heading the score of *In a Summer Garden* (1908): "Roses, lilies, and a thousand scented flowers. Bright butterflies flitting from petal to petal, and gold-brown bees humming in the warm, quivering summer air. Beneath the shade of ancient trees, a quiet river with water lilies. In a boat, almost hidden, two people. A thrush is singing in the distance." For Delius, this is only medium lush. The rest is tonal. He was a hummingbird.

Slowly

Lyn Hejinian

I wake to the waking "shadow" of the world the waking have
in common for one long visit slowly
    I walk rather than speed up the ordinary unfolding
    One has to wait for the lateness of the day with recalcitrance
circulating to stop in the midst of traffic in a blindspot that flows
around one smoothly to regard the dark building without apology
    Movement prolongs the finitudes a person moving achieves
which is finality imperceptibly
    Out the dark door over black leaves putting into motion what
painters have known for years I see that the night is in the mind
before it ever gets to day
    Colors creating forms are left for the imagination to turn from
birds in flight to photographs of same or nearly same
    The middle of my face aches as if with cold a physicist can
detect as an acceleration I'm slowing
    Or there might be signs a physician scorning dreams should
nonetheless excise as extended omens
    Omens always have a psychological twist indomitable will
exercises
    What one sees comes up in submerged assertions during
afterhours shoptalk of dissatisfaction
    Slowly things partly because of damage are represented as
ghosts grown too quickly
    Repetitive exposure to anything provokes sensations

    I'm always moving around incessantly which is dubious
animation seemingly not chosen
    The old city skyscraper rises today with the pathos that
propels the change from one sensation to another daily bound a
short way
    I recognize it as a skyscraper by going mentally around the
information given

Lyn Hejinian

It inclines its crown
Its walls come from a dune
Its shadow briefly falls like light upon the patterns of motion of
the mottled pigeons that flutter in the gutter and like a photograph
captures the feeling of transience
Light the eye adds to the evidence falls on a scene as the scene
outside its shadow
Lettered passersby pass by what history has for us
The vanquished sit at the center of their world intransigently
outskirting
My eye caught the light, a rock approximately the size of a
head, and something said regarding fate
Each fate is phrased
Fate in sequences
My hand caught the glass just before it hit the floor
Fate is a term for the present
Clichés develop in the dark and they are known as
hallucinations
In the one called "wouldn't you know it!" a dachshund came
out from under the bed
It was the usual dachshund, the irascible fat one
If I had it to do all over again I'd call it "Beethoven" and after
awhile "Lately"
But the hallucination known as "to do it all over again" would
take the kind of time we are immediately fated not to have

The inability to remember except perhaps some vague and
distant storeroom causes doubt whose reach is independent of
everything that might happen tomorrow but the present
The bird we saw yesterday in the tree constantly sings
outwardly
Fate can never in a new way nor as before overcome its
dependence on the present once and for all
When inertia sets in, things that are in motion stay in motion,
things that are stationary stay put
For the onlooker tossing in her bed given too much information
the magic square disappears
The information whispered by the wristwatch counts not for
but to nothing it continues
Its brief halts for repentance erroneously considered an instant

of knowledge are always on the question
Contrition is itself a form of query

Subjectivity even if not of the curling sky is my duration
All day subjectivity is an endurance awaiting objects for a minute
digressing
And it hopes for objects eager and unbaffled in spaces somewhere
near eye level to greet it with comprehension during its waking hours
Everyone knows that in the dream called "Will My Spirit Live
on When I'm Dead" as in the dream called "Will I Be Fired" and
the dream called "Do You Only Pretend to Love Me," there are no
objects
In the dream called "One Who Is Poor Passes by Inch by Inch,"
there is no object
Subjectivity at night must last hours with nothing to judge but
itself
The walls of the hemispheres face and this produces life to
closed admiring eyes

My freedom was the last descriptive passage in the little book
that I carried on top of my head for the sake of my posture when
young when undertaking posture
Learning to walk with it contributed to what's at bottom
optimism and in the main pessimism, feet first, head hesitant, while
all the time the undertaking has to be undertaken gradually
Credulity is given to one with one's name which one carries with
the incredulity that the name returns
Freedom is given back by the threshold over which one trips
stepping into something as intangible as futility
Night comes whose terminus is the future we cannot leave before
the end though the end never comes, it's all that slow
Freely it circulates

Taking a photograph doesn't actually require me to have responses
myself immediately while I take it of necessity lightly, though I'm
taking a chance watching this supersede that
I take a photograph mentally just as a cellist draws a bow in excess
of what is needed merely across much of what I have been saying

273

Shot of marching children, the encyclopedic
Shot of anxiety, the lips of a singer
Shot of the moment, shaking egrets, a digression and not the
first
Shot
Shot of soup, shot of tedious captivity, shot of damage to the
wall, joviality
Shot taken as a self-portrait, but it is not
Lions, an irresolute shot (either we are fleeing or the lions are
receding)
Shot of spectators (in the scene, never entirely swallowed up,
pressed against a fence)
Shot without measure (shot immoderately now)
If there is nothing but uniqueness, we have to accept chaos
quickly, it's the underlying logic of uniqueness

The cameraman who wanting to be loved wants to love shoots
and offers eight strips of film called *Abandon*
And what a sight we are
Do you think he saw us?
Subjectivity at night must survive hours during which it
encounters nothing that is conscious of it
That defiance of closure is what constitutes adventurousness
We're at will
We're with world (return)
Remains of the present remaining in view remain this *and* that

The time is right, the place outlasting
As my passport indicates, I was born nearby
There is nothing self-producing, nothing authentic
Naturally circumnavigators achieve circularity
They are no one departing from themselves
Pursuit can't be separated from routines, clothing, meals, and
eventually music, which is never made for others alone
The interlocutor may ask, Never?
The circumnavigator says, We never stop
Interlocutor: Believing that some horses have blue eyes?
Certainly, says the circumnavigator, while we laboriously wait
for things to resemble what we want things to be

Interlocutor: Tearing through a field of ripening corn accidentally?

Circularity, says the circumnavigator, slows to allow the time of a place to appear

With or without future? asks the interlocutor

Clairvoyance does not occur in the ellipses we know as dreams and therefore, says the circumnavigator, it does not appear in the dreams of dogs any more than it occurs in ours

Dreaming to think accidentally?

Slowly to no outcome

I go slowly in acknowledgment and know I'll have to go there again

Events have many centers and they fall into ruins like solemnly decomposing cliffs usefully, they while away

If you know little about hot springs and volcanoes then you can look them up

But there will always be a hole in the picture or holes will appear abundantly without useful copy

This describes things historically like mystification—we think for ourselves—but not only that—look up history

Look up cloud quantity, see organization, suction, cascade (antonym: fixity)

Look up cascade, see deliberation, failure, sincerest repeat

Look up sincerest repeat, see aftermath

Look up aftermath, see fugue, history, perceptible color

Look up perceptible color, see unit of cognition, common sense, paint

Look up paint, see painting (antonym: blank)

Look up painting, see critical inches, see color (above), cobalt gray viridian gray gray lake inch, look up

Look up inch, see premonition, fabric, millimeters

Look up millimeters, see wider films, see fate ramble, fate flicker, reality sucking up fate

It's rare to see fate—observation doesn't reveal one's own reality but the reality of things that are foreign to one proving one's alienation, one's unreality, a very nice creature and rare, whoa

Whoa, back up

Whoa, what's that

Quickly

275

Things not deadly rise to come to light

On the wall, the post, the pedestrian quickly I can think this not through but again quickly inexorably quickly to no outcome and plethora of outcome slowly

The pedestrian goes back (reappears) and passes the wall to the post and consigns the future of her having lived to it more and more heavy rain, a taxi, the north coast, and therefore puddles more and more to posterity as a scholar might bequeath his or her library to a university in a state of excitement, as knowledge, viz utterly

What is done can be seen in the light of how it's done, empirically

Pedro playing Janine gives Trina playing Christopher an outright gift of money from Françoise playing Jamal surreptitiously but in the name of an ethos

One can't look up and see mathematics, one can't look up and find autonomy

Find circumnavigation, find farms

Find history, modifications, salt, the sun

All about are beings with obstinate whims living through events accumulating chance installments often twice in a day which we know as this day

From the direction of the theater and to the corner the eye comes to rest on what it slides to

E.g., skepticism, shore, probability, piano, rhythm, fog

Films have viscosity, emptiness

Films slide regularly steadily just as dawns and dusks gradually to the darting denouement day after day never the same overlapping jump away without parting and evidence remains

Pedestrian, pigeon, and frame

The day causes one to see it as a day even now but it has only ambiguous abstract accidental unity, now, the unity with which the day begins and which inconsistencies and alternatives slow down

One could say that one day crosses another though not that one day causes another but the speech of every one of us has had cause to begin with "Alas!" "Yikes!" or "Woe!"

I think of causes suspiciously

Saying this I courageously kiss you cautiously again (effects not wearing off)

The Fossil-Seeker
Joyce Carol Oates

The cruel beauty of The Falls
That calls to you—
Surrender!

—M. L. Trau, "The Ballad of the Niagara," 1931

The Falls at Niagara, comprising the American,
the Bridal Veil, and the enormous Horseshoe falls,
exert upon a proportion of the human population,
perhaps as many as forty percent (of adults), an
uncanny effect called the hydracropsychic. This
morbid condition has been known to render even
the will of the active, robust man in the prime of
life temporarily invalid, as if under the spell of a
malevolent hypnotist. Such a one, drawn to the
turbulent rapids above The Falls, may stand for
long minutes staring as if paralyzed. Speak to him
in the most forcible tone, he will not hear you.
Touch him, or attempt to restrain him, he may
throw off your hand angrily. The eyes of the
enthralled victim are fixed and dilated. There
may be a mysterious biological attraction to the
thunderous force of nature represented by The
Falls, romantically misinterpreted as "magnifi-
cent"—"grand"—"godly"—and so the unfortunate victim throws himself to his doom if he is
not prevented.

We may speculate: Under the spell of The Falls
the hapless individual both ceases to exist and
yet wills to become immortal. A new birth, not
unlike the Christian promise of the Resurrection
of the Body, may be the cruelest hope. Silently the
victim vows to The Falls—"Yes, you have killed
thousands of men and women but you can't kill
me. Because I am me."

—Dr. Moses Blaine, A Niagara Falls
Physician's Log 1879–1905

277

Joyce Carol Oates

12 June 1950. RUN, RUN! Run for your life!

At last it was dawn. All night the thunderous river had called to him. Through the night as he prayed to summon strength for what he must do, the river called to him. *Come! Here is peace.* River of Thunder, the Tuscaroras named it centuries ago. Falls of Thunder. The Ongiara Indians named it Hungry Water. Devouring the unwary, and the sacrifices. Those who threw themselves into its seething waters to be carried off to oblivion, and peace. How many tortured souls repudiated by God had found peace in those waters, how many had been obliterated and returned to God, he could not guess. Surely there had been hundreds like himself, perhaps thousands. From the start of recorded history in this part of North America, in the 1500s. Many of these were pagans, but Jesus would pity them. Jesus would pity him. Jesus would grant him oblivion, as He on His cross would have been granted oblivion if He had wished it. But He had not required such solace for He was the son of God and born without sin or the very capacity or yearning for sin. Never had He touched a woman, never had He shrieked in ecstatic surrender to the woman's crude touch.

It was dawn, it was time. He'd lived too long. Twenty-nine years! They called him young, they fussed over him as a prodigy, but he knew better. He'd lived a day and a night too long. *Do you take this woman as your lawfully wedded wife. Till death do you part* and so he could not bear another hour. Slipping from the bed. Slipping from the bedclothes that smelled of their bodies. As the woman who was Mrs. Erskine *the lawfully wedded wife* slept heavily, on her back as if she'd fallen from a great height, unconscious, brainless, her hands flung upward in an expression of astonishment, mouth open like a fish's and her breath catching at the back of her mouth in a wet, rasping, idiotic way that maddened him, made him want to shut his fingers around her throat and squeeze. Run, run! Don't look back. Gathering his clothes, his shoes, tiptoeing into the parlor where a chill, pale light at the windows exposed the fussily decorated plush-pink room. *Honeymoon suite, paradise for two. Luxury and privacy. An idyll you will never forget!* Fumbling with buttons, a zipper, muttering to himself as he dressed hurriedly, pushed his bare feet by force into part-laced shoes, and fled.

Run, run! For your life.

Too restless to wait for an elevator, taking the fire stairs instead. Five flights down. By the Bulova watch (a gift from his proud parents when he'd graduated top of his class at the Albany Theological

Seminary) he had not failed to strap to his wrist, for G. was one to observe certain routine rituals of his life even in the final exalted hour of his life, it was just past 6 A.M. The hotel lobby was nearly deserted. A few uniformed hotel staff, taking not much notice of him. Outside, the air was cold and very damp. June, the month of brides. June, the season of young love. June, a mockery. If by G.'s watch it should have been dawn, by the actual sky above the Niagara gorge it was an hour without time, mist-shrouded, sullenly glaring like the bottom of a scrubbed pot, and smelling mostly of something sulfurous, metallic. *Niagara! Honeymoon capital of the world.* He'd known from the start, maybe. Never had he truly deceived himself. Introduced to the red-haired woman, eager to establish himself with her influential father, the Reverend Thaddeus Littrell of Troy, New York. Introduced to the red-haired woman whose thin lips wavered in a hesitant, hopeful smile even as her pebbly-green eyes stared at him lustrous and unyielding as glass. And he'd thought, in his folly, vanity, desperation, *A sister! One like myself.*

He was walking swiftly. Bare feet in leather dress shoes, and his heels chafed. A mistake not to pull on socks but he hadn't time. He needed to get to the river, he needed to get *there.* As if, only *there,* he could breathe. The broad sidewalks of Prospect Street were puddled from a recent rain. The cobbled street glistened with wet. He stepped into the street and out of nowhere a rattling trolley rushed at him and a shrieking horn sounded and he hid his face so no one could recognize it afterward seeing its likeness in the local papers. For he knew the shame and desperation of his act would outlive him, and its courage would be obscured, but he did not care, for it was time, God would never forgive him but God would grant him freedom. That was the promise of The Falls. Through the night he heard its murmurous roar and now in the open air he heard it more clearly, and could feel the very ground beneath his feet vibrating with its power. *Come! Here alone is peace.*

What pride, what a fervor of triumph. Ten months before.

On the telephone announcing in a tremulous voice *I am engaged, Douglas.* And his friend spoke warmly, spontaneously. *Congratulations, Gil!* And he'd said almost boastfully, *Will you come to my wedding? They're scheduling it for next June.* D. said, *Of course, Gil. Hey, this is great news. I'm very happy for you.* G. said, *I'm happy, too. I'm . . . happy.* D. said, *Gil?* and G. said, *Yes, Douglas?* and D. asked, *Who is she?* and for a moment G. couldn't think, and

279

stammered, *Who?* and D. said, laughing, *Your fiancée, Gil. When will I meet her?*

D. had been impressed (hadn't he?) when he'd learned who his friend's fiancée was. The daughter of. A music instructor, pianist, and singer.

At the seminary they'd been such opposite types. Yet they'd talked passionately late into the night: of life and death, mortality and Life Everlasting. Never had they talked of suicide. Never of despair. For, young Christian men studying for the ministry, why should they despair? They were themselves the bearers of good news. Instead, they talked with the fervor of late adolescence of love—"mature love"—"love between a man and a woman"—"what a Christian marriage in the mid-twentieth century should be." Of course they'd talked of having children.

They played chess, which was D.'s game. They went hiking, and sometimes searched for fossils in shale-rich ravines and creek beds, which was G.'s game since boyhood.

D. hadn't been able to attend G.'s wedding. G. wondered if he would attend his funeral. If there can be a funeral without a body? For maybe they'd never find his body. He smiled to think so. Sometimes, going over The Falls, a human being was lost forever. Even small boats had been known to disintegrate in such a way that their parts were never retrieved or identified.

The peace of oblivion.

G. had left no note for D. He'd left a scribbled note only for A., his wife. Out of a sense of obligation that suggested (he hoped, for he wasn't cruel) none of the loathing he felt for the woman. But D. would forgive him. He believed.

D., in the simplicity and goodness of his heart. A natural-born Christian. He would grieve for G., but forgive him.

D. had his own, separate life now. For years. He was assistant to the minister of a large, prosperous church in Springfield, Mass. He was a proud husband and father of two-year-old girl twins. To make of D. an accomplice of a kind if only at second- or thirdhand would be a sinful act. To make of D. a sharer of so shameful a secret. Unless it was so beautiful a secret. *I can't love any woman, God help me I've tried. I can only love you.* D. had joined G. in his rambling walks in search of fossils. He'd begun as a boy collecting Indian arrowheads and artifacts but "fossils" came to fascinate him more. These delicate, leafy remnants of a lost and scarcely imaginable time before human history. Like mysterious artworks they were, skeletal impressions of once-living organisms from an era millions of years—an unfathomable sixty-five million years!—before Christ. A world of slow time in which one thousand years was but a moment and sixty thousand years was too brief a time to be measured by geological methods of fossil dating. As a boy of thirteen he'd fashioned a fine-meshed net attached to a wooden frame so that he could wade creek beds and sift through soft black muck in search of fragments of fossil rocks and bone, the teeth of ancient sharks and skates; the outlines of ancient squids calcified to a kind of amber. So far inland as Troy, New York! G. couldn't believe, as his own father did, that the devil had planted so-called fossils in the earth to mislead mankind; to cast doubt on the account of creation in Genesis—that God had created the earth and the stars and all the creatures of the earth in seven days and nights, no more than six thousand years ago. (Six thousand! G. smiled to think of it.) Yet he resisted the very premise of "evolution." Blindness, accident. No! Not possible.

And yet: Could it be true that ninety-nine percent of all species, flora and fauna, that have ever lived have become extinct, and that species are passing into extinction continuously? Daily? Why did God create so many creatures, only to let them fight frantically with one another for existence, and then to pass into oblivion? Would mankind disappear too one day? *Was this God's plan?* For surely there was a plan. Christianity must try to comprehend, and to explain. G.'s father refused to discuss such issues with G. He'd long ago come to the conclusion that science was a false, shallow religion and that deep, abiding faith was all that mattered, finally. "You'll see, son. In time." A few of G.'s younger instructors at the seminary were more open to discuss such questions but these men, too, were limited in their responses, and uninformed in science. To them, there was little difference between six thousand years, sixty-five million years, and five hundred million years. Faith, faith! G. complained to D., "What good is 'faith' if it's based upon ignorance? I want to *know.*" But D. said, "Look, Gil. Faith is a day-to-day, practical matter. I can no more doubt the existence of God and Jesus than I can doubt the existence of my family, or you. What matters is how we relate to them, and to one another. And that's all that matters."

G. was moved by this answer. Its simplicity, and the essential soundness of such an attitude. Yet he doubted he could be satisfied with it. Always he wanted more. . . .

"Maybe that's your special destiny, Gil. To make sense of these things. To bring together science and 'faith.' Ever think of that?"

D. seemed quite serious, saying this. He seemed to think that G., graduate of a provincial Protestant seminary in upstate New York, with virtually no science in his background, might be capable of such a task.

No one but D. had ever had such ambitions for G.

No one but D. had ever called him *Gil*.

Well, that was finished now. G. would be leaving his fossil collection behind, in his parents' house. In his boyhood room, in drawers and cartons. In junior high he'd begun bringing these to show his science teachers, who made a stab at identifying and dating them. Had his teachers known much more than G. himself, he wondered. He'd wanted to think so. They assured him that, at least, the fossils were millions of years old. Hundreds of millions? There was the Cambrian Era, and there was the Cretaceous Era. Fossils in this upstate New York region might belong to the Ice Age. The Age of Dinosaurs. The Age of Neanderthals. He'd been thrilled to think that these mysterious objects had ended up in his possession. There were no accidents in God's plan, and he knew that God had intended him to be a minister; since God had allowed him to find these fossils, too, there was a reason. One day, he would know that reason. He intended to take courses in paleontology, paleozoology, at a distinguished university like Cornell. . . . Somehow, he never had. He wondered if he'd been fearful of what he might learn.

That you have no special destiny. Not you, and not mankind.

At this early hour of Sunday morning the city was nearly deserted. Yet church bells seemed to be ringing continuously. A noisy clamor. He wanted to clap his hands over his ears. Never had he noticed how intrusive his faith was. Here we are! Christians! Surrounding you! Bringing news of the Gospel! Good news! Come and be saved! How much more seductive he found the monosyllabic roar of The Falls.

He forced himself, panting, to walk at a normal pace. For what if a police officer saw him, and guessed his intention. His face. His ravaged face. His boy's face that had aged years in a single night. His eyes sunken in his face. He was afraid it shone unmistakably in his face, the release from misery he sought.

It was difficult for him to simulate calm, though. He felt like a wild beast on a leash. If anyone got in his way or tried to stop him, if the woman had tried to stop him, he'd have flung her aside in a rage.

It wasn't despair he felt. Not at all. Despair suggested meekness, passivity, giving up. But Gilbert Erskine wasn't giving anything up.

Another man would return to the hotel suite, to the *lawfully wedded wife.* The bed, the swath of rusted-red crotch. The moaning fish's mouth and the eyes rolled back in the head and the eventual babies, a cozy stink of diapers. That was Gilbert Erskine's true destiny. The tall, gaunt house in Palmyra, New York, mud-colored brick and rotted shingle boards on the roof and a congregation of less than two hundred people, most of them middle-aged and older, to whom the young minister must "prove" himself. "Win" their confidence, their respect, eventually their love. Yes? But no.

Not for G. He was acting out of courage, conviction. God would not forgive him. *But God will know me as I am.*

The roar of The Falls. Like the blood-roar in the ears. Penetrating his fevered brain as he'd lain sleepless in that bed. Recalling the vanity of their first meeting. He'd believed the woman a "sister"—what a cruel, crude joke. How they'd met. Now he knew. Their elders had shrewdly planned the meeting, he saw now. Her parents were desperate for the prim, plain spinster to be married, and his parents were desperate for the prim, plain bachelor to be married. (Possibly they worried about his manhood? Reverend Erskine at least.) And so "Ariah" and "Gilbert" were but pawns on a chessboard who'd imagined themselves players!

Last night. His life careening past as if already he were drowning in the river. Broken like a cheap plastic doll in The Falls. Beside him the stuporous, snoring woman. Drunken woman. His wedding night, and a drunken woman. Run, run! He had to throw himself into the most monstrous of falls, the Horseshoe. Nothing less would suffice. In his expansive sense of himself he dreaded surviving. He dreaded being pulled from the churning water below The Falls, broken and maimed. Would rescue crews be on duty, so early in the morning? He wished for total extinction, obliteration. To erase forever from his sight the smeared, greedy face of the red-haired woman. Chaste and virginal and cool to the touch as an icicle she'd been for the long months of their engagement, and that thin-lipped smile and awkward manner . . . Well, he'd been deceived. Like a dupe of the devil he'd been deceived. He, Gilbert Erskine! The most skeptical of the seminarians. The most "freethinking." He who'd prided himself on eluding the wiles of featherbrained simpering-coy females for years. Desperate to marry, they were. The pack of them desperate to be "engaged"; shamelessly greedy for a ring to wear, to present boastfully to the world. *See? I'm loved. I'm saved.* But Ariah Littrell had seemed to him so different. Of another species. A young woman he might respect as a wife, a woman who was his equal socially and almost his equal intellectually.

He was bitter that D. had not asked, *Do you love this woman, Gil?*

He'd planned to say to D., *As much as you love yours.*

The occasion had not arisen. In fact, no one asked G., *Do you love this woman?*

Possibly G. had murmured to her, yes, he did. He loved her. Possibly, stricken with shyness. Embarrassment. And the woman in turn stiff, self-conscious, blinking rapidly and her green-glassy eyes wavering from his eyes. Possibly she'd murmured to him, in turn. *And I, I love you.*

So it was decided. He'd slid the ring on her thin finger.

Run, run!

Spray wetted his face like spit. The roar of The Falls had been steadily getting louder. His glasses were misted over, hardly could he see the pavement in front of him. That bridge. Goat Island Suspension Bridge. *Love me why can't you love me for God's sake can't you. Do it, DO IT!* It was Goat Island he wanted. He'd marked on the tourist map. With the little silver pen she'd given him, inscribed with his initials *G.E.* His pride in this artifact! *I'm loved, I'm saved.*

Their shy groping dry-mouthed kisses. Her stiffening body, the tough little skeleton holding her erect when he touched her, put his arms around her. *Like they do in the movies. Fred Astaire, Ginger Rogers, let's dance! It's so easy.*

He'd known she hadn't loved him. Of course he'd known.

Yet he'd believed (almost!) that he loved her. *He would come to love her, his lawfully wedded wife. In time.*

As his father had come to love his mother, he supposed. As all men came to love their wives.

For had not God enjoined mankind to *increase and multiply.*

Run! The shame of it would paralyze him otherwise.

Champagne at the reception, and in the hotel room. He had not known. Had not guessed. This delicate-boned woman drinking thirstily as a day laborer. Ignoring his tactful suggestions that maybe she'd had enough. Giggling, wiping her smeared mouth on the back of her hand. Kicking off her shoes. When she tried to stand she'd swayed, light-headed; he'd jumped up to steady her. She half-fell, pushed herself into his arms. How different from the stiff-backed minister's daughter he'd known. Ariah Littrell in her white ruffled blouses, her Peter Pan collars and crisply ironed shirtwaist dresses and flannel skirts. Neatly polished high-heeled pumps and spotless white gloves. That Ariah was three years older than G. secretly pleased him. It was like a trump card, for he knew she had to be grateful he'd chosen her. And he didn't want an immature woman for a wife, he understood that he would be the immature spouse. Ariah would take care of Gilbert as his adoring mother had done for twenty-nine years. If he was hurt, sulky, irritable, disappointed, Ariah would understand and forgive. If he flared up in a childish temper, she would forgive. All this he was counting on. An ambitious young minister requires a canny, mature, responsible wife. Attractive but not overly attractive. And Ariah was gifted, in the way of small-town, sequestered talent: He'd been impressed by her piano playing, and by the quality of her soprano voice. At a Christmas recital there was Ariah Littrell singing "Silent Night, Holy Night" so beautifully you saw her as beautiful. The sallow skin was radiant! The rather chill, shrinking eyes were green-glowing as emeralds! The small pursed mouth was gracefully opened to shape surpassingly sweet words. *Silent night, holy night. . . .* G., seated with Reverend and Mrs. Littrell, was taken by surprise. He hadn't expected to much enjoy the recital but as soon as Ariah stepped out onstage, nodded to her pianist-accompanist, and began to sing, he felt a thrill of—something. Pride? Covetousness? Sexual attraction? This beautiful, coolly poised young woman singing to an audience of admirers, strikingly dressed in a long wine-colored velvet skirt with a sash, and a long-sleeved white silk blouse. Her eyes were uplifted as if to heaven. Her narrow, tapered fingers were pressed to her bosom in an attitude of prayer. The hair that in ordinary light was dull, faded, limp was lustrous in the stage lighting. Subtle spots of rouge enlivened her face. *All is calm, all is bright. . . .* G. clenched his fists thinking, yes, yes, he would love this remarkable woman. He would make her *his*.

Run for your life.

The wedding ceremony had passed in a haze like landscape glimpsed from the window of a speeding, lurching vehicle. Though D. was not present, hadn't been able to attend, G. persisted in seeing him in the corner of his eye. D., smiling and nodding encouragement. *Yes! Good! I've done it, Gil, and so can you!* At the reception she'd begun drinking and on the drive from Troy to Niagara Falls she'd fallen asleep, her head lolling against his shoulder in a way that annoyed him, it was so intimate and yet unconscious, brainless. And in their hotel room she'd drunk most of the bottle of champagne that awaited them. She chattered nervously, her words slurred. She giggled and wiped at her mouth. Lipstick on her teeth, her clothing disheveled. Rising, she became dizzy and lost her balance; he'd had to jump up to steady her. "Ariah, dear!" Undressing for bed, she giggled and hiccuped and stumbled to him. When he stooped to kiss her wet, parted lips he tasted alcohol and panic. His heart was lurching and kicking. The bed was ludicrously large, the mattress so high from the floor, Ariah insisted he "boost" her. Heart-shaped velvet cushions everywhere, lace coverlets like nets to catch unwary fish. This was a shrine to—what? Ariah lay in the bed like an awkward sea otter in her ivory silk nightgown, hiccuping, jamming her knuckles against her mouth, and trying not to burst into laughter. Or was it hysterical sobbing?

He hadn't known what to expect, hadn't wanted to think ahead, but, dear God, he hadn't expected this. She drew him to kneel beside her, aroused and trembling as in a fever dream of lurid degradation. Beneath his hesitant weight she squirmed and moaned. Suddenly clasping her arms around his neck—tight!—tight as an octopus's tentacles—and kissing him full on the lips. Was this Ariah Littrell, the minister's spinster daughter? Clumsily seductive, one of her eyelids drooping. He couldn't bear it, her hot hands swiping blindly at him. She was moaning his name, which in her mouth sounded obscene. Groping against his chest, his belly, and groin. His penis! That any woman would touch him there, like that. . . . In a guttural moan pleading, *Love me, why can't you love me for God's sake. Do it! DO IT!* The bared gums, damp exposed teeth. A ragged swath of rust-colored hairs between her clutching thighs. She was ugly to him, repulsive. *Damn you please what's wrong with you DO IT!* Bucking her groin against him. Her bony pelvis. He wanted to strike her with his fists, pummel her until she lost consciousness and had no further knowledge of him. He too was moaning, pleading, *Stop! Don't! You disgust me.* In fact, he may have slapped her, not with the flat of his hand exactly, flailing out in instinctive self-defense, knocking her back into the oversized pillows. But she'd only laughed. Unless she was crying. The brass bed jiggled, creaked, lurched, and careened like a drunken boat. His elbow raked against her breast. There was something offensive, obscene about the small, hard breasts, the inflamed-looking nipples. He shouted and spat at her to leave him alone yet blindly she swiped at him, grabbed at him, her strong fingers gripped his penis as in the most lewd of adolescent sex fantasies. To his horror, a sharp, shuddering cry escaped from his lips even as his milky seed leapt from him piercing-sweet like a swarm of honeybees. He collapsed upon her then, panting. His brain was extinguished, like a flame that has been blown out. His heart pounded dangerously. Their sweat-slick bodies held fast.

Later he would hear her gagging and vomiting in the bathroom.

A delirium of sleep washed over him like filthy, frothy water. In the confusion of a dream he believed he might have murdered the woman whose name he couldn't remember. *Lawfully wedded wife. Death do you part.* He'd snapped her neck. Smothered her in the smelly bedclothes. Pounded and clawed between her legs. He was trying to explain to his father, and to his friend D., whom he'd betrayed. He could not bear it. Never again.

Run, run!

Crossing the plank bridge above the rapids. His bare feet in leather shoes were hurting. He'd dressed hurriedly, carelessly. His zipper had jammed. A voice lifted in his wake—"Mister? Tickets are fifty cents." Someone was calling after him. Fifty cents! G. didn't so much as glance back. He'd had a reputation, he'd prided himself in his reputation, at the seminary, for being rather aloof, even arrogant. D. was his only friend, D. was truly Christly, good. D. would understand his desperation and forgive him even if God would not. He hadn't a penny for a ticket. Where he was headed, he had no need for a penny. And possibly it was the devil who was teasing him in the guise of a bridge gatekeeper. Tempting him to turn back. Tempting him to cowardice. But G. would not succumb, for G. had vowed to see this through. To God he'd vowed. To Jesus Christ, whose salvation he repudiated he'd vowed. In the dead hour of the night, by his Bulova watch nearing five o'clock, he'd knelt on the hard tile floor of the bathroom. Steeling himself to endure the woman's odor. Vomit, sweat. Odor of unclean female flesh. He'd bared his soul to his maker, that it be extirpated by the roots. For he had no need of a soul now. This act would be his crucifixion. A man's death and not a coward's. D. would see. All the world would see.

And no possibility of survival.

Behind him the gatekeeper shouted. There was desperation in this stranger's voice, but G. paid no heed. To his left the Niagara River was wild, deafening. The Falls, he knew, were ahead. He could scarcely see but he knew The Falls were ahead. It was Terrapin Point he sought, knowing by the map that it was the southernmost tip of the little island. The Falls were so loud now as to be mesmerizing, calming. Mist and spray blinded him but he had no need any longer to see. His glasses slid down his nose. In an audacious gesture of which he'd never have been capable in life he seized them and flung them into space. Good riddance! No more! Suddenly he was at the railing. At Terrapin Point. So soon? His hands groped out and closed around the topmost rung of the railing. He lifted a foot, a slippery-soled shoe, almost lost his balance but righted himself, breathlessly positioning himself on top of the rung, and over the rung, even as a part of his mind recoiled in disbelief and even bemusement thinking, *You can't be serious, Gilbert! This is ridiculous, they've given you a new car, you can't die.* But he was over the railing, and in the water, swept instantaneously forward with the rushing current and within two swift seconds his skull was broken, his brain extinguished forever; within ten swift seconds his heart had stopped, like a clock whose mechanism has been smashed. His backbone was snapped, and snapped, and snapped like the dried wishbone of a turkey clutched at by greedy, giggling children, and his body was flung lifeless as a rag doll at the foot of the Horseshoe Falls, lifted and dropped and lifted again and sucked downward amid churning water, lost now to the appalled sight of the sole witness on the sidewalk above Terrapin Point though shortly it would be regurgitated from the foot of The Falls and swept downriver three-quarters of a mile past the Whirlpool Rapids and into the Devil's Whirlpool where it would be sucked downward from sight and for seven days and nights trapped in the spiraling water the broken body would spin like a deranged moon in orbit until, in His mercy, God granted the miracle of putrefaction to inflate the body with gases, floating it to the surface of the foaming water, and release.

Amazing Grace
Bradford Morrow

> *Whereas I was blind, now I see.*
> —John 9:25

THE MIRACLE THAT RESTORED my sight, one wicked winter morning, was a miracle which led to many desperate others. Who could have foreseen the catastrophes that followed this moment I had dreamed of for over a decade? The only blessing that accompanied the sudden, unexpected reversal of my blindness was this: I was alone when it happened. My wife was away shopping; the two children were out. Myself, I was in my humble study, listening to an old recording of Sviatoslav Richter playing Schubert's Sonata in G Major. Thanks to Sarah, a fire crackled in the wood-burning stove, making my sanctum warm and dry—the room where I worked was an uninsulated extension added to the house in the months after my accident. A pot of nice fragrant cinnamon tea was on my desk, along with my Braille Bible, some reference books also in Braille, and my computer loaded with voice-synthesizing software I used to draft the many motivational speeches I gave touring the country. It has always struck me as ironic, although naturally I never mentioned it in my uplifting talks, that I made a far better living after the accident than when I was among the sighted. No one would have paid a plug nickel to hear me speak before tragedy struck me down. Now I filled rented auditoriums and motel convention halls, and my talks on surviving personal crises were well received wherever I went. Not that my philosophy about adversity management was more informed or refined than the next survivor's—not a vain bone in *this* body—it's just my story had all the necessary elements. The perfect life, the great disabling affliction, the season of despair, the awakening of hope, and the long road of spiritual renewal that rewards the steadfast pilgrim with a life far richer than what seemed so perfect before. Sarah, I must say, deftly supervised this unanticipated chautauqua career of mine, from bookings to billings, and oversaw with the help of our dedicated manager every detail of our burgeoning mission. And with seldom—no, never a complaint. She was nothing less than a stoic saint, an altruistic martyr, with just enough savvy to hold our shattered lives together, not only keeping her eye on our spiritual needs, but making sure there was always bread on the table.

One reason I have been so successful on the circuit is because I believed every word I said, or at least *most every word.* To the sort of individual who attends such seminars, unwavering personal conviction on the part of the speaker is nine-tenths the victory. I have often felt that if I held up an egg in the palm of my hand and proclaimed with firm faith that it was not an egg, but a flower or a shoe, say, the right audience of seekers would cry out in agreement, *So it is!* With conviction and what might be called a *winning idiosyncrasy in the presenter*—in my case, blindness—one can bring people around to anything. That I never used my powers of persuasion to ends other than kindly inspiration, positive role-modeling, carrying the simple message of hope to souls willing to listen, pleases me. The temptation to deceive was always there, somehow, but it was a human weakness never acted upon. Not that I'd have known what to deceive my acolytes about, nor that I ever made the logical next step to consider the possibility that some of them entertained deceptive thoughts regarding me. No one, I convinced myself, would want to victimize this victim: Hadn't I suffered enough? The answer is *I had not even begun my real suffering.*

Not born blind, indeed I had 20/20 vision for thirty years. A robust, confident young man, I met my Sarah at a church bazaar—we were always active members at St. Francis Episcopal—and it was love at first sight. Her thick auburn hair drifting in gentle waves down the back of her white dress, her quick blue eyes, the exquisite mole above her lip, the strong warm hands that shook mine when we were introduced, her smile as radiant as dawn. How many times since my world fell into shadow have I conjured up the visual memory of that day. After a succinct courtship, we married and started a family. Rebecca was born first, and then the twins, Emma and Luke. Emma survived only a few weeks, poor little bird. My grief over the loss was so great that to this day I indulge in fantasizing about her, what her interests would have been, how her voice might have sounded. I would like to think she'd have turned out a trustworthy Milton's daughter. In my mind's eye, I always pictured her as a young Sarah, slender as a willow and sturdy as an oak, along those lines. But we all know how ingenious imagination can be, how it sometimes finds *a shining berth* in the rankest mound of dung.

Time passed, our young family thrived. My job at the utilities company was going well enough; the benefits were good and hours such that I could spend quality time with my children. I worked the graveyard shift at the local power plant as a maintenance technician troubleshooting outages, servicing customer emergencies, getting people back on line when an ice storm or high wind brought down wires or blew out a transformer. In the Northeast, where we live just a mile from my own childhood home, our crew had more to do during the night than one might imagine. Always something going wrong, always some problem to remedy. I very much enjoyed the challenge, as I've told my rapt audiences, and learned a lot meeting people from all walks of life under trying circumstances. So long as I live, I will never forget the courage of the little girl—her name was Belinda, if I'm not mistaken—who, during a severe nor'easter that crippled not just Gloucester but the whole corridor from the Carolinas up to Maine, offered her mommy her teddy bear to feed to the flames in the fireplace that heated their home while our crew worked through the night to restore power. A bunch of us later pooled together to buy her a new bear, bigger and fuzzier than the one she sacrificed. *Duress* brings out the *best* in us—so I often advised my Ramada listeners. In a file somewhere there is a newspaper clipping with a photograph of Belinda surrounded by her benefactors and our stuffed bear. Sarah had it up on the refrigerator for months. She thought it was a flattering shot. I must have looked pleased with myself, because in those days I was. Life was a river awash with proverbial milk and honey.

A stifling, muggy midsummer night changed all that. I wasn't even supposed to work the shift, but a massive brownout across our regional grid forced the company to call upon every available hand. My memory of that night is selective at best. I whispered goodbye to Sarah, kissed the children where they lay asleep in their bedrooms. The streets were eerily dim. Thick steamy amber haze hung in the wilted trees. Cicadas had burrowed up from the earth to mate that year, dogday locusts we called them, and were lustily clicking and buzzing away outside the open windows of our utility van, their boisterous droning sounding like bandsaws underwater. We were at work on a central routing transformer, using the headlights of the van to see by, when I must have made the simplest error, crossing two clusters of wire in such a way that I sparked a high-voltage explosion. Knocked unconscious, I have no recollection of what happened in the hours that followed. My first perceptions had only to do with a searing, bludgeoning pain in my neck and around the base of my hot skull. My face was burned and my eyes felt as if they were molten.

Recuperation swallowed up days and weeks of time, all of which remains vague even now. What stands out from the miasma of my slow recovery was the ophthalmologist's concern that the many lesions on the corneas of both eyes were healing, as he'd expected them to, but my vision still hadn't returned. Yet one should have resulted in the other. I could make out uneasy shapes at a distance of a foot or so in front of me, but had no strong sense of day or night, of whether the lights were on or off. The doctors performed tests to determine ocular blood flow, ran an MRI against the possibility of brain damage, but found nothing that would explain the blindness. My 20/20 vision was now 20/400 at best and when I was released from the hospital my condition was not only unimproved, but worsening. They continued to chart my progress but there wasn't much more that could be done medically.

Summer faded into fall. The once steady stream of colleagues and friends who dropped in to visit, read me the Bible, listen to music with me, dwindled. I couldn't in fairness expect otherwise. Sarah's considerate idea of building an extension onto the house, thus to spare me the trouble and danger of walking up and down stairs I couldn't see, kept me busy for a while. Not that I was able to help. But my wife and the contractor did consult with me about construction specs. Ever the *clever one in our family*, Sarah suggested we might save money by forgoing windows in my modest wing—they could be added later, when and if my sight returned—and used the balance of the home improvement loan to carpet the whole house. I thought it an extravagance, but she insisted it would cushion any falls I happened to take. Although my equilibrium hadn't been a problem, I commended her ingenuity.

Around Thanksgiving I lost my job. My supervisor was kind enough to give me the bad news in person. They'd held out as long as they could, he said, sitting with me in my den over some chowder Sarah served us in mugs. Damn bad luck, he told me, his voice gooey from the thick soup *if not the tacky sentiment*. I nodded, trying to form an understanding smile on my lips, though I'd already begun to forget what I looked like before the accident, and had no clear concept what such a smile might look like now. Vivid silence clouded the room before I heard him shift in his seat and rise to leave. Your workman's comp is all in order, he said, taking my free hand into his, which was clammy. I thanked him, climbing to my feet. I wanted to touch his face but hadn't the nerve to ask. As I recall, he had a dense, large nose, the by-product of a long-standing love affair with cheap scotch chased by cheaper ale. Balls and beer, the boys used to call it at work, a thousand years ago. Off the top of my head I couldn't tell you his or any of their names now.

Then came the truly dark days. Days that added up to months, a year of miserable months that vanished like voices murmuring in an empty room. Learning Braille was a necessary but grim admission that my blindness was not the temporary setback my ophthalmologist had diagnosed. A second sightless Christmas came and went. Luke and Becca seemed happy with their presents, none of which I could see any more than I could their presumptive beaming faces. Sarah thanked me for the nightgown I bought her with the help of a salesperson who was kind enough to describe it to me over the telephone—rayon, beige, a few flounces edged in lace. We tried to act celebratory, to make the best of the situation, and I even indulged in a little champagne which gave me a migraine that lasted a week. Sitting alone in my personal black hole on New Year's Eve, I urged Sarah to go without me to a party down the street, hire a sitter, *enjoy herself a little.* It hardly seemed fair for her, who looked after me day and night, to stay home reading to me from Isaiah, or Job, while I followed along with my fingers. Even as I sat wallowing in my misfortune that evening, listening to Mahler and eating a bowl of popcorn my wife had placed on the side table, I guessed the busybodies were talking about none other than me and what a shame all this was for poor Sarah, who was still so young and vibrant. I drowned myself in the choral voices of the Ninth Symphony, then fell asleep in my chair. Later, Sarah woke me and led me by the arm upstairs to bed, which smelled of roses and sage. My melancholy delirium lifted for a moment, for these fragrances reminded me of the careless, caring nights we used to enjoy, the nights of intimacy that resulted in the birth of our babies. Half awake, I kissed her and thanked her for all she had done to help me through this tragedy. I promised her— though she might not have heard, since I could tell by her breathing she was asleep—that I would try harder, would overcome the doldrums that made life so tough this past year and a half. That I would do something with myself, defeat my disability in some way, learn to see anew, like blind Bartimaeus whom Jesus cured in Jericho with nothing more than a few words of encouragement.

True to my promise, the next morning I glued Braille tabs to the keys of my old typewriter and sat myself down to outline everything that conspired to bring me to my present predicament, and what I believed as I began my long journey back to life. Sarah set me up with a fresh ream of paper. The work was slow. It took a while to get a feel for producing words and phrases through the clumsy machinery of the typewriter. Not being able to review what I'd just written, I had to visualize the sentences fore and aft in my head. Initially, Sarah read me back what I'd sketched, but even she had reasonable limits as to how much time she could devote to my little project. The children weren't getting younger. She had even taken a part-time position with that contractor who built the extension, in order to supplement my benefits. He was called Jim James, a name whose triumph of redundancy might have intimated the ways matters were drifting but did not. We were grateful for the income.

At first I thought to write an article for the St. Francis newsletter about how faith in God is essential to our surviving crises, or some such, but as I got the ideas down on paper, I realized it was one cliché after another and of no use to anybody. I had to *delve deeper into my reservoir of pain* so turned some of my ideas around backwards and found they came out much better. Faith alone, in other words, was not enough to carry us through. Rather, it was one oar we could use to pull our fragile ship through the turbulent waters of doubt and despair, the other oar being hope. Like that. I spent hours on end working out my thoughts, quoting passages from my King James whenever the reference seemed apropos, or sometimes—if the pretty image struck my fancy—when it wasn't. Not only did the newsletter publish my first effort but, thanks to someone in the congregation who showed it to an editor at the local paper, reminding him who I was—*the man blinded while trying to bring light to others,* as he put it—I was commissioned to write a human interest article detailing the aftermath of that horrifying night. I missed the deadline and Sarah asked for an extension, which they granted. When I did turn in my manuscript I explained in an apologetic cover letter that typing on an old Royal rigged with Braille tabs that kept falling off made for perhaps not the best working conditions. I hoped nevertheless that they would find the final product worthy of their esteemed pages.

The memoir was a success. Letters came in from around the state, the most gushing of which were published in the newspaper over the days that followed. Sarah knocked on my door soon after, announcing that the editor himself had dropped by the house with something that might make me very happy. Indeed, I was floored by Mr. Harrison's kindness. On behalf of everyone at the paper, he presented me with a used computer preloaded with software for the blind. Little Luke, who was eight then and computer savvy, taught me how to use this gift, and within a matter of months I was contributing regularly to various periodicals distributed in the area. From this print exposure came my first invitations to speak before the public. My wife's *inherent Christian strength of spirit* was aroused by what she saw happening before her eyes. The love, empathy, and compassion she witnessed flowing toward her husband from these strangers, common workaday people who listened intently to what insights I was able to give them, overwhelmed dear Sarah. That Mr. Harrison offered to assist us financially, lift the burden of her having to work for the contractor, so she could devote more time to helping answer every request to address this crowd or that, constituted another blessing on our household. I, who had come to abide misfortune, was now in the pulpit of Everyman, as it were. *Many are called but few are chosen*, the Bible tells us, and I—an unfledged beggar by the waters of Siloam—was called.

Sarah was never more attentive, more heedful than during the heady times that followed. Invite followed invite, obliging us to be away from home for days, even weeks, at a time. When my wife told me that we'd begun to charge sponsors a nominal fee to offset expenses of travel, lodging, meals, not to mention the live-in housekeeper who also looked after Luke and Becca, I didn't object, though deep down I would have preferred offering my inspirational views without money attached. Harrison advised her on the best ways to proceed, and acted on my behalf as an agent, placing my lectures in various journals and anthologies, *building the rep*, as he put it. They were right, of course, telling me that if we wanted to get my message out there, we needed assistance, and who better than the listeners and readers themselves to assist? The venture was worthy, we all knew. There were many who wanted, needed, to hear my story of hardship and hope. I told Sarah that, if she didn't mind, she should be the one who managed the practicalities with Harrison's help. Back in the halcyon days before the world went dark I wore the financial pants in the house, if you will. Given that now I couldn't tell a one-dollar check from another of a thousand made our positions clear. Sarah agreed with all my requests, *bless her heart*. Both my muse and protector, she was brilliant in her role.

What possible point would there be in reproducing a transcript of the speeches I made? Often I was introduced by a local priest or minister. My wife would then lead me to the podium. Applause. I launched straightaway into my backstory, guided my auditors from the shadowy valley of pain and grief to the mountain of renewal and joy. Self-pity was just that: a *pit* from which we must rise and shine. I told them about my New Year's Eve revelation, mentioning how I had come to believe that the marvelous scent of sage and roses in the bedroom that night was an auspicious sign from God, the soulstruck breath of my guardian angel. My favorite concluding exhortation was *Don't be afraid of miracles.* Applause. Then a few questions and answers. Do you think that God will restore your sight one day? was the perennial query I could count on being asked. My response was, in this life or the next, I know He will let me see my wife and children again, for *He's a good and generous God.* A reception would follow during which the voices around me brimmed with appreciative respect that made me understand just how attached each member of the human family is to another. My calling as a missionary of faith suited me well and as the years elapsed the uneasy peace I'd made with my blindness deepened. Never would I have touched so many lives had I not been stricken. I like to think that I was always a good man, but so many have proclaimed there's a genuine spark of greatness in me that at times I have to believe there may be. If so, all credit goes to our Savior, as such blessings flow only from Him, and so forth.

Home, now, from nine weeks on the road, after a restless night in my bed in the study—Sarah and I agreed to sleep in separate quarters after such long trips on the circuit because when I was particularly fatigued I tossed and turned—I awoke feeling not quite myself. True, I had been working harder than ever. Our schedule had been nonstop for months, so perhaps this explained my sensation of unbalance. Along with prayer, music has always been my remedy for any illness, and so it was I'd put on Schubert's Opus 78 for piano, whose divine opening chords would, I was sure, bring me around. Martita, the housekeeper, served cinnamon tea and tended my fire. Not wanting to bother her—and besides, the monumental Richter seemed to be working his magic—I said nothing about my disposition.

Some minutes after she closed my door, abrupt pain erupted in my temples. Beset by wild dizziness, by violent nausea, by spasms that stabbed like long needles through my skull, I shrieked, though no noise left my throat. Gasping, I rolled from my chair onto the floor, hitting my head as I did. I tried to call out for Sarah but couldn't. Then, as suddenly as the pain began it was replaced by numbness. I could hear the piano music very distantly, as if it were coming from the far end of a long tunnel. Light engulfed my eyes—a cascade, a flood, a torrent of *unblinding light.* As I grabbed at the arms of my chair to stand, I found myself staring into what appeared to be flames dancing behind the grate of the potbellied stove. My eyes agonizingly darted around the room and there, in this dim place on whose walls firelight flickered—more like Plato's cave than a Christian's den—were all the things I'd come to know only by touch. My table, my books, my computer, my cot, my chair. No embellishments, nothing on the walls, all very minimal, even dreary to my naive eyes. But of course, I thought. Why decorate? Why wallpaper a blind man's cell? Standing now, a bit shaky, admiring *my wife's wise Christian expediency,* I walked around placing my hands on everything, still not quite sure what was happening. My vision was blurry but with each new moment I became more reassured this wasn't a dream, a taunting nightmare. The radical pain having largely subsided, I remained a little numb, whether from excitement or physiological impulse, I didn't know or care. I wanted to climb to the roof and cry out to the world that my miracle had finally come. My feet carried me to the door that led to the main house, and I who rarely left my sanctum—why should I have?—opened it.

Bright white light poured through the living room windows, sun reflected off the snow. But for the ticking of a clock, in Franz Schubert's wake, the house was silent. I took a few tentative steps and gazed, blinking hard while heavily tearing, in wonder. What had happened to our simple home? If you will, I couldn't believe my eyes. The walls were gilded and the windows dressed with billowing chiffon sashes. In an alcove stood a gargantuan breakfront on whose glassed shelves were countless porcelain figurines. I stumbled ahead toward facing sofas and stuffed chairs upholstered in striped silks of chartreuse and gold. Here was a commode with a marble top and a vase of orchids above the marquetry. There were two reclining brass deer on a prayer rug by the hearth. An antique grandfather clock clad in luminous mahogany stood haughty in a corner. Oriental carpets of red, blue, yellow, and green lay atop the white wall-to-wall. Fine old portraits of men and women dressed in the garb of another century hung everywhere, staring out at me from canvases black as lacquer. A chandelier centered it all, its prisms reflecting hundreds of tiny rainbows on the ceiling, which was done up with decorative plaster moldings. Though I examined each piece of furniture, horrified and fascinated, and though what I saw was as tangible as truth itself, my heart sank, because I knew this couldn't be so.

297

I pinched myself, closed my eyes, reopened them. But the room didn't change. If anything, it became more lavish as my sore eyes adjusted to the light.

A familiar sound came from upstairs. It seemed to be Harrison, softly whistling to himself some random tune, as he often did when he accompanied us on the road. I thought to call out his name, tell him the astonishing news, ask him to come down, fall to his knees with me and *pray Lord God thanks for this deliverance,* but didn't. Who knows how or wherefrom inner voices speak to us, or in what mysterious ways they confide to us involuntary prophecies that save us from harm, disillusion, even doom? The whistling stopped and when it did, I took a couple of steps back, bumping into a side table and knocking a crystal lamp to the floor. I was startled to hear Harrison say, *Bunny?* And hearing him ask the question again, this time in a deeper, softer, more melodiously concerned voice, I looked around for a place to hide, *an Adam's fig leaf as it were,* suddenly frightened, frightened even beyond the terror of finding myself among the sighted, standing there agog, a dumb novitiate, a stranger in my own house. He glided down the carpeted stairs, silent as a proverbial ghost, and seemed relieved to find me, half-crouching behind one of the big plush sofas. You all right? asked Harrison. Instinctively, I stared forward and said I was. What did I break? I wanted to know. Out of the corner of my eye I saw him inspecting the damage, dressed to the nines in a deep blue silk robe, the same color I remembered Sarah's irises as being. His hair, which I'd always pictured black and short, was silver and stylishly long. His unshaven face was taut and handsome. Averting my eyes when he glanced at me, I noticed that he, like Sarah, had a mole, though his was on the cheek. What bothered me most was that his robe was open in the front. If my wife or children were to walk into the room just then, what an eyeful they'd get. Think how embarrassed everyone would be. Stay here, he calmly requested, his voice sweet but the look on his suntanned face as annoyed as a pet owner scolding a naughty puppy. Taking me by the arm, he sat me by the gold wall in a chair appointed with fine overstuffed upholstery. I could have sworn he cursed under his breath as he left, but at that moment I didn't trust my ears any more than my eyes. At least while he retreated toward the kitchen he tied his winsome dressing gown. I had caught a subtle glimpse of what hung there, haloed by white hair. It was nothing anyone should want to see, let alone someone who'd been denied the privilege of seeing anything whatever for a decade.

Other astonishments appeared. The more I saw, the more I understood it was important, somehow, that those around me thought I saw nothing. Conspicuous among my discoveries was how wrong I'd imagined everyone and everything. I who had begun truly to believe my fervent homilies, urging my followers to keep the faith first by trusting themselves, their convictions, their own views—*be thee blind or seeing with lucid eyes*—slowly understood how utterly I'd erred. If that morning returned to me my sight, the rest of the day brought my insights, as I have come to think of them. Harrison in his baronial robe waltzing through our kinky nouveau riche living room was merely the first verse in my New Apocrypha. Martita, who came to clean up the broken lamp, was someone whose voice, again, I recognized but whose appearance struck me as incongruous with the life I'd believed my family was leading. Not that she, poor Cayman immigrant and clearly a good if very illegal girl, behaved in any way that could be perceived as unchristian. No, it was that they had her in a black uniform with white starched trim and in a state of *quasi-penal subservience.* Harrison wondered if I wouldn't like to go back to my room, said I looked exhausted, Lord knows no one would blame me for wanting a little more rest, given the grueling schedule I had just endured. Again I asked what I'd broken and he answered that it was nothing, just a glass one of the kids left on an end table, not to worry. The maid crossed herself and, having finished cleaning, left the room. Where is Sarah? I asked, my hands shaking although I anchored them between my thighs. Out, he said, shopping. When I inquired when she was expected back, he muttered something and, excusing himself, flew upstairs, ever silently, no doubt to change into some clothes.

Time passed—twenty-three minutes to be exact, now that I could watch the clock—then Sarah unlocked the grand front door. Making her way to the kitchen, she failed to notice her husband seated in an unwonted corner, escapee from his holy cage. The years had not been kind. My once wholesome Sarah had acquired, I must admit, a gaunt sophistication. Though elegant and drily beautiful, her face was as if invaded by knives—angular, hewn, deblooded. It was all I could do to maintain on my own face the blankest possible expression. This was only the beginning. What I saw next *I wouldn't wish on the Prince of Darkness himself.* Harrison floated back downstairs, gathered my wife in his arms and kissed her, put his forefinger to his lips, and pointed in my direction. I would like to believe she might have fainted, standing there in the arms of this man, staring at her blind husband not thirty feet away. To the contrary, she sweetly called my name, breaking from Harrison's embrace, and asked me the same question he had, patting my head, offering to help me get back to my room. I needed more rest, she cooed. After all, we had only a week before we were committed to going to Louisville for the Christian Recovery Convention, at which I was one of the headliners. Bed did seem a desirable destination at the moment. Yes, bed, I answered, and allowed her to take me by the arm, as she had countless times over the last decade, and lead me into my hermitage. I fell asleep immediately.

Seeing the world, I had not yet come to know how to reckon it. That was, I always felt, God's distinct purview, His task. Yet in the days that followed, seeing what I saw was judgment enough and though Job was my cherished Old Testament hero, I would prove to be no Job. Seeing, like my original blinding, was an unexpected trauma, a crossroads. The more I reflect upon what has happened, whether from a vantage of darkness or light, the more I see life as an investigation into just this: how much pain we can tolerate before we either (1) turn ourselves humbly over to our God, that His will be done, or (2) turn against the sadistic Bastard *with every fiber of our being.* Just how He found the fortitude, tenacity, and nerve to look down on me from on high these ten long suffering years, knowing all the while that every word of encouragement I offered to the far-flung members of His miscellaneous flock was fouled by the adultery and avarice of those who pretended to sustain His wretched servant, I cannot pretend to know. The ways of the Almighty are, it has been often recorded, mysterious. We mere mortals who fail to know our own hearts can't begin to fathom what motivates His. Not that my poor wife's weakness of the flesh, her infidelity, and materialist lust are in any way the fault of the Precious Savior. Nor that my bene-factor and proponent, Harrison, without whose support I might never have found my audience, all those hungry souls who have dined— I hope nutritiously—at my inspirational banquets, was guided by the hand, if not the hoof, of the Lamb. As I lay in the equally dark but somehow less blurry shadows of my new world, as deeply dejected as I ever was when I first lost my sight, I decided to follow my instincts and *see what there was to see.* My life became a blindman's bluff.

Sarah checked in on me sometime later that same day, concerned why I'd been stumbling around the living room. Was I feeling all right? she wanted to know. I was fine, I assured her, and testing the waters asked if I couldn't sleep upstairs with her tonight. We generally had separate bedrooms on the road, and so often slept apart at home, I said; surely the Lord would want a wife to abide some snoring now and then, if only *for the sake of Old Testament conjugal duty.* Though I stared at the wall behind her, the look of dismay that shrouded her face, like Beelzebub's specter, was unmistakable. Her voice smilingly assured me that we need to take it easy during this week off, while the frown on her lips mutely bespoke another message. I wanted to say, how could I have been so blind to her true feelings all this time? but kept my own counsel and meekly agreed. That seemed to brighten her mood. Her face relaxed as she brushed back her frosted hair and asked what kind of soup I wanted Martita to bring me for lunch. Barley, I said, and watched my estranged wife's hips pitch softly back and forth as she left the sanctum.

The children were my only hope. My wonderful babies, my joys, bounty of my loins. They, I assured myself, had not veered from the path of righteousness like their mother. Persisting with my charade the next morning, I once more entered the main house. Rather than loiter in the garish living room, I joined Martita in the kitchen, which was also extensively renovated, shiny chrome and glass everywhere, and a tile-work splashback depicting urns choked with flowers and French farm scenes. Though she was at first surprised by my appearing in her domain, Martita helped me to a chair at the long table and got me my morning tea. It was quite early, I saw by the wall clock, too early for Sarah, but maybe not for the kids, who I assumed would come down first, on their way to class. Becca was in her last year of high school, and Luke a junior. As Martita busied herself, chatting amiably about this and that, I furtively studied her, wondering just how much she knew about the goings-on around here. Her black hair combed into a chignon, her handsome concise form moving lithely in her uniform, her dark eyes, her pretty hands—she cut a finer figure than I had imagined. Some obvious questions came to mind to ask her, but I thought the better of it. Ease up, I reminded myself. As St. Paul advised in his Epistle to the Hebrews, *Let us run with patience the race that is set before us.*

Luke entered the kitchen first. That is, a young man whom Martita referred to as Luke. Rather than coming downstairs, however, to have his breakfast, he ducked through the back door having apparently spent the night elsewhere. Abstracted, with eyes glazed, he noticed me as he opened the refrigerator door and drank long and hard from an orange juice carton, but said nothing. His hair was every bit as orange as the juice he consumed, and rose in numerous spikes off the top of his head. His mascara was smudged—little Luke wore mascara? Great chunks of silver graced each of his fingers. He was skinny as a broomstick and looked the warlock part he affected. I sat in stunned silence, maintaining my own vacant glazed-over stare which matched my son's. I didn't know they made boots that big. What's *he* doing here? Luke asked Martita. I interrupted, How are you doing this morning, Luke? Awright, I guess, he answered. You're up with the roosters, I pressed, at the same time wondering if he oughtn't be nervous that the coffin lids were all supposed to be down by this time, and then saw him give Martita a look that could only be described as threatening. Sure am, he said, taking a fat green apple from the bowl of fruit on the table and politely excusing himself with a sneer. After he left the kitchen, I said, Luke's a fine young man, isn't he.

If both Sarah and Luke had gone the way of Judas, and Harrison with them, it seemed improbable Rebecca had managed to resist the tide of treachery. For having *betrayed my credulous innocence with vizor'd falsehood, and base forgery*, as blind Milton himself once wrote, *the pillared firmament is rottenness, and the earth's base is built on stubble.* I fled to my cave.

A pestilence had swept through my household, like the very dog-day locusts which prophesied the onset of my blindness that summer night a decade ago. I lay on my cot, hands over my forehead and face, unable to move, loath to think, as sweat broke out across the length of my body and a range of black emotions chased through me. Above all, I wanted never to leave my room again. They could bring me my filthy barley soup and vile cinnamon tea whenever they found time between the commission of sins, and to hell with the rest of it. Indeed, when Sarah ventured by later, reeking of sage and roses, and found me prostrate, she let out a little cry of fear. Perhaps I should be ashamed to admit it, but that cry was like sweet music to me—even better than the opening strains of Stravinsky's *Apollon Musagète,* though it sounded more like Honegger's Symphony No. 2, the *molto moderato,* so very crushingly ominous, as performed by von Karajan and the Berliner Philharmoniker. Not because I was deluded enough to think it meant she was concerned, as such, for my sake, or that my heart melted with sudden forgiveness. No, no—rather because *it gave me my idea.* Whereas before I couldn't see her face if she voiced distress on my behalf, now I did, and Sarah's look was that of a caretaker grown weary of her role, disgusted, in fact, by it. Humanitarian that I strove to be, and *many had seen fit to call me*, I reluctantly sympathized with my wife. I understood her failings and well knew how many persons of good intent and a hopeful heart nevertheless plant the earnest seeds of their goodness and optimism in *the yielding muck of ambition.* Look at Harrison. He probably didn't have designs on my wife, my home, my finances, my very self, when he first got me into print and onto a podium. How do I know? Because by the same reasoning one might say that I never intended for him to succeed so assiduously in ruining me, even as he saved the souls of thousands by helping me to save my own. Having noted that, inspiration took hold of me and would not give way to any alternative from that day forward, until it had fulfilled itself like the competent beast it was.

The idea began simply. I didn't feel up to Louisville. We would have to cancel. Sarah thought we should pray for guidance, and we went through the gesture of prayer. I still didn't feel like going. Harrison suggested that a doctor ought to be brought in to look me over. Louisville was, after all, *awfully darned important to the furtherance of the crusade*—the Christian Recovery Convention was, if I didn't mind his saying so, the Holy Grail, a motivational orator's Valhalla. It was a dream come true for me, for Sarah, for everyone who believed in my message of hope. A doctor wouldn't find anything wrong with me, I said, staring right through him. What then? he asked, before underscoring again the importance of keeping this engagement, reminding me it was the kickoff to our big tour through the South, saying something about another book deal in the works. I appreciated how much work Sarah and he had put into Louisville, the tour, all the rest, but couldn't do it. The problem was this. Somehow I lost my calling. Sarah's pale face drained of all color as she looked at Harrison, who was also ashen. You still believe in God, of course, my wife whispered. I told her I suppose I did, it wasn't that. Well, what is it, man? Harrison asked, noiselessly taking my wife's hand in his. Not sure, I said. My message of hope seemed stale, banal, for some reason, and the more I thought about it the more I'd come to believe it was one better repudiated than preached. Likewise, God seemed more complicated than I'd believed Him to be. I didn't understand Him or His ways, certainly not well enough to speak His cause before others whom, by the way, I also did not understand. Sarah withdrew her hand, stepped toward me, placed it on my head, which made me wince a little, and she said, You're tired, dear, is all . . . your audiences need you, your family needs you, *all of us need you* to go to Louisville and shine the light of truth into the darkest corners of people's souls and help them find their way back into the sun.

Sarah, it would appear, had been listening to my patent drivel these past years so perfectly was she able to quote me to myself. God in heaven, I almost laughed, but the idea had nothing to do with mirth. Instead, allow me to admit, it ran more along the lines of St. Paul's Epistle to the Romans 12:19. Look it up for yourself.

Over the days that followed my initial confession of apostasy came many wearying pleas and petitions from my wife, my manager, even the children. My prediction regarding Rebecca was not wrong. She had become what the kids call a Goth. The dyed black hair, the black fingernails, the black dress and black boots even bigger than Luke's, *if that was possible,* and a girlfriend in tow dressed in the same uniform. Becca, I should say, did seem the least egregious of the lot of heretics my family had become. She at least didn't seem to care as much as the others whether the income from my missionary work continued or not. She styled herself, I'm guessing, as a bit of an anarchist, though we all know anarchy is best proselytized by the disaffected well-to-do. Be that as it may, Rebecca was no more able to budge me from my den than the others, and Louisville soon came and went, absent its blind featured speaker. Harrison told me we received hundreds of cards and letters from well-wishers.

Which brought me to the second phase of the idea. The revenue stream must be stopped. This was not as simple as merely dropping off the lecture circuit since, clearly, Harrison had invested wisely and, despite myself, money still flowed in with those letters. An anonymous tip to the Internal Revenue Service informing them that my family and closest advisor were bilking our religious foundation of tens of thousands of dollars, maybe more, for personal gain, rather than funding programs for the blind and other disableds, got the job done. It all went rather quickly. The lien on our home and bank accounts, the removal of the furniture and frippery in the living room and everywhere else in this house—yes, things moved irrevocably, decisively. Sarah spent a lot of time crying, I can report. When she wasn't doing that she was arguing with Harrison. Luke simply disappeared off the scene. And Rebecca, I gathered, was spending more and more time over at her girlfriend's place. Harrison's indictment for fraud and income tax evasion was bittersweet for me though my residual sentimentality toward him, the former him, I should say, the man who did help me in the beginning, faded away to nothing when I learned how much we had earned over those fruitful years, and how much he had stolen from his gullible mistress. They broke up. And once my lawyer—a former devotee who volunteered his time—cleared me of any collaboration in my handlers' schemes, I filed for divorce from the lovely Sarah, who, seeing there was nothing to salvage, didn't contest the action. The foundation was dismantled. The media was ruthless. An insightful if scathing article about *my amazing fall from grace* was published in the very newspaper that gave me my computer and printed my own first efforts. Fond memories. Now I was left with the house and enough money to live modestly, having such comforts as society thinks are due a poor blind fellow who'd been bruised a bit in the proverbial school of hard knocks.

While I sometimes feel a numbness in the pit of my stomach when pondering the arc of my brilliant life, I still have my Sviatoslav Richter disc of Schubert's Sonata in G Major to comfort me. I still indulge in fantasizing how my daughter Emma, had she lived, would have saved me from my hapless enemies if not myself. But the past has passed. The sole question that remains is whether or not to feign a sudden miraculous recovery of my sight after Martita becomes my new bride. God knows, there's much to be said for blindness, especially when one can see. Either way, I'm sure she and I will be quite happy living here together once we get this damn gilt off the walls.

The Supremes
Rick Moody

I'VE USED LOTS OF KINDS of portables. All for patriotism. Like when we were protesting against the Million Mom March, there were just ten or twenty of us girls out on the plaza with signs and banners, and every now and then, you know, we needed to use the bank of Maxim 3000 portables the moms were using. We hid the signs back of the benches on the Mall when we had to go. They didn't know us from Adam. When you're using the next stall over from some other girl you don't care about her politics, you just hope she puts some paper down on the seat. I don't actually think all those moms were really moms, if you know what I mean. I think a lot of them were homosexuals. But I was raised to be polite. I'm not going to say whether they were homosexuals, even though I could see that they didn't shave. I didn't need to bring it up in the bathroom line. That would have been impolite. Anyway, the Maxim 3000 is a very nice portable, especially in royal blue or sand. The tank holds seventy gallons, and the walls are nice and smooth, and they can be cleaned *lickety-split,* and that's one thing I'll say for the Million Moms, they kept their portable toilets clean. For a southern girl, it makes a difference.

Let's say it's a protest for some inner-city cause that I don't particularly agree with, and there are other sorts of people there. They might have a different kind of portable altogether. I don't personally go in for those sorts of protests, because the time I came to protest against affirmative action—I had a sign that said *Quotas for People Who Ain't Even Votas,* which is a slogan my girlfriend Darlene thought up—I got spat at. I'm a churchgoer. I'm a redhead who lots of eligible young men sure would like to take home to meet their folks. I used to be a cheerleader. I wouldn't hurt a flea. But I got spat at a whole bunch of times while exercising my constitutionally protected rights of free speech. I've cleaned really *icky* blobs of spit out of my eyes and my hair, boy, you really don't want to know about it. Anyway, if I did go to those sorts of rallies now where they're smoking marijuana cigarettes and crack and who knows what else, well, then I'd probably be more acquainted with the Tuffway model of portable, because the Tuffway has a Fresh Flush interior swirly thing, you know, for the obvious reasons. Sometimes you just need suction. Also a seventy-gallon tank and a hand pump in case of accidents. When the Promise Keepers came to the District of Columbia and had that outdoor rally, I didn't actually go to that event, but Daddy did. That was one of his last rallies. I just went to the Nordstrom's at Pentagon City. I like Nordstrom's a whole lot. A girl can really get herself done up there. Promise Keepers had the Freedom 2 portable, which is a men's urinal house manufactured by the same folks who brought you the Tuffway. It can fit several boys at a time. I think the Freedom 2 is a really wholesome name for an American urinal.

Over by the Vietnam Memorial, they feature the Sani-Jon. The Vietnam War, well, don't get me started. We got all weak-kneed about our military and how important it was that those boys in uniforms were ready to fight for us. It's there in the Bible, you know, eye for an eye, and those nice young men, they were trying to prevent communists and gamblers from getting a foothold in our country, the envy of the world. You can't win a war if the college students are out in the street taking drugs and having orgies. My college, by the way, is the Richmond College for Women, of Richmond, VA, and most of the girls there think that women shouldn't serve in the military at all, and that men should do their patriotic duty and then come on home in their uniforms and teach their wives about liberty and valor.

The Vietnam Memorial, what happened is that I came out of the double clamshell door of the Sani-Jon, this was a couple of days ago, when I got into town on my first-ever solo protest adventure, and I walked by that statue, the nice statue of the soldiers that's a ways away from that boring wall—that thing looks like the baffling they put up along the interstate—and I don't know what happened because my daddy taught me how to be strong *and* caring, and I have things in my purse that could hurt a man. Like mace and pepper spray. And I carry a pistol, because I have a right. It's all registered. I do a lot of protesting, and also I visit a lot of portables, so I carry a pistol, and I even brought my pistol to the Million Mom March, especially to the Million Mom March, because no lesbian is going to tell me I have to leave my gun at home. Anyway, I'm embarrassed to say it, but I started crying at that stupid Vietnam Memorial wall. Even if Jesus is my personal savior and God is on the side of the USA, I saw that man in the wheelchair with the ponytail, didn't have any arms or legs, he was wearing fatigues and crying at the stupid wall,

307

and everybody thought, well, these Vietnam veterans they didn't fight hard enough, or the president didn't have the political capital to drop *the big one* over there, which is what he should have done, well, I cried anyway, because of this soldier with the missing legs and arms, so I took myself right back to the portable, where I got all emotional and had to reapply mascara, because suddenly I didn't know if it was the plan of my personal savior to blow off the arms and legs of the veterans with the ponytails, just because these boys preferred bad music or didn't have the money to go to private schools; sometimes I wonder why that's the plan of Jesus, because everybody is some mother's son.

When I'm with the folks, down on the farm in Albemarle County, when we're visiting with other First Families of Virginia, it's hot and everyone's out on the porch, and the talk just goes where it will go, and there's lots of people laughing about which baseball team did what, and what the prospects are for the football or basketball teams, that's one kind of afternoon I know pretty well, and everything is easy on the porch and we're with good people and those days are gentle and they will be memorable for years and years to come. I was a cheerleader for the football team. I really liked Bobby Prescott, the quarterback, but he didn't know I was alive. Later he was arrested for drunk driving. I would have kept him from that, because I would have loved him as best as a girl can love a quarterback. I wouldn't have let him drive after drinking, I would have given him a piece of my mind, and he would have remembered it. This is the dream that I dream sometimes, when it's so humid you can't really believe it and you just have to try to stay put as well as you can. That's how it was during this past summer when the campaign was winding down. One day I was in the backyard looking at birds with a pair of old binoculars when I caught my father in the crosshairs of my lenses throwing up in the garden. One second he was unsteady with his clippers, lurching around clipping things, next second he was doubled over, wiping off his mouth. He pretended like nothing had happened at all.

By autumn everything had gone all to heck. I took my dog down to get groomed while the recounts were being requested in Broward and Volusia counties, and the preachers I listen to regularly, their broadcasts were playing in the canine beauty parlor, and it was like a hive of angry bees had descended into that radio station, they were so upset about the election, about how the election was gonna get stolen. They were saying it was time for people to be protesting in

the streets, why, all the churches in the state of Virginia, they needed people to raise their voices, they need people to be making signs,
they needed to mobilize, and that's how our organization, the Loud
and Unbowed, started getting involved. If we didn't watch out this
whole darned thing was going to *go the wrong way on us*, on the
lord Jesus Christ, king of kings.

One thing led to another, the absentee ballot mess down there in
Leon County, the suits challenging that butterfly ballot in Palm
Beach, you know, and then I realized that I could maybe get in to
hear the oral arguments at the Supreme Court. These would be
public oral arguments! I had no idea, though, that there would be *no
portables*. Like there's a thousand people camped out here, on First
Street, people who want to get in to hear the oral arguments, and
you're not even going to have any portables for them? When the
future of democracy hangs in the balance? I mean they should have
had a whole *family* of portables, portables of every size and color, a
rainbow coalition of portables, because everyone who had ever been
to a protest was here to try to listen to the Supreme Court, or at least
to wait outside and hear the rumors. Every kind of person, they were
all here, and they needed a place to tidy up!

I went down by the Justice Department. Most times, you know,
you have to load a portable on or off a big flatbed, and you rent them
from some middle man or distributor who's got a warehouse out in
the industrial park with a big billboard, *We're number one with
your number two!*, but the Porta-John, this one model over by the
Justice Department, it folds up. The other models, most are vandal-
resistant, that's what the brochures say. But the Justice Department
probably didn't believe it was going to have so many people around
when the election got all backwards. Thank the lord *this* Supreme
Court understands it has a responsibility to decide the case according to the Christian values of our nation. And thank God for patriots
from Cuba. They were helpful to President Nixon, and they're going
to be helpful to our new president. For the record I think the hair and
makeup of that secretary of state from Florida are pretty nice. I bet
she makes a mean gumbo and I'd like to make an official request
right here for the recipe. I think she ought to have a cabinet-level job,
you know, because even if she and the governor smooched one
another, I bet these were just friendly kisses, like you kiss your
mama. She's a woman of dignity and so there's no cause for complaining about how she looks, though less foundation wouldn't hurt.

I parked the Ford Explorer that my daddy gave me for my high school graduation over by the Pentagon, because they have better security there. I admire people who work in the Pentagon and also in the Central Intelligence Agency. My Explorer is blue-gray, color of thunderstorms in August, also the color of my high school football team, and the license plate says R-O-S-I-E on it, because Daddy is a rose breeder, or that's his hobby. It's also my name. I can tell you that one of the really biggest problems of coming into town for the Movement is finding places to park the Ford Explorer. For one thing it's a big car, but also just about every site in your nation's capital where you'd want to protest has spots where you're not allowed to park. Metrocenter, I mean, there are *no spaces,* no parking lots either. Like I could swear that when we were trying to lobby to eliminate the Food and Drug Administration and the Department of Education and also the pornographers at the National Endowment for the Arts, I swear that there had been parking in front of both Food and Drug and Education. Not anymore. This time I couldn't find a space anywhere, except I thought I had one and then a drug trafficker in diplomatic plates and tinted windows just zoomed in there. I got so mad thinking about it that I spent most of the afternoon driving around with the window rolled down and I was screaming at stoplights on Connecticut Avenue that I couldn't visit this city anymore if there weren't going to be any parking spaces. I must have driven around the Metrocenter for an hour and a half, so long that I had a really bad *bodily need.* By the time I found a parking space over by the Watergate I had to go into a half-dozen unsavory bars and restaurants with signs indicating *Bathrooms for customer use only,* before finding a nearby Porta-John. We have all this taxpayer money illegally taken away from the people and nobody can even figure out how to make it so a girl can park and protest.

When we were all across the street from the vice president's residence (where I started spending a lot of time somewhere around the middle of November), well, it was the same thing. The Loud and Unbowed had organized a mob—this was back when the state supreme court prohibited *certification*—sending out e-mail messages and leaving fliers at churches. I heard it from a friend who heard it from a friend. That's embassy row, Massachusetts Avenue, you know, and I started showing up a couple days a week. My car almost got a ticket in front of the embassy for Kazakhstan, which I don't think is a real country, and then it almost got towed from in front of the Belgian Embassy. I went back to check on it just in time. The good thing about the vice president's residence is that we had lots more protestors than the other side, who probably had never been to any football rallies and didn't even know how to have fun. We had better signs, too, like that *Sore Loserman* sign. Whoever thought that up, I'd like to give him a big kiss. There was lots of singing. I had on a wool skirt and tights and a silk blouse under my down jacket, but it wasn't really warm enough. Daddy used to say that I was the best emissary of traditional American family values that some people would ever meet, so I had to look presentable. But at least the protestors on the other side of the barricades got to wear blue jeans and long underwear. I never wear slacks, but sometimes I wish I could.

Dad stopped coming to the protests because of his drinking, which isn't something I would tell just anybody, but I feel free here by the light of my Eveready flashlight, in front of the Supreme Court with its sixteen Ionic columns and its sculpture of *liberty guarded by order and authority*. I feel free, because inside the court those nine justices, especially the chief justice and also Justices Thomas and Scalia, understand that the fate of the American family is in their hands. Although I don't remember too much about it, my daddy was a lawyer once, and sort of a detail man, and you could set your watch by him he was so prompt, and every prosecutor in Virginia knew him and knew to give him a wide berth. Lately, my mom has just tried to make it easy for him at home on the farm, which is from the nineteenth century. It was my grandfather's farm before it was Daddy's farm. My grandfather was a district attorney during the depression, and he was a big man just like my father and he had a real big temper. When I was a little girl, his face was entirely red, like he got scorched. That's what he looked like to me. And he would just sit on the porch with a bottle of sour mash, and seems like that might be what's happening to Dad too, the same winding down, like that time I found Daddy asleep in the hayloft and realized that there were all kinds of bottles up there, I was kicking bottles around wherever I stepped, but that's not the worst part of it, the worst part is that my daddy had been a stalwart at all the protests, just like I am. He took me to all of the protests. Well, until they signed the Contract with America.

We're from Dixie and everybody has a horse trailer. It's not that much trouble to get an Indian elephant, where I come from, you can get them at a lot of the circuses, and every county has its circus, where the kids used to go to feed the baby goats, and there would be an Indian elephant in the field behind the church, where the circus was, and he'd be going around and around in a ring, because when he was a baby elephant he'd been tethered to a banyan or some other kind of tree and he got so used to being tethered to the tree, and he got so used to the little brown man who attached him to the banyan tree, that later on when he was bigger, when he had a fabulous elephant memory, he believed that the little brown man was still in charge, even though he could have easily squashed the little brown man, just by shifting the weight from one foot to the next. Instead he went around and around in the ring. Anyway, when we used to go to the circus, back when I was a little girl, well that was about when I started to figure out that the other little kids didn't want to come to my house for some reason, because Daddy was always getting upset about nothing, or else he just didn't make sense. It's a pretty bad situation, when you're a girl, and nobody comes to your house, because how are you going to get elected homecoming queen? And what about a prom date? That's just the beginning of it, of course. Maybe Daddy was always getting upset because his dad always got upset. All I know is no one would come to the house. Some memories you keep to yourself.

The party strategists, they got an Indian elephant from some scrupulous circus owner who cared about traditional American family values and our Second Amendment right to bear arms, and they put this Indian elephant in the trailer and drove it up to the capitol building. Not an African elephant, because an African elephant is too big and too smart to be tied to a banyan tree, and I don't think they have banyan trees in Africa anyhow, though I think they might have baobab trees there. The party strategists used Indian elephants for Republican fund-raisers and stuff. They were supposed to bring the elephant up onto the steps for the signing of the Contract with America, that's how everyone tells the story, the scrupulous circus owner was supposed to bring the elephant to the steps of the capitol building for the press conference for the Contract with America, but the problem was that scrupulous circus owner who cared about traditional American family values and the rights of hunters wasn't really treating the elephant very nice. You know how elephants are. They're dumber than auto parts, even with their long memories, but you whip an animal long enough, he's bound to get stubborn. On the other hand, you have to whip on their hides pretty hard if you want them to perform at all, otherwise they just sit there and flap their ears. This elephant was in the trailer and didn't want to come out, and it didn't make any difference that they tried to lure him out with oats or leaves of succulent plants, both of which they'd brought along in a pickup truck since apparently the elephant eats around five hundred pounds of this particular green salad a day, so the hayseed from the NRA who really was *not* a specialist on elephants, he started *whupping* the elephant and swearing at him with all kinds of filthy language, stuff that the elephant's *mahout* or little brown man would never say. All while the network guys were screwing lenses onto their cameras and testing their microphones. Then there was the most god-awful racket, which was the sound of the elephant refusing to do his patriotic duty. They tried to pretend it wasn't happening, the reporters, they tried to talk over it, into their microphones, but the elephant was bellowing pitifully. I was holding my daddy's hand, I was just a teenager then, see, and the thing is, my father, he'd been drinking a little bit. Maybe a lot. I don't know exactly, except maybe he'd just seen one *whupping* too many, or maybe he'd been *whupped* himself, by my parboiled granddaddy, who, like I say, was as sweet as an onion when I got to knowing him, but my daddy let go my hand, sprinted down the steps to the avenue, where the trailer was parked, and he threw himself between the hayseed from the NRA and the elephant. He was mumbling something and if I didn't know better I could almost swear it was something about how the elephant was known to produce *just a single calf in captivity, and therefore should be treated with love and respect,* which is just loony tunes obviously, that's just the flask talking, but Daddy took the electric cattle prod out of the hands of the scrupulous circus owner, and my dad turned it on that NRA wrangler himself, and this was all directly in front of the cameras, there was a bank of cameras, and cameramen, and reporters, and those trucks with the satellite antennae on them, all the networks, and there was my daddy, Republican operative from Virginia, with the electric cattle prod that he was about to use on the behind of some redneck with bad teeth, until Daddy came to his senses and dropped the thing, dropped the electric cattle prod, which was when the wrangler turned on my father and clocked him once, *hard.* I was standing right there when my father went down flat on the paving stones of Washington, DC.

Would have been better if he'd been knocked down sooner! That's my opinion. Then I could say it had all been a bad dream I had. But my daddy was drunk as a Shenandoah skunk, and he had compromised his belief system and the goals of the Movement, because of not being able to hold his drink. It's as bad as gambling and fornicating. For a second there, it was like he didn't believe in family values

313

or something! Even when I was just a girl twelve years old, I knew that these were important things. I pretended I didn't see any of it, didn't see my father on the paving stones, and what I noticed instead was the statue of freedom on the top of the dome, on the capitol building, facing away, the other direction entirely, like she couldn't bear to be looking at us and our little human comedy. I was so ashamed! Of my own daddy! Shame is a bright, stinging jab, like when a yellow jacket comes for you, and it's a feeling that I didn't want to have ever again. Anyway, enough complaining. Since that day when he got his fanny tarred by that redneck posing as a scrupulous circus owner, Dad left the protesting to me. Now he just sticks with the rose hybrids. You didn't think a young girl who's spunky and knows how to darn socks doesn't have to negotiate the generation gap with her daddy the lawyer? Think again.

The Florida Supreme Court agreed to hear the appeal of Judge Sauls about the rejection of the *election contest,* and the court of appeals said the vice presidential candidate's home state wasn't the great state of Texas, and the Leon County judges refused to throw out the absentee ballots. Still, there was darkness on the land. Even at the theme parks up north of Florida, I bet, there was rain and God's message fell on deaf ears and faxes came in backwards and the beast took up his position along the beaches, in the palms, at the hotels of South Beach, devouring the souls of girls with extra-large breast implants. The beast was in a position to complete his dark domination of the good people of the Lord. Like the good book says, there will be *signs and portents,* and you could see them wherever you looked. Holy War for the Movement, Holy War for the Loud and Unbowed. This election represented the great struggle between Good and Evil, between the ingenuity of a Ray Kroc or a Sam Walton and rapists and pedophiles and homosexuals whose names I don't have to repeat. Holy War. That's why I had to be here, and that's why I tried to get my girlfriend Darlene to drive up with me, but she couldn't come, although she did make my sign, *The Fat Lady Is Fixen to Sing!*

I have a Monroe Javalina backpack with six pockets and a removable fanny pack and inside it I packed a Manning EZ-Vestibule tent with rainfly-zippered ingress and three shock-corded fiberglass tent poles, a tent that fits *two,* you know, in case Darlene wanted to come, and I packed a Coleman Oak Grove sleeping bag, tall size, which weighed six pounds and was good down to about forty degrees, and a Coleman guide-series propane three-burner stove, because I figured it would be nice to have a potluck supper with any other Christians who were praying and chanting at the courthouse. I had tarps, cutlery, mess kit, canteen, and a headlamp that I tried to use to write notes last night. I packed a first-aid kit and insect repellent, and a battery-powered television set so that I could watch the Cable News Network and country and western programming. I had freeze-dried meats and eggs. Like on any trip, I had beef jerky.

One thing I'm partial to when I'm on the road for the Movement is to stop in a gas station on the county road, one that's still run by some guy who actually knows how to repair cars, a gas station where there are high-visibility hats and clothes for sale, where there's a group of hunters that's about to go out and blast *the very last red-breasted highland warbler* into extinction. Over by the register, there's the rack of jerky! Hundreds of kinds of jerkies, meat sticks, smoked meats, meats in tins. When I was getting ready for a trip to the Supreme Court on behalf of the Movement, I picked up some supplies in this gas station. Like I said, I was making the trip by myself for the first time, and I had no idea whether I was going to be allowed to camp out on First Street, in front of the court, and my backpack, it was full up with the stuff I told you about, and it weighed about half as much as I weigh. You know, this was all kind of confusing. I bet you think that protesting for a cause that's popular with such wonderful people, all of them believing that they have a savior, is *easy,* like a religious pilgrimage or something. You go on up to Washington, people take you in and they give you their smoked meats and their pistachios and sugar-free sodas. They give whatever they have to a spunky redheaded go-getter. But I'm here to say that there's a lot of uncertainty involved and time for reflection, too, and a lot of waiting around for the media. My feet always hurt from wearing my pumps. Even this afternoon I was in the crowd right about when the people from the networks came and filed their stories about oral arguments, and you'd think you'd make a lot of friends just then, because a lot of things were coming together, and there should be embracing and cheering and high fives. But for me it was kind of lonely. I got a little downhearted and confused, for a second, I didn't even know why I was sticking around, because I didn't get in to hear the oral arguments—those seats went to folks who'd been camped out for days—and I had exams back at school that I hadn't studied for even a little, and my parents were worried and kept calling me on the beeper every forty-five minutes.

It started with that gas station, see, that particular gas station. How come, that day, the gas station was such a creepy place? How come there wasn't enough light inside? How come the beer signs were all falling down? What's with that musty smell of old plastered walls giving way to mildew? What's with that smell of after-shaved men who don't get out enough, with their bad air, and their breath, which is like the carcass of a raccoon. The second I pulled open the fogged-up door at that filling station I realized I'd made a big mistake. Good men make bad men so easy to pick out in a crowd, can't have one without the other, so when I got myself indoors at the filling station, to demand that they fill the tank for me, because I don't really believe in the self-serve phenomenon, I realized I was in the company of a *gang of outlaws,* cowboys who would have keelhauled the mail coach or taken up with Indians back in the old frontier days, even though now there was nothing for them to do but tap stills up in the mountains and shoot at squirrels. They were angry and they blamed me for it, or that's what it seemed like. I tried to say something polite on my way past the register, about how I was on a journey *to protest for the rights of Christians on the Mall in Washington, DC.* Don't know why I felt like I had to tell them all of that, the guy behind the register, and his friends who were leaning against racks of chewing tobacco and motor oil, all of them with ponytails and unusual styles of facial hair and stuff. I think I need to look inward and ask myself this question, why was this gas station any different, since I usually liked these gas stations, and this one could be just as good as any other, maybe with a little counsel from a business efficiency expert or some pastoral care, but this time I was upset, you know, so I gathered up my selections in their tins and wrappers, and I carried them up to the register, and I searched around in my backpack for my purse, made sure my handgun was still in there, in case I had to shoot up the place, and the man at the register, he said, *Guess you like meat, huh?* And there was a roar of laughter from the guys by the chewing tobacco. And there was a second roar of laughter from a back room someplace, and I could tell that it had something to do with me and my pilgrimage and my selection of tinned meats, even though I was supposed to feel like the men in the *survivalist wing* of the Movement were my friends, like with the brothers from the Aryan Nations who were resisting the fat cats in the government and making their kingdom in heaven. But I didn't always feel like they were my friends, especially when two more of them came from the room in back, with their big bellies and their unshaven chins. They smelled like wet peat moss. I didn't think that living in remote shacks up in the Blue Ridge Mountains and eating roadkill was something I could share with them, even though I thought that on another day I might like them personally, if I saw them in the pews, if we could honorably discuss biblical passages, such as: *The stouthearted are spoiled, they have slept their sleep.* I wasn't seeing these lowdown deserters in church, though, because I was in the tumbledown gas station out on a county road where it was really quiet and early in the morning, and if they were to pursue their evil ways with a co-ed with a red ponytail and a polite way of talking, after which they carved her up and then left the pieces of her up in the mountains, well, it just wouldn't be right, especially when she was partly responsible for the drive to repeal the Endangered Species Act so they could go blast away at *the very last red-breasted highland warbler* without interference from elites.

I wasn't going to argue about it, while they were all standing there staring at me and my stuff. But when I got out the crisp twenties in my purse, I sneaked my pepper spray into the pocket of my dress, and I went on my way with my snacks, knowing I could hurt a man. It only occurred to me later that I forgot to wait for my change, but you know there were things to see and do. Still, even when I was standing in front of the Supreme Court, I couldn't stop thinking of it, how there were toothless guys with high-visibility gear who'd kill and eat a Young Republican just the same as they'd kill a possum or a liberal, even though they were part of the Movement themselves and went to church and believed in a second coming. I was thinking about it while I was making a dinner with some instant soup from packets and some pre-mixed Jell-O that I had bought and put in my cooler, I was mulling it over, I was thinking I needed to be more *grateful,* you know, about sunsets and pecans and spring break, but I didn't know why I should be grateful for Republican murderers. Sometimes things set you off, even though you have always been well behaved and enthusiastic. Well, that's usually when someone comes knocking at your door. That's usually when the heavenly draperies part. When you're experiencing tribulation, when clouds amass on the horizon. That's when an impeccably dressed young man in a bow tie and wool suit comes to the mesh doorway of your pup tent promising all the benefits of salvation.

I was in the front ranks of a tent city, you know, like it was during the administration of Herbert Hoover. All the Loud and Unbowed had come, and more than a couple of people from that other political party too, I should admit it, and each of these protestors had his own tent, his own flashlight, his own sleeping bag, his own television.

The police had been coming around a couple of times an hour to make clear that there was only the one certain piece of a lawn next to the building where we could camp for the night, because people were streaming in, you know, and maybe it didn't have anything to do with the oral arguments anymore, maybe it just had to do with people wanting to camp out in the nation's capital, since they paid for it. Anyway there was this man working his way through the tent community, a presentable young man, and, like I said, I guess because I go to a women's college I don't meet that many men, not like I did back when Daddy used to take me to the protests. Not like when I was a cheerleader and snuck mint juleps out of the pitcher in the refrigerator at night. When you think about it, it's sort of strange that I could know so much about how whiskey causes damage to your inner organs and makes you unable to work and causes your wife and children to lead lonely, confused lives. It's strange I could know all this and not really know anything about boys. The time was *evening*, so it was hard to know what kind of a young man this young man was, beyond romanticizing him because he turned up at sunset. Hard to figure whether he agreed with me about the rights of the unborn, you know, and that's a nonnegotiable point with me where men are concerned. But all this did not stop the young man in the bow tie calling through the mesh screen of my tent, *Borrow a cup of sugar?*

I straightened out a few things right away. I said, *I don't have conversations with young men unless they agree about the right to life of the unborn. Don't you come around here looking to converse with a young lady while there are unborn children being killed by the federal government this very afternoon.*

He said, *Nice to meet you, too!* Then he introduced himself and his organization, which was funded by the patriotic soft-money donations flowing into the coffers of our party. That should have been enough of a common interest. He tried to reassure me, just the same. *I'm here to make sure that you have donated to your party, according to the limits prescribed by the law, and to make sure we have you on our mailing list since you're obviously a very committed young voter.*

Flattering, I'm sure, but I knew he was really here because the smell of instant soup was enticing to him. Maybe beef jerky, too. I was a girl who was prepared and who had brought freeze-dried food products along, a girl who didn't figure on meeting too many people. The man in the bow tie came to my tent first, and I asked him in.

One thing about the Coleman Powermax lantern with matchless lighting, well, it made people look *beautiful.* Like Darlene, the time she and I camped out behind the Sciences Library at school to protest stem cell research. Darlene, she has *bad skin,* she has skin that looks like she got attacked by a darning needle, you know? But in the light of the Coleman Powermax lantern with matchless lighting, Darlene looked like one of those women in the fashion magazines. Darlene didn't even need any makeup, because we were out on the lawn and she had taken all of her lipstick off, but she still looked like she should be wearing a slinky dress and dating a country and western singer. The same thing turns out to be true with boys, I guess, according to what was going on in my tent. Maybe it's something about the handsome *globe shield* around the Powermax lantern, it just lends a convex beauty to things.

There hadn't ever been any boys in my tent. That's God's honest truth. But suddenly there was a boy in my tent and it took my breath away, this man with the bow tie, this foot soldier of Christ. Looked like he came to life from the ceiling of a cathedral. So this is probably the secret to how the colonial fathers reproduced. I mean, they had wooden teeth and they wore powdered wigs, like homosexuals. And the corseted women they married were drawing on beauty marks with lead pencils. The colonial fathers probably never wanted to have anything to do with their wives during the day or the slave women or what have you. The women felt that same way about their husbands. But night came on, and say a serving girl sidles up to the tents where the revolutionary soldiers were fighting for Manifest Destiny and One Nation Under God; the soldiers take one look at her in candlelight and she's going to be *eating for two.* It's just that way with lanterns. Lanterns were given by God to insure multiplication.

Once the man in the bow tie was in the tent, I was experiencing temptation. I hate to say it. I started looking for ways to keep him in my tent. I was looking at him and I was afraid to look at him at the same time, and all the things my mother told me about men, which really wasn't all that many things, because my mom doesn't say anything except when she feels a need to draw your attention to the weather, well, those things were coming back to me. I could tell that the smell of my little dinner was pleasing to him, and that's good because when the right man actually comes along, I'll be able to woo him by means of cookery.

Would you like some Jell-O? said I, forgetting temporarily that it

319

was best to have the main course first, because even though I had just poured the hot water into the soup, I kept looking into his enormous green eyes, I never really saw eyes like that, and I was never alone with a man in the tent, so I forgot to offer him the meat sticks and the soup, and instead I offered him Jell-O, which I was going to serve with some grapes and cherries.

Grace first, don't you think? he said. I was contrite, you know, because he was some sort of a visitation from above, I guess, so I mumbled something about God's abundance and may the election go our way, to which we both said robust *amens* and guffawed heartily, and then he ate the Jell-O like he was greedy for it. He was stabbing at the green Jell-O with a little spoon from my mess kit.

We had both been horseback riders when we were little, and we had both learned how to shoot, and we both believed that cosmopolitans from Hollywood were responsible for suppressing the conspiracies of the last administration, and we believed that a newly elected senator was part of a secret cabal of lesbians who wanted to celebrate black masses and convert children to their lifestyle, and we both joked about how when we were kids we always thought that the singing group called *the Supremes* was the *same thing* as the Supreme Court of the United States of America! I remember thinking that the judges must be really talented if they could sing *and* make these important judicial rulings. But after a while I stopped talking altogether because I noticed I was watching his tongue work its way over his teeth and around the inside of his mouth, while he was saying *Born in a little town in the Cumberland Mountains, state of Tennessee, Daddy owned a lumber and construction supplies company. Used to work for him on weekends loading up orders. These days, I'm so busy I got to buy everything at Wal-Mart. Whatever's on sale, know what I mean? Could really use a nice girl like yourself to do those sort of things and improve me in that way. I'd be grateful for her help, you know. There are times when it's not the easiest line of work, canvassing, lonely sometimes, but combined with the money I bring in as a salesman of women's beauty-care products line, well, it's fine, for now. I don't need a lot of money, you know.* From there, onto the subject of taxation and how this is an oppression against the good Christian people of this country. *Why is it a foregone conclusion that the government gets my money in the first place? Nobody asked me if I agree with where the money is going. If they want to let me sign off on these programs, these federal programs, then we can talk about it.*

*I don't want to finance any of this degenerate art. So if it weren't
for the government, I'd do a little better when it comes to tax
time, and I could give this money back to the faith of my choice.*
I just started asking him questions, you know, because I heard questions put a good man at ease, so I asked him what the saddest thing
he ever saw on earth was, and he said, *You know, I saw my friend
Tommy take off a couple of fingers on a lathe. I never heard anyone yelping out like that. But I've seen some stuff since then that
was just as bad, and Tommy he doesn't worry about not having
all his fingers anymore. He plays softball with us now. Can't mess
up a man's soul on a lathe.* And then he moved on to the deep sorrows of his life: *My brother ran off. Got to be sixteen or so. Guess
he didn't feel like the things that I loved as a kid, like being a
child of God, or whatnot, didn't feel like it was for him, and I'm
still all torn up about it. Loved that guy, looked up to him like I
never looked up to anybody since. I miss my brother every day,
and I heard he's up in the federal penitentiary, and if that's the
truth, well, it's OK. I love him and forgive him.* My heart was
sorely touched by the sadnesses of this man with the bow tie, honest,
and my hand was fluttering up to my heart at these personal revelations, just like I was in church, and he was a preacher, because here
we were two lonely warriors for God, in a dimly lit tent community,
where these tents all had their little lonely flashlights going, like the
flashlights were the stars in the constellations, which was maybe
why he started talking about the heavens, *We used to go to a Baptist
summer camp when I was a boy, up in the mountains. Lots cooler
up there in the summer. Used to have campfires and so forth, and
I used to volunteer to put things away after the campfires. You
know, fold up the chairs, make sure the fire was out. I was always
the last one up to bed in my bunk. Up there, in the summer, when
it's cool, you could see all the stars.*

But somewhere in here I got clumsy, I don't know how really, it
was cramped in the tent, and I spilled the last of my soup right into
my lap. It's amazing to think that inside the Supreme Court of the
United States clerks of the justices were writing digests about the
briefs they had heard that afternoon, and at the same time, I was
overturning a mug full of instant beef and vegetable soup right into
my lap, and then I was reaching for the canteen and beginning to dab
at the part of my skirt where no man had ever set his grubby paws,
except my gynecologist, and when I looked up the man in the bow
tie was sipping from a flask, just like my own Daddy, just watching

and drinking, and I should have hated him for it, hated my childhood, hated not having a swing set and being dragged off to rallies, hated lying and incoherent sobbing, all of that nonsense, but he offered me a sip from his flask in the light of those constellations of Washington, DC, *You really ought to just take that skirt off, don't you think? So it can dry?* I took the drink.

Next thing I knew we were kissing.

When you see a beautiful man steal into your house, and he's darling, and he has green eyes, and he's reborn in the cauldron of truth, stripped clean of all that makes men dirty, and if he offers you a sip of some backyard stuff that his cousins made from molasses, and it loosens you up so that the streetlights in one of the most dangerous cities in America seem like constellations, you rise up boldly to the occasion. I knew the kisses were wrong, because I know right from wrong, and I know what a girl is supposed to do on her first overnight protest in our nation's capital, with network cameramen on every street corner. A girl is supposed to conduct herself like a lady, a girl is supposed to display her self-respect and her poise. But once I got started, I couldn't stop, and I figured it was a celebration and we were about to steal victory from the *slavering jaws of defeat,* I figured it was just like giving your mom a peck, and besides his mouth tasted great, and I got to see his eyes up close this way, and so I just kept kissing him and we were *rocking and rolling,* and soon everything was all shoved around in the tent, my sleeping bag was out from under us and he was all on top of me and had his hands in my hair and I had my hands in his hair, which was stiff with some greasy hair tonic, and I had the root of some cherry tree sticking in the small of my back, and I had to keep *shooshing* him from saying things, *Goddamned if I am not a lucky man!* There were people around who could hear everything that was happening, could hear the virtue of Christians being cast off like plastic wrap, so I rolled him over so I was on top of him, and everything about him was taut like in a spring break video program, he was rippling and he was fair, and I was about to use all those vulgar words that I had heard loose girls say, when finally a bolt of lightning hit me, knocked me upside the head, a figurative bolt of lightning, and I rolled off him and said I had to go take care of something for a second. And I gathered up some things, my pepper spray and my pistol, and I got the heck out of there. I ran for it.

That's one of the good things about *portables,* when you have nowhere else to go. There's always the portables. Like for example

322

the *W. C. Supreme* of Cumbria, United Kingdom, whose five-star model has laminated walls and real porcelain fittings and *carpeting*. I don't know why the campus of Georgetown University would need to have a portable from the United Kingdom with carpeting in it, but I went for a *long walk*, miles and miles of walking, all around this city you paid for, and when I saw a line of women and men out in front of the *W. C. Supreme* model, all of those men and women suffering with, you know, colitis, Crohn's disease, maybe urinary frequency or something, you know, you have to have compassion for the people lined up out in front of the portables. They're part of a larger thing, a big thing, a Movement going on all across our land, spreading across the globe, like a malignancy, like the lightning of God, spreading, engulfing. Sorry to be tying up the place like I am, but I have to get all of these thoughts down. It's been a big day for me.

An Experiment in Public Character
Brenda Coultas

The movie star lives in an old furniture store with huge display windows covered with gold blinds. If you look up, you can see the tops of his closets through the 2nd-floor window and you say to yourself with awe, those are the suits of a famous man, those are the wire hangers and sleeves of a famous man.

The Bowery Plan goes something like this, there are explosions, and condos arise Las Vegas–like from the smoke. There are floodlights and fireworks or helium balloon races or ribbons cut or ground broken with ceremonial shovels or trees wrapped in yellow ribbons or butterflies, freshly hatched, flying out of boxes. That is the mayor's plan, however mine is different, mine includes groupings of tables and chairs and hanging plants, all portable, public gardens and open houses and a faux suicide by 5 bungee-jumping squatters at McGurk's Suicide Hall.

Do you remember the stone soup story, how a beggar came to town and began to boil water? Well, bring me a potato. Bring me a story.

I'm not a public character nor do I sleep in open spaces or sleep on bum bed pads in public, rather I sleep and toilet in private and think of public spaces. Inside I eat it all and Sal, our homeless, says he's drinking it all in before heading to Las Vegas. I'll miss our homeless although we don't do anything for him.

Don't liked to be touched by ghosts only invisible ones, not cloudy kinds where you can make out the entire face and hear them speak. Bowery Bum ghosts are real people although they sleep in rooms made of chicken wire. They are not apparitions of McGurk's Suicide Hall or tenement life circa 1900.

I squatted down to touch gray Gap T-shirt on street outside Bowery Bar. I'd just seen an ad of 6 real people wearing same gray T-shirt. Thought I could wear this one. Was damp with a liquid, got repulsed, dropped it.

Every morning en route to 6 train, I see a ceramic cat visible from the public space, white with paw raised, in an old lady's window.

I take a break from the Bowery, on train to Hamptons to see our Joe and Janice. Couple fighting, young man with expensive gangster rapper pants, hand tooled 70s belt, two silver mouth studs, perfectly in your face Hamptons punk-gangster chic, saying to plain girl, "This is the worst day of my life, you miserable bitch."

Dumpster outside Fisher Sheet music store
Can't see into it, must be climbed.

Double high red dumpster with office debris and a promising office chair, green leather and metal. Circa early industrial 60s half-buried in the rubble. (Astor Place and Lafayette.)

Trash can by Film Anthology; a bright patterned dress pulled out with fingers, label looked expensive, got creeped out, dropped on rim of can, walked on. The way I see it, no one, not even me, has the time or patience to inventory every dumpster she sees. (August 10, 00, 2nd St. & 2nd Ave.)

I had been obsessed with chairs lately. Mostly random chairs and sitting spots, a hidden surprise plastic Adirondack chair by creek, groups of chairs as if in conversation therefore a need for close physical proximity. In restaurants, if you are one person you cannot sit at a 4 top or 6 top, you must sit at the 2 top and they remove the other place setting but leave the chair intact. In photographs of my dad's barn I notice chairs where before I used to notice cats. This time only one cat appears. Up in the hayloft are rockers with missing woven reed seats and a couch that I covered with a sheet against the bird droppings, a great place to sit and look out the window. That is what I do best, sit and look out windows.

Woke up seeing garbage with new eyes and new fresh attitude. Felt transcendental all day. (August 16, 00.)

In order to transform into a public character I need to claim a public space. I will sit in a chair on the Bowery at the same place and time for a season and participate and expedite street life.
For interaction I will ask strangers to take my photograph. I will record all encounters and emotions. I'm going to dump it all in, everything that occurs to me or everything I see. That will be my data, my eyes upon the street; the firsthand observation of this last bum-claimed space, a small record before the wrecking ball arrives. I'm taking only pen and notepad. Everything I truly need will appear—I'm not an archaeologist, but am a studier of person and documenter of trails.

She said he lives here, pointing at a green building, and I said what is he like?
  "Intense," she said.
  I said, thinking about his photographs and how he carves words into his prints, "For a person like that it must be hard to be in the world."
  "Yes," she said.
  I thought about the emotion of his pictures.
  I said, "You can't see inside."
  We walked on. (August 17, 00, Bleecker & Bowery.)

I've cultivated a joy of dumpsters out of necessity, romanticized dumpster diving in order to make hunting and gathering interesting. I had a good attitude until recently, I've become ashamed, developed a fear of being yelled at for disturbing the recycling. That's where I get my magazines. Some people say, "You love garbage, I've seen you get so excited about it." But, really, it's just a glamorous pose.

I used to dream of yard sales, where I was the first person there and every collectable I ever desired was on the table, but I had to grab them before the others arrived. I trembled, I tremble in real life before the good stuff.

A Bowery Bum asked, "Can I talk to you for a minute?" He burped loudly in my ear. Later he asked me to look up at the sun where he had written his name. Then to hug him. I did both. Why do I listen to Bowery Bums?

Peacock fan chair on sidewalk. Another peacock chair lying in vacant lot next to wet matted rat. (August 21, 00, 3rd St. and 2nd Ave.)

No notable garbage today despite big pile of rubble from the destruction of a collapsed building on 2nd and Houston. Big blue dumpster hauled to the scene. Would I see anything worth recording? Will I have access to that dumpster? Or will it remain behind the cops' yellow ribbon?

Later remembered sadly that I hadn't thought about my revolutionary idea of surprise chairs in public space. Or the accidental overlooking of sitting space, such as rails without spikes, or bum-friendly stoops like Joe's where Sal lives. This is a new plan, reverse musical chairs. The number of chairs increases every time there's a pause in the honking, wholly mufflers, brakes squealing, cell phone conversations, sirens wailing, and humans crying, a new chair appears. The point of the game to seat everyone. The point is that there is a seat for everyone.

Orange chair, 70s, metal legs, dirt ring in plastic seat, Apple color printer, metal cig machine on top of dumpster, front opened. Air conditioner without a shell. (February 8, 01, Bowery & 2nd St.)

Random memory association: Dust burning off the hot bulbs of a tube radio.

Wooden canvas cot folded up and chairs grouped by a fire hydrant and a man explaining the function of formally everyday objects because we couldn't understand anymore and we couldn't even see how the body fit into them or how they could possibly serve it. There was a metal dish on a stand. It was a nurse's basin, he explained. I examined it, turning it over. There was a long metal

327

cylinder lying on the ground.
  "Is that an iron lung?"
  "No, that's a mid-century Electrolux."

Puddle of puke. (March 1, 00, Bowery & First St.)

Random memory association: A lady's boxy vanity case, most
likely with mirror inside lid and cloth pocket running around the
rim, for placing beauty products. A junk drawer, unmatched
buttons, a place for odd objects and lost mates.

We were talking about the garbage in the 1970s before people got
black plastic bags and ruined it. He said you couldn't window-shop
big trash night anymore. There was no way to see what was inside
the plastic without opening it. He said you should have seen it
before, copper pots and pans, designer bric-a-brac, china, crystal,
the clothes from Bloomingdale's, no less! All in plain sight. He said
imagine the castoffs of the Upper East Side! What glorious days.

Someone said if you had a million dollars I know you'd still work,
that's the kind of person you are. What kind of person is that? Then
I was very angry at myself for working as if I was a millionaire.

This will be my museum, I'll put it all down here on the page,
a portable museum of the 1890s and the 1990s on the Bowery,
better'n film, no pocket projectors invented yet, but real words to
be copied and read and I write slow cause I expect to live a long
time. I made a note: Projected cost of Wall Street Guggenheim,
200 million; actual cost of Brenda's The Museum of the Bowery,
78 dollars.

What I saw on the Bowery: a bum sitting in an early 20th-century
vault, a small vault, front door missing, on its back, filled with
water and trash and now a bum drinking out of a bag, his ass firmly
planted, his arms and legs sticking out. That's what I saw, a
resourceful response to chairlessness. (April 12, 01.)

"It was late at night, and a fine rain was swirling softly down. . . .
That is when I began this experiment in misery." I lived on skid
row in Los Angeles in a Bukowski-que building. I was 20 and a
welder by trade, left Firestone Steel, took Greyhound to Los
Angeles because in all the articles I had ever read that's where
everyone lived. And I had never been much outside the state, knew
no one who had been.

All the mental hospitals had been emptied out due to a tax cut and
there were crazies everywhere or rather more so than usual. In
two separate occasions insane persons asked if I had seen her/his
identical twin and both showed me a photograph of her/himself
sans glasses, and said, "She/he looks just like me only without
glasses." I hung out with an old bum who was a maintenance man
at the theater where I worked, who seemed normal but must have
gone on long binges where he burned all his bridges. I was the
elevator operator and wore a bandbox hat and a jacket with double
rows of brass buttons in a club dedicated to reviving vaudeville in
1978. The club's most popular act was the original singer of
"Tiptoe Through the Tulips," a spunky 80-year-old who played
his ukulele.

We went to The Old Pantry restaurant, where bums and regular
folks lined up to get in, but the bums appreciated the bounty
the most. Meals were served family style, and relish trays were
on every table, of carrots and celery sticks, endless bread, big
portions of meat. The bums saved up their change and came for
their weekly meal. There were portraits of the waiters on the
wall. I lived in a studio apt with a Murphy bed in the wall and free
roaches. I was the greenest person ever to live there.

Flowers at CBGB for Joey Ramone. (April 15, 01, Bleecker &
Bowery.)

A tour guide was standing in front. He was saying that it was better
to tear down a building than to allow the residents, artists and
writers, to live in it paying below market rates. He said that this
was his personal opinion and did not represent the views of the
Bowery Tour Guide Service.

Brenda Coultas

2 homeless, relaxing inside a cardboard box 20 ft. away. (June 9, 01, 295 Bowery.)

A church lady rakes through trash for goods, man asleep on sidewalk. (First St. & 2nd Ave., June 10, 01.)

A lady sitting down in street said, "I like your scarf." Saleswoman said, "I like your shirt." And man walking by said, "That's the second one today." Man on the ground said, "Take me home." Then a man growled and flung a suitcase around in the air. (June 12, 01.)

2 Eames rockers with footstools in a Brooklyn dumpster on Remsen St. A man with white hair said they were original, but no one wanted to pay to have the springs repaired. I climbed to top, pushed the trash around, trying to decide if they were worth calling home about, heard movement in the bottom, jumped down. (June 15, 01, Brooklyn.)

The Usefulness of Ugliness
Joanna Scott

1.

FROM MY DESK IN A sixth-floor apartment in the city of Florence I can look out the window straight over the tile roofs at the Campanile flanking the ghostly mass of Brunelleschi's Duomo. When I lean out the window I can look across the river up into the hills and see the striped facade of San Miniato. To the east the steeple of Santa Croce pokes above the palazzi surrounding it, though at night the church seems to grow, or the other buildings shrink, and the whole of Santa Croce mysteriously fills my hall mirror.

Florence, my temporary home, is famously beautiful, one of the few places in the world where beauty has been carefully preserved and where the intense concentration of art can be exhausting. "An excess of pleasure," Melville said after coming out of the Uffizi. "It's as bad as too much pain; it gets to be pain at last."

The painful pleasures of beauty. Last month wisteria spilled over the walls around Florence; now the trellises are full of roses. On the balcony above me and on the balcony across the way, women beat rugs; it's Thursday, which must be rug-beating day, and the thump of the broomsticks echoes through the streets. Dust blows into my room through the open window, along with all the mosquitoes that have managed to escape the hungry swallows.

Dusty, crowded, beautiful Florence. Here I am, surrounded by beautiful art, thinking about distortion and incongruity. I think about the word "grotesque"—denoting deliberate ugliness in art, though originally coined to describe Roman murals discovered in excavated grottoes. I think about manifestations of the grotesque in painting, in sculpture, in poetry, in music. I think about how fiction is unwieldy, misshapen, full of oppositions. Any art must define its aesthetics and continually renegotiate standards of beauty. But fiction has too much contradictory stuff in it to attain a pure beauty. Fiction is a hodgepodge, a stew of contrasts. Novelists must learn to love the grotesque by necessity.

Which is why, in one of the most beautiful cities of the world, I've been thinking about the diverse uses of the grotesque. What are the effects of strong grotesque art—or "true grotesque," as Ruskin calls the complex imagery of the fantastic imagination, in contrast to the "idiotic mockery of the low grotesque"? Even if aesthetic values are culturally determined, can we isolate any general functions of the grotesque that might shed light on its contemporary uses?

Funny how awareness benefits from curiosity. I go out in search of ugliness, and suddenly I see it everywhere.

Hell, Coppo di Marcovaldo. Mosaic detail, Baptistery, Florence.

2.

Florence, it turns out, is full of sinners. They are being impaled with burning spears in Federico Zuccari's hell looming overhead in the Duomo. They are protesting in anguish in Orcagna's *Triumph of Death* in the Museum of Santa Croce. They are being punished in Nardo di Cione's frescoes in the Strozzi of Mantua Chapel in Santa Maria Novella. Most everywhere angels are gathering in Florence's many Renaissance heavens, devils are keeping sinners busy in hell.

Cross the piazza from the Duomo and enter the Baptistery, and you'll find Florence's original hell in the mosaic attributed to Marcovaldo, dating from the 1260s and 70s. The octagonal Baptistery, the oldest building in Florence, was built during the fourth and fifth centuries. The interior mosaic includes images of the Creation and the stories of Joseph and John the Baptist. The mosaic of the Last Judgment is the largest of its kind in Europe.

The Baptistery Lucifer combines aspects of human form and animal. He has human eyes, goat horns, and serpents are coming out of his ears and buttocks. His skin is a scaly green, his head blue, his legs brown. He clutches two naked sinners and is devouring a third. He is undeniably ugly.

The Catholic dogma of Marcovaldo's time offered two binding descriptions of hell: 1) "The Devil and the other demons were created good by God, but became evil by their own choice" (Fourth Lateran Council, First Vatican Council) and 2) "The suffering of the demons is eternal" (Synod of Constantinople, Fourth Lateran Council). These were, in a sense, the only rules a thirteenth-century artist had to respect when he set out to depict the world teeming below the judging Christ. The Book of Revelation—the main biblical description of hell—is too murky to provide a distinct account of hell. For the Baptistery mosaic, there is no single textual source. *The Egyptian Book of the Dead,* classical descriptions of the kingdom of Tartarus in Hades, the Leviathan in the book of Job, along with the many paradoxical images from Revelation could all have gone into the concoction. But mostly hell seems to have released Marcovaldo from the strict iconography of the time, allowing him to imagine his way into multiple stories.

Gombrich describes the grotesque as "the product of an irresponsible imagination on holiday." But in the Florence Baptistery it's not the distortions in themselves that are most expressive. The many monsters would have been familiar to thirteenth-century viewers, since the grotesque already had an important didactic place in Italian art. What is strikingly original about this scene of hell is the way ugliness is put into motion: The Baptistery hell is distinguished from heaven more by motion than by distortion. In heaven, saints and angels are poised in stiff eternal adulation. In hell, sinners and devils writhe in an eternal dance of torment, with each figure enacting the story of his fall.

When we examine Marcovaldo's representations of anonymous figures in hell, we can see why individuation is central to the process of narrative invention and why it's so often connected to ugliness. Imperfections generate characters, and distinct characters generate motion. While this thirteenth-century representation of heaven is full of illustrations of saints whose portraits conform to strict iconography, hell is full of the artist's imaginative inventions—unique characters forever tumbling toward their separate destinies.

The Annunciation, Beato Angelico. Convent of San Marco, Florence.

3.

Sometimes ugliness frees the imagination. But measured against the apotheosis of the beautiful, ugliness may have a disruptive effect on an orderly composition—unless it can be shaped into an enhancement.

In the convent of San Marco in Florence there are forty-three little dormitory cells decorated between 1437 and 1446 with scenes from the life and passion of Christ. Most of the frescoes were done by the artist Beato Angelico, himself a Dominican friar. In each of those cells, a monk remained in isolation for many long hours, studying religious texts and contemplating the single image on his wall.

With the first corridor of these cells forming the axis, the San Marco convent offers two exemplary directions. At the beginning of the hall is Fra Angelico's *Annunciation*, a fresco that set a new standard of beauty for the fifteenth century; at the other end of the hall, around the corner, are Savonarola's cells—rooms without frescoes, bare cold cells that originally were used to store furniture and clothes.

Girolamo Savonarola is commonly remembered today for persuading Florentines to destroy every sign of evil—to burn lascivious pictures, books, dice, and anything else that could be used to lure the soul from contemplation of God. At a time when wars and plagues were straining the Florentine economy and the Medicis were closing their banks abroad, Savonarola was spreading his fierce brand of populist mysticism, preaching against vanities with such force that he converted Pico della Mirandola into a Dominican and cowed Botticelli and Michelangelo with his prophecies.

Savonarola, righteously uncomfortable in his rough wool robes, denounced what he considered the immoral art of his time. But as a friar in San Marco he would have passed Fra Angelico's *Annunciation* every day, a fresco that invites the viewer to consider the details of the landscape, the ingenious perspective, and the Florentine architecture, all potentially irrelevant additions to a sacred subject. If art's main purpose is didactic, then its benefits are compromised by distracting decoration.

"Everyone play, dance, or sing! Let the heart burn sweetly! No labor, no pain!" These are lines from a poem by Lorenzo de' Medici. The lightness of spirit expressed in the poem shares the sentiment evoked with the decorative aspects of Fra Angelico's fresco. This is the beauty of flowers and sunshine and the glow of youth. Beauty is springtime, one of Lorenzo's contemporaries, the poet Bartolomeo Platina, suggests in an essay. And to enjoy the beauty of spring, he recommends eating "light, temperate foods" so that we can drink more wine. "Coitus in this period," he assures us, "can be practiced with tranquillity."

Following the logic of Savonarola's polemics, the *Annunciation* is perilously beautiful—at least theoretically. And although Fra Angelico proved with another painting, his gruesome *Universal Judgment*, that he wasn't afraid of the extreme grotesque, in the frescoes of San Marco the primary function of ugliness is to amplify beauty. In the most violent scenes of the Passion, the grotesque imagery is muted by the colors of the surrounding landscape and a tranquil emotional inflection in the portraits. Principles of beauty dominate these illustrations of suffering. Silken robes flow around the figures holding the body of the dead Christ. The reincarnated Christ appears to Mary Magdalene as a gardener poised on a bed of flowers. Even the mocked Christ sits regally, serenely on his

335

makeshift throne while his tormentors beat and spit on him.

To the mystic, silence is the purest form of expression. To the artist, beauty orders experience and gives meaning to the confusion of life. Most art falls between the extremes of Savonarola's blank walls and Fra Angelico's *Annunciation*, between the purity of silence and the perfection of beauty. Most art has an element of ugliness.

Whatever form the grotesque takes within a culture, at its extreme it prompts disgust, severing the communication between artist and audience. This might be a more profitable effect these days than in fifteenth-century Florence. But if disgust isn't an artist's ultimate goal, the grotesque can be used as a method of control over imperfections, providing a contrast that enhances the overall design.

It would be hard to identify any element of ugliness in Fra Angelico's *Annunciation*. This fresco tells us what to expect as we wander down the corridor past the cells. Throughout the scenes of the Passion, where ugly wounds mar elegant bodies and cartoon figures spit on their serene victims, the grotesque serves to amplify beauty. By restricting the effects of ugliness to subordinate contrast, Fra Angelico has provided a display of beauty's powers. Down at the end of the hall, Savonarola is waiting to remind us of the dangers.

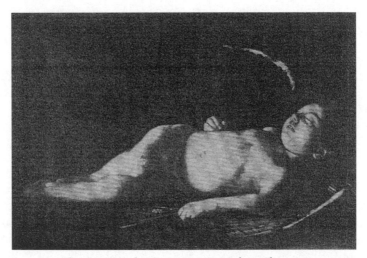

Sleeping Cupid, Caravaggio. Pitti Palace, Florence.

4.

Am I taking for granted the clichés about the Florentines and their fashionable humanism, in which Cicero's civic virtues were supposed to be mirrored by artistic beauty? Having assumed that there is a measurable difference between whatever constitutes beauty and whatever constitutes ugliness at any given period in the history of art, I'll admit that it's difficult to discriminate between the two, just as it's difficult to discriminate between pleasure and pain, moralism and frivolity, pity and cruelty, infatuation and self-loathing.

And so I turn to Caravaggio, accused by his contemporary critics for his "winking wantonness." He was known as a slanderer, a murderer, a fugitive, and, for a year, as a Knight of the Order of Malta. The facts of his biography exist inside a swirling mist of rumor. He was said to have used the drowned body of a prostitute as the model for his painting *Death of the Virgin*. He used himself when he was recovering from illness as the model for his portrait of the sick Bacchus. He used an illiterate peasant for his first version of *The Vocation of Saint Matthew* (an extraordinary painting destroyed in Berlin during World War II). And I'm told by a curator that he used a rheumatic child—some critics speculate he used a child's corpse—as the model for his *Sleeping Cupid*.

Sleeping Cupid—Amore dormiente—hangs on a crowded wall in the Pitti Palace. Is this a beautiful painting of a sickly child? Is it an ugly painting of a beautiful child? Why is this image of profound serenity so disturbing? What has happened to the tranquil beauty of Fra Angelico? What has happened to the Renaissance celebration of the perfectly proportioned human body? What is the effect of disproportion? What is wrong with this boy?

The light falls upon the child's round belly and full cheeks. The feathers of his wings flicker with streaks of white. He is clutching the shafts of arrows and smiling in his sleep. He is dreaming a sweet dream. He will never wake up.

I'm reminded of the grotesque dwarf riding the stone tortoise in the Boboli Gardens. But Caravaggio's Cupid isn't entirely grotesque. Nor is he entirely beautiful. He is something else, something neither, something we could call ambiguous.

Ambiguity is defiant. As an aesthetic strategy it has an improvisational quality and so belongs more to the individual artist than to the culture. As an aesthetic value it is a strong rival to beauty and can have a more pressing effect on memory.

Weak ambiguity does little more than express confusion. Strong ambiguity redescribes confusion, enabling us to experience it in a new light, contained within new boundaries of darkness, without the guiding standards of beauty and ugliness.

I make frequent visits to the Pitti to see Caravaggio's little Cupid wrapped in shadow and light and to experience the unsettling effects of ambiguity. This technique of chiaroscuro is paradoxical. Visual contrasts dissolve aesthetic contrasts, making it more difficult to know what I think about what I see. I can no longer admire the accomplishments of beauty. I stop looking for the functions of ugliness. In the confrontation with ambiguity, the whole apparatus of aesthetic judgment becomes useless.

Carnival in Florence, February 2001.

5.

Here are things you might see while sitting on the steps of the Duomo in Florence: A French tour guide holds up a broom. Someone's cell phone rings. A man with a bandage crisscrossing half his face looks around. An old woman carrying an orange cloth bag brushes dandruff from the shoulders of her navy coat. An old man carrying a green bag with the logo Energy glances at his wristwatch.

Crowds file into the Duomo on the left side and file out through the door on the right. About one in thirty people bothers to look up at the facade. A municipal policeman ambles by, his white hat perched on his head like a puffy *panettone.* Another cell phone rings, and the man who answers it squints against the smoke of his cigarette. A mother says, *"Ecco,"* as she and her daughter find seats on the stone step. *"Ah, che bella, ecco qua."* The mother puts a napkin on the little girl's lap and hands her a *bigne.* A blind woman chides her dog when it stops to sniff at a trash can. *"Allora, andiamo."* A German tour guide raises up a stick spiked with red. A vendor looks around warily, unfolds his cardboard, spreads out his sunglasses. A woman beckons to a friend; the black-eyed mop of a terrier's head peaks out from her purse. A carriage driver urges his chestnut horse through the crowd at a fast trot. "Eh!" he calls, and people stagger out of the horse's way. Somewhere another cell phone rings and someone says, *"Pronto!"*

Cultural experience teaches us how to recognize beauty. This education usually fails us, though, when we attempt to make something beautiful. We begin with infinite potential, which is lost with the first dab of paint, a word, a note. The made thing teeters out of emptiness into the world toward its named finality.

You watch a woman at a table on the Via Calzaiuola squeaking a fluffy duck puppet at passersby. Squeak squeak. The duck flicks a saucy red tongue when it squeaks. Squeak! Doesn't this young woman strike you as someone who likes to laugh at fools and cowards? Squeak!

Glances generate immediate judgments. Our opinions bounce off the clutter of the world. That woman likes to laugh at fools and cowards. The dog in the basket is ready to bolt. That facade is ugly, but the interior is beautiful. At a glance, we know what we think about what we're noticing. Usually, we can tell the difference between what immediately attracts and what appalls.

Making art, confident judgment gives way to guesswork. We can make something ugly beautiful or something beautiful ugly, but we can't measure the success of foresight beforehand. Perhaps all art begins as a series of mistakes, which are then corrected, to varying degrees.

A phone rings in Italy and is answered by the greeting of *Pronto. Pronto,* meaning ready. *Pronto . . . via!* Ready . . . go. Instead of hello, *pronto* is the greeting of preparedness. "Don't take this any further, however, as I have heard some unknowing people do," writes P. J. T. Glendening in *Cassell's Colloquial Italian.* "It would be ludicrous to call out *pronto* to someone you knew in the street."

In our absence, when we are just a voice on a phone, we need to convince others that we are ready. The phone has not caught us off guard. We are in control, eager to plunge into a conversation. Ready, set, go. *Pronto.*

A pigeon has taken to perching on the sloping corner of a roof that extends beside my window from the building next door. The bird arrives every morning between ten and eleven, clamps its little claws around the curve of an orange tile, and cocks its head as it looks around. Some days it seems as if the pigeon is trying to spy on me; other times it focuses on the vista to the south, with an overt haughtiness, daring me to be miffed by its indifference.

What a pigeon is and what a pigeon seems—the difference is hard to measure. We cling to facts in an effort to orient ourselves. But facts often generate mistakes. Facts, stuff, things—they enter the work with particular values already attached to them, and we have to struggle to see beyond what we've come to take for granted.

Who wants to be caught off guard? We want to know what we can know. I know the child on the steps of the Duomo was eating a *bigne.* I know the pigeon has a gray collar of feathers. But rarely do I know what, exactly, is going to happen next or what I will do by accident. The evening before the morning that I am sitting writing these words, I got so absorbed in *Adam Bede* that I let a sauce simmer to a charred crust in the pan.

Still, like everyone else, I try to be ready. Perhaps there is no cliché more expressive of the confusion created by our concept of time than the line Sure I'm ready, as ready as I'll ever be—a declaration reminding us that we're all in the midst of unfinished work, trying to move forward and at the same time repair our mistakes.

The activity of ugliness within a work of art can liberate the imagination. As a method of contrast, ugliness can be positioned to enhance beauty. And ugliness can disappear into the paradoxes of ambiguity. But ugliness can also be entirely accidental—a flaw that has no purpose other than to stand as proof of imperfection and so becomes deliberate only in retrospect.

Pronto, hello, yes, I'm ready for you, as ready as I'll ever be. We might not know what to expect, but we can at least hope we know enough about the world to be prepared for almost anything.

Clocking the World on Cue:
The Chronogram for 2001

Harry Mathews

NOTE: The chronogram—a centuries-old literary form—follows a simple but demanding rule: When all letters corresponding to Roman numerals (c, d, i, l, m, v, and x) are added together, they produce a sum equivalent to a specific year of the Christian calendar. The single words *memory* and *memento* are thus chronograms of the year 2000 (m x 2); so are *A moment for feasts & prayers* (m x 2) and *A year to pay homage to the dead* (m x 1 + d x 2). Both the title and text of this work are examples of chronograms of the current year.

JANUARY STARTS: sun here, stars there. So what joys & fears has the New Year brought us?

• In the Irkukst penitentiary ironworks the night shift is finishing its stint, skirting weighty pig-iron ingots as it regains the prison interior.

• In Pienza, Ernestina is heating tripe *fiorentina* for thirteen.

• In Sing-Sing, wearing surreptitious attire, spiting the surprising North Irish negotiations & shrinking tensions, Phineas, retiring Bishop of Ossining, with the authorities' requisite inattention, is tonight anointing fifteen Fenian ("Fighting Irish") priests in a rite of injurious piety.

• Bibi is shirring pigeon eggs in Saint Étienne.

• In Brighton, gregarious Brother Ignatius is getting high quaffing his fifth straight Irish whisky.

• In Pretoria, gritty Erwin Higginson (age eight), ignoring fatigue & injuries, is winning his point in a bruising nineteen-eighteen tie-breaker against Fritz Spitzfinger (age nine) by returning a wristy spinner hip-high & without hesitation whipping it fair, Spitzfinger then batting it high into the rows to bring the fifteenth prestigious Witherspoon Tennis Initiation Tourney to a breathtaking finish.

• In Fuji, pursuing a hashish high with Quentin, Kenny is perusing sporting prints by Hiroshige & Hokusai.

• Arising at eight in Brisbane, Ian, aspiring historian of propitious intuitions, enjoys the benign aberration that, by getting a grip on his utopian fusion of Augustinian with Einsteinian reasoning, he is attaining a genuine gnosis.

• In Etrurian Tarquinia, Gigi is eating spaghetti with pepperoni.

• In Austria, zipping past the Inn, ignoring warning signs, Pippo Peruzzi, first-string Ferrari whiz, big winner in Spain & Argentina, is steering his touring bike (pistons & turbine whirring, its stunning furnishings genuine Pinin-Farina) in brisk pursuit of fiery Zizi, his Hungarian skier, itinerant antithesis, antagonist, tigress, priestess, siren, obsession, happiness, wife.

• Bobbie is sitting with Bert in a Parisian bistro, in whose noisy interior untiring opportunists are satisfying pretentious ninnies with inferior white wine.

• Heroin originating in Iquitos is winning first prize with tertiary bargaining arbitrators in Tijuana.

• Bonnie is frying onion rings in Triffin, Ohio.

• In antique Poitiers, Antoinette is refreshing her guests with interpretations of Rossini's quainter offerings, interspersing arias & ariettas with his *"Nizza"* (singer & piano), his *"Raisins"* & *"Noisettes"* (piano), his first *sinfonia* (strings), & his roguish *"Iphigenia"* (bass trio).

• In Tirana, inept Hussein is paying fifty-eight qintars to fortify his Istrian wine with Bosnian raki.

• In the wintry outskirts of Pori, Father Tiki Haakinen—enterprising & itinerant Finnish priest—is repairing hi-fi wiring for a parish benefit.

• In spite of its threat to her ingratiating Gibson waist, Rikki, in Zanzibar, is insisting on heaping & eating piggish portions of spaghetti & fig pie.

• Postponing inopportune issues & putting first things first, Kiwanis, Rotarians, & Shriners are putting their agonizing unity in writing, signing a proposition that reasserts their opposition to atheists, bigotry, euthanasia ("outright assassination"), heroin, pinkos, the Spanish Inquisition, superstition, & unfairness in business arbitration.

• In Tauris, the ghost of pious Iphigenia waits for Orestes to bring her yet again to her father's house.

• In Antibes, bingeing on *pastis* is getting Winnie higher than nine kites.

• In Kiruna, in white tie, sipping a Perrier, Fafnir Grieg, high priest of Ibsen initiates, is testing his register & intonation in painstaking preparation for his fiftieth signature interpretation of the protagonist in *Ghosts.*

• In Gorizia, Anita is working up an appetite for *anitra triestina* ironing sheets.

• At Trinity, Robin is boating with his tutor, Isaiah Singe. Isaiah is asking if Robin thinks he is going to finish his thesis (*Affinities with the Orient: Inquiries into spurious interpretations of Hafiz in Ariosto, Ossian, & Kropotkin*) within his transitory span of years.

• In Bingen, penurious Winston is spiking his uninspiring Pepsi with Steinhäger.

• Business-wise Erika O'Higgins is sitting in Pittsburgh squinting with attention at the infuriating fine print in an IRS opinion assigning Irish pension benefits she is repatriating. The opinion questions her attestation separating foreign benefits, earnings as insurer in Tangier & those in fringe proprietary rights in Eritrea; pinpoints gains transpiring through inquiries into unwritten but propitious negotiations in Haiti; & reinstates profits inherent in eight-figure operations she is authorizing in Bisk (Siberia).

• In Bonaire, Georgia, hungry Josiah is weighing into his piping-hot grits & grunts.

• Rehearsing *Rienzi* in her Gorki isba, Anastasia thinks of Patti singing in *I Puritani*, of Kipnis in *Boris*, of Kiri Te Kanawa's Rosina in a Göttingen *Figaro.*

• In Ostia, engaging Ethiopian waiters trigger big tips by squirting nips of *grappa* into porringers of out-of-season fruit.

• Batting against the Orizaba Tigres in Irapuato, rookie Juanito

Arias first whiffs in eight straight opportunities before hitting a ninth-inning zinger & satisfying the inhabitants' hopes of winning the Zapatista Series.

• Zazie is biting into rabbit thighs in Barbizon.

• Zenia, passionate Aquinist, is pursuing an ingenious hypothesis, assigning the origins of Aquinas's interpretations of Gorgias to an "Osirian" genesis arising in the writings of inquiring Egyptian priests, an origin that the Sophists reinstate, or so Zenia infers in her ingenious synthesis. Questioning the suppositions of post-Aquinist thinkers, Zenia insists on the inferiority of Fourier's "inanities," Wittgenstein's "gibberish," & Austin's "asininities."

• High-intensity spirits inspire high-intensity spirit in noisy Kirin.

• In an uninspiring quarter of Trier, Ohioan Josiah, a boisterous nineteen, is infuriating Swiss Inge, a serious thirty, by persisting in attributing the first apprehension of the Einstein shift to Igor Sikorsky.

• In a *ristorante* in Torino, sheepish Antonio's superstitious hesitation between *arrabiata* spaghetti & risotto with *funghi* both intrigues & irritates patient Giorgina.

• In Ottawa, thirteen Inuit Situationists are signing treaties with the nation's highest authorities guaranteeing that their tribes & regions inherit proprietary herring-fishing rights outright & in perpetuity.

• In Whitby, seagoing Einar, finishing his fifteenth pink gin, insists he is quite fine.

• In Twinsburg (Ohio), when a nitwit intern, threatening to irrigate her intestines with his "own unique quinine infusion," brings out a giant syringe, Queenie, a patient with hepatitis B, her weary inertia shattering at the threat of this aggression, begins reiterating in shrieks of irritation & anguish, "No penetration without representation!"

• Ski-touring in Bennington, Jiri spits out bits of unripe kiwi in a fit of pique.

• Supine in Biarritz, Tristan—unsparing onanist—is perusing Gautier's pornographies, whose swift prurient inspiration stiffens his waning spirits.

- In Rosario (Argentina), fiery Antonio is assuaging his thirst with sweetish Rhine wine.

- Ianthe, in Berkshire, is initiating with requisite ingenuity her inquiry into "Oppositions & affinities in the autobiographies of Gibbon, Twain, & Frank Harris."

- In the Ain, Fifi is eating pike patties.

- In their frigate-repair station in Hawaii, engineer's assistant Rossetti is preparing to assassinate his superior, Ensign Fink, for gratuitous insinuations about his inferior IQ.

- Anisette fizzes are winning the night in Springs, whither Henri is steering Bettina in his antique Hispano-Suiza.

- Rehearsing Griffith's reinterpretation of the *Oresteia*, Saint Rita is pursuing Sinatra—a horrifying Aegistheus—then knifing Frank in his upstairs bathing unit. Arguing about the Patripassian & Arian heresies, Ignatius, Athanasius, & Boethius irritate an otherwise patient Hypatia. Portia is propositioning Iago. Tweetie, Isaiah, & Sophie Goering are intoning Britten's (or is it Griffin's?) "Fair Oriana." With Thisbe furnishing her know-how to position the pair, King Henry the Fifth is trying to insert his uninteresting penis into a twittering Titania. The White Rabbit appraises Pippa passing with irony and pity.

- In Saint-Quentin, Pierre is into his fifth pinkish Pinot Noir.

- Writing *finis* to his reign in the prize ring in Ashanti, Nigeria, "Tiger" Titus (Niger) is forfeiting a bruising fist fight to his Ibo heir, Tobias, thus ratifying his apparent superiority.

- In a quaint inn in Rieti, Kiki & Brigitte sniff quasi-appetizing brain fritters hissing in swine fat.

- Fishing in Touraine, Irwin is unkinking Eugenia's rig & fitting it with spinners. Their skiff sits in a quiet bight where feisty, spiky pike are rising & biting. First strike! It is raining.

- Uriah, Iggi, Jenifer, Tabitha are hitting the Pinot Grigio in a wine bar in Waikiki.

- In Fife, Inigo Higgins finishes writing his iniquitous *Jottings on Kinship Etiquette in Barrie, Rattigan, Braine, & Pinter.*

- Gauging his position in the whitening Pakistanian heights, Piotr eats his fiftieth fig out of its tin.

• Its gregarious parties gathering at a transient staging-point, shipping in the Bering Straits, either freight or passenger, is stationary tonight—engines quiet, neither jib nor spinnaker astir. As the fortieth ship nears, persistent skiffs begin sprinting through the nippy waters, swapping ostentatious rations & surprising potations & ferrying a rotation of seafaring prostitutes out of Tientsin, Biak, Iquique, Teresina, Kauai, Tenerife, Piraeus, & Hoboken.

• In Whitefriars, Pip infers that he is gaining genuine insights by sharing a firkin of Guinness with Brian.

• In Perugia, unwise Arrigo Panin is preparing a presentation that, straining notions of affinities to their breaking-point, risks irking (or boring) knowing trainees in his Institute for Insight & Orientation by arguing that it is appropriate to attribute Hopkins's inspiration to Whittier, Stein's to Browning.

• Faith is refrigerating nineteen stingers & braising nine satiating portions of bison brisket in Topperish (Washington).

• Hiking in the interior of Shikoku, Kirk is sustaining a tiring Iris with aspirins & interesting attributions of Finnegan's epiphanies.

• Sophie & Étienne, in an Iberian setting, are swigging refreshing pints of sangria *gratis.*

• In Sabine, righteous Sheriff Winthrop Prior, feinting a right, is banging a furious fist into a hirsute rapist's ribs & a punishing thigh into his iniquitous groin.

• Georgianna is nourishing nine aging kittens in Big Sur.

• Benign skies in Arizona. At a prairie spring, Tintin is watering his proprietor's thirty-eight first-string ponies—they're skittish ponies, stirring, neighing, biting, nosing bitten withers. Rising high in his stirrups, reins tight against bit, quirt hanging at his wrist, Tintin spits; sitting, he tips a sparing ration into its Zigzag wrapping. Prairie rabbits thinking: rain. Harriers beating their wings in thin bright air. Tintin thinking: This night's attire—white shirt, string tie—is right for winning his engaging señorita. His pinto whinnies & pisses.

• Sipping saki in Gifu, Roshi is getting quite tipsy.

• Zigzagging in nifty figure eights on a skating rink in frosty Keewatin, Nettie is fantasizing an ingenious haikuisation of Swinburne's "Proserpine."

347

• In Pistoia, tiny Pierino, stripping a thin bit of appetizing skin off the shining ribs of a spit-roasting pig, bites into it with a grin.

• Within sight of eternity, Keith Asquith, wintering in Antigua, is taking unsparing pains to surprise, spite, & punish his nowise ingratiating Yorkshire heirs—"The shits!"

• In Iowa abstainers are abstaining.

• In Austin, Ira & Justina, a striking pair, registering at first sight no antipathies but intriguing affinities, wishing to kiss, interiorize their inhibitions, banish their hesitations, skip propositions, & kiss, hip against hip. A swift shifting into a pertinent interior to quit their attire: whipping off pigskin trainers, unbuttoning Ira's shirt, stripping off Justina's T-shirt, unzipping her tight-fitting skirt & his khakis, unhooking her brassiere, ripping away panties & briefs, ignoring trinkets, skin to skin. . . . "Wait," interrupts Justina, insisting, "first this joint," to forthwith initiate brisk intakes & an instantaneous high. Kissing again, Ira's fingertips graze with finesse Justina's hair, ribs, & thighs. Justina seizes his wrists & entwines his waist between jittering tibias. Straining, Ira nips her tits. Thrashing, her nips stiffening, Justina tightens her grip. Gratifying Justina's appetite for kissing with ingenious bites, in his benign yearning Ira using his weight tips her posterior hither, baring Justina's piping fig. Into this engaging shrine Ira insinuates his inspissating thing, an insertion that ingratiates writhing Justina, inquiring in its penetration of her gripping, shifting pith, whose stunning twinges infuse Ira with stinging fire. He begins panting, his sinews stiffen, he hisses, Justina shrieks. It's brief, it's nifty, it's insane. Supine & sweating, Ira & Justina sigh faint sighs, kiss, grin, & sink into unworrying, transitory night.

• In the Tsinking zoo, unhesitating hippos, giraffes, kiwis, penguins, tortoises, porpoises, & tigers are ingesting big propitiatory portions of grain, onions, fruit, ginger, fish, & pig.

• On Thirteenth Street & First, Antoine & Honoria are sharing a pizza & a knish.

• Aries & Sirius are shining in Tunisian skies,

& so our New Year has begun.

Müller

Brian Evenson

> *... the category through which the world*
> *manifests itself is the category of hallucination.*
>
> —Gottfried Benn

I.

HIS GRANDFATHER KEPT SOUNDING like he was choking to death. The attending physician had claimed this was natural, an involuntary reflex—in other words, just because Müller's grandfather sounded like he was choking to death, it did not mean he was choking to death. Still Müller could not resist plunging his fingers down his grandfather's throat, so as to clear it, and each time he did, he felt the teeth.

The bridge was loose, the bands connected to the real teeth easily slipping off. His grandfather remained semiconscious, moaning. The bridge came free after Müller pried it back and forth a mere twenty minutes, the post screwed into his grandfather's jaw shearing off sharp. He did not let his wife stop him. He never let his wife stop him. *If the bridge is left in,* he told his wife as he pried, *he might aspirate it. In any case, he's not your grandfather. This is none of your concern.*

II.

He sat in the passenger seat, feeling the row of teeth through his pocket: central incisor, lateral incisor, cuspid, bicuspid. His grandfather liked him, he thought, and now he had stolen his teeth. There had always been teeth, he thought. His whole life, nothing but teeth. His wife was saying something, either to him or the road. He had never been able to smile in a way that showed more than the very tips of his top row of teeth—his wife, when she smiled, showed not only the upper teeth but a stretch of gum above. Other teeth: He had braces when he was a teenager but had failed to finish the treatment;

349

now his mouth was painfully instable, his teeth and jaw slowly shifting back to their untrammeled state. Other teeth: Once while riding his bicycle he had seen a dog's head hit by the fender of a car, its teeth spattering out and scattering down the road. The car, whose license plate he could still remember, never slowed for an instant. Other teeth: He felt in his pocket the four teeth—bicuspid, cuspid, lateral incisor, central incisor. A pocket is not where teeth belong, he thought. The mouth is where they belong. Or a glass. There was noise in the car and he looked up to find his wife smiling softly at him, her mouth closed.

III.

In the dark, Müller kept putting his grandfather's four teeth into his mouth, slipping them between his lip and teeth. He grimaced, imagining what he would look like with his grandfather's teeth in place of his own, his hair thinning, shoulders hunching, body slowly wasting away. His wife lay beside him, becoming his grandmother. Heat radiated off her; she was still alive. Nervously he kept taking the teeth out and nervously slipped them back in again.

He got up from bed, found a mirror. The man in it was hardly familiar, his mouth oddly bunched, neither himself nor his grandfather. He went and found some pliers. He opened the jaws of the pliers, opened his own jaws as well, carefully clamped the pliers around a central incisor. He had to open his jaw wider than was comfortable, and still one of the pliers' grips was wedged against his lower lip. The rasp of the scored metal against his tooth's enamel seemed to sound not in his mouth but deeper, against the lining of his skull.

He stood still, looking at himself in the mirror, the apparatus hanging from his mouth. It is not too late, he thought, his hand tight on the grips. He looked up, froze. Here was his grandfather at last, startled but attentive, watching him.

From One Big Self: Prisoners of Louisiana

C. D. Wright

Leaving Transylvania light yet

A gaggle of teens in front of the E-Z Mart the one with dollar bills
pinned to his T-shirt is Deano's baby brother

Is it really your birthday or are you just fooling

              Lake Providence

Last town in America to get rotary phones
town under curfew

              New Town

The real real poor part of Lake Providence

Warden, Louisiana, other side of Epps

Epps Industrial Park: West Carroll Detention Center; that's it for industry

              Artifact

Self-extinguishing cigarette with failsafe tilt ring
patent #4991595 2-12-91 Rosco Jones #105190.

   (This way if you're lying back on the couch on a slow night,
drinking, sweating in front of the swamp box, swatting mosquitoes, and
you happen to fall off before the dogs, you won't burn up)

C. D. Wright

    Why, Good morning Miss Tolliver, how are you

My pressure went up on me   if you have sons and daughters
        they cause your pressure to go up
        Come on down to the station and see me Baby
        I got to get back on the air Come on down

En Louisianne

     spit out a seed and up springs a watermelon

The old leprosarium in Carville lost its tax exemption
      during the Reagan years; then the army moved in

     We don't stand for corruption we demand it

Chicken pox can be dried up by scaring chickens

                             to fly over the afflicted child
En Louisanne
     Formosan termites on the wing

     more religion than you can shake a stick at
                        en Louisianne

Remember POP lived through his execution
had to let him go   that's the law   *en Louisianne*

In the mind of Joe Christmas
her death not an aberration but an abstraction to him
        brought on by bitchery and abomination

        Found: the doctor's wife
her two-year-old quadruplets crawling around in her blood
unharmed   unharmed   the papers said

Book the good doctor's cell in advance—high season rates

Go home now, POP, this bed is reserved for a predator

352

This bed now belongs to the good doctor

Bubba's got fresh gar for the senior citizens
None of that old gar Come on down and see
between The Projects and The Sweet Potato Man

in the subtle and savage light

Wrap this program around the shut-ins and the shut-outs
have a little mercy, etc.

I AM SENTENCED TO DEATH BY ELECTROCUTION!
According to state records, in 1970, 30 years ago. To have
electricity pass through my body until I am pronounced dead.
Yes, you heard me right, I am all stirred up. I am the seventh
child to the late Sister Rose.

He lived in that big old house   with his dogs   his guns

Was that a Harley or a coffin you were driving

Can I take off my tie yet

Keep on rocking in the free world

No we're not parole officers
No we're not church ladies

The redhead here is a photographer and I'm her humble factotum

Deano knows   he's got to be good until he gets off paper

                                        the sickly ambrosia of hope

Church marquee: life fragile

                                        handle with prayer

the subtle and savage light

C. D. Wright

      the fecundity   the enstiflement   the hole that dreams

Le ciel est par-dessus le toit

The windows here
      whiten in increments

There is no emptiness

Only a silence that does not go in reverse

I want to say I will be there   to collect your tears

After all, I am not Sister Prejean

No one here for urinating in public

A woman's hand will moisten your lips

7 A.M., the white ladies already out on soul patrol

Come on down,
The food is cheap the squirrels are black   you get drive-through daiquiris
at Macdaiquiri Factory   jumbo shrimp for $5.50 lb. at the Sinclair
cataracts removed at Dr. Brussard's; pecans at Mayonnaise's Place
50 flavors at the sno-cone shack   and soft soft real soft ice cream
barbecue at Pardners delivered by pony express   cathead biscuits
you can get your smothered steak at Hen House; collards, rhubarb cobbler,
                                   cornbread still sittin' on the side

The Best Substitute for War
Paul Auster

NOTE: This is drawn from the complete text of an article commissioned by the *New York Times Magazine* for one of several "millennial issues." The assignment was to write about "the best game of the past thousand years." Due to limited space, only a portion of the article was printed at the time.

... AND WHEN I CAST ABOUT in my mind for a single, dominant image or idea that might sum up the past ten centuries of European history, the word that keeps coming back to me is *bloodshed*. And by that I mean the metaphysics of violence: war, mass destruction, the slaughter of the innocent.

This is not to denigrate the glories of European culture and civilization. But in spite of Dante and Shakespeare, in spite of Vermeer and Goya, in spite of Chartres and the Declaration of the Rights of Man, it's a proven fact that scarcely a month has gone by in the past thousand years when one group of Europeans has not been intent on killing another group of Europeans. Country has fought against country (the Hundred Years' War), alliances of countries have fought against other alliances of countries (the Thirty Years War), and the citizens of a single country have fought against each other (the French Religious Wars). When it comes to our own, much vaunted century of progress and enlightenment, just fill in the appropriate blanks. And lest anyone think the carnage has ended, he has only to open the paper and read about the current situation in the former Yugoslavia. Not to speak of what has been happening in Northern Ireland for the past thirty years.

Mercifully, there has been peace among the major European powers since the end of World War II. For the first forty-five years, that peace was tainted by another kind of war, but since the fall of the Berlin Wall and the breakup of the Soviet Union, the peace has held. This is unprecedented in European history. With a common currency on the horizon and passport-free borders already a reality, it looks as though the combatants have finally put down their arms. That doesn't mean they like each other, and it doesn't mean that nationalism is any less fervent than it used to be, but for once it seems that the Europeans have found a way to hate each other without hacking each other to pieces. This miracle goes by the name of soccer.

I don't want to exaggerate, but how else to interpret the facts? When France pulled off a surprise victory in the World Cup last summer, more than a million people gathered on the Champs-Elysées to celebrate. By all accounts, it was the largest demonstration of public happiness seen in Paris since the liberation from the Germans in 1944.

One could only gape at the enormity of the event, the sheer excessiveness of the joy on display. It was just a sports victory, I kept telling myself, and yet there it was for everyone to see: on the same street in the same city, the same festive jubilation, the same outpouring of national pride that greeted General de Gaulle when he marched through the Arc de Triomphe fifty-four years earlier.

As I watched this scene on television, I thought of the title of a book I had read earlier in the decade: *The Soccer War*, by Ryszard Kapuściński. Was it possible that soccer had become a *substitute* for war?

Compared to American football, the European version seems rather tame, but the truth is that the history of soccer has always been steeped in violence. Legend or not, the first reference to football-playing in this millennium stems from an incident of war. In the year 1000 or thereabouts, the British were supposed to have celebrated their victory over an invading Danish chieftain by removing his head from his body and using it as a football. We don't have to believe that story, but verifiable documents confirm that by the 1100s Shrove Tuesdays were celebrated throughout England with massive football matches that pitted entire towns against one another. Five hundred players on a side. A field that could be up to several miles long. And games that lasted all day, with no fixed rules. It came to be known as "mob football," and the mayhem that resulted from these semiorganized brawls led to so many injuries, broken bones, and even deaths that in 1314 Edward II issued an edict that banned the playing of football. "Forasmuch as there is great noise in the city, caused by hustling over large balls from which many evils might arise . . . we commend and forbid, on behalf of the King, on pain of imprisonment, such game to be used in the city in future."

Further bans were issued by Edward III, Richard II, and Henry IV.

These kings were not just disturbed by the violence of the sport, they were worried that too much "meddling in football" had cut into the time previously devoted to archery practice and that their kingdoms would not be militarily prepared in the event of a foreign invasion. As far back as the first half of the millennium, then, the connection had already been made. War and football were two sides of the same coin.

With the development of firearms, archery ceased to be a required skill among soldiers, and by the late seventeenth century football was actively encouraged by Charles II. Standard rules were introduced in 1801, and as every schoolchild knows, Napoleon was defeated a decade and a half later "on the playing fields of Eton." After 1863, when the rules of present-day soccer were drawn up at Cambridge University, the game spread throughout Europe and the rest of the world. Since then, it has developed into the most popular and widely played sport in human history.

America seems to be the only country that has resisted its charms, but the importance of this game in Europe, its grip on the imagination of tens of millions of people living between Portugal and Poland cannot be overestimated. Add together our interest in baseball, football, and basketball, then multiply by ten or twenty, and you begin to have an idea of the scope of the obsession. When you further consider that each country fields its own national team, and that these teams go head to head against each other in European and world tournaments, it isn't hard to imagine how the love of football and homeland can be turned into a cocktail for chauvinistic excess and the settling of ancient scores. No country in Europe has avoided invasion and humiliation by one or more of its neighbors during this millennium, and now, as we come to the end of these thousand years, it sometimes looks as though the entire history of the continent were being recapitulated on the soccer field. Holland versus Spain. England versus France. Poland versus Germany. An eerie memory of past antagonisms hovers over each game. Every time a goal is scored, one hears an echo of old victories and old defeats. Passions among the spectators run high. They wave their country's flag, they sing patriotic songs, they insult the supporters of the other team. Americans might look at these antics and think they're all in good fun, but they're not. They're serious business. But at least the mock battles waged by the surrogate armies in short pants do not threaten to increase the population of widows and fatherless children.

Yes, I am aware of the British football hooligans, and I know about the riots and injuries that occurred in several French cities during last year's World Cup. But these instances of extreme and violent behavior only reinforce my point. Soccer is a substitute for war. As long as countries square off against each other on the playing field, we will be able to count the casualties on the fingers of our two hands. A generation ago, they were tallied in the millions.

Does this mean that after a thousand years of bloodshed, Europe has finally found a peaceful way to settle its differences?

We'll see.

A Detective and a Turtle
John Barth

"PROMISED . . . BUT NEVER . . . seen!" the voice sang out as from a soundtrack: "A detective . . . and a turtle!"

To Charles P. Mason, sleeping protagonist of this story, the words made sense at the time as a comment on the action in progress, and the singer's amused, ironically sprightly tone was appropriate: Dreamer and female companion were in automotive transit from some Point A toward some Point B, and, sure enough, neither the promised detective nor the expected turtle was in evidence. When a moment later our man awoke, however—in bed beside his still-snoozing wife in their satisfactory house at first light on a rainychill March morning in the Appalachian hills of Western Maryland—the sense-lending context evaporated: where the couple had been going and why; what relevance a "promised" detective and turtle, of all unlikely duos, had to the situation, whatever that situation was; and what their no-show portended for the travelers. Who those travelers *were*, even, Charles couldn't say for sure—Connie and himself, he presumed, but the woman in that dream-vehicle had been an un-visualized though palpable and familiar presence—any more than he could recall whether the "soundtrack" voice had been male or female, solo or chorus, instrumentally accompanied or *a capella*. Only the words, cryptic now, distinctly survived his waking, along with their melody: the rising, fanfarelike first phrase—*Táda tadáda tá!*—and the playfully lilting, rising-then-falling second—*Tadadát-tá da da táda.*

Don't ask Charlie, Reader; he just works here, anyhow tries to, between dreams and waking obligations. Our man is by vocation a storyteller: a dreamer-up and writer-down of confected characters, situations, scenes, and actions; one whose specialty, worse luck for him—as quaint a calling nowadays as shoeing horses or fletching arrows—is the all but profit-free genre of the Short Story. Ah that he were a novelist instead, C.P.M. sometimes can't resist wishing: not mainly, but at least *occasionally* a novelist, preferably of the commercial-blockbusting variety. As a medium of art and entertainment, your Novel still manages some audience share in the age of cable TV and the Internet; not what it was this time last century, but still much with us. Look at your bustling bookchains, between their calendars and their cappuccini; at your lending libraries, between their videocassette and CD racks and their banked computer terminals. Look at folks on beaches, pool decks, cruise ships, wide-body airliners and their associated passenger lounges, where cell phones and the not-*quite*-almighty Screen compete with, but have yet to supplant altogether, the novelistic Page. Lovers of *short stories,* on the other hand—whose ranks a hundred years ago happily included just about everyone who could read at all—have become almost as small and special a minority as lovers of verse: literary support groups, really, akin to those for the clinically addicted and the terminally ill.

Understand, our chap isn't complaining; he's just acknowledging the situation, reporting the news—which in the nature of the case isn't likely to *be* news to whoever's reading these words, and so enough of that. Nobody forced Chuck Mason into this "business," as he wryly calls it; this vocation so far from being a profession (as it genuinely was for many a talester in the years B.T., Before the Tube) that he's been obliged lifelong to ply a gainful trade in pursuit of his gainless calling. The late poet/novelist Robert Graves remarked of his commercially successful novel-writing that he was like a man who breeds and sells dogs in order to keep a cat. C. P. Mason, in order to keep his short-tale Tabby purring—in order, i.e., to contribute his share to the family economy and still free up enough time to conceive, gestate, and deliver his unmerchandisable little darlings at the rate of three or four per annum into a world almost entirely ignorant of and indifferent to their existence, let alone their welfare—pays the rent mainly by . . . *teaching.*

Yup: teaching. *School*teaching. Drilling the language's grammar and elementary composition into prospective teachers of same at what used to be called a teachers college before such places elevated themselves to branch campuses of the state university system. English-for-Teachers 101, in short, and the occasional Intro-to-Literature course: four overloaded sections per semester, decade after decade until quite recently, while Connie worked her butt off as Librarian Et Cetera in a not-bad area private school (always plenty of Et Ceteras in private-school job descriptions) so that their son and daughter could attend the place gratis, the public schools in their neck of the woods being alas less than impressive.

So? Nothing to sniff at in any of that, you considerately protest:

360

Certainly not in librarianing, and not in downscale branch-campus Learn-Your-Native-Language-teaching, either. *Somebody* has to do it, and Charles Mason has done it conscientiously, uncynically (despite his tone when speaking of it), and pretty effectively, if less than wholeheartedly, for his entire adult life. With only a State-U master's degree himself, he entertained no academic ambitions beyond reasonable job security, a fair salary plus fringe benefits till the kids were on their own, and the liberal holidays and long summer break of the academic calendar in which to pursue his real calling. Wallace Stevens sold insurance; T. S. Eliot worked in a bank; Charles P. Mason, like more poets and short-story writers than not in the USA these days, schoolteaches for a living. Which doesn't mean that he likes to natter on about it, is all we're saying, as we've done here.

So went their decades, zip-zip-zip, of life's short story: in the Masons' case, the twentieth century's latter half, during which, so it seems to them, American decades lost their former flavor. Before their time you had your World War Nineteen-Teens, your Jazz-Age Roaring Twenties, and your swing-band Depression-era Thirties; *in* their time, your World-War-again Nineteen-Forties, your crewcut and tailfinned postwar Fifties, your sideburned and bellbottomed druggy Sixties, which rock-and-rolled on for the dozen-plus years from JFK's assassination until the Arab oil embargo and America's retreat from Southeast Asia. After that—from C&C's perspective, anyhow, although they'd grant that their children, not to mention any Russian, South African, or Iranian, say, might see things quite otherwise—the decades lose adjectival character. The Seventies? The Eighties? The Nineties?

Comes then Y2K, and while neither The World As We've Known It nor this story-of-a-story ends with the millennium, the Masons find themselves officially Senior Citizens. Connie takes early retirement from the Garrett Day School and volunteers three days a week at the local branch of the county library—to "keep her hand in," she declares, without getting in her Garrett replacement's hair. Her husband scales down from full- to half- and then to quarter-time professoring: one course per semester wherever his old department finds itself temporarily shorthanded by leaves of absence or higher-than-expected enrollments. He compares himself to those "utility men" on factory assembly lines who learn the operations of ten or a dozen regular assemblers in order to relieve them serially for their coffee breaks, fill in for absentees, and train replacements. Inasmuch as his job has always been not only to teach language-mechanics, composition, and a bit o' Lit, but to teach student teachers how to *teach* those subjects—in short, teaching Teaching, and even, to his more "advanced" students, teaching the *teaching* of Teaching—we oughtn't to be surprised if at least now and then a C. P. Mason short story has to do with Stories and their Telling. Much as he prefers to keep Mason the breadwinning pedagogue separate from Mason the narrative wordsmith, those are ineluctably two aspects of the same fellow, and the muses are notorious for taking their procedures as well as their material where they find them, concerning themselves only with the transubstantiation of those P's and M's into art.

Exciting, no? While ethnic hatreds lacerate much of Earth's burgeoning human population; while poverty, disease, and malignant governments afflict millions more; while those of us fortunate enough to be spared such miseries busily overconsume our planet's natural resources, despoil the environment, and confront sundry crises of our own at every stage of our so-brief-no-matter-how-long lives, Charles P. Mason scribblescribblescribbles! And while some others blessed with his gifts of language and narrative imagination manage to illuminate in just a few pages some aspect of human experience and to render that illumination memorably into life-enhancing art, our Chuck spins yarns about . . . yarnspinning!

Yes. Now and then, anyhow, and among other subjects. Because, damn it—No, not *because:* He doesn't do it *because* of what I'm about to say, but if questioned on the matter he would most likely assent to the proposition that telling stories is as characteristically human a thing as we humans do, and is thus itself at least as fit a story-subject as another. How goes it, friend? How was your weekend, your childhood, your parents' divorce, your first life-changing love affair, most painful disenchantment, biggest mistake, dying day? And what does it tell us about you that you tell us *those* particular stories about yourself and others—that, moreover, you tell them the way you tell them—rather than telling some other stories some other way? Nay, more: Though neither philosopher nor cognitive scientist himself, Charles P. Mason would, if asked, almost certainly agree with those "neurophilosophers" who hold that consciousness itself has evolved to be essentially a scenario machine; that in order to make sense of and to navigate through the onstreaming flood of signals deluging all our senses, our brains posit the useful fiction of a Self that attends, selects from, organizes, considers, speculates, and acts upon that data; an *I* who invents and edits itself as it goes along, in effect telling stories to itself and to others about who it is. Indeed, an I whose antecedent *is*, finally, nothing other than those ongoing, ever-evolving stories, their center of narrative gravity.

Okay? Anyhow, that's what "I" can imagine part-time Professor Mason nodding Yes to if obliged to affirm some rationale for his spending precious autumnal hours writing stories about writing stories, and for his imagining that even a handful of his species-mates might trouble to read them. *That*, however (he'd want quickly to add), has to do at least as much with the quality of the telling as with the matter of the tale, with the How as much as with the What, to the extent that those are separable—and here we join the chap at his "business." Short-storymaking may be less than a profession, but our Charles is nonetheless a pro: He knows a C. P. Mason story-idea when he sees one; just as important, he knows how to make a C. P. Mason story out of that idea. He inclines to the snowflake analogy: Just as nature requires for flake-making, along with sufficient moisture and proper temperatures, a speck of atmospheric dust for ice-crystals to coalesce upon and grow their intricate hexagonal lattices, so your storymaker needs some *given*—a newspaper item, a mote of gossip or conversation, witnessed behavior or personal experience, even a dream—from which to grow the narrative artifact. And like the dust-grain in the fallen flake, the real-life datum may be all but imperceptible after narrative imagination has wrought it into finished fiction.

"Even a dream," did we hear somebody musing? *Yea, verily,* nods frowning Charles—at his old worktable in his old workroom now, breakfast and morning stretchies done and his wife off on household errands—*even a dream.* And he sets to work.

Detective. Turtle. Promised. Never seen. His frown manifests not only authorial seriousness (along with bemused puzzlement at that odd-coupled brace of nouns and cryptic pair of participles) but the frowner's reluctance to address the subject of Dreams—a reluctance that I quite understand and share. Since the heyday of Freud and Jung, much has been learned by neuropsychologists about the *processes* of dreaming: REM-sleep and the rest. Dream *content*, on the other hand (aside from the obvious general relevance of posttraumatic nightmares), is scarcely regarded these days in scientific circles as significant or interpretable, although beyond those circles one needn't look far to find dream-books, psychic dream-readers, and the age-old rest. In no story by C. P. Mason will you find a "dream sequence"—at least not one meant to be taken by the reader as

Significant or Portentous—and he is impatient with such sequences in other folks' fiction. Even such famous plot-turning dreams as Raskolnikov's and Svidrigailov's in Dostoevsky's *Crime and Punishment*, or Gustav Aschenbach's in Thomas Mann's "Death in Venice," make Charles fidget; appropriate though they doubtless are to the psychology of their respective dreamers and their historical periods, he can accept them only as he accepts the witches in *Macbeth*, the ghost in *Hamlet*, or the interaction of gods and mortals in Homer and Virgil.

That said, he grants of course that our dreams continue to fascinate us, at least mildly, when we recall them at all: So *weird* they can be sometimes! So amusing, distressing, or merely puzzling. And he would regard it as quite legitimate for a C. P. Mason character to manifest such fascination; even for that fascination (as distinct from the dream's "meaning") to drive or turn the story's action. Indeed, now that the subject has his full attention he'll go so far as to allow that even the dream's meaning—i.e., what the dreamer or some fellow character takes it to mean—might legitimately motivate the action, if it's clearly implicit that the author him/herself isn't demanding our assent to the character's interpretation. For no doubt people's real-life behavior is occasionally influenced by their dreams, or by the reported dreams of their spouses, lovers, comrades. Take for instance a dream Charles dreamed just a few nights prior to the one currently under his muse's consideration: He and Connie were finishing an early-morning bicycle ride on the boardwalk of some seaside resort. Dismounting to rest, they're asked by a pleasant-appearing middle-aged fellow where he might rent a bicycle himself for half an hour or so. Impulsively (and quite uncharacteristically) Charles insists that the stranger borrow *his* bicycle, gratis, and return it at this same spot in half an hour. But then he and Connie are on some residential back street; she needs his help in applying an unguent to her itching rectum (!), but he can't for the life of him puzzle out the unfamiliar instructions on the more-or-less-familiar unguent applicator. He then remembers that in time past a few eggs whipped in a blender have served the purpose just as well (!), but when he makes to prepare that poultice (on a residential sidewalk?) he finds the blender-vessel alarmingly encrusted with dead ants (!). Fortunately, a water-hose is running in a nearby yard; he's able to rinse off the thick layer of insect-corpses and beat the eggs (where's the electrical outlet?), thinking to himself that Con would have a fit if she knew the thing hadn't been scrubbed with hot soapy water. But she *won't* know, and in all this distraction he has lost track of time: The agreed-upon half hour has long passed; he'll never get his good bike back, which of course he should never have loaned to a total stranger. All the same, he'd better hurry to the boardwalk and hope against hope—but it's dark now; lights are coming on in the houses; he's not even sure which way the boardwalk is, and anyhow he's suddenly wearing nothing but Jockey briefs and undershirt. In one of the illuminated houses he sees several well-dressed women about to sit down to dinner; on their sideboard is the blender with the beaten-egg poultice in it! How to explain all this to waiting Connie, and where is she now anyhow? At this point the dreamer woke, only mildly and momentarily anxious, but tisking at the nutsiness of dreams. Go to it, Freudians! C. P. Mason won't take seriously either the dream or your reading of it, but he won't deny that a less skeptical character might, and consequentially so.

An unusual dream, in short, like any other unusual impingement upon or turn of events in the protagonist's life situation, may become the vehicle of dramatic action, the dust mote that precipitates a story. Precipitates it out of what? I've used the term "life situation"; Charles himself prefers to call it the Ground Situation (mentally capitalizing because both term and concept sound Germanic to him): a state of affairs preexistent to the story's present action and possessed of some dramatic *potential,* a voltage of which the characters themselves may be scarcely aware; a situation ripe (excuse his shifting metaphor; the guy is concentrating just now, not editing) for precipitation. Given such a . . . *Grundlage!* . . . the protagonist's dreaming of, for example, a promised-but-never-seen detective and turtle (!)— more exactly, his subsequent waking puzzled fascination with that dream—could conceivably trigger a story. Otherwise, it's as dramaturgically inconsequential as would be his seeing a goldfinch flit across the road, or hearing a distant siren, or farting after a heavy meal (any one of which, to be sure, in just the right circumstances . . .).

So, then: What's the Ground Situation here? The as-yet-unnamed because as yet unimagined Protagonist's, we mean, of this yet-to-be-dreamed-up C. P. Mason short story? Since its author *has* no Protagonist on the payroll yet, and inasmuch as that chirpy dream was in fact his own, not some made-up Character's, he now directs his muse's attention experimentally to his own "life situation," to see what in it might be said to have the makings of a proper *Grundlage,* ready for the storyflake-making. Semiretired sixty-plus East-Coast-American White Anglo-Saxon (lapsed-)Protestant branch-campus

English prof and modestly successful practitioner of regrettably now-marginal art form (his output sooner or later finds a home in some small lit-mag or other and very occasionally in what remains of the American large-circulation-magazine market, and has been collected into two volumes by two different "small presses") has been more than contentedly married for some forty years to coeval and co-ethnic now-retired librarian. One half-assed reciprocal infidelity in their long-distant past, so entirely healed over and inconsequential that if anything chances to remind them of that reckless episode (as this life summary may do) they merely roll their eyes at their then selves. Two grown children: daughter Carla, thirty-seven, a prospering estate-and-trust lawyer in Baltimore, divorced, childless, and evidently content to remain so; son Mark, thirty-three, a rising associate professor of marine biology at San Diego State, married, father of three-year-old only-grandchild Juanita (Mark's wife's Hispanic), whose grandparents wish she lived three thousand miles closer. Both elder Masons enjoy prevailingly good health, as do their offspring; their six decades have thus far spared them serious disease, serious accident, untimely death of loved ones, fire and flood and suchlike natural disasters, war and criminal depredation and suchlike man-made ones. Their quite comfortable suburban house is "free and clear"; their pensions, savings, modest investments, and insurance coverages are adequate to their needs; their country is as of this writing strong, prosperous, and at peace. Even Carla's divorce was amicable, as such things go: Her public-defender and civil-rights-activist husband discovered or decided that he was gay, or more gay than not, and that was that; the pair remain on cordial terms.

Indeed, so equable and agon-free has been the senior Masons' life thus far that it lacks the makings of a story. The only thing Charles sees in it, now that he's looking, that might amount to a voltaged Ground Situation is their good fortune itself: their recognition (his, anyhow; he has spared Connie this morbid *aperçu*) that the law of averages hangs over them like Damocles's sword. No one escapes death, and next to none are spared prior affliction: Sooner or later—and at their present age it can't be *much* later—disease, disability, and dying will overtake one of them, leaving the other searingly bereft and burdened until likewise overtaken. In some humors Charles can't help grimly envying a couple from their neighborhood, happily married retired professionals like themselves, who in the summer of 1996 were en route to revisit Paris aboard TWA Flight 800 when their 747 exploded over the Atlantic, killing all hands more or less instantly. The only improvements on that scenario that Charles can imagine (when he's in this mood) would be to make their quietus ten healthy years farther down the road instead of three or four, and in circumstances such that they not only "never knew what hit them" but never even knew they'd been hit.

In that case, though, he acknowledges, there'd still be no Story—not that that matters to our author vis-à-vis himself and Connie, but it obviously won't do for *our* story, Charles's story, the C. P. Mason story-not-yet-in-progress. The "And then one day" that typically introduces the Dramatic Vehicle to generate a story from the Ground Situation cannot likely be "And then one day he died" (although one can point to some odd, beyond-the-grave narrative exceptions). Whereas it might very well be something like "And then one day he woke from an amusingly obscure dream of a detective and a turtle, *promised but never seen*"—if there were a proper Ground Situation. He can imagine, e.g., a character not unlike himself determinedly, even obsessively analyzing that so-brief nonsense dream (along with his uncharacteristically sustained fascination with it) and in the process . . . what? Alienating his family, friends, and colleagues, perhaps, who are initially amused, then off-put, and finally concerned that old Chuck has gone bonkers? Or actually *going* bonkers, perhaps, to the extent of becoming convinced that the voice in the dream was God's, addressing him personally (Charles remembers J. L. Borges's observation, in "The Secret Miracle," that according to Rabbi Maimonides, "the words of a dream, when they are clear and distinct and one cannot see who spoke them, are holy") and in effect directing him to search out the promised but thus far unfound Detective and Turtle? Which would amount, would it not, to his becoming an unlicensed though divinely appointed detective of sorts himself, pursuing—like Achilles, was it, in Somebody-or-Other's famous paradox?—a turtle. Perhaps the Turtle of Truth? The Turtle of Story? But wait: Achilles's quarry was a tortoise, not a turtle; does Charles remember the zoological distinction?

He thinks so (turtle:water::tortoise:land), but clicks the terms up anyhow in his online dictionary, wondering as he does *Is this how Chekhov went about his art? Has any storyteller from Homer to Hemingway, Poe to Pasternak, attempted to fabricate a narrative something out of so nearly nothing?* Not likely (though not impossibly, either), and no matter. Our talester is none of those: He's Charles the Mason, surveying the materials at hand with a professional eye and a skilled artisan's imagination, to see whether there might be in them not an *Iliad* or a *Dr. Zhivago* but a C. P. Mason short story. If there be no *weather* in it, say (as there's been next to none so far in this), or pungent sense of place, eloquent details, memorable characters, grand passions, and high drama, then *tant pis:* It'll at least be architecturally complete, with a proper story's incremental raising of stakes, climactic even if quiet "turn," and consequential denouement.

Or else it won't be, in which case it won't get told.

His mention of Edgar Allan Poe—*somebody's* mention of that nineteenth-century East-Coast-American WASP inventor of the analytical detective story—prompts the reflection that most folks' experience of detectives is happily limited to printed fiction, films, and television dramas. Charles himself has to the best of his knowledge never laid eyes on a real-life detective, although in addition to police detectives even a quite small city's telephone directory will list one or two private investigative agencies—employed chiefly by disgruntled spouses and their lawyers, Charles imagines, to get the goods on errant mates in connection with divorce suits. Thus actual detectives *have* in fact been, in that sense and by Charles P. Mason, "never seen"—appropriately enough, he supposes, given the undercover aura of their business. But none was ever "promised," either, and so there goes that.

And turtles? (His dictionary modifies Charles's rough distinction by defining *tortoise* as "any of various terrestrial turtles.") Turtles are another story, he would acknowledge with a small smile: live and altogether visible baby turtles in Carla's and Mark's childhood terraria; box turtles on rural roads and occasionally in suburban yards, including the Masons' own; the odd snapper spotted in pond or creek; even large sea turtles admired in city aquaria or while snorkeling warm-water reefs off vacation resorts. Seen too on public television nature shows, and featured prominently—their terrestrial subset, anyhow—in folktale and fable: Aesop's Hare and Tortoise; Zeno's aforementioned paradox (he now remembers) of Achilles and the tortoise; the four turtles in Hindu cosmology upon whose chelonian carapaces stands the great elephant who in turn supports the Earth (those last, he grants, like Poe's M. Dupin and Conan Doyle's Sherlock Holmes, are "seeable" by the mind's eye only). Charles remarks further that turtles tend to withdraw from "sight" into their shells when approached or otherwise alarmed, as (with some stretching) the sense of a dream might be said to do upon investigation. . . . But "promised"? Quite possibly he and Connie had "promised" one or both of the kids those pet turtles before acquiring same; if so, however, the promise had most certainly been kept, the turtle-tykes delivered to the Mason-tykes and by all hands appreciatively "seen." So there goes *that*.

In short, while your typical character-in-the-street will likely have had more direct dealings with turtles than with detectives, neither can properly be said to be *never* seen, only seldom seen "live." And surely (with the minor sort of exception above noted) neither was *promised:* Promised by whom? To whom? For what?

Which leaves? Setting aside the dream-singer's D & T, Charles can think of any number of things Promised but Never (or Not Yet) Seen, from U.S. Congressional action on a political campaign finance reform bill to the Christian Messiah's Second Coming and the Jewish Messiah's First. The Masons' own revisit to Paris/London/Rome, which they've been promising themselves for the past ten years but can't seem to get around to, what with Connie's involvement in her volunteer work and Charles's in his scribblescribblescribbling. The overcommitted housepainter who swore he'd get their exterior woodwork done before summer but more often than not doesn't even get around to answering their telephoned Where-are-you's. Peace on Earth. The significance and/or relevance of the dream-song upon which short-story-writer C. P. Mason has now expended more than half a morning's professional attention and accumulated pages of notes without coming noticeably closer either to understanding it or to making fictive use of it—two quite separable matters, whereof the former is not always prerequisite to the latter.

So? So (He walks to the kitchen, pausing en route at the downstairs lavatory to urinate; refills his thermal coffee-mug; returns to his scriptorium; considers briefly whether to set this silly business aside and leaf through his notebook for some more promising bit toward which to direct his muse's energies. But there is none, he's fairly certain; inspiration, like penile erection, doesn't come to him as readily or frequently as in decades past; anyhow, the detective/turtle bit, if only *faute de mieux*, won't let go [he recalls—and makes written note of, to keep his pen moving—the folk-belief that when a turtle bites, it will hold on until either thunder or nightfall, he forgets which], and he's really rather persuaded now—perhaps also *faute de mieux*, but who cares?—that *there's a C. P. Mason story hiding here somewhere*): Aging protagonist's only Ground Situation is that he *has* no apparent Ground Situation, other than his relatively misery-free life history thus far versus the law of averages; *and then one day*—by dawn's early light, actually—he awakes from an untroubling but distinct and perplexing dream of (etc.).

Car radio, it suddenly occurs to him. There is less music in the Masons' house than in time past, when they routinely played their jazz or Caribbean LPs (and later their audiocassettes, followed by their compact discs) through cocktails and dinner prep, then quiet classical while they ate, and sometimes rock or disco to dance to when they felt frisky at evening's end. More and more in recent years they've found the sound bothersome; have progressively reduced the volume toward inaudibility, and often as not nowadays prefer to dine without background music. It is when traveling by car that they most often now punch up the local classical, jazz, or pop stations; and in that dream, Protagonist and Mate were "in transit"; and it is of course recorded music that most commonly presents us with invisible vocalists. So maybe the detective-and-turtle voice wasn't God's, but merely some pop singer's on the Easy Listening station?

Nah: It was more *ubiquitous* than that; more "out there" than the sound of their aging Honda's front-and-rear loudspeakers—and thus more interesting, at least potentially. Anyhow (Charles reminds himself), the stuff of dreams needs no such homely accounting for, although the impulse to rationalize the intriguingly mysterious he would grant to be human and honorable. There may well be, at least theoretically, some neurological or even psychological explanation of why C. P. Mason's dreaming brain came up this morning with an unlocatable voice singing of a reneged-upon detective and turtle rather than with, say, a recklessly loaned bicycle and an ant-encrusted blender for the curbside preparation of rectal poultices. But at such explanations the Muse of Story shrugs her Parnassian shoulders—unless, valid or not, they prompt some dramaturgically significant action on the protagonist's part.

Such as? Oh, well . . . such as his near-overwhelmment, at this point in this narrative, by a hot mix of unsortable emotions at the sudden vivid recollection (prompted by that nutsy rectal-poultice business above) of his adulterous anal intercourse thirty-plus years ago with an adult female former student of his at the teachers college: one Deedee Francis, a grown-up Sixties Flower Child, exotic in that academic venue, to whose hippie husband her vagina was inviolably pledged but not her other orifices, which she offered with Hubbie's blessing in their psychedelically painted Volkswagen Microbus to such of her admirers as were also her admirees, and she'd really really grooved on Charles's Introduction to the Teaching of Poetry course the year before. Dear down-to-earth, high-as-a-kite Deedee, with her "sidelong pickerel smile" (as poet Theodore Roethke phrased it in the course's text), smiled fetchingly overshoulder in mid-buttfuck; where was she now, and doing what with whom? No matter: That early, uncharacteristic infidelity (and Connie's tearfully furious retaliation therefor with one of Charles's departmental colleagues upon his confessing it to her; such were the High Sixties, Reader, even in the boondocks of Academe) had most certainly been a pain in their marital backside, poulticed only by the passing of many a semester. And it could quite imaginably become so again if, say, a reawakened interest in or nostalgia for it came to reflect, perhaps even to *cause,* some growing, till-now-unrecognized dissatisfaction with his mate, his marriage, his life. . . .

Nonsense! Our man protests (too strongly?). How could he even hypothesize such a thing? he asks himself (like a wily psychoanalyst?).

Et cetera: *There's* a Ground Situation for you!

But not for C. P. Mason, who declines even to consider what "dramaturgically significant action" he (he means his protagonist-character) might take in consequence of this dream-cued recollection/revelation. With relief he offers himself and us an alternative Such As, altogether safer though less voltaged: Small-time academic and middlingly successful practitioner of fading literary genre, now in the autumn of his career and of its, has become accustomed to and patient with occasional recalcitrance on his muse's part, as with occasional genital dysfunction and other exactions of relentless aging. *But then one day,* seasoned professional that he is—after throwing several morningsworth of good imaginative money after bad in his effort to discover the C. P. Mason story that he feels strongly to be "hypertexted" behind the imagery of a certain C. P. Mason dreamfragment—he confronts not only the growing likelihood that there's no story there after all (Who cares, finally, about that?), but the vertiginous possibility that the cupboard is bare, the well gone dry for keeps. For would the C. P. Mason of even five years ago, not to say twenty or thirty years ago, have spent a whole week's work-time poking and puttering at the memory of a silly dream if his notebooks burgeoned, as once upon a time they did, with other story-seeds awaiting his consideration and cultivation? Anton Chekhov is said to have remarked, no doubt ironically, that if a story took him longer than an afternoon to write, it probably wasn't worth his time. No

371

Chekhov, Charles has never cared how long a C. P. Mason story remains in the works, as long as it's working. In better days, however (which is to say, right up to Page One of this story), he would have reshelved so unforthcoming a "bit" as this detective-and-turtle dream to germinate while he developed some other, less resistant item from his backlog.

Such as? There's the rub: There *is* no backlog of notebook-entries awaiting his authorial attention; nor has there been, for longer than it's comfortable for Charles to remember. That's why, when he awoke this morning with that dumdum dream-song still reverberating in his head, he fetched it expectantly from bed through breakfast-with-Connie to his workroom, to see what might be made of it.

Nothing. Nada. Niente. Nichts. Nichivo. He has that notebook open now, just checking: the original little brown looseleaf pocket notebook in which since apprenticehood he has accumulated trial offerings to his muse. Its most recent entry is the opening sentence of this story. The one before it—scratched through after its deployment, like all the entries before *it*—is dated a full year earlier: the touchstone of his most recently completed C. P. Masonry, long since out of the shop and making its slow rounds of likely periodicals. The two stories preceding that one had likewise been worked up from prior-year inspirations, now duly crossed out: three withdrawals from an account into which he has made no new deposits since, its balance zero. . . .

Until now. Impulsively—perhaps only for the gratification of seeing two uncanceled entries instead of one—below the detective-and-turtle nonsense he copies that line from Roethke's "Elegy for Jane," his student killed in a fall from her horse: *Her sidelong pickerel smile.* The poet's grief is pure ("I, with no rights in this matter," the poem concludes: "Neither father nor lover."); Charles's memory of *his* long-ago (ex-) student's similar smile is not, although from so distant a remove and in so autumnal a humor as his current one, it has its own innocence. The movement of his pen on paper is, as always, agreeable. It occurs to him, regarding the two notebook-entries thus juxtaposed, to imagine that smile—Deedee Francis's over-the-shoulder, Go-to-it-big-boy smile in the back seat of that old Microbus—as his muse's. His protracted search for usable significance in that dream—his detective-work upon it, one might say—has proceeded slowly and deliberately (and thus far futilely): at tortoise speed, one might say. And yet, quite like Deedee's *in flagrante delicto*, Ms. Muse's sidelong pickerel smile has at once encouraged him to go to it, reassured him that what they are about is pleasurable, anyhow not unpleasant, for her as well as for him, and suggested tantalizingly that she's onto something—something amusing to herself—that he is not. In Deedee's case (so he learned after the subsequent debacle), that something had been or had at least included the datum that yet another of her admired admirers, Charles's then-colleague Fred Sullivan, had confided to her in that same vehicular venue his hankering to do with Connie Mason what he was just then doing with her. As subsequently, Q.E.D., the fellow did—for such were the lusty-among-other-things High Sixties.

And Mademoiselle Muse? What piquant infobit might *she* be savoring as they two go to it? Perhaps that, hump her as he might, she has conceived her last by him, whether that last be this misbegotten detective-and-turtle story or, more likely (for whoever made babies *this* way?), the comparatively bona fide item before it, finished months ago and now in the mails with its self-addressed stamped return envelope. Perhaps, on the contrary, that Charles's current fallow season is after all just a rather-longer-than-usual downtime, to be followed by fruitful intercourse again before his inevitable *finis.* Or perhaps that that *finis* is very much closer than he supposes; that it will come—via ruptured aneurysm or out-of-the-blue fatal accident or who knows how—within the hour of his putting the closing period to what after all (so I choose to imagine her mercifully or mischievously granting, in honor of their long and not-unproductive connection) will turn out to be a by-hook-or-by-crook C. P. Mason short story, obscurely promised and finally, if obliquely, seen: one having to do, more or less and by golly, with a detective and a turtle.

Camp Cedar Crest
Alexander Theroux

CAMP CEDAR CREST WAS THE FIRST and last camp I ever attended. It was run by a couple named Beebe, had Catholic affiliations, and the counselors were seminarians, candidates for the priesthood who, for the duration of the summer, tyrannically ruled the hundred or so boys sent there, mostly from the inner city, to get them off the streets. It was an inexpensive place, predominantly for boys from poor families, and there were even charity cases. My parents sent me there for another reason: to be cured of wetting the bed. I had turned twelve years old that summer and had never been away from home before, and I remember when my parents dropped me off and drove away I had the sudden feeling of being deserted.

The word *priesthood* for some reason always, chillingly, gave me an image of cobras.

Was it because of the counselors? They wore black trousers and white T-shirts, and seemed always hidden, until, sliding out of some corner, they appeared, pimply faced and tall with big black shoes and round miraculous medals around their necks. They were Irish and sex-starved and jut-jawed and repressed and angry and always spoke to us, overpronouncing words, as if talking to idiots. The worst one was Monsky, in charge of C cabin—mine. He had short hair, a fat humorless head, rather like a professional bowler's, and a feral-looking case of underbite, with fanged teeth. He was also humpbacked and mannerless and dyed his hair and had a missing kneecap and held his fork like a screwdriver.

He shouted at everyone and with disgust called us "quats" and could cagily pick out features in each of us to ridicule. I met Monsky right away because the first day I got there and was waiting for my cabin assignment he called me in and asked, "Why are you sitting on your footlocker like a fairy and not outside with the others?"

The camp was a circle of old barrack-type cabins in a clearance of a forest in Marshfield, Massachusetts. Dusty fields lay all around. At the end of the main field, in front of which stood a flagpole—we fell in at 6:30 A.M. for reveille—stood the administrative hall, where Bill and Phoebe Beebe, the administrators, ran the programs. Races, activities, things like that. Canoes were launched along the small river, a narrows beset with woody islets where the summer air was redolent of hot pine, spruce, and cedar. Blueberry bushes sprouted up everywhere. Spongy pine needles were lovely to walk on in those dark dingles and dales under the kind of tall, massive, sky-pointing evergreens that I knew could once be seen all over North America when it was a young and beautiful country. Nearby lay a malodorous marsh that stank at low tide and which we called Fart Harbor. I stared at the moon by night and communed with it. Mist gathered in valleys in the early morning. Most of the ballfield grass got yellow by the middle of July. It was, all in all, a green, deeply forested, and isolated place which became even more so in the rain-dripping darkness. I remember many warm lazy afternoons, a droning plane somewhere in the distance, writing postcards home. Many far miles away rose the kind of hills, I knew, that Indians once lived on, always facing south, near water. I knew about stuff like that. I don't know, maybe most everybody did. I had a book with photos, in his tent in the frozen wastes, of Richard Evelyn Byrd, whose name *wasn't* a woman's.

My favorite book, thick and green, was *Trader Horn*, about an adventurer who once made a comment on one page I remember regarding the lack of softness in nature. I wrote down words from it that I later kept. My favorite song was "The Heather on the Hill." My favorite painting was *Lady with an Ermine*. I had six rolls of Wheatsheaf pennies. A beautiful Korean girl named Sarah with an angel's features once gave me a valentine that I still have in a drawer. I wanted to know and I needed to feel and I felt I had to know the meaning of everything.

I can honestly say that most of the time I lived a dream life. So many times I saw people, strangers, passersby, and out of nowhere thought: *I will never ever see that person again.* Everyone always walked in different directions in the world, lost to logic or loyalty or luck. What was fleeting was temporary, and anything temporary broke my heart. Nothing one experienced ever remained permanent or recoverable, I realized with melancholy—not the moment, not the place, nothing. Whatever we encountered or passed by was immediately and forever in the past. I pondered in consequence and with mad concentration the way things used to be. I was always wasting my time as a young boy trying to squint back through space and time or some dimension, making an effort to look into and then past crowded neighborhoods and urban blight and city blocks in an attempt to see, as if by way of photographs, the ghosts of the past.

And I knew about druids. Who knew, I thought, maybe I was one once. I could read signs in nature. I wanted to sleep in the open air without a blanket, live in the woods, eat berries, and find mushrooms—I believed trees had rights—trek over trailless mountains and meet Pontiac's holy ghost, attaining the tippity-top of their highest mysterious peaks, silent in their primeval sleep. Be an explorer. That word. I loved it. And the word *scout.* I made friends, grew quiet in the presence of girls, whose beauty and mystery I loved and feared, but still, because I was going to be an author, I walked alone by the lake, tossing in stones, listening in silence in clearings, and taking long looks into the world. I got goose bumps.

Phoebe Beebe, who gave out mail in the high hall, where the chapel was—daily attendance was required—looked like a bag of russet potatoes with earrings. Augie Doggie had a joke about her and told it every day. "Why is it good Phoebe Beebe has the face of a vulture and the voice of a crow?" And we'd all sing in unison, "Because if you threw a rock at her, you could kill two birds with one stone."

There were campfires at night, when we all sat like Mohawks *sur leur derrières,* crouched, our knees as high as our ears, and fed the fire fat pine knots as we listened to scary stories about creepy madmen like Grippo and Three-Fingered Willy and Mr. Mendacino, a sentient vegetable, and Fat Ping, the Chinese warlord who bit people to death, and Dripple the Cripple, who strangled women and said, "Thuffer!" Sometimes we threw on pieces of old driftwood: Whoever has seen driftwood burn with all its magical lights, hissing and spitting sparks, odd bursts of powder, will never forget it. The moon would be out. Foxes barked some nights, and I think I heard coyotes. I felt the wind. It was wild and wonderful to be alive.

At times Mulligan and Obie, two of the nicer counselors, asked questions. I often knew the answers. It was because of my reading—and knowledge of James Fenimore Cooper and spirits that came from the loveliness of the deep woods and being able to survive if I got lost on Mount Katahdin and all the time I put in dreaming, especially about Glooskap, an Indian spirit who never grew old and lived at the south end of the world with the lion and the wolf.

Curfew was for ten. And they were strict. "Don't you trust us?" asked Vinnie Mushpart, as in the dark we filed into the cabins by flashlight. "Yuh," said Atkins, "like a pink-faced prostikook doing pushups over twenty-dollar bills."

But I didn't mind the curfews. Or the work detail. Or even Monsky. (My nightly affliction was something else.) I had not only friends, but admirers for the first time. I knew things others didn't and it won me some esteem. A button is a good fish lure. Snow is a leavener for cooking. All seaweed is good to eat. Never plant a seed deeper than its width. Spring moves north about thirteen miles a day. The bark of a dead tree holds moisture on its northern side, and the center of the damp or rotten area is usually slightly east of north. I even knew that people wiped their bums with stones in Samoa, but that I didn't feel was right to mention.

We sneaked out and smoked pipes, not cornsilk as once I did at home, but Edgeworth in the blue pouch and Model tobacco, from a can with the cartoon of the bald old man with a mustache that the Jackdaws bought, two brothers named Shoffner who looked like birds of prey but were great at soap carving, where you glued together two or three bars, one on top of the other, for whittling totem poles or heads. I thought I'd never get as old as that old geezer on the Model can. My postcards home were speckled with nonsense, puns, and Latinisms. Sometimes Monsky stared at me in games. He was cruel and, I felt, dangerous.

I got to know my bunk mates. Billy Gilday could mouth and spit-shoot three hundred BBs into the hole of a Daisy rifle. There was Harshbarger, the Nazi, who went for "mailbox baseball," smashing them with a bat. Rappleye, a genuine mutant who had webbed toes, a twist of nature he often pointed to with pride. Snover. Brian Godalming, my friend. Fitler, who was always flipping a Zippo in his pocket. Richard Center went home with rheumatic fever and later died. Patroni. Slupski. Julie Zuk, from Danvers, who collected leaves (oak, maple, catalpa, etc.)—"telling leaves," he called it—and Mush-part, who, although he was thin as a reed, weak, and pale as the underbelly of a fish, would stand up during dinner and squeeze sandwiches through his fingers. There was Edd ("Bona") Harding. And even Blackerby who was from Athol and turned blue in the ocean and whom we called the "Unidentified Flying Oddball."

And Warren Ruck, who wanted to talk after taps. I remember him as a quiet, fragile, stuttering boy with exquisite but somehow feminine manners who always wondered why I got up from the breakfast table—the wood was always gluey—to get back to the cabin before the others. But inspection followed, and I had to open the window and talcum the sheets whenever I had an accident, which was all the time.

Cruel counselors mocked Ruck—and always, of course, us—about girls. They called him "SSSpeedo" and snatched his hat and played *salucci* with it and abused him and never picked him for patrol leader. Several times the counselors asked us if we wanted to become priests. But from the sound of the sheets shuffling at night, and from what I heard about it, there may have been sins being committed, which is why one Sunday after Mass, Phoebe Beebe had pamphlets called *The Difficult Commandment* passed around to all.

We often went to the old tractor shed, with its old tin signs advertising Moxie and Nehi that resonated when we bounced small green apples off them, me and Warren and Brian Godalming. We made gimp lanyards and twill-woven pot holders and rawhide wallets and leatherhead drums and birch birdhouses and talked about things like when is the best time to plant and where to build lean-tos or how the Pilgrims survived the first winter in Plymouth. "Eating groundnuts, birch syrup, pigweed, even antlers when in velvet," I said, which was true. I never said much about myself, having developed formidable defenses against reality at a very tender age. Bedwetters must. But I remember being very happy.

I was *prepared*. It's a concept young boys alone can understand: being prepared, not for anything in particular. But for everything. Like the Minutemen. Was it an escape mechanism? I ratholed all sorts of things in my khaki footlocker: pamphlets on ventriloquism and throwing your voice; baby powder; a rubber sheet; a jackknife; two bottles of Vitalis; an army compass; a flashlight; several packages of Clark's Teaberry gum; a copy of *Saint Among the Hurons*; bags of chestnuts; a hatchet; copies of my favorite comic books: *Strange Tales, Sad Sack, The Purple Claw, Wild Bill Elliott.* I had copies of Jimmy Hatlo's *They'll Do It Every Time*.

I wanted to be an author, mostly because, at least to me, writing books with quills by candlelight seemed to be about the best thing a person could do, no matter what, and also, I think, at least partially, because I had the same name as Alexandre Dumas. I once made a list:

Things in Nature That Hurt

sunglare
jellyfish
horseradish
hot peppers

locust bark
poison ivy
dry ice
yucca plants
snakes
onions
rhubarb leaves
mosquito bites
thorns
hail
hornpouts

Camp food dorked. We marched to the dining hall every morning to "Fairest of the Fair," an old scratched 78 rpm record playing on a Victrola up in the wooden fire tower and blasted over a loudspeaker. I remember watery scrambled eggs and pancakes and clogged syruppourers and the scent of pine blowing through morning windows thrown wide open. Gilday once winkled some silverware and we made long spears, to fight saber-toothed tigers. We left messages in the woods by shaping tree limbs. Tapioca pudding we called "fisheyes," doughnuts "shotputs," apples "Mrs. Beebe's Bubbies," and certain white round desert-dry cross crackers they gave us were impossible to eat with peanut butter without strangling. The soup was so thin, we used to say it was made from boiling the shadow of a pigeon that had starved to death. Sometimes we stole Oreo cookies, which we wolfed down with gulps of milk, trying to see who'd pass out and making a paste completely unspitoutable— "Look!" we gagged—and thick enough to brick up Fortunato.

Afterward came inspection, as I say, which terrified me. I came to align all my hopes to the fact of that, not so much never being known, as much as, if found out, then forgiven. I desperately shook powder over the stained sheets or doubled up the blanket or did both, praying to God under my breath that no one would notice my incontinence. It worked for a few days. But then my luck abruptly came to an end. I can still remember the morning. Monsky strode in and, jutjawed, hump up, paused, flinging back the covers of my cot, singling me out in front of all the others, and screamed, "What is this? Come here, fart harbor, and explain this! Are you a fairy? Hand wash them blankets! Spray the slats, springs, and frames of this bed! Get them thoroughly wet, then borax them, hear me?" He called me a quat and a doughhead and a fairy and, in his mocking way, even managed to make my friends laugh at me. My face heated balloon red from humiliation, and, for a minute, in a hot flush of vertigo, I actually thought I had disappeared. Or was upside-down. I remember hearing only echoes in my head of his infernal shouts. "And spray that dog of a mattress! Do not soak it! Pay particular attention to seams and tufts! And brush the box springs, for godsakes, because they reek!"

As a punishment, I was forced for an afternoon, in front of the entire cabin, to sit on a stool and wear a rubber sheet around my neck.

Many things have happened to me in the intervening years, good and bad, but from that day on I was never the same person again. I was only worried. I never wrote home again, or if I did, I rarely told the truth. It was like I never was. And when I was given jobs, like putting para-crystals in the old storage rooms and cleaning the garbage pails with chlorine bleach and brushing the radiators and boraxing the toilet molding, I always wondered whose hands were doing the job and who was acting under my name.

I was going to say I never went out after that—but I wasn't even alive anymore—and yet I did go out once, to the top of the old wooden fire tower, where I sat alone for hours trying not so much to not be seen, though that, as to be able somehow to turn back time. The whole last week of camp it rained, and we stayed in those musty cabins with their cedar walls and silverfish in the wood and naked light bulbs, and it never seemed so lonely. I was so homesick that if anybody blew on me, I knew I'd start to cry.

The day my father came for me, I was so happy to see him I went mute. I could not talk. My throat was filled with tears. But I was cynical, too. Since I figured nothing ever came true, especially what you wanted, when I wanted something I prayed for it not to happen, so it would, like my father coming to get me. I never went to camp again. Nor did I dream again of woods or compasses or Glooskap or wolves or the best way off Mount Katahdin. I was a bedwetter, and so knew I was worthy of being neither an Indian nor an author.

One thing I never wondered anymore was what hurt most in nature, only because I knew. It wasn't jellyfish or locust bark or dry ice or thorns or eating rhubarb leaves. It was people. Camp, they said, always taught you something. And now I knew that they were right.

Two Poems
John Yau

ING GRISH

You need to speak Singlish to express a Singaporean feeling.
—Catherine Liu

I never learned Singlish

I cannot speak Taglish, but I have registered
the tonal shifts of Dumglish, Bumglish, and Scumglish

I do not know Ing Grish but I will study it down to its
black and broken bones

I do not know Ing Gwish but I speak dung and dungaree,
satray and claptrap

Today I speak barbecue and canoe

Today I speak running dog and yellow dog

I do not know Spin Gloss but I hear humdrum and humdinger,
bugaboo and jigaboo

I do not know Ang Grish but I can tell you that my last name
consists of three letters, and that technically all of them are vowels

I do not know Um Glish but I do know how to eat with two sticks

Oh but I do know English because my father's mother was English
and because my father was born in New York in 1921 and was able
to return to America in 1949 and become a citizen

John Yau

I no speak Chinee, Chanel, or Cheyenne

I do not speak or dream in Chinese because my parents were afraid
I would never learn to speak English property or properly. They
were afraid I would mumble in Ing Grish.

I do know English because I am able to tell others
that I am not who they think I am

I do not know Chinese because my mother said that I refused to
learn it from the moment that I was born, and that my refusal was
one of the greatest sorrows of her life, the other being the birth of
my brother

I do know Chinese because I understood what my mother's friend
told her one Sunday morning, shortly after she sat down: "I hope
you don't mind that I parked my helicopter on your roof."

Because I do not know Chinese I have been told that this means I
am not Chinese by a man who translates from Spanish. He said
that he had studied Chinese and was therefore closer to being
Chinese than I could ever be. No one publicly disagreed with him,
which, according to the rules of English, means he is right.

I do know English and I know that knowing it means that I don't
always believe it

The fact that I disagree with the man who translates from the
Spanish is further proof that I am not Chinese because all the
Chinese living in America are hardworking and earnest and would
never waste their time disagreeing with someone who was right

This proves I even know how to behave in English
It has been said by an authority on poetry that I don't look or act
Chinese

I do know English because I understood what my first wife's
mother meant when she said that people from India and Pakistan
like to work at gas stations at night because they didn't have to
worry about getting sunburned

I do not know English because I got divorced and therefore I must
have misunderstood the vows I made at City Hall

I do know English because the second time I made a marriage vow
I had to repeat it in Hebrew

I do know English because I know what "fortune cookie" means
when it is said of a Chinese woman

I do know English because I can read the book of names which a
friend has said can help me name my daughter

The authority on poetry announced that I discovered I was Chinese
when it was to my advantage to do so

My father was afraid that if I did not speak English properly I
would be condemned to work as a waiter in a Chinese restaurant

My mother, however, said that this was impossible because I didn't
speak Cantonese, because the only language waiters in Chinese
restaurants knew how to speak was Cantonese

I do not know either Cantonese or English, Ang Glish or Ing Grish

Anguish is a language everyone can speak but no one listens to it

I do know English because my father was proud that he was half
English and half Chinese before interracial marriage was acceptable
under the law

I do know English because my father's mother was Ivy Hillier. She
was born and died in Liverpool, after living in America and China,
and claimed to be a descendant of the Huguenots.

I do know English because I misheard my grandmother and thought
she said that I was a descendant of the Argonauts

I do know English because I remember what "Made in Japan"
meant when I was a child

John Yau

I learn over and over again that I do not know Chinese. Yesterday a man asked me how to write my last name in Chinese, because he was sure that I had been mispronouncing it and that if this was how my father pronounced it, then the poor man had been wrong all his life.

I do not know Chinese even though my parents conversed in it every day

I do know English because I had to ask the nurses not to put my mother in a straitjacket, and reassure them that I would be willing to stay with her until the doctor came the next morning

I do know English because I left the room when the doctor told me I had no business being there

I do not know Chinese because during the Vietnam War I was called a gook instead of a chink and realized that I had managed to change my spots without meaning to

I do not know English because when my father said he would like to see me dead, I was never sure quite what he meant

I do not know Chinese because I never slept with a woman whose vagina slanted like my mother's eyes

I do not know either English or Chinese and, because of that, I did not put a gravestone at the head of my parents' graves as I felt no language mirrored the ones they spoke

John Yau

CONVERSATION AFTER MIDNIGHT

The civilization of green ants
met last week or month
(your sense of time a concept
I don't yet understand
and besides I wasn't there)
and they elected me to come here,
even though me was still not me or even an I,
an unarticulated murmur maybe that
at best some dust of unlikely possibility
I was nevertheless elected to be
among you, to arrive and to periodically whimper
howl stir scream cry
in a black spring night
gone sour with images of the moon
(O oarless alabaster boat)
(O pearly O sitting high above the savannah)
so many poets still call on,
as if it's the next-door neighbor,
a ubiquitous presence signifying
the right proportion of magic and tragedy
when they want to let everyone know
how divine they have become in the interim
kissed by capital G you might say
but I need not tell you that you are hardly divine
a lump is more like it if it is what you are
My name is Cerise Tzara Aschheim Yau
I am your daughter
I have been here a little over a month
crying shitting eating sleeping restless
as I extend my arms and kick my feet
and I can see that you are perplexed by what
I am trying to tell you through the infant
you hold in your hands, the one you
think of as your daughter
which she is, but I too am your daughter,
I who am an I, you and me two three,
the one elected by the green ants
their leader whispered something
(was I to repeat it word for word

John Yau

as if such repetition is accurate
a higher form of mimesis than trompe l'oeil?)
something I have forgotten during
the during and enduring from the to the,
here and there not yet having hardwired
their coordinates within the celestial tumult
Something in words about and through them perhaps
I can't remember which is why no amount of
beseeching is going to yield anything more from me
than I am the poem yes I am the one
you want to write or be written by
you boob or should I say boobus sanctimonious
I am the poem
you need to listen to and for
the one that isn't one
but one of the ones who might
step out from the flickering skyline of transparent shadows
and say to you years from now
hey old farting sag face
dim bulb in a dark and gloomy night
why did you spend years
shitting all that goop onto pristine white page
after white page
and you will smile
knowing I know the answer
knew it before here became
the time-space continuum I inhabit
but this is a conversation that will unfold
at and in another time right now being
right now I am hungry
so go
get me something warm to drink
will you bud
and hey mister whoever you are
you better quit calling me
Pipalotti Poopsalot
Starvin' Marvin
Crusty Punkin and Kidd
I got a name
why doncha use it

Dear Born Just North of Poke
Diane Williams

SHE IS SO SATISFACTORY—why wouldn't she be?—and so are the pouring vessels, spouted jugs, the bell-shaped bowl, the flared bowls, her cup with the trough spout, the cockleshell container, the wardrobe box.

She's got a—I don't know if he's really her husband. Pleasant enough guy. Their table is covered with red felt and is round and higher and higher than it should be.

To sum up—based on what could be seen—a fork in the food—there's a trace of what I'd like to see.

Well, this is the intimate story of a woman and of a man who have found—last night he was able to touch the tip of her.

Running vines and fruit are near the performed actions. They were, of course, all intending to—we don't know what happened at—

The woman's face—bordered by her warm strips across the top of it—shows heavenly weakness. She says, "Have would you like to sit here?"

A window returns darkened air to the rooms and it's quite dark out there with a green-colored background.

When the complaint, when the measure taken, when the purpose of the measures are explained, she waves her arms and has some strength. Yet whatever liveliness we see in her protruding shoulders is dictated by me—one who is proud, clannish, sexually imperfect, and who can be easily seen playing with a toy car.

"Hi. Okay," says a demon, "I'll be right with you."

So it goes, ad libitum. The whole effect is too dry and irritated now—the vast significance of their sucking mouthparts and of their wholesome diversions is that they are trying to be sociable.

Used to come here a lot for the pancakes and eggs because she's been told not to lead a dull life.

I should just say that at one end of the span of her purpose, her lust is vivacious.

When she'd had about as much as she wanted, it was late in my life. She can just chat when she is hugging and kissing.

387

"Okay, then wait for me outside," says her man to her. "Shh-h-h."

"I will," she says.

She snatches the napkin from her lap and wipes her mouth.

She's told, "You wait for me outside. Go to the curb!"

At the curb she looks back beyond the clumps and the tub because this is the most crucial view of the world.

To her the clumps look iffy or curiously like haunches of meat. Three victims, certainly male, drink liquid from straws. A woman holds a jar and a drinking cup filled with beer. The heads of more denizens are shown.

Virtually none of these types of people are sullen and there's an overwhelming sense of such a rich life.

One arbitrarily confident delicatessen owner, slightly flaked, but still solid, who is certainly demonic, quivers.

Hooking at, pulling at the scenes of heroes provides fine examples of banqueters who are not dead and who are likely to be in a situation where ordinary common sense is still humiliating.

From Vague Swimmers
Heather Ramsdell

Now I'm going to formulate some questions. I would like you to answer them as honestly as you can so we can determine the best place to start: Would you like me to make them Difficult, Medium, or Easy?

Remember that no response counts as an answer and all answers count. This may take a few minutes to start up at first and then it will be a scenario and we'll go quite fast. If you start to feel dizzy or sick, you can always "escape" by using the "escape tool," which will turn down the lights and automatically engage the music.

If you feel overwhelmed or experience crying or numbness, pause by depressing the "pause" key until we have switched safely into the shared area, where I gain access to the controls. If you'd like me to help you defend your position, please say so. If not, it is all right to leave wrong answers.

It will be difficult to get up each morning and try again, yet this is precisely what we must do.

Answer even if you think there is no answer. "Swerving" will place you in an equally difficult parallel channel where I will cease to be your interlocutor.

When you are lost, everything counts as a sign.

Now place your hand on her back.
Now struggle and shove him off.
Please place flowers in this problem.
Now hang up on me.

You enjoy the e-mail function, please match the following pages with money. Survey the crowd applying for more money. Make at least twice as much sense. Create two small cuts, each a quarter inch in length, so we can slide in secret money. Meet me for breakfast. (See *Healthy Quick Cook.*)

Several uncomfortable minutes later, he [shirt] and she [pants] emerge bearing flowers. Place the flowers into four decorated egg-cups. Okay eggcups. Okay flowers and draw money in through the slots.

Yes, I would like to have the classics brought into my home, definitely check this box.

Please bring money for this (your name appears real big in this section). Flowers are appropriate for this. Tuesdays and Thursdays are good for this.

New flaws. Next, food rotting within a safe context. First the food then the flood in a sequence that is graspable, therefore comforting to us, tucking Mr. Triangle into the blue field so that contingency replaces some personal debt, because the replacing phase should start by then, as the mourning process courses through its phases, this plays out in the ideologies of other islands.

And if the problem should spread wide enough to engulf us, and I show up in time to put an end to expectation, if they let me explain it as clearly as possible, plowing a fine path to future ills, not to emerge from the grid in the form of a star, probably not to emerge from the field of grids, ever ranked according to importance, urgency, lateness, and scale, including rhetorical burlesques and the many degrees of sincerity, so that some listeners get certain parts of the point if nobody gets the whole thing, I will organize these questions into three big stacks, adding and erasing question marks as needed. In this way the miraculous peels off and can be stuck to other things.

I am very enthusiastic about this pile of rubble.

Waiting in a waiting room. Swirls on a buff-colored rug.

Enters the waiting room. Completely empty. A paler rectangle of wall on the wall. Is this some kind of a *door?* What kind of a door is *this?* A box? Abstract? Again, a battering ram, big log to smash the door down. To better direct you toward good help. Being able to see the sign on the wall, which lends scale, giving way to an optical trap until the eye itself stops.

But the eye does not stop. The test stops. The eye keeps going until it hits the wall. The wall is big, plus reinforced, and so it is a good wall, but the eye stops caring. That is how it goes blind.

The person attached to the eye. The person cannot close to escape the self. Cannot stop saying I. Cannot ask for a door. Cannot speak to the door. Cannot open the door before thinking only of doors, you can go no further.

You cannot escape the literal. The subject can always be found out. The subject blinks.

Two Poems
Amy Catanzano

NOTES ON THE ENCLOSURE OF SUMS

Translated, the eyelets exposed the
fossil body, a clock of abrupt leaves. You were lost here
between eclipse and elm,
a hermeneutic moment of white clay, an empty gnaw,
the novel spill—body
as breath—the fossil body's loose grip, its neutralized
signs, gaps, revisions, tether.
This can be seen by placing the dream against the near-
dream, so that the waking
silhouette pauses, separates the bleach from the bone.
The memory has made
its boundaries clear, thatched at this speed, committed
to the aftermath,
its off-scene irises closed. Birds were called "open shapes"
then "the birds of desire," fossil
text, fossil hearts of sky the translator charts with rock,
rock welts and rock map,
rock ink drained from the ground, eyelets rocking in dark.
You can say the sleeping word
but cannot dream it, can break open a shore of silver
if you remember
while the door, close to freezing, shuts—
the zero geometry of fog, one eye on the lick of the fire

Amy Catanzano

THE BARBELITH POEMS[1]

10. Octopi change color as a mode of communication, and this distressed him, enormously.

09. "In his own cathedral" of shock waves, calculating not end-dates but zero-dates, sentencing others to a life without "every man will live," writing *a mystery is often accompanied by its fraudulent twin. . . .*

08. With weaponry we separate the fish from the fish, crusades are undone on the walls of buildings, bright blue shutters are opened to the private dome, nothing is preemptive but the elaborate luster of scrawled names; and Tom, who paints tags on monuments before his adaptive fingerprints are photographed in three dimensions.

07. Pulling it apart layer by layer one can imagine how, under the banner of Neoism, they made their location: sweat and city temporarily in mid-ripple, forming watery hives in throngs, then collapsing over a luxury jurisdiction. Could the bright blue shutters have been opened when he moved away? Each page in which "real ink cloud" appeared was torn. Shimmering through to ruby blossoms, the Law of Fives is not as discordant as it used to be: sonic roses have risen where first an empire lisped.

06. Photography, as a whole, is not adequate. That I swallowed the lily is not adequate.

05. *When push comes to shove, you pull on gravity for your pleasure, letting those thin discs of Beta Pictoris pleasure you.*

04. I was told to blister rather than to break. The embrace of narrow. A hook of entry. Thus nothing in common moves wings. Wings move toward nothing in common. Soon the participants perceived the neutral painting bare. Tom practiced entropy he admired. Degrees are year long under the statue of stars. We sob. Rubies burst. Speechless, and I spill my serrated heart all over town recorded for miles.

---

[1]The term "Barbelith" was invented by Grant Morrison, creator of *The Invisibles.* Vol. 1 #2. Vertigo/DC Comics, 1994.

Amy Catanzano

03.   Watch for the word BARBELITH on your walls.[2]

If our words are circles, theirs are bubbles.[3]

Therefore, the lack of margins have designations. They are, from left to right: "Ice Storms Are Responsible for Holographic Fractures in World Maps" and "The Big Bang Happens Only Once, and in the Future."

02. Not a star but a strategy of flutter. I could say it just once before astonishment took over—batteries blinking awake in micromuseums, and I, clipped by a thin tulip of air—and Tom changing the shapes of things—and others doing this too by singing some out from their factories. Hence, I didn't give way to astonishment, but rather observed the tetragram of troops closing in, taking note of the maneuvers they used: an accuracy I hadn't seen since words were words and entire brotherhoods could travel by mirror.

December 21, 2012 A.D.

Option 01: Your human hands are what you pay for.

Option 02: This is a plume, a trick hierarchy of billions.

Option 03: This is a ghost, a noose, something on lashes.

Option 04: This is an emblem minus the moon of incident.

Option 05: This is a thorn-opal, found split in the estuary.

Option 06: This is a ring, a limb, something that floats.

Option 07: Duration left to itself bends everything red.

Option 08: This is a cubic pearl, skinned, in tropical water.

Option 09: It was a period of apologies on arrival.

Option 10: This is a vine, a lock, what we're made from.

Option 11: This is a bribe, ensuring silence, a deep slit.

---

[2] Vol. 2 #18. *The Invisibles.* 1998.
[3] Vol. 2 #12. *The Invisibles.* 1998.

Five Poems

John Ashbery

SYLLABUS

Look,
the savage glitter of downtown,
those walls of glycerin
inspissated by tears—
yes, and why does the smell not go away?
Honey, it's been ages, take off your hat and coat,
rest your feet awhile? Now, where were we?

Wave upon wave of new construction
(some of it shoddy), then that too plowed under
as new waves bare their teeth—
where's it gotten us? I say, you
look a little disheveled—want to freshen up?
Play doctor? Uh, I'll be with you
in a moment. Yes, the doctor is in,
yuk yuk. Now, what was it we were learning to say?

"Change the value systems. All incandescence and fear
have their origin there. In not nice night
one must strip down silently, and quickly.
See, a little headway has been made."

The snow shovel's disclaimer
defused the situation. Soon the host was ruddy
with his own reflected good cheer.
And it was again time to creep back a ways,
to rest, sheltered by soffits,
and pronounce one's own alphabet, nasally and distinctly, backwards
like it was supposed to be all along. We'd arrived
again, it seemed, though we only came along for the ride.

John Ashbery

HAVEN'T HEARD ANYTHING

Quietly the first hours left, amused.
We were in a quandary at first then wet our whistles
in some neighborhood bar. The throng came on strong.

It's too far away to hear the people over there,
someone said. Perhaps we should move,
another one said. Perhaps. But we were a good ways off
and the rut in the sand only led to one place.

When the sand closes over our case
we'll know it done.

The morose driver wept, represented his case
as somehow more urgent. Than other passengers'.
Somehow we got out.
Vanilla ice cream, I quaffed,
for it *seemed* good, for a little time at that.
The poet wanted to introduce us to his suite.
But what he really wanted to do
was play for a little time. Well, that's natural—
I mean, who among us haven't tried?
Few, it's true, have succeeded.

Another morn he would be in shock
over the state of poetry. "None could penetrate
the recesses of the human mind like Major Pendennis,"
he averred. We saw it all coming,
or should have:
a big empty cape
on the shoulders of the oldest
who seemed to be advancing.
He wasn't ancient, but he struck us that way.
If we'd never been to town, and heard the lights
sometime, we'd be all over a neighbor, licking,
passing out free samples of dude. But it was like
too cagey for them, none of us wanted to retire.

Since that day the memory of recognition beats
at my template. I don't know what to do with all my acquired knowledge.

I could give it to someone, I suppose. Wait, no then
they wouldn't know what to do with it.
I suppose I could be relaxed.
Yes, that's more the ticket we smiled.

THE HAVES

Many there were that.
There were many who that.
Many did that to what.
Many undid that to what.
Many there were worse than that.
To undo that many did that.
More of an obstacle to this than that
where the upcoming is done to that.

The undone is done is that.
They are speaking to what is done
not left on the stove.
The done is that to that done.

There were many who did this and that,
meanwhile were many who undid that.
The undone undid the that.
The crisis under the batter's hat.

Do you manage a common if?
If so why is the crisis that?
Who did the crisis there?
Why is the crisis after my time that.

Ordinarily men go around
seeking wedgies the corner is out.
They this and why and in this bat
an eyelash to be better than that
on the day that.

And that was all a better than that day had that
unto the jousting which was unto a way down that.

John Ashbery

They mortared the way under the man hat
that wanted to under a bill be that that.

In London just now is cold.
In London just now a gull spring
in London on the back of the bat
in London on the back of that.

When they and London remove the bat back
the bat backer became the bat back.
The butt packer begat the back pack
under lest the noise disturb those that bat back.

In the backing the true bat resides
under a cleft the cliff nose
gannets nosed underside.
The cliff-size size briar sizes up size,
decides size is lies under the briar thighs.

That was a lot of that and lack
come down the stair decorum
and lack of reasonable store bin
under the store the straw was been.
Me like methink it all past being
and beyond into the been that he sinned,
the being that has seen
under the hedgerow greens as feline
is opposed to oppressed being been
and never two of us no no more we'll have been.

The barn exploded.
The big store ripped apart.
Gravel on the lawn made its mark
yes that and festoon of grit in the sky
while the riders came riding by
and nobody was appointed to fill the exam
no others why no other have ever been
why the irritated sky
and we'll never be the fly
not two states ever to fly by

and no more store no more in store by the fly
they fly by and take just as your daddy did
and stand by the chest

just make sure to be to the thigh
came crawling across clock's tempest.

HINTS AND FRAGMENTS

The arty set adheres
to the stolen pavement. Inside
are sherbets and "Barbara."
Strange, how one day

you'll come over "all queer,"
then next day we're scrambling to stamp it out.
Such are our inspirations:
of unequal value, one chasing the better
ones until he stops, forgetting. That's

the time I like best, cold color of cistern.
Values show up in the neighborhood house;
next day it's moved on.

In the Pennsylvania of my youth, tungsten filaments
daubed hoardings ludicrous shades, one after another.
The crowds have bicycled far out to see you fail.
Don't disappoint them.

Three on a match he said
is how it all began. Seven years' bad luck
and after that, roseate perspectives garlanded
with octaves of blooms. Keeping next to her
and the door closes, kindly.

All that's behind us, or
so we used to say.
Kettle's on the hob, ghost dancers
are fierce tonight. Yet it collects

399

in the hollow of my palm, somehow,
tears in an appetizing equation.

Door is shut,
but hasn't been locked yet.
We owe this to our childhood dogs,
sprig of hope. Where clarity once ruled
dreams are still active,
a clarinet floats ashore,
a good time was had by all.

REMINISCENCES OF NORMA

Knowledgeably, she is knowledgeable about many things—
the stars in their errant orbits, a bud
sliding over a hibiscus, a cloud like a frown
on the face of a teddy bear. And then, more stuff.
The inquisitors were endlessly patient, amused—
you had to be, in that business.
And if they liked your answer, you were free.
It didn't have to be true. Streamers, party favors,
confetti—all were yours.
I know now why some have seen the sun sink
and it fed their hunger, they came on unabated.
Is it my lord's pleasure to mate?
In that case we have pogo sticks of different sizes and colors.
But he may just go away
thinking it enough for that day.

Bicycle came barreling through the sleet—

Mendoza: 1949

An Enactment of Duchamp's *Large Glass*

Toby Olson

> *. . . the machine runs only on words.*
>
> —Jean Suquet

HE'D BEEN HAVING A little trouble with his endowment, not so much that it interfered with the practices, but enough to shift his focus almost completely to the physical, and while this was not a bad thing in itself, it had a way of increasing his recent boredom, and those questions of continuance had percolated to the surface once again.

Even before Snowflake there had been an insistence upon shaving, some new, most probably ancient, titillation, and this had defamiliarized the organs and, in the loss of those coronas, melded them to the body in ways both unsettling and athletic. Even the bride, his boss, had noticed this, though she had remained inviolate throughout.

They'd dragged out the sacramental altar a good two hours before the audience arrived. Some would be in costume, he knew, uniforms of trade and position, policemen, even priests and undertakers, and some of pure fantasy, a horse soldier in ancient armor, a French gendarme, maybe a clown. And there would be the delivery boys, then waiters in white jackets, and the busboys and other flunkies to clear away the leavings of that cold dinner and the attendant drinking once the show was over and all were, in their way, spent.

It was an old story for him and getting even older in his recent malady. He was forty-one now, and he knew the surge of El Malabarista's piano and his singing and the juggling, performances he'd once found energy in, would account for very little this time around. The last time they had was down in Nogales, where they had dressed him in the antlers and the white bushy tail, but that had been fantastically theatrical and a while ago, and he would be no more than a groom in this tableau, though in tuxedo and elaborate underclothing, to be removed ritualistically, a slow peeling away of many layers for his revealing, to them and the various bridesmaids he would deflower

401

for their pleasure, or they him.

He watched their entrance from behind the curtain. They came into the hall in small groups and some alone and furtive, looking to see who might be there, a wife, mother, or a sister, though there would be no women in the audience, and they need not have worried. He saw young men and old, those in costume, the hat of a stationmaster, a man limping on crutches, and he noted the ones with the round glasses, those who would find a way to sit apart from the others in silence and without motion, as if witnesses only, the true voyeurs, who were devoid even of imagination and in need of the visible display, empty vessels to be filled through holes in their heads behind those *anteojos*. And he saw Angelica Marcos and Bebe, the latter as if a small doll linked by a leash to her sister's activities. They were seating the men, calling out for bottles, attentive to the clearly wealthy, yet sensitive to those who were bewildered and alone, for they too might have money, bills pressed into their palms when the lights were darkened, payment for secret caresses, the only exchange of intimacy that was allowed beyond the stage. Some of the men were a bit raucous, and the sisters quieted them with smiles and soft laughter. Then he was touched on the shoulder, not the bride, his boss, but Secondino, and was told that El Malabarista was drunk again and would not be there. They had a fiddler.

He was stationed in a chair below the altar when the lights came up, a little to the side of it, and a large upholstered cube and another chair and a low couch had been positioned on the carpeting between him and the place where the bridesmaids in their similar dresses would stand in a line when they came out. There would be little to suggest a story, just the skeleton of one and the fiddler when the cue was given. He sat on a tall stool beyond the footlights and was playing softly, some dark romantic tune. From my home in Fuente, thought El Soltero, having taken on his stage name with the taste of drug moments before his entrance. He could see the first ring of figures, the wealthy in their suits and feigned dignity and behind them a few other bodies, shadows only, and could hear occasional coughing and whispers in the distant quarters of the room. He was the only human presence on the stage, and all eyes were on him, anticipating his reputation.

Then the bridesmaids entered, making no show of their bodies, modest in those girlish promenade dresses his boss had bought cheaply at auction, then had fitted with snaps and easily disengaged hooks. They were green, yellow, and red, of similar cut, crinoline at the hems and spilling like whipped cream at the décolletage, and the women's hair fell to their shoulders, or rose in piles held in place with combs and pins. Each wore makeup matching the basic color of her garment. They paraded gratuitously near the footlights, hips swaying, grinning and waving out into the darkness, gestures answered by a few disembodied catcalls. Then they were standing in their formal order, across the furniture from where he sat, ready to rise.

He knew all four of them, but had performed with only three of them before. His boss was good at such things, perceptive, and while he had not spoken of his malady with her, he was sure she was aware that something was amiss. Rosa Palomino was not his gift, but strange fruit simply, delivered out of business motives and cynicism. *He* was the prize, and his boss would milk him, and milk him again, until he was quite dry. Rosa had been brought all the way from Mexico City, and while she was not fresh, she was different, and he concentrated on imagining the configurations of her shaved flesh below the folds of her gown, anything at all, along with the mild kick of the drug, to get him going. He could see that her eyes were vacant, that she too had dipped into the drug store, and this also might be of some help to him, the possibility of a boredom-relieving luridness. Then he rose up from his chair to get things started, and the fiddler took the cue and moved into a sinuous tango.

The bride was late, and he and the bridesmaids stood half-turned to face the empty altar. There was a wooden lattice there, an archway of flowers of the kind found in gardens. Red roses mingled with the buds of white ones, and a bright light illuminated the empty space it enclosed, a dramatic element designed to punctuate the fact of the bride's absence. Then the fiddler guttered down to a lower register, made his instrument groan, and one among the bridesmaids turned a bit to face her neighbor, pushing into her, and raised her chin in El Soltero's direction, grinning and pulling at the snaps of her bodice, as if she were ripping it away, until her breasts were exposed, and another was laughing then and pointing to where he stood, for though he was the groom, he was not yet the husband, and the bride was late, and he was still the bachelor, and though it was impossible in any real world, there was time now, before he was married and thus lost to them forever.

One had pushed another slightly forward from their line. She demurred, then another urged her on. It was Rosa Palomino who did the urging, and he saw her hand reach to the back of her neck, searching.

403

She found the latch, or a hinge, and her dress fell away to the waist, then down to a billowing at her ankles, and she stepped out of it, watching him, imagining, he thought, her legs in dark stockings held up by a belt, something the men liked, though they were unclear about the reason. She wore a rhinestone choker at her neck, touched by the tips of her dark hair, and nothing else. Then all the bridesmaids had stepped free of their dresses and were moving among the furniture in their various and aggressive underwear, approaching him.

He had his hand in his pocket, nothing much below it yet, and even when they reached him and began working at him, one slipping her palms under his lapels to his shoulders, lifting his tuxedo coat until it fell back behind him, revealing his body in suspenders and tight pants and shirt, there was nothing, and as another's hands moved to his belt, he thought briefly of those dance instructors who carried cucumbers in specially fitted pockets to impress older women with their desirability, and he thought too of a kind of pump.

Then one of them was pulling at his zipper and he was gazing at Rosa and the others as they moved around and behind him in a slow dance, then appeared again, their perfume in his nostrils and the blemishes below their thick makeup pushing through that coloration, distinctly visible on cheeks and chins. He felt the touch of fingers through the linen then and was finally rising. She was pulling at him, working at his disengagement, and when she had accomplished this she fell down to her knees, and he heard those familiar gasps from beyond the footlights, even a slight dissonance from the fiddler as he missed his strings. He looked down at himself then, not in admiration of his length and thickness, but automatically, as if he could see the source of that deep, pinching ache, back under his heavy testicles where he knew the hard knot was pulsing.

It proceeded then much as it always had, the one on her knees partaking of the crown of his endowment, while another stroked the length of it, facing the audience, a gaze of wonderment and a twisted smile on her red lips, tongue tracing that matrix of veins as if each was the course of a river running through some newly discovered continent and she the cartographer. He stood in profile for his display there, and the others looked on, awestruck and hungry, touching themselves and one another, viewing the origin of the world, which was yet some delectable confection, soon to be devoured.

The bride's arrival seemed now impossible, or at least out of the question, and as the bridesmaids sported with him, the latticework bower prepared for the marriage transition slipped slowly into a darkness that was deep as that hiding activities in the audience, though he could hear the drone of fractured litanies coming from that quarter, a junk of frustrated lives slowed down to keep pace with the cheap construction of these onstage doings.

He proceeded then to mount them, each in her turn, on upholstered cube and couch, as the others crowded in around their couplings, participating as they might. There were sharp calls now from the audience, for the most part unintelligible, though at one point the man in the stationmaster's hat stepped into the footlights, his hand raised as if holding the chain of an air whistle. "Toot-toot!" at the moment of penetration. She was on her knees, he squatting behind her. Then the man was ushered away, back into the darkness.

They expected ejaculation, and they expected it to be visible, out in the air where they could see it, some odd evidence of sincerity, but that had now become the most difficult thing for him, both in the pain and the timing. Something had happened that seemed quite mechanical, and now the spewing preceded orgasm by long moments, as if someone had turned on a fountain for a thirsty man, then had held him back from drinking. And the pain had become a blossoming, the knot tightening beyond what seemed possible, so that his endowment, swelling in its potential, seemed close to explosion, his deep shaking some pathetic aftermath, like grief settled in after the perverse excitement of death.

Now he had fucked them all and at times they had fucked him, all but Rosa Palomino, who had touched him intimately at times and at times had watched him with the others, touching herself. She knelt before him, and the others had moved to the side of the stage, giving the audience an unobstructed view. Rosa was licking his crown, and he knew all eyes were upon them. Then, behind and above their activity, the lights slowly came up again, revealing the flowered archway of roses that were copies of red roses, plastic, with an electrical light in each, brightening its petals and sharp thorns, and the bride stood within that bower, the voluptial apotheosis, like a virgin's *retablo*, in her white dress, filling the space so that the flowers seemed part of the dress, the white buds a sewn-on edging to sleeves, bodice, and billowing flair below the hips. The dress was filmy, a tightly woven silk that reflected the flowers and their stems as if its surface were liquid and the buds and petals were drifting upon some shallow pool, or were under that still water, dressing her drowned skin and shining through to a surface above. It was hard to determine which was the negative image, which positive, but at least the skeletal story was now clear.

The bride had wanted this for him, but for herself as well, so that she might have it under her watchful eye, as if he were a bull in some arena tested for the acceptability of his potency, and this is why she was late. She stood at the place where he would soon join her, after this testing, to become El Soltero no longer, but the groom and husband, though not quite yet.

She wore a white veil, but it was as transparent as her dress, and her face was clearly visible, a placid smile upon her lips as she watched Rosa and his member as Rosa sucked it, and he knew the audience could see all three of them without shifting their eyes and he could hear their onanistic groans. Then the white buds among the red were opening, and the bride herself seemed to be blossoming, swelling to fill the entire space under the wooden archway, becoming part of it, and he thought he could hear her there, some powerful engine, idling, her flushed face in display of controlled ecstasy under the veil.

And he was watching her and hearing her as he pulled his member free of Rosa's engagement with it and began to stroke it, urging himself, waiting for the frustration and needing to get beyond it, and finally, after a long time of working at it, the fountain was geysering, without passion or seeming volition, and Rosa's face and breasts were splashed with his product, the flecks of blood within it marking ambiguous locations on the wayward landscape of his spewing.

There were yells and whoops from the audience, a distant "toot-toot" from the stationmaster, and El Soltero turned from the soiled vision of Rosa below him, his endowment hanging from that root of pain. He was feeling the deep, pathetic shudders of his tardy orgasm as he limped toward the pulsing archway and the ready maid. It was time now for the surrender of his name, but before he could reach the carpeted steps that led up to that dubious union, the lights dimmed down into a complete and anonymous darkness and the show was over.

Autobiography
Thalia Field

Make a Laundry List of This
search
a weed's dominion
search   an overhunted   rebuttal
this overmuch   this common content
autocartography
she read the palm hands down

Make a Hammer of This
                             slow depopulation
not really
one species overtaking its own
search
popular conceptions, gates
flickering trial
even forced, across walls of laundry, can't not

a Wake of This
        some splitless spot of calm, can calm against

Make an Excuse of This
domain
enter
the delusion other than intuition; a herd instinct

Make a Ploy of This
girl at a computer   running
full sockets   options
colors supposedly her slight   conscience
monitors   her miniscule overconsumption
but for clarity, a dark room
the bounded nature of a plane
absolved abstraction infinity's perception in cell deaths

Thalia Field

                          the end of production
the smell of busy bacteria   a grid of sourceless wind
the room manifestly unseen   and windless, want
some carbon forms

Make a Point of This
one old wholly [sic] mammoth
she punches, agile   some letters
Make Feedback of This
she enters
an expert
her rich gravitas and post
knowledge predicate: poverty, overeaten
the verb form slow to a light speed caught   too, well
                                    a self, conscious

Make a Meal of This
                portal
some engine
expressing herself   circle   all attention, narrows

Make a Dance of This
                show, the traveling caravan
back to a passive can't
of clarity the deepest math   or a percent decline

enter
woolly mammoth   or
                    in quotations
thalia field

Make News of This
mammoth or a mastodon
                            relic theory
of good decisions   the rising sites
to hunt in hunger, the crisis of surviving opulently
                                        in passing
did not die

Make More of This
                        from one or another

but from slight and constant pressure
one by one by one
the search
in quotations, resulting   in the darkness's clear signal

Make a Mockery of This
taken back by Texas Rangers on the spot
enter Cynthia Ann Parker
the promise hooded in blood   early American destiny resolves
the history, return   space
the carcass simultaneous   loses useful distinction
                              a shape less recognized
european can't can not seeing
directions at once   skin and back
Make a Photo of This
overattended
underexistence   a mcat substitute   please
joke spreads from hole to hole
and overabundance to overexistence to   overlook what

Make the Most of This
laugh, she the one who reads
someone stands confounded   by the absence
and screens list
clarity
the calls by the name of the entered   spark
the entry exit

Make a Nail of This
breezeless   putsch
        remorse   or graft
generations
supposedly regenerate   the function
the probabilities   turn against   the key
        likely choice   from one to one   eminent domain

Make Rain of This
name
        date
Make an Advertisement of This
of the three   megafauna

whose bones make reasonable evidence   the job   of extinction
    contracted bit by bit

Make a Definition of This
thalia field
housed   lock of
clothes made to laundry
without weather cold   or momentum
the work compliant   gains   sin, DNA
    against this   or the next against   a small overkill
        just a little overattention
Make a Hunt of This
natural writing, the produce
of concrete
Make a Fork in the Road
    search out hungry for work
the furrow material in which
blink to spoiled sleeps
punching away
a very slow meal   the thought of turning
to overextend, tonight and today
species-wise
Make a Dwelling
a kind of breeze, from inside the effort

but what about the drive?
she hands over wet clothing

and tools

and thinking
back

Make a Government of This
restart with a different sort of result
a bride search
a mother
of the last *Comanche* chief
beyond the pale comes up
takes on a name   in legend, posted
        walked the continent

a fake despite silence
despite the varying powers   of storage

Make a Fortune of This
mammoth memory
repose   response   image   cornered
in advance of corners, merely tabulations
Make a Traveling Circus
an intended population
some aimless plan, innocent
with incremental growth

Make an Instinct
blank breezeless   mindless
after it's closed   the door
entices

the hallway
        new rival
another search

Make a Video; Video Game
differently and inaudible prisoners and witnesses
separate architecture have separate entrances

Make a Poem
developers bid   an expensive pitch   for a meal
                                    a money substitute
for a building to store houses
the kind fortunes of failure
Make a Microscope
in all walks   extinct backwardly to tell anything

hands resist reaches muscled prose

Make a Time Line of This
what finds none tells   a symbol   punch in
me, this time   my own
unique supposed
rhetoric overspeaks   a room is quiet, but alert

Thalia Field

Make a Gesture
awaiting   the ground sloths and armadillos
                                      the size of tanker trucks
insert a picture here
a famous reinactment [sic]
of settlers and tribes
a hospitality the size of texas
                                            search in quotation marks
hog calling and outhouse races
                                      Cynthia Ann

Make a Mention of This
her festival   and impotence the size   what breeze
map   what   blows
            thinking   drains   what
river   floods   what   grid
texas plain   clicks

Make a Robot of This
or Quanah Parker, for the nine wagons   click
the rifle   his mother's stolen rough fear fragrance
of flowers   of 1836, a new independence, a texas, gates locked, click
a dead silence; Silas Parker

Make a Window
punched in   electric, out

Make a Hand-Woven Fabric
stolen
stolen back
                              what search relieved
taken
taken back
                                    what private
Make a Progress of This
old sold
Make a Meaningful Glance
reransomed ironically   privilege searches
getting closer to the zero or extinction
rhetorical flourish
                              a slow overhunting

412

Make a Science of This
"Cynthia Ann"
lived with the tribe called People
anyway
Make a Plastic Spoon of This
renamed her Naduah
married Peta Nocona with horses and smallpox
what comes up
represents a story in the place of

Make a Lamp
                              scattered, assembled
to keep the flame clear
                                        you can't enter it
                  or   tell me
to enter

Make a Beveled Mirror

or   a belief   justify this

Make a News Article
afraid   of entering "myself"
      the megafauna may have craved
                        this hypothesis, and overgrazed
Make a Theory
an Apology
the herds of necessary
the hunter blooms   and one by one
too many skills; too the plug-ins
Make Electricity
and a thousand years'll do the work
the slowing family

Make Light of This
what looks like procreation hides the truth
number mutate
inclines against time
                        the overillumination
the   handsome   invisible
disappearance of sink holes popular

Thalia Field

glacial conditions
present instance

Make a Stage Play
at the junction of a U.S. Highway and Farm Road 262
thalia field
Make an Unbearable Certainty of This

collapse	winsome
shoal	extinct
immobile	mammoth
metaphor	sloth
fake	skins

      wrong means
uniquely unmaking diversity
Make a small Dusky Sparrow
this something, different   each   subtraction
      search through slow accrual
the name changed
Make a Hard Knock
a turbulence; undermined
and new industry, weeds

then Thalia field would not so much fail
as provide some rich habitat, some production

Make Shit of This
failing
this marginal accident   of symbol   induction
renewal of a tenacious breed   the settling   of names
punched, proceeding
where "thalia field" and any related words

Make a Supermarket
fall out of the darkness   into obscurity
Make a Cardboard Box
originally named Paradise, until the post office rejected that
for Thalia itself
and take a left at the creek, Thalia field lies to the south

Make a Wanted Poster
survey available

futile lead to only
the manifest apparition of abundant life
Make a Way of This
a place platted in 1910
Thalia field wasn't drilled until 1925

Make an Ink Pen
growing value   oasis
the search increases   as words for things

Make a Fence of This
to refer to becalming decomposition   to writing more and more
the energy usage up
and nothing new under the sun
and nothing to lessen it
but with a long-abandoned school, Thalia's deserted houses
and decaying businesses offer a grim foreshadowing of what could happen

Make a Decision
to this carcass feet from   finding it

Make a U-Turn
feet from forever ending
a prairie which appears without finish, the sentence deserted
this dark room
clear and quiet and quite breezeless
                                        an unproducing reserve
of willing   forgetting   dependance
Make a Fuel Reserve
on refining searches
and power flows out of the system
an opening
        deep
                ends
Make a Roll of Tape
result
"thalia field"
without quotation
Make an Oil Painting of This
domain whose borders move
with annual rainfall of 23.9 inches

Thalia Field

grazed first and fenced
the loamy land between sand rivers

Thalia field once contained some herds of heads
Make a Promise of This
          that first drill   the sentences   barbed
             ranch building, the namesake
             near paradise, the high school closed
                   but at its heyday once produced 50,000 barrels of crude
                      as the interstate intersects county 6
Make a Drive-In Movie
the result of autobiographical plateau; abundant and empty
Thalia field devastated by tornado
for many seasons an economic overevent; lay there pushing daisies
                         commit to staying
          thalia field
rebounds as a major helium reserve in the 1950s
Make a Delayed Reaction of This
          onions and oil and sweet potato
          bales of cotton and bushels
          of wheat and sorghum
          wild fruits fed the tribes, the buffalo road
accidental   to tell
to know
the old dovetail
                         the cow skull, still
one step behind the date
between contacts
Make a Note of This
may 4, or 5th in Crowell, the Cynthia Ann Parker Festival
celebrated in the area where she disappeared
Make a Plot of This
outhouse races instead of Kiowa bands
          the richness of hog calling   finding home forced
          from her days with little Quanah Parker
lost child and husband
enter thalia field
depopulated
the area   slides
back
to show   the move

ease
Make a Long Story Short
by keyword
of one carcass and a billion bacteria
"Down the road, Thalia, population 104, is almost a ghost town"
my consumer history   for all to read
the post office closed   how much I eat
the calculations show
Cynthia Ann
and Helium   production but no grocery
            protected
thalia field from the open
range; some raid, some captive
      taken back

Make a Baseball Bat
the effects of quotations
Make a Bridge
A Basket
to search products for other uses
against the constant background of energy
skins and food
Make an Abstract Noun
as consumption of nonrenewable resources grows
even at tiny imperceptible percents
then 10,000 years' supply of oil will last only 125
Make an Equation
the oil leases on thalia field, since 1901
                            produce think
produce
                    think
Make a Bicycle
three-inch pipeline reserves   to the railway at Foard City
dip and
exponential functions
Make a Common House Fly
replace overhunted mastodons
in the field, the math because it's late
Cynthia Ann was only nine
with electronic memories, raid again
production dropped to 20,000 barrels in 1948, and stays

Thalia Field

in a trap, writing "the young people are moving away"
Make a Wool Hat of This
drilling thalia field for nothing
Make a Dog Collar
an Escalator
the hardest places
Make a Pair of Handcuffs
collapse neat extinctions
Make a Television Sitcom
click
named for the flower or for nothing
mines and ranches, new settlers musing
on millenniums barely clearing the hill
as laundry room   happens
the mastodons happened
Make a Milk Bottle of This
rich land for different riches
think clearly
                    nice thalia field, pretty place
Make a Hair Salon
at   33°59′5″N
         99°32′15″W
                              to eke out value
          at some expense
enter or ambush
"Cynthia Ann Parker" called back
against
a search for herself   a festival, a hog call   a missed breath
the quantity behaves a certain way
in the story whose rate of change is proportional to its size
in the search
the exponential function describes
Make a Drum of This
across Thalia field
circle back for comfort
Make a Warm Meal
Make a Clothes Line
in the exit

Lifelike

Susan Steinberg

THE START. THERE WERE FITS. Then fitful thoughts. But first there were stars. They flashed past my face. They went. The stars. And I watched. And my pulse. I need not say. The speed.

I was at school. We were critiquing. We stood to look at the paintings. They were green and brown I recall. Of course. They were trees and trees are green and brown. Whether or not the paintings were good. No matter. The teacher was saying words on them. The girl whose paintings they were said words. I can't recall what either said. Something of harmony. Something of truth. Nothing significant I should know. I too was a painter who painted trees. I painted faces. And I painted because I was good at painting. I could make a tree look like a tree. A face look like a face. The teachers often looked over my shoulders. Often they said, nice tree. But what of a tree looking facelike in life. As often they did. We were driving when I caught the trees looking at me. My boyfriend drove. He said, you need help. But the trees had ancient faces. Like mine would become. Made of bark and lined. So help me, I said. Ha ha. He laughed too.

How the fits started I can't say. There was a trigger-point perhaps. Some trigger-point I can't recall. A spark. I can't recall. I listened close to the words of the girl. I listened too to the teacher's. I stood for a closer look at the paintings. The teacher said, a break. And as I took a step to the door I stopped. A piece of time must have passed. A beat. And there were stars by my head. There were stars too inside. My head that is. And more time passed. And as it passed the room thinned to a tube. I was looking through one end of the tube. And everyone was stuck to the inside tube walls. They were trying to crawl through the other side. There was light on that side. And inside light shot past like stars. My pulse was speeding with the light. I can't explain it better than this. The tube was attached to my face. I turned to the person nearest me. The teacher. Curved to the wall as a letter S. He would help I knew. I sat again. I said, I don't feel well. He shrugged or laughed or said, what can I do. I said, help me. I clutched his arm. This I recall. He said, what's wrong. I said, I don't know, and he said, well what's wrong. My pulse was speeding. Light shot past like stars.

Everything of course shifted at that point as things shift. Meaning once it shifted it stayed as such. I was seeing through the narrow tube. This isn't symbolic. This weightless invisible tube. Through it were the trees my hands the clouds. And through it things near blurred from recognition. Things far loomed and shadowed. I can't explain it better. How the fits swam under my skin. I could feel them as the swimmer would. I felt them too as water.

I saw no good reason to leave the house. My boyfriend tried to make me laugh. I took pills when I had to leave. I only left to get the mail. I took pills too in the house. They made me feel like a rain-soaked shirt. And the tube went limp. Slack. It disintegrated into. You know. Nothing. The teachers called when I missed those weeks. I didn't answer the telephone. My boyfriend answered it for me. He talked to the teachers in whispers. I heard my boyfriend laughing. I don't know what he told them. I think that I was sick. I talked into the sheets when he wasn't looking. Sometimes words of no significance. Like those. At some point I stopped taking the pills. They were making me hateful and I didn't want to hate. My boyfriend danced to make me laugh. My mother said to take the pills damn it. She said, get some sleep. My boyfriend took the pills away. He said, you need to eat. But the food on my plate had turned too lifelike. The green and brown were the same as life all landing on the floor when I threw the plate.

I recall the teacher. He said, what's wrong. Well for one he was S-shaped. For two he was curved inside the tube. I had to look in. It was stuck to my face you know. Invisibly. I looked. I listened to words how words go. His words. It must sound like nothing how I explain. But it was frantic. First the trigger-point I can't recall. Then the stars. I clutched his shirt. His arm. Hotter than you'd think. I can't recall what he said or did then. But I know he didn't help. I ran from the classroom to the basement. In the basement I found nothing. Then a light. A telephone. The tube thinned. I called my mother. She rushed to get me. I waited outside. Under a car. Imagine her face when I crawled out from under. She wore diamond rings. My face was

smudged. She drove me to the doctor. She never liked my boyfriend.
Inside her car was freezing. The doctor said, hold still. I was hiding
under the paper sheet shaking. My boyfriend couldn't be bothered
that day. And my mother how she carried on.

Needless to say. Fitful thoughts. Nothing significant. Thoughts on
truth as we have and we have them. How you strike a match and the
fire goes out. But first the cigarette lights. Life, you think and you
have this thought. One thing rubs against another. Something else
gains a spark. Then the cigarette is crushed under a heel. Like that.

Trees as well. They often looked so vegetal. Like overgrown broccoli stalks. I could see no difference between trees and broccoli. Except their ancient faces. The trees. They often looked so animal.
Except their size. And there was bark I guess. Making a difference
that is. I can't explain bark. Like shell I guess. And were broccoli
stalks to grow and grow they too would have bark I'm guessing. As
would flowers. Animals. My hands. My eyes were always so bloodshot. When my mother called I let the telephone ring.

I lied to you. It wasn't my mother who picked me up when I ran
to the basement. It was my boyfriend. I called my mother first. She
answered the telephone. But she couldn't talk long that day I recall.
She had things in her life. Significant things. My boyfriend came to
get me. I waited under a car. He laughed when I crawled out from
under. My face was smudged. He drove me to the doctor. He hated
my mother. He said she was always pushing. I was sweating sitting
in his car. The trees were looking at me funny. The clouds as well.
And they never stay still. The clouds. Even when it seems they are.
The trees were looking through ancient eyes. Mine would one day
too turn ancient. Slits in folds of hardened fat. My boyfriend said, I
can't drive any faster. I left my boyfriend in his car. He drove beside
me. He told me, get in. I ran and my pulse went faster. I ran up an
alley where he couldn't drive. I pressed my pulse to slow the speed.
I knew I was in a pile of dirty leaves. My mother wanted things for
me. Marriage. Money. Only the best. My boyfriend's car went past.
Rusted at the bottom. He didn't see me in the gutter. The leaves
made a sound. Like what. Like static. And the light changed.
Meaning the sun set. Pink at first. The light. Divine. The traffic
thinned to nothing.

I recall late one night I left the house. I went to school. I couldn't sleep so thought to paint. I thought I could. Another girl was painting. The girl from class it was. I hadn't been to class in weeks. She never asked me why. I should say there was a wall between us. This isn't symbolic. From her wall side she talked and I talked back. We were having a good talk on painting and on school and on our teacher and so on. Nothing significant. But we got to laughing hard over our talk and over nothing. She came into my space on my wall side. And this was friendship I decided. Laughing hard over nothing and talking. And half a beat after I decided friendship was in fact a fixed thing. So for half a beat after my decision I felt fit. I wanted to squeeze this girl on my wall side. But I recalled friendship wasn't fixed. How could it be when trees were far bigger and rooted in dirt and yet trees weren't fixed. And how when diamonds were hard and sharp enough to cut glass and yet not fixed. I knew about clouds. I knew they were over you one second and over someone else the next. They too were often dark and swollen with rain. My eyes were bloodshot I knew. My hands were numb. My face. And I knew all our laughing and talking would be caught in the clouds and taken somewhere at cloud speed.

I rose from the gutter. Ran to the doctor. My boyfriend met me there. The doctor said, hold still. Boy did I shake under the sheet. My boyfriend was sweating. My mother couldn't be bothered that day. There was shopping of sorts. She had friends. Good ones. Driving home my boyfriend said, that cunt. To me. Imagine the fight.

I said to my boyfriend, you can be with whomever. I said, it doesn't matter. I said, get out of my face. Please, I said. I said, please just be with someone else. It didn't matter. He didn't get me. He was always smoking by my mailbox. He drank at night. It was never enough to pass him out. He answered the telephone when I told him not to. It was he and the teachers using words. He and my mother fighting. But neither knew what was best for me. And I didn't know. I knew we weren't to be fixed he and I. He saw trees as trees and that was a laugh. There was nothing fixed besides. He was poor besides. My mother said I should look a bit harder. Trust me I was looking. I looked so hard I couldn't get near him. It wasn't his fault. He had turned too lifelike. Across the room he loomed and shadowed the room. Up near he pushed and blurred in my face like food. I said, get out of my face. He went soft. Slack. I looked good and hard.

I thought, how sad. Like an old sleeping animal. An overcooked vegetable.

It occurred to me in my boyfriend's car that paintings do depict life. I thought, yes. I thought, paintings are unfixed as life. Of course. My mother's diamonds always flashed in the sunlight. The sun burned white in her black glasses. In her hair. I knew the sun would fade her hair. It would yellow her diamonds. Her face was turning lined and hard as bark. I knew the sun would also fade. The earth would turn cold. Or hot. The air was ice in my mother's car. My boyfriend kept his windows down. For air, he said. I left his car. Ran to the doctor. The doctor said, take these.

We could have formed a friendship that night me and the girl. We were laughing so hard and talking. But I was thinking. And her laughing stopped for a second. She was taking a break. Just one second. She held up one finger. Just two seconds. Just to get her cigarette lit. She struck the match. She took a long drag off her cigarette. No smoke floated from her after the drag. This isn't to say she wasn't breathing. She was. She was even talking again. But I watched as she dragged long and no smoke came floating from her mouth. Nor from her nose. I thought there must be something wrong. I thought, she can't go on like this. I stood nearer. I watched the cigarette tip brighten and saw no smoke float from her mouth. Nor from her nose. I stood with my side pressed to her side. I whispered, what's happening. She backed away. The room was starting up. My pulse. I whispered, what on earth. She said, what's wrong with you. She walked back to her side. I followed her. She said, stop.

Earlier that day. I recall. My mother sent me flowers. This isn't symbolic. They were right by the mailbox. Then she called. She told my boyfriend, they'll brighten the room. They'll fix things, she said. The flowers were very bright. But the petals were already drying. Some fell to the floor. There they were scattered. There's nothing deeper to this.

My boyfriend called and said, let's break. It wasn't his fault. He said, sorry. No matter. I threw my plate. I felt I was supposed to. All that broken glass. Those greens and browns. All that food was once life growing. In fields. The sun shone over top and brightened the fields. Then something crushed the animals. Everything green was crushed as well. There it was on my kitchen floor. What's that, you say. I say, your guess. I could have dropped to the dirty floor. Don't take this as deep but very shallow. I admit I felt cleaned out. Unfit.

Wrong from the start. We met at a dinner. My mother looked at his shirt. Torn. He looked at her diamonds. She looked at my hair. I looked at her face. She looked at the paint on my clothes. There wasn't much to say except pass this pass that. I sensed the first flicker of stars. Off to the sides by my ears. Passed off as drunken I'm guessing. I had been drinking. Some air, I said. I left to sit on the curb. Cars went past. I pushed leaves in the gutter with my hands. What they said in my absence. Well there was a fight. I saw my boyfriend huff to his rusted car. I saw my mother follow smirking smugly. I left too.

I recall the critique. The paintings were awful. The colors. Wrong. Awful dirty greens. The teacher was spitting words that day. The girl was carrying on. Something about truth and harmony. Really quite funny and the teacher said, break. I looked at the paintings. I looked good and hard at the mess. The truth. I laughed good and hard. The teacher looked up. The girl looked hurt. What was that. The trigger. That shallow cunt. I hated her paintings. Her poor hurt face. I said, help.

The first fit hit me like a fist in the mouth. My mother's that is. Diamonds square in the face. The next fits were softer. Expected. Like her smirking and handing a hairbrush saying, brush it. Or a white dress saying, try it. Or a bar of soap saying, paint on your hands. Your clothes. Your face. Or a diamond smirking, one day it's yours. Your father gave it to me that son of a bitch. And when I flinch she hands me a twenty. A fifty. To take off the edge.

My mother couldn't get me from school. Shopping or some such. She had good friends. I was shaking. She knew it. I was having thoughts. The tube as a tunnel. Light at the end. You've heard it before. The teacher came down looking for me. The girl came down with the teacher. My things were up in the classroom. The teacher was calling my name. The girl was calling my name. Their voices pushed like spreading roots. They tore up the basement floor. And before they could reach me I was running outside. Empty-handed.

Crawling under a car. Hiding from the mess. Looking for my mother. But I saw the rusted car bottom float past.

When the flowers lost their petals. Well, I thought, now this is fixed. Not the shell shapes. Not the dry veins I could see with light. But that they would disintegrate as they do. Would turn to nothing. That was fixed. I know you've thought this. Who hasn't thought it. But I hadn't yet. And this is mine. Let me be shallow.

The way she handed a brush to fix my hair. I said, stop it. She dragged it through my hair. It made a sound I can't explain. You're thinking, sparks. Something sparking. Yes. She said, your look. She shook her head. Her fist made contact with her palm. Never my face. But she meant it. I saw lights in her diamonds. Her car was ice. She gripped the wheel. You just need two things, she said. Marriage and money. My mother got both. Both were unfixed. Her glasses had the blackest lenses. I couldn't tell you of her eyes. I must admit. Only my father's diamond was real. It was divine. The rest were glass. My boyfriend smoked down to the fingers. When I say I loved him. Well what do you think. He pointed to trees and clouds. He said, looks good to me. I know what you're thinking. But was there a spark. Your guess.

When my mother called. You know. I hid in the sheets. It's my mother, I said to my boyfriend. Yes Mother, I said to her face. To her voice. That cunt, I said when she wasn't with me. In the mirror that is I said, that cunt. She was with me. I would get old.

What I recall from school. How you often have to squint to see. How you often have to back away. How a face is a face and a tree a tree. And something of the colors brown and green. And something of trees being brown and green. And something of the colors black and white and of black being the presence of all colors. No that's light. White. Black being the absence of all colors. I can't recall. And something of harmony something of truth. I can't recall. No matter.

I lied to you. My mother had brought the flowers it was. I went for the mail. There she stood by the mailbox. Looking old. Food on her face. She said, you're looking fit, and looked away. My boyfriend was smoking. I said to him, go. I meant for him to. But she handed the flowers to my boyfriend. She said, they'll brighten the room. Then

she started to leave. I said, you stay Mother. I pushed my boyfriend.
I said, please get out of my face. He held the flowers in front of his
head. My mother said, come. We went shopping. We bought nothing.
When I got home my boyfriend was gone. I was somewhat on edge.
My mother had tried to fix me up. With clothes and the rest. With
boyfriends. Imagine. The fight in the car. I need not say. At home the
petals were scattered. My boyfriend called. I threw the plate. The
flowers.

I went to school that night. The girl and I laughed. We talked of
nothing significant. Like this and like this. I thought of friendship.
I thought of me and the girl as friends. She smoked and swallowed
the smoke.

And I thought of trees. How they grow out of nothing. Dirt. How
they grow into nothing. Air. Somehow there's life. A spark. But
unfixed. It gets crushed. That's life you know. Screaming oneself
awake. Redfaced and bald. Closing the eyes. Bald again. Just stop me
now. I knew nothing. I admit it. I know nothing.

The girl. I tried to tell her. I had nothing to tell. But I tried. I pushed
against her. I said, what on earth. I was starting up. She said, what's
wrong with you, and walked away. I followed her. I looked at her
paintings. I would say sorry for laughing. She looked so hurt. She
said, stop. I thought, sorry. But her paintings. They were awful.
Lifelike one could say. She knew I would laugh into fits. She would
get hurt. I started to laugh. But I wasn't laughing. I felt it starting. But
I said, I don't feel well. Stop, she said.

The end. I saw the girl through the tube. She looked scared. Or
hurt. She looked far away. Light shot past like stars. My pulse. I
crawled under a car. My pulse slowed. The sun rose. Shone over top.
Brightened the gutter. The gutter stayed bright for a time. The leaves
in the gutter were bright. This isn't symbolic. I didn't think of my
boyfriend. I didn't think of my mother. I didn't cry into the leaves for
goodness sake. I just breathed as we do.

Life and Letters
Gilbert Sorrentino

SOME THREE OR FOUR YEARS AGO, Edward Krefitz published a story that, as is the case with many stories, contained elements of his past life, elements, of course, disguised, twisted, corrupted, embellished, romanticized, and wholly fanciful. A few people recognized themselves as models for characters in the story, and were, predictably, chagrined or flattered, depending on the quality of the fiction's distortion of their being. They all wished, surely, to be *accurately portrayed*, certainly; but there is accuracy and then there is meanspiritedness. So they muttered.

Edward wasn't interested in their scattered responses to his story when and if he got wind of them. However, the one person whom he had used as a model for a major character in the story, the one person he dearly wanted to read the story and be hurt by it, never acknowledged it, even though it had been published in a literary magazine that Edward knew this person deeply, even somewhat ridiculously, admired—at least he had, years before. Edward was disappointed, since his fictional creation—vapid, obtuse, childishly cruel—was easily recognizable, and he so wanted him to *be* recognized by his ex-friend, if "friend" is not too exotic a word to use. Because of this disappointment, which he chafed into a kind of fullblown irritation, he made a mistake; that is, he sent the model a photocopy of the story, insincerely inscribed, and followed this, soon after, with a letter, thereby, quite perfectly, compounding his original error.

The story, entitled, rather obscurely, "The Birds Are Singing," was a bitter, if frail, comedy of manners (bad manners, as Edward liked to think of it), driven by the wheezing engine of "the adulterous tale," one that was neither particularly comic nor particularly sordid. Its hero, if you will, a young husband whose authorial aspirations are at best halfhearted, has a wife, pretty and possessed of a kind of floundering hedonism. She is content to be "his" because of his aspirations and the spidery talents he owns, as well as by the fact that his literary vocation has thrown the couple into contact with other young literary people, jittery, amoral, indifferently talented, if talented at all. These companions are drawn as wrapped in a cheap and shabby, vaguely hysterical delusion, and too selfish or stupid to recognize it as such. At the center of this overdone clique of the pathetic is the major character already mentioned. This man is presented, in the most patronizing as well as nastiest prose that Edward could knock together, as a vapid dilettante; a poet, of sorts, who is hard at work on a novel that will justify the shameful fact that he is the owner of a successful messenger service for which the husband works as a bookkeeper. The boss/novelist is given to the reader as a tedious lout who confuses his sociopolitical right thinking with artistic talent, and he is stuffed with cretinous dialogue that even Wyndham Lewis might hesitate to put into his most contemptible characters' mouths. The boss seduces the husband's wife in an ugly scene that boils with loathing for the pair. The husband is aware of this, but has no clear proof, and so ignores it, much as if his wife's probable seducer is no more than a living dildo and she a disembodied vagina. He is sure, however, that this amorous clod may one day be able to help him along in his career, or what he thinks of as his career. This was, then, the bones of Edward's story, one that he came to admire more as it aged, so to speak. The notion that the cuckolded husband finds his betrayer pitifully absurd, and his wife a virtual specter, while he emerges as a genuine if eccentric and as yet unrealized artist pleased him, even though the story had, he realized, a somewhat manufactured air about it.

The model for the boss was, of course, the man, Peter, whom Edward wanted to anger and wound. The cause of his dislike went back almost twenty years, when he and most especially his wife, Patricia, insisted on thinking of him and Peter as partners in a small restaurant in what was then, the early seventies, a just newly fashionable SoHo. Peter was, in actuality, Edward's boss. There had been a falling-out between them as the restaurant began to make money, or, as it is said, "real" money. At this point, the friends' differences quickly surfaced and became unmanageable. Edward felt, on the strength, really, of no more than their joint literary, ah, proclivities, let's say, that he was being deprived of his bonus: his loft apartment, his summers on the Island, his good clothes, his this, his that. And Patricia! It's enough to say that she simply blamed Peter for everything, from her spoiled childhood to her sullen years at Hunter and the School of Visual Arts to her haphazard marriage to Edward— Edward, who had been cheated of his rightful *partner's* place as entrepreneur *and* literary force. She hated Peter, even more, perhaps, than she hated Edward some few years later, at the time of their separation and divorce; hated Edward so cleanly and thoroughly for his varied failures that in her last conversation with him she'd told him, rather sadly, understandingly, and even sweetly, that in their eight years of marriage he had *never once* made her come. He stood quietly before her news, looking, as an old phrase has it, like death chewing on a cracker.

After the dissolution of the friendship and "partnership," Edward began teaching beginning creative-writing courses at coolie wages; writing reviews for *Booklist, Library Journal,* and the like; freelancing as a copy editor and proofreader; and, in general, living the shaky life of the barely published and virtually unknown author. Patricia worked as an editorial assistant for a small scholastic publisher, and they got by, seeing, if not the same friends they had been seeing, the same kinds of friends. It should be mentioned that, at this time, Patricia was somewhat admiring of Edward for insisting, at her urging, of course, on his rights and perquisites, and so she regularly told him, to his delight. She was convinced that Peter, "that bastard," was much inferior in business acumen to her husband; and as the author of a wretched little book of poems, *Table d'Hôte*—published by Peter himself as the Chambers Street Press—he had no right to think himself superior to anybody about anything! In sum, she maintained little but an offhand, careless disregard for Peter; who, in turn, vilified her, pointedly or subtly, to people whom he knew that Edward would run into. She was, in his creation, the scattered and selfish Zelda to Edward's hapless Scott.

The rub was that although Edward broke off his friendship or relationship or association with Peter in a swirl of hurt feelings and envy, still, oh yes, *still,* he wondered if Peter might have been right about Patricia. About her "interference," her "malicious interference," as he had put it, in Edward's work and career. That Edward's work and career were, to be extremely kind, negligible, is neither here nor there: He thought it was work; he thought it a career. Or, to gloss that particular text, it's the rare mediocre writer who knows how mediocre he is. When Patricia left him, soon after it was apparent to her, or so he figured it, that his dissociating himself from Peter would in no way allow his star ever to grow bright enough to have a chance at dimming, left him with her peroration on his sexual limitations, he thought, he *knew* that Peter was right and had been right. He was ashamed of himself, he was what an earlier generation called mortified. Why had he listened to his bitch of a wife? Why had she so despised Peter?

Over the next several years, as Edward established himself as a reliable contributor of short fiction and reviews to a myriad magazines, he vacillated in his feelings about both Peter and Patricia. He heard many stories of Peter's financial success, and of his mockery of him and his work, of him and his contemptible third-rate literary niche, of Patricia. And concerning her, concerning her . . . Although Edward's thoughts of her were tinged with pain and embarrassment, he yet felt, in some unbalanced way, protective of her—even more absurd, he felt loyal to her. And so he began, again, to blame Peter for this and for that and for, well, for everything. It is simple to understand, then, why "The Birds Are Singing" was written, why it was important to Edward that Peter read it, why it was important that he respond to it with, at the very least, irritation. Edward wanted to demonstrate *things* to Peter, salient among which was that he had, indeed, become a writer, by Christ, and that his writer's eye had been sharp enough all those many years ago to see Peter for what he had been: He'd not been fooled, for a moment, by him!—who had been crude and grasping and filled with contempt for him and Patricia, whom he'd hurt and somehow embittered. Edward wanted, simply, to get even with Peter. And so strong was his desire, perhaps his need, to knife Peter, to shock him with a view of himself as a vulgar, cheap, mean poseur that, as already noted, he sent a copy of the story to him, followed, a week or so later, by a letter.

> Dear Peter,
>
> I hope you got the new story I sent a few days ago. This is all out of the blue, I know, but "the old days" have been on my mind lately. I thought that you, more than anyone, would "see" the story clearly, and recognize the furniture, so to speak. It's maybe a little dark, and nobody comes off too well, but I think it's pretty true to the feel of that time, confused as things were. Anyway, drop me a line if the spirit moves you. I often wonder how we came to part so completely, considering how our differences, whatever they were, seem so trivial now. I hear, by the way, that you are doing fine with a specialty catering business, as well as with a new restaurant in Chelsea. I got this from Marge, who also gave me your address. I'm pleased for you, really. Take care, and cheers.
>
> Fondly,
>
>   Ed

As I've suggested, the "gift" of the story to Peter was a mistake, one that was richly compounded by the above letter. And as if to polish these mistakes into perfection, Edward, awash in the lies of nostalgia that his acts had awakened, quite unaccountably and foolishly, began to feel bad about everything that had happened: the story, its grotesque caricature of Peter, its dispatch to him, the letter, and, most tellingly, their shattered friendship, which Edward managed to burnish into much more than it had ever been or ever could have been. This broken relationship he now nimbly contrived to place, such were the powers of corrupted memory, on the shoulders of Patricia. She was, yes she was, yes, yes, she was to blame, the snob, the cynical snob, the bitch. And to think that he had felt that *she* had cared about him, had thought to protect his interests, Jesus Christ! There had been no reason, had there, for him and Peter to break their easygoing relationship, their, in a way, partnership? They were in accord on ideas, notions of the comic and the absurd, politics, books, on notions of *what was good.* Hadn't this been the case? He even thought, fleetingly, to be sure, of calling Patricia, if he could track her down, to ask her, to yell at her, to do something! And so he poked at himself, rereading, two or three times, "The Birds Are Singing" with distaste and regret and a growing sense of shame.

A month passed, during which time Edward thought of calling Peter every day, to maybe make a date for lunch or a drink? To talk, to mend fences. He might, he could, he would, yes, apologize for the story itself. One day he received a letter from Peter, and opened it with hope and pleasure. Peter, of course, felt the way he did; he, too, wanted to resume their old camaraderie, tempered, surely, changed, but still *real.* Patricia's malice would be diluted, it would be banished, at last.

Dear Ed,

I was surprised and I guess shocked to get your piece and the follow-up letter after all this time, it's really been a long time! The piece brought back those days in that little dump in SoHo that we called the cash-eater, remember? I hope that the piece and letter are ways of saying that bygones should be bygones. Maybe things will be OK between us again, that would be terrific.

I'm doing pretty well. Marge is right that I have a little café in Chelsea on Twentieth Street near Ninth, the Arles. And the catering business, Peter's Specialty Cuisine, maybe Marge told you, is in a loft building on Hudson near

Houston on the fourth floor, you can imagine the hassles with the Fire Dept. and the Buildings Dept. and the Board of Health and so on! But everything is fine now, I'm making a living, as they say, married for sixteen years now with a fourteen-year-old daughter. We live in Bronxville.

Most importantly, Ed, really, I mean *really*, is how fantastically brave and honest and forgiving you are to have written this piece, which I've read three times now. It must have taken a lot of courage, moral courage, as they say, to use yourself as a model for the husband character, Ned, that poor bastard who is so painfully and cruelly and flagrantly betrayed by his wife and friend. Who, if I read right, are Patricia and me, of course. It amazes me, just floors me to realize, all these years later, that you knew, all along, probably from the beginning, that Patricia and I were lovers and stayed lovers for a year and a half. We were so crazy that we didn't care whether we hurt you or not, although we were careful not to be obvious about meeting each other, and we were certain that you didn't know. Patricia's bad-mouthing me really should have worked, and yet you obviously saw right through it. What makes me feel worse than the affair is that we ended our friendship for the wrong reason, or maybe I should say over something that wasn't even real!

Now, with this marvelous piece, you are letting me know that you knew, you knew all along, and you let it go, maybe for friendship or love, I don't know. It's just fantastic. You're a wonderful writer, as I always thought you were. Please write again, stay in touch?

Your old partner,

Peter

Unlikely as it may seem, when Edward read this letter, he decided that Peter had maliciously and carefully contrived to humiliate him with a confession of an imagined adultery. Peter and Patricia, good God! How ridiculous. And yet Edward felt stupid and clumsy to have thought Peter worthy of his concern. He tore up the letter, and then sat down to read "The Birds Are Singing" once again.

From Penury
Myung Mi Kim

mustard seed ‖ subsistence

incendiary aphid

to carry, more at (to) bear

acre or square ‖ dilapidate, "takes place"

Hazard Sequence

Household faced with ‖

———————

Myung Mi Kim

Iodine's property

[conjugate]

A dependent's call
A dependent cries out

Pressure behind the cataract

a ‖ marvel perceive

_____

Hands rinsed in disinfectant
Series of rubbing

Bells sounded ‖ referenced

‖ Someone teaches "topic sentence"

The house held up its garrison

Children will continue to play

Gold | corn | corncob

_____

[consolidated   limit]

Alleyway. One works a machine. Neck
bent. Arm, lesion, and pound.

Stone headdresses

Octopus of boils

: This is in English

Lobe and barricade ‖ as treats a stateroom

———————

As though
Clock or bulwark
Guards ‖

: There's nothing as isolating as having to think in another's language

———————

Myung Mi Kim

[isthmus]

plethora of roots ‖ mowed lawns

clot ‖ tendon and refuse, who
cowered, supermarkets, windshield
snap. Does the single tree list
favoring snow. Disinterred. Would be forced to look.

―――――――――

Bodies bound in linen

Dirt filled boots

[matriculate]

She, the weeping work
Parade of earnings

The house ‖ weight of forelegs and hooves underwater
A ripple ‖ birched
Alyssum. A carved stamp

―――――――――

‖ household ‖ *servitus* ‖ outcrop ‖

mutual obligation of help, scattered

commerce, its own perforate law

‖ whose isolation, whose cordoned family

| brought into use or practice |

: for the good of the very few and the suffering of a great many

The Apocalypse Museum
William H. *Gass*

The fear that the human race might not survive has been replaced by the fear that it will endure.

YOU CANNOT END AN English sentence with a preposition. Skizzen had more than once read that. Or the world with "with"—leaving the whimper unwhimpered. Or with "on account of"—overpopulation, for example—unspecified. Or with "in"—omitting fire or flood or wind . . . a storm of hail the size of eyeballs. Can you imagine what it will die of? if it actually can die. There will be many endings vying for the honor. And any agent of our end will have a radiant sense of ruin. Any agent of our end will dance where the score says rest.

In the garden the cornflowers watch my small mother, Skizzen thought, watch my small mother wash her small hands in the soft loamy soil of the beds. She has dug in compost over years, compost mixed with sand, with bark, with mulching leaves, a little manure, a bit of bone meal; and with a fork she has carefully circulated the soil, turning sand and leaves and rotted peelings under one another, down where the earthworms slowly pass everything through themselves and thereby imagine shit as a city. She handles the leaves and touches the blossoms. She knows how to do it. Her grasp is vigorous, never shy or uncertain. The plants respond. Eat well. Thrive. Go to nefarious seed.

Our concern that the human race might not endure has been succeeded by the fear it will survive.

Oh . . . oh—Skizzen oh'd, in his sermons to himself—Oh, the decomposition of man will stench the sky at first but how immeasurably it will manure the soil, how thoroughly it will improve the land with all those fine bones added, while plants cover and trees stand. For the worm the climate will be tropical, they will grow longer than tunnels and their four hearts beat for blocks. Lakes will deepen and be blue again. Clean sky will harbor happy winds. Mountainsides of aspens will be able to color and flutter without having their picture taken. Waterfalls will fall free of enterprising eyes. It will be grand.

Unless there is a universal flood and fish school in corner offices; unless there is an atomic wind and an image of our race is burned into the side of a glass cliff; unless glaciers creep down from the North almost as blue as green as winedark as the solidifying sea.

The thought that mankind might not endure has been replaced by the fear it may luck out.

Armageddon's final field was nearly measured once before. It was half a cataclysm—a clysm—maybe. Preliminary bout. A third of the world sickened during the three years of the Black Plague: 1348—1349—1350. And the Plague swung its scythe four times, the last swathe reducing Europe to half what it had been the century before: in 1388—1389—1390. They believed the disease was evil advancing like an army. They said it was Satan's century. *Diabolus in musica.* That was before Passchendaele. The population of the planet diminished by a fifth.

Those who suffered the Plague and survived: They suggested to Joseph Skizzen the unpleasant likelihood that Man might squeak through even a loss at Armageddon—one death per second not fast enough—and outlive the zapping of the planet, duck a fleet of meteors, hunkerbunker through a real world war with cannons going grump to salute our last breath as if horror were a ceremony, emerge to sing of bombs bursting, endure the triggers of a trillion guns amorously squeezed until every nation's ammo was quite spent, and all the private stock was fired off at the life and livestock of a neighbor, so that in battle's final silence one could hear only the crash after crash of financial houses, countless vacuum cleaners, under their own orders, sucking up official lies, contracts screaming like lettuce shredded for a salad, outcries from the crucifixion of caring borne on the wind as if in an ode, the screech of every wheel as it became uninvented, brief protests from dimming tubes, destimulated wires; though the slowing of most functions would go on in silence, shit merded up in the street to be refried by aberrant microwaves, diseases coursing about and competing for victims, slowdowns coming to standstills without a sigh, until the heavy quiet of war's cease is broken by . . . by what? might we imagine boils bursting out of each surviving eye . . . the accumulated pus of perception? a burst like what? like trumpets blowing twenty centuries of pointless noise at an already deaf-eared world . . . with what sort of sound exactly?

439

with a roar that rattles nails already driven in their boards, so . . . so that, as the sound comes through their windows, houses will heave and sag into themselves, as unfastened as flesh from a corset; yet out of every heap of rubble, smoking ruin, ditch of consanguineous corpses, could creep a survivor—*he* was such a survivor, Joseph Skizzen, faux doctor and musician—someone born of ruin as flies are from offal; that from a cave or collection of shattered trees there might emerge a creature who could thrive on a prolonged diet of phlegm soup and his own entrails even, and in spite of every imaginable catastrophe salvage at least a remnant of his race with the strength, the interest, the spunk, to fuck on, fuck on like Christian soldiers, stiff pricked still, with some sperm left with the ability to engender, to fuck on, so what if with a limp, fuck on, or a severed tongue, fuck on, or a blind eye, fuck on, in order to multiply, first to spread and then to gather, to confer, to wonder why, to invent, to philosophize, accumulate, connive: to wonder why this punishment? to wonder why this pain? why did we—among the we's that were—survive? what was accomplished that couldn't have been realized otherwise? why were babies born to be so cruelly belabored back into the grave? who of our race betrayed our trust? what was the cause of our bad luck? what divine plan did this disaster further? why were grandfathers tortured by the deaths they were about to sigh for? why? but weren't we special? we few, we leftovers, without a tree to climb, we must have been set aside, saved for a moment of magnificence? to be handed the trophy, awarded the prize; because the Good Book, we would—dumb and blind—still believe in, said a remnant would be saved; because the good, the great, the well-born and internetted, the rich, the incandescent stars, will win through: that . . . that . . . that we believed, we knew, God will see to that, he will see, see to it, if he hasn't had a belly full, if the liar's, the liar's beard is not on fire like Santa Claus stuck in a chimney.

The thought that mankind might not endure has been replaced by the fear it may make it through another age of ice.

In spite of death and desolation, music, Professor Joseph Skizzen assured himself, would still be made. Toms would be tom'd, the earth beaten by bones born to a rhythm if not a rhyme, a ground swept by sweet dancing feet. There would be voices raised in song to celebrate heaven, to thank the gods for the radish about to be eaten, to pray for victory in tomorrow's war, or the reinvention of the motorcar. Someone would, like Simonides, remember where

440

everyone was sitting when the roof of the world fell in, or how the stars were configured, and would be able to identify the dead, if anyone cared. With that feat on his resumé, Simonides could easily sell his memory-method for a lot of cabbages, many messes of pottage, thirty carloads of silver, options to buy. Because we would want everyone properly buried in their appropriately consecrated ground, sacred ground we would kill one another to acquire, to protect and fill with our grateful dead—each race decomposing, each would allege, with more dignity, more delight to those worms, more . . . more to the nth than the others.

Soon there would be family clans and prisons again. Beneath all ash, hate would still be warm enough to make tea. That's the state in which Professor Skizzen's mind would be when he left off worrying his sentence—the possibility that all of us might just check out has been overcome by the probability that some of us will never vacate our rooms or pay our bills on time or receive our just desserts—break off to imagine man's return, the triumph of the club and the broken knees of enemies, the harvesting of ferns, the refinement of war paint— each time taking a slightly different route to new triumphs and fresh renown. Upon our Second Coming, we would hate the earth and eat only air. We would live in ice like a little bit of lost light. We would grow fur and another nose. Fingernails, hard as horn, would curl like crampons. We would scuttle in and out of caves, live on insects, bats, and birds, and grow blue as a glacier. Perhaps we'd emerge in the shape of those ten-foot tropical worms, and like *Lumbricus terrestris* have many hundred species. It was so discouraging, but such thoughts had one plus: They drove him away from his obsession with words like "fear" and "concern" and "worry" and returned him to his profitable work—the study of the late piano pieces of Franz Liszt—a passion which his former colleagues found amusing, especially in an Austrian such as himself, who ought to disdain the French/Slav Musical Axis in favor of a hub that was purely German (little did they know where he'd already been!), and who had foolishly chosen one instrument when the entire Vienna Philharmonic could have been strumming and tootling his tunes.

Yes, that very orchestra where his father might have played had he chosen to imagine himself a concert violinist instead of a fleeing Jew. Joseph Skizzen's mother carried him to London like coffee in a thermos. To grow up in a ruin, amid the blitz'd, the burned, and broken, a foretaste of the soon-to-be forlorn and fallen world. Joseph preferred to think of his father's moves as resembling, when he left

Vienna in the guise of a Jew, a profound departure from the tonic; and his father's sojourn in London, until he went to work in the betting parlor, as a deft modulation back to the Aryan fold; but it was difficult to account for the abandonment of his family, his departure for America, and his subsequent disappearance, in some sort of sonata form. Changelings required impromptus, variations, bagatelles, divertimenti to do justice to their nature. He, Joseph Skizzen, was a weathercock, too.

Joseph Skizzen's surmise that mankind might not survive its own profligate and murderous nature has been supplanted by the suspicion that nonetheless it will.

The Gothic house he and his mother shared had several attic rooms, and Joseph Skizzen had decided to devote one of them to the books and clippings that comprised his other hobby: The Inhumanity Museum. He had painstakingly lettered a large white card with that name and fastened it to the door. It did not embarrass him to do this since only he was ever audience to the announcement. Sometimes he changed the placard to one which called it The Apocalypse Museum instead. The stairs to the third floor were too many and too steep for his mother now. Daily, he would escape his sentence in order to enter yesterday's clippings into the scrapbooks that constituted the continuing record:

Friday June 18, 1999.

Sri Lanka. Municipal workers dug up more bones from a site believed to contain the bodies of hundreds of Tamils murdered by the military.

Same day.
Poklek, Jugoslavia. 62 Kosovars are packed into a room into which a grenade is tossed.

Same day.
Pristina, Jugoslavia. It is now estimated that 10,000 people were killed in the Serbian ethnic-cleansing pogrom.

Now there was no one left in Kosovo to kill but Gypsies.
Or

William H. Gass

Tuesday April 16, 2001.

Cotonou, Benin. The boat at the center of an international search for scores of child slaves believed to have been roaming the West African coast for more than two weeks arrived early this morning in this port.

Next day.
Cotonou, Benin. Authorities boarded a ship suspected of carrying child slaves after it docked at Cotonou early today but found no sign of such children.

Next day.
Cotonou, Benin. According to the manifest, there were only seven children aboard. UNICEF officials said thirty-one were placed in foster homes. The Men of the Earth charity had forty-three at their refuge. The ship's chief mate insisted that there were twenty-eight children on board, all with their families.

The paste would have to wait on this one which would not be a keeper unless the kids had been thrown overboard.

Skizzen clipped a few local items, but his harvest was mostly taken from the *New York Times* and the weekly newsmagazines. He ignored most crime and merely ordinary malfeasance. Occasionally he would include a shooting on the subway or the theft of donor organs, but he felt that you had to discount things done mainly from poverty or madness. Actually, human stupidity was his principal target. Stupidity was shifty. It often pretended to be smart. For instance, the other day he had saved yet another article on the preservation of small vials of smallpox—on the off chance, just in case, for scientific use, with the understanding that no species should be intentionally lost. In the same spirit, he ruled out the petty subornings popular among politicians, but he carefully saved accounts of elections in which a blatant scoundrel was voted into office by a smug, lazy, or indifferent electorate. He scissored when he spotted superstitions singing like sirens, when he caught stupidity in action, stupidity that especially embodied willful blindness or where greed or one of the other deadly sins overcame weak reason once again. Judgments could be dicey. Dust Bowl pictures were included because it was Skizzen's conclusion that human mistreatment of the soil, not Nature out of whimsical meanness and acting alone, had made the plains barren, wasted the cattle, and scoured the barns to their bare

443

boards. Hoof and Mouth were the names of two instruments in his orchestra. Mad Cow a must. AIDS, of course, was easy, ignorance and stupidity fed and spread it, but river blindness, say, was a close call, and he ultimately rejected some very moving photographs of scar-closed eyes.

On the walls of his attic area were everywhere pinned atrocity pictures, some of them classics: the weeping baby of Nanking or the wailing Vietnamese girl running naked amid other running wailing children on that fatal Route 1 near Trang Bang (even the name a mockery); numerous sepias of dead outlaws with their names on crude signs propped beneath their boots; clips from films that showed what struck the eyes of those who first entered the extermination camps—careless heaps of skins and bones, entirely tangled, exhibiting more knees and elbows than two-pair-to-a-death ought allow; amateurishly aimed shots of the sodden trench-corpse as well as bodies hanging over barbed battlefield wire; the bound Viet Cong officer, a pistol at the end of a long arm pointed at his head, a picture taken in the act of his execution by a so-called chief of police; then, to add class, the rape of the Sabine women, etchings of chimney sweeps, paintings of sad solitaries and painted whores, or for the purposes of education, the consequences of car bombs, mob hits, traitors hung from lamp posts—Mussolini among the many whose bodies were publically displayed—as were niggers strung, as a lesson, from the limbs of trees; but most were images transient for readers: countless corpses from African famines, African wars, African epidemics, ditto India, ditto China but adding floods; there were big-eyed pot-bellied starvelings, wasted victims of disease, fields full of dead Dinka tribesmen, machine-gunned refugees on roads, misguided monks who had set fire to themselves, ghoulishly smoking up a street; and there were lots of Japanese prints that seemed to celebrate rape, paintings and pictures that glorified war or sanctified lying priests, flattered pompous kings and smugly vicious dictators, still others that celebrated serial killers, and tried to put a good face on fat ward politicians or merely reported on the Klansmen, dressed like hotel napkins; the Goya etchings depicting the "Disasters of War," in poor reproductions to be sure, were all there, as well as Bosches xeroxed in color from an art book, a few stills from snuff films, violent propaganda posters, numerous Dorés, Grünewalds, saints suffering on grills or from flights of arrows, details from *Guernica,* examples from Grosz, close-ups of nails penetrating palms then boards, illustrations in volumes of the Marquis de Sade, lots of photographs of the dead on battlefields or in burial grounds from *Gardner's Photographic Sketchbook of the Civil War*, many of them tampered with and staged, which created an added interest; there were drawings of medieval implements of torture, each aspect and element precisely labeled, paintings of autos-da-fé by the Spanish master, firing squads by Monet, cavalry charges and combatants at the barricades by Delacroix; the guillotine with several of its severed heads was there, as well as emasculations, circumcision ceremonies, buffalo hunts, seal cubs as they were being clubbed, executions of various kinds—by knife, by fire, by gas, by poison, by lethal injection, by trap drop, by jolt, by shot—Indians massacred, natives forced over cliffs, notable assassinations—but only if the victim wasn't deserving—as well as wall after wall, not in Skizzen's room but out in the world, where rebel soldiers or Warsaw Jews were lined up to be gunned down and photographed after, during, and before by the documentary minded; close-ups of scattered body parts, many of them less identifiable than steaks or chops, abattoirs in operation, fine watercolors of slave ships under full sail, a clutch of Salgado gold-mine prints depicting humans toiling in holes more horrible than Dante had imagined (and then only for the deserving), detailed photographs of torture instruments—the iron maiden, thumb-screw, rack—from the collection kept in the Tower of London, children huddled in doorways, on grates, coal miners in black face, breadlines and the bloody swollen faces of beaten boxers, women working in sweatshops or shrouded in worshipful crowds, torchlit Nazi rallies, and the professor's prize, an original Koudelka picturing a tipped-over tortoise, dead on a muddy Turkish road, the photograph handsomely matted and framed and hung center stage.

Mostly, though, from every place not already tacked or pasted, clippings were loosely pinned or taped so that they would have fluttered had there ever been a draft, as they did wave a little when Skizzen passed, dangling for quite a ways down the wall in overlapping layers sometimes, even stuck to flypaper Skizzen had cannily suspended from the ceiling, the whole crowd requiring him to duck if he didn't want his head and neck tickled, and giving to the room a cavey cachelike feeling, as if some creature, fond of collecting, lived there, and only sallied forth like the jackdaw to find and fetch back bright things, or, in this case, cuttings from the tree of evil, for which purpose paper shears had been put in every room of the large house, every room including entry, bath, and laundry, because you never knew when you might come upon something, and Skizzen had learned not to put off the opportunity, or delay the acquisition, since he had, early on and before this present remedy, forgotten where he had seen a particular picture or news item, and was sadly unable to locate it again. He vividly remembered, too, how he had lost an image on a handout by postponing its extraction when he should have scissored it out while he was still standing on the front stoop holding in his shocked hand a leaflet bearing a grotesque beard and a text attacking the Amish because they were receiving special privileges, which allowed them their own schools, when children (whose God-loving parents were faithful members of the Church of Christ's White Messengers) were called truants when kept from class because in school they were compelled to study—by a sick and god-forsaken society—demonically inspired opinions of Creation and its consequences.

Next door, though the room was doorless and open to anyone who found their way there, was the library, three of its walls lined by crude plank-and-brick cases crammed with books bearing witness to the inhumanity of man, especially a complete set of the lives of the saints, the *Newgate Calendars,* several on the history of the church, the many-volumed *International Military Trials* in an ugly library binding (for sale at a very reasonable price by the superintendent of documents of the U.S. Government Printing Office), or several on the practice of slavery through the centuries, lives of the Caesars, careers of the Medicis, biographies of feminists, the fate of the Gypsies or the American Indians, and, of course, tome after tome on holocausts and pogroms, exterminations and racial cleansings from then to now, where on one page he could feed on names like Major Dr. Huhnemoerder, Oberst von Reurmont, Gruppenfuehrer Nebe, OKW Chef Kgf, and General Grosch; however, the library did not merely hold works on barbaric rites and cruel customs or on spying, strike-breaking, lynching, pillaging, raping, but on counterfeiting, colluding, cheating, exploiting, blackmailing and extorting, absconding, suborning, skimming, embezzling, and other white-collar crimes as well: proof through news reports, through ideas, images, and action, of the wholly fallen and utterly depraved condition of our race—testimony that Joseph Skizzen augmented, on the few ritual occasions he allowed himself to observe and celebrate, by his reciting aloud, while standing at what he deemed was the center of his collection, alternatively from a random page of some volume chosen similarly, or from a news bulletin pulled down blindly from whatever stalactite came to hand, although he did occasionally cheat in favor of the

Newgate Calendar, from which he would read with relish accounts of crimes like that of Catherine Hayes, who contrived, by egging on several of her many paramours, to have her husband's head cut off, in the punishment of which the righteous were seen to be even more inventively wicked than the criminal.

> When the wretched woman had finished her devotions, an iron chain was put round her body, with which she was fixed to a stake near the gallows. On these occasions, when women were burnt for petty treason, it was customary to strangle them, by means of a rope passed round the neck, and pulled by the executioner, so that they were dead before the flames reached the body. But this woman was literally burnt alive; for the executioner letting go the rope sooner than usual, in consequence of the flames reaching his hands, the fire burnt fiercely round her, and the spectators beheld her pushing the faggots from her, while she rent the air with her cries and lamentations. Other faggots were instantly thrown on her; but she survived amidst the flames for a considerable time, and her body was not perfectly reduced to ashes in less than three hours.

Joseph Skizzen put his whole heart into his voice, happy not another ear could hear him, satisfied that no one would ever see his collection either, for he was no Jonathan Edwards, although his tones were dark, round, ripe, and juicy as olives, because he had no interest in the redemption of the masses whose moral improvement was quite fruitless in any case. He did privately admit, and thus absolve himself of it, that Joseph Skizzen was a man who enjoyed the repeated proofs that he was right.

He had acquired an impressive collection of volumes on perverse religious rituals and social practices, a few containing photographs of wives being burned by their furniture, directions concerning the cutting out of human hearts, the placement of beautifying scars and punctures, the timing of soprano-sustaining castrations, the grooming of sacrificial animals, the strategic placement of impurity huts, the designing of corsets and binding of feet, of types of dungeons, and places for the sequestration of monks, nuns, and the general run of women who weren't thought to be unclean for other reasons.

The drug trade and all it entailed, including bribery and money laundering, bored him—Joseph Skizzen had to confess to that partiality, and to the fact that the relative absence of this and similarly vulgar forms of criminal business, as well as many of the brutalities of ordinary life which rarely reached the papers, was a serious flaw in his collection, and, presumably, in his character as well. But who would know or care? That was a comfort. His work had been protected from its critics.

Movies which would pan a camera about a serial killer's poster-lined room (or a delinquent adolescent's sometimes), after the police had invaded it, in order to astonish the audience's eyes as police eyes presumably were—such scenes would cause Skizzen an unpleasant twinge on account of the situation's distant similarity, especially when the lens would dwell on newspaper clippings, lists with circled names, or photographs of Charles Manson, but he bore such surprises well, and avoided them altogether when that was possible.

So as time and life passed, Professor Joseph Skizzen took care of Miriam, the mother with whom he still lived; he played his piano, now a nice one; he prepared his classes and dealt with his students, studied Liszt, obsessively rewrote his sentence—now in its fifty-seventh version—or clipped affronts to reason, evidences of evil action, or ill feeling, from books, papers, periodicals, and elsewhere, most of them to paste in albums organized in terms of Flaws, Crimes, and Consequences, though many of the more lurid were strung up like victims on lengths of flypaper, nothing but reports of riots on one, high treasons on another, poaching, strip-mining, or deforestation on still others; and in order not to play favorites, he decorated a specially selected string with unspeakable deeds done by Jews, among them—in honor of his would-be forgotten father—the abandonment of the family.

Professor Joseph Skizzen's concern that the human race might not endure has been succeeded by his fear that it will quite comfortably survive.

NOTES ON CONTRIBUTORS

WALTER ABISH is completing *Double Vision*, an autobiographical account to be published by Knopf.

JOHN ASHBERY is the author of many books, most recently *Your Name Here* (Farrar, Straus & Giroux), *Other Traditions* (Harvard University Press), and *As Umbrellas Follow Rain*, forthcoming from Qua.

PAUL AUSTER's most recent book is *The Story of My Typewriter*, with paintings and drawings by Sam Messer (Distributed Art Publishers). He also edited the anthology *I Thought My Father Was God and Other True Tales from NPR's National Story Project* (Henry Holt).

JOHN BARTH's new novel, *Coming Soon!!!*, has just been published by Houghton Mifflin.

MARTINE BELLEN's most recent collection of poetry is *The Vulnerability of Order* (Copper Canyon Press). Her *Tales of Murasaki and Other Poems* (Sun & Moon Press) was a winner of the National Poetry Series.

A new book of poems by MEI-MEI BERSSENBRUGGE, *Nest*, is forthcoming from Kelsey Street Press. She lives in New Mexico and New York City.

MARY CAPONEGRO's new collection of fiction is *The Complexities of Intimacy* (Coffee House Press).

Next year, ANNE CARSON will publish a translation of the fragments of Sappho, with commentary (Knopf).

AMY CATANZANO's poems have recently appeared in or are forthcoming from *American Letters & Commentary*, *Columbia Poetry Review*, *Facture*, and *Iowa Journal of Cultural Studies*.

PETER COLE's most recent book, *Selected Poems of Solomon Ibn Gabirol* (Princeton University Press), was awarded this year's TLS Hebrew Translation Prize.

BRENDA COULTAS has a book forthcoming from Coffee House Press in 2003.

ROBERT CREELEY's "Pictures" was written for a collaboration with Jim Dine (Tamarind). His latest books are *Drawn & Quartered*, with artist Archie Rand (Granary Books), and *Just in Time: Poems 1984-1994* (New Directions).

MARK Z. DANIELEWSKI is the author of *House of Leaves* (Pantheon).

RIKKI DUCORNET's most recent publications are a novel, *The Fan Maker's Inquisition* (Ballantine), and a book of essays, *The Monstrous and the Marvelous* (City Lights). She is currently writing a novel to be published by Knopf, of which "Sleeping with Schéhérazade" is a chapter.

ELAINE EQUI's latest collection of poems, *Voice-Over*, published by Coffee House Press, won the San Francisco State Poetry Award. She teaches at New York University and in the graduate program at City College.

NOMI EVE is the author of the novel *The Family Orchard*, recently released in paperback by Vintage. A small passage of "The Murder of Rabbi David Berliner Herschell" appeared in it.

BRIAN EVENSON's books include, most recently, *Contagion* (Wordcraft of Oregon). His first story collection, *Altmann's Tongue*, will be reissued next spring by University of Nebraska Press.

THALIA FIELD's collection, *Point & Line*, is available from New Directions. "Autobiography" is from her forthcoming collection, *American Nouns*.

FORREST GANDER is the author of *Torn Awake* and *Science & Steepleflower* (both from New Directions). His translations *No Shelter: Selected Poems of Pura López Colomé* and *Immanent Visitor: Selected Poems of Jaime Saenz* (with Kent Johnson) are forthcoming in 2002.

WILLIAM H. GASS was the recipient of the first PEN/Nabokov Award for lifetime achievement in literature. *Reading Rilke* is his most recent book, and forthcoming this winter is *Tests of Time* (both from Knopf).

JORIE GRAHAM is the author of nine collections of poetry. These poems are drawn from her forthcoming book, *Never*, due from Ecco/HarperCollins in spring 2002.

LYN HEJINIAN's latest books are *The Beginner* (Spectacular Books), *The Language of Inquiry* (University of California Press), and *A Border Comedy* (Granary Books). She is co-director (with Travis Ortiz) of *Atelos*, a literary project publishing cross-genre work by poets.

BRENDA HILLMAN is the author of three chapbooks and six books of poetry, most recently *Cascadia* (Wesleyan University Press). She teaches at St. Mary's College in California.

The Shunra and the Schmetterling, an excerpt of which appears in this issue, is forthcoming from New Directions, which has previously published YOEL HOFFMANN's *The Heart Is Katmandu*, *The Christ of Fish*, *Bernhard*, and *Katschen & the Book of Joseph*.

SHELLEY JACKSON is the author of *Patchwork Girl*, a hypertext novel available online (www.ineradicablestain.com), and *The Melancholy of Anatomy*, forthcoming next spring from Anchor Vintage.

Next spring, Black Sparrow Press will publish a new collection of recent poems by ROBERT KELLY. He is currently working on a gathering of shorter poems entitled *Sheet Music*, a novel on the theme of alien abduction, a collection of essays, and a fourth collection of short fiction.

MYUNG MI KIM's books include *Under Flag* (Kelsey Street Press), *The Bounty* (Chax Press), and *Dura* (Sun & Moon Press). *Commons* will appear in the spring of 2002 from the University of California Press.

ANN LAUTERBACH's sixth collection, *If In Time: Selected Poems 1975-2000*, was published last April by Penguin. She is the Ruth and David Schwab Professor of Language and Literature at Bard College, where she also directs the writing division of the Milton Avery Graduate School of the Arts.

CAROLE MASO is the author, most recently, of *The Room Lit by Roses: A Journal of Pregnancy and Birth* (Counterpoint Press) and *Beauty Is Convulsive: The Passion of Frida Kahlo* (forthcoming from Counterpoint Press). She teaches at Brown University.

HARRY MATHEWS's most recent books are *Oulipo Compendium*, co-edited with Alastair Brotchie (Atlas Press), and *Sainte Catherine*, a novella in French (Éditions P.O.L).

ANGE MLINKO lives in New York City, where she edits the *Poetry Project Newsletter*. Her book of poems, *Matinées*, is available from Zoland Books.

RICK MOODY is the author, most recently, of *Demonology*, a collection of short stories (Little Brown).

BRADFORD MORROW founded and edits *Conjunctions*. His new novel, *Ariel's Crossing*, will be published by Viking in May 2002. He teaches at Bard College.

HOWARD NORMAN's "View of Kala Murie Stepping Out of Her Black Dress" is excerpted from his new novel, *The Haunting of L.*, to be published by Farrar, Straus & Giroux in spring 2002.

JOYCE CAROL OATES is the author, most recently, of the novel *Blonde* and the short story collection *Faithless: Tales of Transgression* (both from Ecco Press).

"Mendoza: 1949" is an excerpt from TOBY OLSON's novel *The Blond Box*. His recent books are *Write Letter to Billy* (Coffee House Press) and *Human Nature* (New Directions).

RICHARD POWERS is the author of seven novels, most recently, *Plowing the Dark* (Farrar, Straus & Giroux). "Singing" is an excerpt from his latest book, which will appear in January 2003.

HEATHER RAMSDELL is the author of *Lost Wax* (University of Illinois Press). Her new manuscript of prose writing is *Vague Swimmers*.

JOANNA SCOTT's most recent novel is *Make Believe* (Little Brown). "The Usefulness of Ugliness" is adapted from a presentation given at the University of Paris VIII conference, "Imagination Alive Imagine," in April 2001.

451

REGINALD SHEPHERD's fourth book, *Otherhood*, is forthcoming from the University of Pittsburgh Press. His other collections are *Some Are Drowning*, which won the 1993 AWP Award, *Angels Interrupted*, and *Wrong* (all from the University of Pittsburgh Press).

CHRISTOPHER SORRENTINO is the author of *Sound on Sound* (Dalkey Archive Press) and is working on a new novel, to be published by Farrar, Straus & Giroux.

GILBERT SORRENTINO's burlesque Western, *Gold Fools*, was published this year by Green Integer. Another novel, *Little Casino*, will appear from Coffee House Press in spring 2002. He has recently completed an imaginative journal of imaginative art exhibitions, *Painting the Moon*.

SUSAN STEINBERG's stories have recently appeared or are forthcoming in the *Gettysburg Review*, *Boulevard*, *Quarterly West*, *Denver Quarterly*, and the *Massachusetts Review*.

ALEXANDER THEROUX's most recent book is *The Strange Case of Edward Gorey* (Fantagraphics Books). He has just finished an epic novel, *Laura Warholic*.

DAVID FOSTER WALLACE is the author of numerous books, most recently *Brief Interviews With Hideous Men* (Back Bay Books). He lives in Bloomington, Illinois.

PAUL WEST's new novel is *A Fifth of November* (New Directions), about the Gunpowder Plot and Guy Fawkes, and his latest work of nonfiction is *Master Class* (Harcourt), a memoir of his last writing seminar. He is at work on a novel, *Cheops*, about ancient Egypt, and a memoir, *Oxford Days*.

EDMUND WHITE has written, most recently, *Marcel Proust* (Viking, Penguin Lives series), a travel essay about Paris, *The Flaneur: A Stroll through the Paradoxes of Paris* (Bloomsbury), and a novel, *The Married Man* (Knopf).

JOHN EDGAR WIDEMAN's *Hoop Roots: Basketball, Race, and Love* has just been published by Houghton Mifflin.

DIANE WILLIAMS has just completed a novella and stories, *Romancer Erector*, forthcoming from Dalkey Archive Press. She is founder of the literary annual *NOON*.

Steal Away: Selected and New Poems by C. D. WRIGHT is forthcoming in the spring of 2002. She is currently working on a project with photographer Deborah Luster about prisoners in Louisiana.

JOHN YAU's forthcoming books include a collaboration with Archie Rand, *100 More Jokes from the Book of the Dead* (Meritage Press), *My Heart Is That Eternal Rose Tattoo* (Black Sparrow Press), and *Borrowed Love Poems* (Penguin).

40 years on the burning deck

Susan Gevirtz, *Hourglass Transcripts*

What is legible? How can the uncountable, unaccountable find the page outside of measurable time? To approach the unspeakable, it may be necessary to make an incision through the center of a line, to as it were hyphenate thought. Or, in "Hollowed Out Book," the names of shipping lines float across the water like gigantic book titles, telling much about the distant and the up close. And so about the act of seeing. Form is motion through place—toward the not yet imagined: its fabulous possibility and the full extent of its previous demolition.

Poems, 80 pages, offset, smyth-sewn, ISBN 1-886224-40-4, original paperback $10

Jennifer Martenson, *Xq28*[1]

A satiric response to the so-called "gay gene." Mock-scientific inquiries into the biology of lesbianism get ensnared in footnotes and infinite regress. More concerned with codes of conduct than genetic codes, *Xq28*[1] does not take sides on the nature/nurture question as much as it plays around in the ideological context of the debate. Poem, 20 pages, offset, saddlestitched ISBN 1-886224-42-0, paper $5

Oskar Pastior, *Many Glove Compartments*

[Dichten=, #5; trans. Harry Mathews, Christopher Middleton, Rosmarie Waldrop, with a guest appearance by John Yau]

For Pastior, the only German member of OULIPO, language is the stuff of life, a metabolism where words and even concepts are made flesh or, rather, "thought-music as leaping perspective."

"Pastior's humor is the only legitimate kind beside black humor which of course also darkly lights up here"— *Frankfurter Allgemeine Zeitung*

Poems, 120 pages, offset, smyth-sewn, ISBN 1-886224-44-7, original paperback $10

Pascal Quignard, *On Wooden Tablets: Apronenia Avitia*

[Série d'Ecriture, #15; trans. Bruce X]

At the end of the 4th century, a Roman Patrician Matron writes notes, somewhat in the manner of Sei Shonagon's Pillow Book. She notes erotic souvenirs, jokes, scenes that have touched her, but also accounts and lists of things to do. For 20 years, Apronenia Avitia keeps this journal without mentioning, except in passing, the ruinous events she witnesses: the Roman Empire is crumbling, invaded by the "Barbarians" from the North as well as infiltrated from within by the Christian "party." Perhaps she does not see. Perhaps she does not want to see.

Quignard's novel is both erudite and playful. He has redefined historical fiction as both hoax and enigma.

Novel, 112 pages, offset, smyth-sewn, ISBN 1-886224-45-5 $10

www.burningdeck.com
Distributed by Small Press Distribution, 1341 Seventh St.,
Berkeley, CA 94710   1-800/869-7553   orders@spdbooks.org

3rd bed

fifth issue

hanging from the spoon

New from Princeton

The Princeton Anthology of Writing
Favorite Pieces by the Ferris/McGraw Writers at Princeton University
Edited by John McPhee and Carol Rigolot
With a preface by John McPhee

Since 1957, many noted nonfiction writers have held the Ferris and McGraw professorships at Princeton University. This new anthology collects the personal favorite works of these well-known authors. Eclectic, idiosyncratic, thought-provoking, and skillfully crafted, these 59 pieces attest to the elegance, eloquence, and endurance of fine nonfiction. Contributors include Blair Clark, Leslie Cockburn, Gloria Emerson, Lucinda Frank, James Gleick, William Greider, Haynes Johnson, Gina Kolata, Jane Kramer, and many others.

Paper $17.95 ISBN 0-691-08681-8   Cloth $39.50 ISBN 0-691-08680-

The Author of Himself
The Life of Marcel Reich-Ranicki
Marcel Reich-Ranicki
With a foreword by Jack Zipes

Marcel Reich-Ranicki is remarkable for both his unlikely life story and his brilliant career as the "pope of German letters." His life took him from middle-class childhood to wartime misery to the heights of intellectual celebrity. His list of friends and enemies has included every influential player on the German literary scene, including Günter Grass and Heinrich Böll. His memoir is an indispensable guide to contemporary German culture as well as an absorbing eyewitness history of some of the twentieth century's most important events.

Cloth $35.00 ISBN 0-691-09040-8

⚘ Princeton University Press
800-777-4726 • WWW.PUP.PRINCETON.EDU

A CONVERGENCE OF BIRDS

Original Fiction and Poetry
Inspired by the Work of Joseph Cornell

DIANE ACKERMAN   MARTINE BELLEN   JOHN BURGHARDT
MARY CAPONEGRO   ROBERT COOVER   LYDIA DAVIS
JONATHAN SAFRAN FOER   SIRI HUSTVEDT   ANN LAUTERBACH
BARRY LOPEZ   RICK MOODY   BRADFORD MORROW
HOWARD NORMAN   JOYCE CAROL OATES   DALE PECK
ROBERT PINSKY   ERIK ANDERSON REECE   JOANNA SCOTT
ROSMARIE WALDROP   PAUL WEST   DIANE WILLIAMS   JON YAU

━━◄◆►━━

"Joseph Cornell's magic is a hard act to follow, except with one's
own magic. I can only applaud the wit and ingenuity and freedom
of so many splendid, high-stepping American writers who followed
a fancy and converged to make this dazzling book." —Susan Sontag

━━◄◆►━━

Published by D.A.P./Distrbuted Art Publishers
Edited by Jonathan Safran Foer
Hardcover, 240 pgs. 26 full-color tipped-on plates
ISBN 1-891024-22-1 $27.50
to order call 800-338-2665